the
'idiot spy'
(the series)
book four of ten

helping friends & chasing diablo

c. benjamin lattimore

helping friends & chasing diablo
Published: December 2020
Printed in the United States of America
ISBN: 978-1-7334945-3-3

a lattidreamer™ publication
© C. Benjamin Lattimore, 2020

To Marisa my bride and number 1 editor!
Thanks for the many hours of experienced, instinctual recommendations, and tweaks that you offered for book # 4.
I appreciate all that you do to improve my passion!
One day I hope to get it right! (hahahaha)

ACKNOWLEDGEMENTS

To my wonderful and canny children, Christopher, Monica, and Courtney, as well as my clever grandchildren, Isaiah, and Desmond for just being special. A unique and heartfelt expression of love to my sister Mary E. and my brother Darryl A. Once again, venerate regards to Maurice Cheeks and Reggie Wilkes.

Special acknowledgements to Marisa, Dawn Marie, Nikki, and Jill.

Lots of love ethereally to my mother, Mary Alice, my father, Walthro M., my little sister, Barbara Ann, and my brother, Walter Eugene.

## CHAPTER ONE

In Washington, DC, the new row was over who was the most qualified to hold the office of the President of the United States of America. Although the front runner for the Republican Party continued to make waves and enemies, he gained support from mainly the rich, the super-rich, the poor, the extremely poor and marginally educated people of a particular persuasion. His fellow billionaires could smell the money and the power. The front-runner's notion of building a wall to keep illegal immigrants from South America out of the country, as well as deporting millions more and requiring all Muslims to register, propelled him to the front of his party, a sad testament to the notion of the Statue of Liberty.

On the other side of the equation, the leading contender was a sitting United States Senator with a less than a sterling record, albeit many of the assertions were based upon conjecture. She had a reputation and knack for getting things done—at any cost. She was also the prime architect for obtaining the Carbon Factor. It was her "trump card", and it would be used to win the election if necessary.

Walter realized he was losing control of the senator as a result of his many botched attempts to gain the secret formula that the entire world was seeking for a powerful, cheap, dirty, little bomb. He thought he had finally obtained the necessary documents and was ready to renegotiate with the person he thought was most likely to win the presidential race. Walter had considered taking the prize to the other camp but realized that terrible things would happen to his family if he attempted to make such a move.

It was ten in the morning when Walter entered the senator's office to present her with the 'crown jewels', or so he thought.

He told her, "I had some of my people with scientific backgrounds, do a cursory review of these disks to make sure that they are legitimate and have what is needed to neutralize the Russians."

The senator looked at the disks and said to a colonel who, seemingly was always by her side, "You know what to do with this, so, let's not waste any more time." The colonel made a call on his cellphone and within four minutes, fifteen heavily armed soldiers appeared in her office.

The colonel addressed a captain, "Are we fully covered with support from the air as well?"

"Yes, sir. I have a full company outside waiting to escort us to the designated facility."

"Good work and, Senator, I will contact you as soon as I have verification that this is indeed the material that you have been seeking." The group left her office and she and Walter began to chat.

The senator asked, "What's the status of those who were previously in control of this information?"

"Unfortunately, there was an explosion at their ranch, and I'm sad to say, there were no survivors."

"Are you certain of that?" The Senator asked.

"Indeed, I am. I was an eyewitness, and no one could have survived that blast. It appears that a propane tank leaked, and there were other products of an incendiary nature in the place and it caused a horrible conclusion of life."

"Do we have any exposure to the Panama Papers?"

"Absolutely not, but I believe your opponent may be mentioned in the upcoming weeks."

"Okay, Walter, make sure all of our work is tight and that there are no loose lips hanging around in hospitals trying to point fingers at you because you know what the results of that would be."

"I'm fully aware. As a matter of fact, I should leave from your side door to minimize scrutiny of our face-to-face contact until after you have a new title. Will you need any resources to support any other campaigns that might be embarrassing?"

"No, just make sure that all boxes are sealed and that we don't have to look over our shoulders for any ghosts."

"I completely understand. Everything is under control."

Two days later, the locals were still trying to extinguish the fires that had spread to the guest house. On occasion, an unspent round of ammunition would discharge as a result of the intense heat which delayed the firefighting task.

Larry, in a state of shock, was mourning the loss of his entire family and all his friends. As he surveyed the blast area, it became crystal clear to him, as well as the others, that no one could have survived the blast, let alone the intense fire. Larry had been crying for two days. He was completely dehydrated, and mentally irrational. His plan was to fly to Washington and kill his stepfather's cousin, Walter. This was neither a well thought out plan nor one that could easily happen. Walter was no longer in Washington, DC, and was making his way to one of his many hideouts that only his family knew about.

Okema, Somara, and Yeshida sifted through the remains hoping to find trinkets or a memento of Brown, Jilkes and John Lee, but everything that remained had been crystalized. It was hard to discern a bone fragment from a melted ornament. It was truly a sad time for everyone, and the community came out in droves, from near and far, to lend a hand for the beloved infamous Vietnam Squad, the FAB 10 plus 2 and their families. The question frequently asked was, "What on earth blew this place up like that?"

As the day began to transition into night, Clyde suggested, "Let's head back to my place and have some dinner and prayer. Tomorrow, we can dig around and hopefully find some remnants of our people. There is nothing we can do today with the fire still simmering and the smoke as toxic as can be. Let's get some food and do some praying."

Later, at Clyde's place, Larry pondered, "I don't understand why we can't find a single body in all of that rubble. Did they use the explosion as a diversion? Did they take them out into the field and slaughter them? No way man, we can't find a single body. Clyde, could they have possibly escaped through the tunnel under the house or could they be locked in the safe down there?"

"Larry, if they were in that basement then they sure as hell perished because there's no air down there. You really can't stay down there for over thirty minutes at a time. Plus, if those bad guys knew about it, that would be the perfect place to herd them to and do their dastardly deeds. Son, we just have to pray for their deliverance and hope that their suffering was not long."

"Clyde, can you explain to me why there are no corpses? I believe they were taken somewhere else and executed, and the ranch explosion was a stratagem. We can't find a single body or bone. We are looking in the wrong place and I think at first light we should divide our group and cover the entire ranch."

"Son, my people would have seen that number of people being moved from the ranch into the fields or the adjacent woods."

"Clyde, there are no bodies in the blast area. Where are the corpses? Where are the bodies, or bones, or skulls or anything that was human? There were none in the blast area and, therefore, I guarantee you, they were moved or that they died in that tunnel."

Okema asked, "Is it possible, Mr. Larry Holland, to use flashlights and locate where the tunnel begins?"

"I'm really not sure, but once we determine the boundaries of the ranch house, I believe we will be able to locate the tunnel entrance. I don't think we can figure this out during the night unless we have high intensity lights."

"You mean those spotlights that you can raise up on a crane or tractor?" asked Clyde.

"Yeah! Do you have any?"

"I do, but I don't think we should ride over a crime scene at night or try to figure out where things are. We should wait until the morning, that way we can see what we're doing and not destroy any evidence or anything."

Okema stated, "Mr. Clyde is correct. I think we should wait until first light to explore our options."

"I guess you're right, but I need one of those big flashlights. I am going back to say a prayer for my children, wife, and the rest of my family and friends. I'm also going to and align myself with Lucifer himself, because those who are responsible for this will truly witness a slow and horrific death."

"Son, your children and family wouldn't want you talking like that."

"My family is dead! I'm now the new +; death to all involved and those who knew about it."

## CHAPTER THREE

At 0500 hours, Larry was dressed and in front of Clyde's ranch throwing rocks. Okema came out, followed by her faithful friends, Somara, and Yeshida. Somara said, "Let us take that vehicle and get an early start rather than having breakfast."

"You know, I haven't thanked you guys for helping me, and I want to extend my friendship to you ladies. Oh, and, Carlos, I appreciate what you and your guys did as well."

"Mr. Larry Holland, we are sad as well because we loved three of your companions and we made this decision to come to America to be with those individuals. We thank you and everyone else who has welcomed us and treated us with the utmost respect," Yeshida stated.

As they were driving to the blast area, Larry looked out of the corner of his eye and saw a lone windmill turning effortlessly, out in the field, away from the ranch house. He wondered to himself, 'why would she have just one windmill'. He became fixated on the windmill and was eventually interrupted by Okema who inquired, "Mr. Larry Holland, why are you staring at that windmill?"

"I'm just wondering why someone would have a single windmill in the middle of a ranch. I don't understand why she would just have one windmill turning unless it had a sole purpose to ventilate a specific area." Larry hesitated a moment and screamed, "That windmill provides air to the tunnel; I'll bet my soul on that!" Larry slammed his foot down on the gas pedal.

Once they reached the blast site, state police were there and had roped the area off and told Larry and his group to leave. Larry had a heated discussion with the lead officer and was calmly shoved back by Okema who said to the officer, "This is an international matter, and unless you want to be retired prematurely, I suggest you let him show you where things were so that he can help you piece together the crime scene. This was not an accident and he knows the layout of this place. Do you officer?"

The lead officer looked at her and asked, "Who do you work for and where are your credentials?"

"If I told you who I worked for, Mr. Officer, you would be involved in an international spy saga which is way above your 'pay grade', according to the slang you Americans use."

"What the hell does that mean?"

"That means if I call my contacts, you and everyone else here will be in trouble for interfering with a White House sanctioned investigation."

"Again, do you have any credentials?" Somara walked forward and flashed her MI-6 credentials and the officer became accommodating.

As Larry began to calm down, Clyde drove up and asked, "Why didn't you guys tell me you were leaving?"

"Didn't want to disturb your breakfast," Larry answered.

Clyde looked at the Police Officer and asked, "How's your family?" Larry noticed the interaction and said to himself, 'it's best to let locals relate to locals, they seemingly are all related'.

Clyde said, "I guess you met young Mr. Holland and his guest from across the pond?"

"Yeah, I guess you can say that. We had some words, but all's good."

"Great, that's what I like to hear in situations like this because we are all here for the same reason." Larry interrupted the kumbaya and asked, "Clyde, why did Asiram have a single windmill out here?"

"I, frankly, don't know why and never really paid any attention to it," Clyde answered.

"Can you figure out where the entrance to the tunnel was before the explosion?"

"I can walk it off because I had issues with the generator in the past. Let me see now, if I am right, this would have been where the door was, and thirty steps straight ahead would lead me to the closet that would take me to the tunnel or should I say basement. I could never figure out what those metal shelves were for."

This caught Larry's attention and he inquired, "What metal shelves?" Clyde looked at him and replied, "Those metal shelves that seemingly got blown off of those hooks and onto the floor."

Larry looked at them and exclaimed, "Shit, those things were on an automatic system—look at the hinges and wires on the side of each one. Someone engaged these things!" As he stood on top of one of them, he decided to tap it with a signal that he and the Sarge had developed years ago when they were doing neighborhood redevelopment and cleansing activities. He did it to pacify himself and to make sure he was doing all he could do to figure out what happened to his family. He found the remnants of a metal bannister and proceeded to tap, "dat datda dat dat; dat dat." There was no response. His next effort began with banging the code. This time, he thought there was a faint sound echoing from the other side of the ranch's layout. He told Okema to bang on the metal shelf and to cease banging when he raised his hand. Larry walked about thirty feet from where she was and gave her the first signal. There was no response, and he yelled for her to bang harder. Okema began to bang on the metal shelf randomly and still there was no response. Finally, Larry said, "I thought I heard a faint sound when I banged on that shelf."

"Perhaps you wanted to hear some sign of life. As humans, we tend to want to believe in miracles. You could possibly be hearing things due to your concussion, Larry," Clyde stated.

"Damn it, Clyde, I'm not hearing things other than sounds being made by someone or something. I am not looking for a miracle unless it comes straight from hell. Then, I'll know that all who knew and participated in the demise of my children, my wife, my father and my mother will learn to recognize the new cacodemon."

"Larry, you're no devil, and never will be. Despite your call for vengeance! Use the word of our Lord to appreciate and honor those who were murdered and let that vengeance thing go, my son. It's disdainful; there is no reward in heaven for seeking revenge!" Clyde exclaimed.

Okema interrupted the sermon and asked, "Mr. Larry Holland, will you once again listen for sounds, I too think I heard something." Larry walked back to where she was standing and placed his ear towards the shelf and rapped the call sign for the Sarge vigorously. From the other side of the shelf came a thunderous reply. Larry yelled, "We need shovels and picks. The Sarge is down there!"

#

Clyde called some of the neighbors and asked them to give him a hand and bring some water. Okema began to speak in her native tongue with Yeshida and Somara. It looked like a vehement argument was taking place. At the end of it, Okema said, "Mr. Larry Holland, I suggest that we don't do this until tonight, unless someone is injured. We are not sure that all of those who were responsible for this have left the area and I don't think Mr. Sarge would want to expose his hand. Also, if too many people are focusing on a single point, it might raise suspicion. This is our conclusion and we think it makes sense to wait until night fall unless someone is hurt."

Larry thought about her statement, then looked at her and said, "It's better that those who did this realize that a day of reckoning is on its way. If I know my father, he will want people to know that they failed, and that he would soon be planning for an accounting. If my family is okay, I want them out of there now, not tonight. Clyde, please make the calls.

CHAPTER FOUR

Five and a half hours later, a bewildered and dehydrated group of people climbed out of the less than religious catacombs of Asiram's tunnel. The Sarge looked at Larry and asked, "What the hell took you so long?" The two men embraced as Larry and the Sarge began to cry.

Larry then kissed his wife, hugged the twins, and said, "I love you guys. Did you miss Daddy?" The responses were unanimous. Asiram looked around at what used to be her ranch and began to cry. Zanthius, in a state of confusion, asked, "Where is the ranch house?"

Larry replied, "You're standing in it." Zanthius pulled Asiram aggressively close to him, and whispered, "On our baby's life, I swear to you that I will make this right and those who did this will pay. I promise you this. I will rebuild our ranch."

Asiram continued to cry and the Sarge said to Mallory, "That woman is going to hate me and never invite me to any place that she lives. This is the third home of hers that I have watched destroyed."

"Sarge, we can get people out here soon to begin the clean-up and planning for the rebuilding of this place. As a matter of fact, we should ask about the status of the farm in Virginia, that may be our only retreat for this many people," Mallory stated.

Courtney told Clyde that she needed to get the Sarge to the hospital to tend to his wounds. Larry asked, "What wounds?"

The Sarge answered, "Thank God, I was wearing a vest because there was a direct shot to my heart and another shot hit me in the side but went clear through. I'll be alright now that I can see the sun and inhale some fresh air. The children and Rashida held up extremely well and I'm proud of everyone who was down in that tunnel. We barely made it to the tunnel when the blast knocked some of my guys to the floor and out cold." Courtney interrupted and said, "We got to get you to the hospital, save your war stories for later."

"Monica and I are going with you for security and probably the two lovers, John Lee and Jilkes, will also accompany us."

"I don't want my family split up. I want them all in one place with my people on guard with sticks and stones as weapons. Mallory, make sure that happens."

"I'm on it, Sarge. You just rest, make sure you're alright, we can plan on where we are going to hide out for a while and plan the ultimate plot of revenge."

Yeshida and Somara asked Mr. Jilkes and Mr. John Lee where they were going and were told they were going to make sure that no further attempts would be made on their leader. Yeshida announced, "Then we go with you to provide additional security." Jilkes looked at her and Somara and said, "That is an excellent idea. Don't you agree, John Lee?"

John Lee looked at Somara and said, "I was hoping that you would want to tag along with us and make sure none of those bad guys do any nasty things to us. I like the idea, and I'm happy that you're going to be right close to me."

Okema said to Brown, "Mr. Brown, did you think I was going to let you die without attempting a rescue?"

"Frankly, the only thing I was thinking about while I was in the tunnel was that I should have told you that I more than like you. I'm willing to forget our first interactions and move to trying to solidify a much more meaningful relationship."

"Mr. Brown, are you saying that you now want to have a definitive relationship with me?"

"All I'm saying is, that while I was down in that tunnel, the only person I thought about was you. After realizing how close to death I was, I decided to make a few decisions. If you'll have me, then I'm yours. I want to make us happy and move this relationship to another level. I now know there is not a tomorrow promised because I surely and sincerely, thought I was going to die in that tunnel."

"Mr. Brown, my heart never skipped a beat, somehow I knew you were still alive. In my mind, when I first saw the blast zone, I thought that you were not among the living, but I also realized that there were no body parts, sorry for saying this, but that is when I decided that somehow everyone escaped that tragedy. Mr. Brown, I would just like for you to claim me as yours. I am yours Mr. Brown, and I arrived at that conclusion after listening to you and experiencing pleasures beyond words when we were in Hong Kong."

# # #

On the ride to the hospital the Sarge said to Mallory, "We have got to figure out who pulls Walter's strings and then we must make a very messy and loud scene to send a message. I mean we have never ever considered killing women and children, but this guy strapped suicide vests on our babies and that is completely unforgivable. I think death is too good for him and yields nothing other than he is no longer here to bother us. Yes, that is too easy. I would like to do to him what my great, great, great grandfather did to one of his foes, cut his legs and arms off, blind him and let him wander for the rest of his life with no eyes and limbs."

"Damn, Sarge, that's a little drastic don't you think?"

"That son-of-a-bitch tried to kill us and wanted to kill our children. I don't want him dead, but so damn close to being dead that he will remember every evil thing that he has ever done to anyone as he attempts to navigate life without critical limbs to get around and without eyes to see. No, just to kill that guy is simply too easy. That is my prescription for my cousin Walter, a message that is loud, messy and makes a statement! You come at our families, then the last thing you see forever, will be the one you remember because I will cut your eyes out!"

# # #

At the hospital, the attending physician emphasized, "I will have to report this to the police because it involves a shooting."

Mallory looked at him and said, "That's fine because I'm the one who accidently shot him, and these people are all witnesses to what happened."

Clyde asked, "So, Dr. Nelson, can I have a private word with you?"

"Sure, Clyde. What can I do for you?"

"We need to keep this one off the books because these folks are big donors to our local charities. As a matter of fact, that new equipment you're trying to get, that X-ray machine, well, on the way over here I mentioned it to them, and they said they would be proud to donate it to the hospital since it will benefit all of the residents. They are good people who don't need to waste their time filling out forms about who accidently got shot by a close friend. You follow me?"

"Well, Clyde, you're asking a lot of me, but I think I can find a way to handle this as something minor. I'll take care of this."

"Thanks, Doc, and I will follow up on that equipment you said you need."

As the doctor began to examine the Sarge he said, "It's a good thing your friend can't shoot straight, another inch to the right and we wouldn't be having this leisurely conversation. I need to get you to the X-ray department so that I can make sure there are no internal injuries. Whoever kept you from bleeding knew what the heck they were doing." Courtney smiled but didn't say a word.

Clyde mentioned to Mallory what was necessary in order to keep this visit off the books. He said, "Not a problem, because gunshots wounds get placed into a national data base and we really can't afford to tip our hand. Good thinking and acting on our behalf. Tell the Doc all we need is the purchase information and the deal is done."

# # #

An hour and a half later, the heavily bandaged Sarge was being wheeled out of the hospital. At the exit, he said to Dr. Nelson, "You never asked me my name."

"I know exactly who you are and what you have done for this community. Clyde asked me to keep this one off the books and that is exactly what this is, an off the book examination."

"We'll get you that equipment you need as soon as you get us the information. Thanks for the discretion and foregoing the form filling out adventure," Mallory said.

# # #

At Clyde's ranch, a disturbed Asiram was still crying about the loss of her ranch. Zanthius attempted to assure her that all would be well and that it would be rebuilt stronger than before. His statements did little to ease her grief. When the door opened and she saw the Sarge, she began to cry even harder. She walked over to him and exclaimed, "Daddy-in-Law, I'm not inviting you to stay at any place that I own, ever again!" Beckmire's eyes watered and Asiram said, "I'm happy you're okay but I'm worried about the safety of my other properties." She broke into laughter and said, "I'm just kidding, because this is one crazy ass family and I wouldn't change a thing. My husband has promised me that he will rebuild it and make it stronger. That's all I needed to hear."

"I'm so sorry about the ranch and the farmhouse, but I promise you they will be rebuilt. You know that they're working around the clock to rebuild the farmhouse in Virginia and the government is paying for most of that work. The ranch will be on us. What say you men?" All thumbs were raised high and the deal was done, not that it mattered because the money wasn't an issue to begin with.

The Sarge huddled with Asiram, Zanthius, Mallory, and Clyde and announced, "We all can't stay here, so do you have any ideas about living arrangements for the next few days?"

"I, for one, don't think that we should separate even if that means sleeping on cots in the barn. We lose our effectiveness when we are spread out," Zanthius stated.

"I agree with you, Son, but in case you haven't noticed, we have added three additional members to our party. The only place that can accommodate us all is the hotel downtown. I suggest we see if we can make reservations there. In two days, I should be able to fly. Then we take a trip to the islands, bask in the sun, consume some fruity drinks, and soak in the salty water."

It was a unanimous decision. The Sarge summoned Jong and inquired, "Can you get us a private hotel or place in St. Thomas or Aruba, for a week or two, until we map out our plan to cut the eyes out of that son-of-a-bitch Walter?"

"Why not just blow his head off, Sarge?"

"You know what? Let's get the team in here so that I can give you my notion of what I want to do to him. Mallory, get the group in here and include Larry."

Ten minutes later, the rest of the group assembled with the addition of Larry and Carlos. The Sarge said, "I first of all want to thank you guys for staying the course with me on this one. I really appreciate all that you people do. Jong asked me why we don't just put a bullet in Walter's head and be done with it. I say that's too good for someone who strapped suicide vests on children and tried to kill us all by blowing up Asiram's ranch. A shot to the head is just too damn easy for him. I want to do to him what my great, great, great grandfather did to one of his foes. I want to cut his arms off at the elbows, cut his legs off at the knees, and then extract both of his damn eyes. I don't want to kill him; I want him to suffer throughout eternity. Those are my plans for my cousin. Any comments or suggestions? Oh, and occasionally, I would like to see dogs cock a leg in the air and do their business on him."

John Lee looked at the Sarge and said, "Now, that be taking vengeance to a whole new level; I like the idea."

Jilkes stood up and asked, "Why don't we castrate his ass as well?"

"If we castrate him, then they'll just place a tube in him so that he can piss. If we leave his nature as is, then he will have to learn to use it with nubs. I want to send a messy, loud message to him and whoever follows him; you mess with us and we will leave a shadow of who you once were to slither around. Secondly, I'm unable to travel for a couple of days. In two days if you guys don't have other pressing obligations, I would like to head down to the islands for some R&R, bask in the sun, consume fruity drinks, and play in the salty water. Are there any questions or comments on that scenario? Also, how many of you need to take some personal time to address your own personal situations?"

As usual, no one had any pressing matters to attend to and the plan was placed into action. Jong began to make calls and seek out secure resorts. He called his pilot-in-command and told him that in two days they would be traveling, probably, to St. Thomas or Aruba and to make ready the planes.

## CHAPTER FIVE

In St. Thomas, Jong was able to book a small hotel that was right on a magnificent private beach. For the next two weeks, the group's only agenda was to relax and exercise once a day. Every evening, the ladies would develop a menu for the next day and present it to the inn keeper. All the meals had a healthy theme to them with lots of fruits and vegetables. Most dinners consisted of chicken and fish with beef only on Saturdays.

Each morning, the men would gather leisurely around 0800 hours and start their day off with a brisk walk that would turn into a run with occasional sprints. The Sarge, other than soreness around both wounds, had totally recuperated and was hell bent on finding and decapitating his cousin. It had become more than vengeance with the Sarge--he couldn't forget the sight of the children strapped in suicide vests.

While he was swimming in the water with Courtney, he asked, "Sweetheart, if someone had their arm cutoff at the elbow, how would you stop their bleeding?"

"What kind of question is that Ben? What are you planning and who is going to lose an arm?"

"Just asking a question. I mean is it that intricate of a procedure that you would need a doctor to do the actual surgery?"

"Ben, it's extremely complicated and I can't give you years of medical school training in a single paragraph, but I will say that if it's not correctly done all kinds of things can go wrong, including infections, such as gangrene. Why are you asking me this?"

"I'm just trying to understand the intricacies of such a procedure, that's all."

"Ben Beckmire, stop the BS. Why did you ask me that question?"

"Honey, trust me, I was just interested in how difficult of a procedure it is. I don't plan on operating on anyone anytime soon, simply curious about the kind of things you learned while in medical school."

# # #

With three days left on their vacation, the Sarge called for a full meeting to discuss the housing issue. He started the meeting by announcing, "Our small group has grown, by leaps and bounds, and there are approximately thirty-three of us, including the children. That is a lot of toilet paper. Does anyone have any ideas as to where we can go unnoticed with that many people?"

"Birmingham, Alabama, we can go there," John Lee announced.

"Great idea, John Lee, but they know where you live."

"They also think that I be dead."

"Excellent point, John Lee. Are there any other suggestions or places that can accommodate a small army?"

"Perhaps we should attempt to find a safe place for the noncombatants, women and children and hide them out until we finish this business," Brown said.

"Just in case you missed the news release, each woman has had to pull the trigger to protect us."

"Sarge, I wasn't making light of that. I was trying to separate the group and see if that makes a difference in our numbers, as well as our defenses. As I think about that statement, I feel that I should withdraw it because if we separate and think that they are safe, we might find ourselves in another tunnel," Brown replied.

"That is exactly my reaction to this problem, because if they realize they failed miserably last time, they won't make the same mistake again. I think our best bet is to stay together, keep home schooling the children, and keep trying to figure out how to get to Walter. We can't separate and leave some people less defended than others."

"Well, it seems like John Lee has the only viable place that can handle all of us. The question I have is, how will we secure our families as we finish this job? Besides, I believe that since Jong randomly cut parts of the formula out for the Carbon Factor, I'm sure it's going to be discovered at some point," Chakes said.

"Okay, we have two more days here so, let's make the most out of it. I was thinking that this place is a perfect getaway, but it needs some serious work. Do you guys think that we should partner with the inn keeper, buy this place, have it gutted and reconstructed?" The Sarge suggested.

"Now, I like that idea because it gives us a wonderful place to call our very own. We can have our meetings here in the winter and commune," Gladstone stated.

"I second that idea and recommend that Mallory, Monica, and Jong pull the owner aside and see what he wants for the place or if he is interested in partnering with us. Other than the rustic nature of the place, I absolutely love its proximity to the wonderful salty water and the peace and tranquility surrounding it. I want to buy it even if you guys don't want to invest in it," Chakes announced.

"Mr. Chakes, I think we're all enthralled with this place and let's see what Mallory, his bride and Jong come up with. It's apparent to me that it needs work. I guess the guy doesn't have the resources to put into it to make it more attractive and marketable. Once again, I think we all should thank Mr. Amazing for finding us another gem in the rough."

Asiram and Zanthius went for an afternoon swim and she said to him, "I want to come out of retirement when we find Walter. I have some really special things I would like to do to him."

"Can't be any worse than what my father is planning for him."

"Oh, I didn't know he had something in mind. What is it?"

"Well, my love, my father is planning on cutting off his arms at the elbows and his legs at the knees."

"Are you serious?"

"Honey, that's only the first part of it. This is what he was told that his great, great, great grandfather did to a foe who was responsible for the death of his wife. After cutting off his limbs, he apparently gauged his eyes out as well. It was a very messy and loud message, but it left the man, who was once rich, a beggar without eyes or limbs to fend for himself. Now, that is what my father has planned for his cousin."

"Now, that's some sick shit. I never knew my daddy-in-law had that kind of a mean streak in him."

"Honey, some of the stories that I have inadvertently heard about my father will cause your blood to curdle. He is definitely not the man you want to piss off or trifle with."

"Is it true that he and those eleven guys killed over a thousand or so enemy soldiers?"

"I don't know if that's true, but since this thing started, they have killed close to 200 mercs, I guess. They are a rare breed of guys and their loyalty to my dad is unshakable. I have never seen men bond like that before and remain committed over a long period of time, it's incredible. Honey, do you want to hear something else incredible?" Asiram swam up to him and began to suckle his breast and play with his already excited member. As she kissed his ear lobe, he began to reach for her most treasured part. Zanthius found the spot and began to gently give attention to the crazy zone on a woman. Asiram began to moan and pull at her thong bikini. Right in the middle of the water, they were able to manifest penetration and after a few minutes of awkward thrusting, the two were able to consummate two terrific orgasms. "I love you so much. You are so great at getting me to that mindless point of pleasure, my 'idiot spy'."

# # #

Meanwhile, back at the hotel, Mr. Richard Brown was being teased by Okema. She was completely without earthly garments; her beauty and sexuality dominated the maladroit Brown who had no clue how to please this woman from another culture. Okema's movements and methods were predicated on her old school teachings. She washed and dried Brown and presented him with a robe. She purposefully touched him in sensitive places and backed off. After fixing Brown a drink, she slid into bed with him and began to touch his breast. This created a new sensation for Brown who was used to "wham, bam, thank you ma'am". She kissed his cheeks, then his lips and began to search his mouth with her tongue, while paying attention to his joystick. After five minutes of intense kissing and touching, Okema said, "Mr. Brown, I am yours to command."

Brown looked at her and asked, "What would you like to do to me?"

"I want to do everything that you desire."

"What would you like me to do to you?"

"You can begin by kissing my love zone until I scream with pleasure."

"Damn, that's it?"

"No, Mr. Brown. That is the beginning, the end will be announced when you have given me all of your juices and when I am satisfied that for the moment, you have no more to offer me other than the comfort of your arms."

#

At the other end of the hotel in his room, Somara asked John Lee, "Are you going to attempt to make me whole?"

"How can I do that?"

"By acting like you did when we first met. We have been in the same room in this hotel for over a week and all you ever say to me is good night. I appreciate the respect you have given me, but I also require some other kinds of attention that are more personal. Today, Mr. John Lee, I would like you and me to act like a normal man and woman and approach the subject of sex. Is that something you would like to talk about, Mr. John Lee?"

"Ms. Somara, I don't want to talk about sex, I want to have sex, but I didn't want to get you all the way over here and make it seem like I can't control myself. You be very special to me and I would like to have intercourse with you."

"You speak in such ancient ways, Mr. John Lee, but I like that about you. This thing you call intercourse is something that I genuinely want to experience with you, but I only wish you would be the aggressor."

"Would you like one of those drinks with them there umbrellas inside?"

"I would very much like the one that is made with coconut."

"Me too, damn it. I'm going to go and get us some of them there drinks and we can sit on the balcony and drink them and discuss our plans and our future, if that be alright with you?"

"That sounds perfect to me, Mr. John Lee, and while you're gone, I'm going to take a shower and try to look sexy for you."

"You don't have to try to look sexy for me because you be done did that already. I think you be as sexy as any girl I've ever seen, and I feel honored to have you as my roommate, but I couldn't cross no lines because that wouldn't have been gentleman like."

"Mr. John Lee, secure the fruity drinks, and we will complete the discussion and perhaps enjoy what is natural between a man and a woman."

#

John Lee entered the bar and saw members of the team. He spoke to them and placed an order for six Pina Coladas to go. McArthur exclaimed, "Oh my, you must be trying to close a deal or something."

"I be trying to order drinks without hearing a lot of pig shit from my friends."

"Come on, Brother, you know I'm jealous but support and defend you at every turn."

John Lee walked over to him and said, "I'm trying to be like a gentleman, and I really don't know much about how them there Asian women think and do things. I'm lost, scared, and Jilkes is having fun with his new friend while I'm simply scared of making too many mistakes."

Realizing how serious John Lee was, McArthur suggested, "First of all, you need to relax your country ass, and think about what it is you want to do without hurting anybody. Take your time and think before you blurt shit out of your mouth. Just relax and be John Lee, don't try to be somebody that you ain't. Just relax, be yourself and you will do well, my brother."

John Lee hugged him and said, "You won't believe how nervous I be, but I'm going to go back there and drink these double drinks and try to relax. Thanks, Mac, and just between me, and you, and the pig pen, I be liking this here woman."

Approximately fifteen minutes later, John Lee entered the room and didn't see Somara and panicked for a minute. He called out her name but there was no answer. Uncommon to her culture, Somara was on the balcony, butt naked enjoying the sun. When John Lee saw her, he dropped the tray full of drinks. Somara salvaged a cherry and bit it in half and offered half to John Lee while it was in her mouth. He got on his knees and maintained that position for fifteen minutes. John Lee provided Somara with multiple orgasms as he sucked her breast, her belly, and her garden. She was more than appreciative of his efforts. She led him to the shower, where she undressed him and began to wash his body. From behind, she reached around to wash and stroke his member and was totally awed by what she was washing. She turned him around and looked at the size of his toy and fell to her knees. She began to make love to his toy, and it grew larger. John Lee pulled her up from her knees, hoisted her into the air and began to open areas within her that she didn't know existed. It was pure bliss. Somara enjoyed every moment and thrust, as well as the momentary pain, from John Lee reaching the stratosphere of her garden.

# # #

In the middle of the hotel, Jilkes and Yeshida had completed their tenth episode in a matter of eleven days. It was only an act of mother nature on her body that impacted their vigorous love making. Yeshida was no longer calling him Mr. Jilkes but had renamed him Mr. Jolt. Prior to the onset of her cycle, Jilkes and Yeshida were opening new avenues within her body. Their first session was a marathon. They cuddled for hours and expressed their true emotions and dreams for the future.

Later, Yeshida said to Jilkes, "I want you to make passionate love to me with your mouth. Are you able to do that for me?" Jilkes didn't respond in words but immediately began to kiss and suckle her most prized region. It was by accident that he found the one spot that created a ghetto response from Yeshida, "Right there brother, right there!" After a mammoth explosion, Yeshida said, "I didn't know that was the place, and I am so happy that you, and you alone know where it is. You make me feel so perfect and I only hope that I make you feel as great." Jilkes gently rolled her over on her stomach, and the two began an entirely new episode, filled with pain and pleasure.

# # #

When Zanthius and Asiram entered their room, Zanthius said, "Honey, the dragon is still with desire."

"No way, I thought we drained him in the water?"

"Honey, come here and take a look." When Asiram saw what was in front of her, she led her man to the chaise lounge, that was in their room, and straddled her legs over his body. She began to pump slowly and methodically, and then like a wild beast. Asiram moved her body in a forward and backward motion that accelerated after each movement. It was as though her movements were that of a well-oiled machine. She stroked her husband backwards and forwards until he yelled for mercy. Each stroke provided Zanthius with a new sensation. He tried desperately to keep up with her movements but realized that he was taking her out of a synchronized routine. She stroked and stroked Zanthius until he continuously yelled at the top of his lungs, "Oh my God! Oh my God!" She rode his roller coaster in every manner possible. He was like a car without an engine, unable to move or talk, just filled with the aftermath of passion, desire and love for his woman. He uttered to her, "Honey, you just screwed my brains out and I can't move a muscle."

CHAPTER SIX

Mallory and Monica spoke with the owner of the property and he frankly told them that he was about to go into bankruptcy because the bank was trying to foreclose on his property. He told them that the bankers were basically small-time crooks who were tied to some seedy people who wanted the property because of its location to the beach. Mallory asked him if he wanted partners who would provide the funds to gut the property, rebuild it as a high-end property, and perhaps pay off all loans depending upon the percentage of ownership he was willing to give up. The owner, Mr. Christopher Carter, said, "Listen, guys, I don't have time for pipe dreams. This is all I have in the world and I'm not going to just give it away."

"Approximately, how much do you owe the bank?" Monica asked.

"I owe about $120k and the interest is outrageous. All I've been doing is trying to make payment on the interest."

"If you were to consider a partnership with us, what would be the percentage of ownership you're willing to give up?"

"I would have to think about that. You people seem like a good group of folks, but I thought that way about the bankers."

"If we paid off your loan today and sent contractors to lay out a refurbished or a completely new place, what do you think that's worth to you? We're expediting our offer because you're facing bankruptcy and eviction. We prefer to have our funds protected and, therefore, we would need greater than 60% of ownership rights."

"Are you people serious?"

"Yes, we are very, serious. We would keep you on as the manager and you would share in 40% of the profits, but you would give up 60% of the business. Think about it--40% of the profits, no bank loans, a salary, and the right to approve any renovations or rebuilding. You would work for us and run this place in our absence. Can you find a better deal than that?"

"First of all, I can't believe that you would do that. And second of all, turning 60% of my life's work over to strangers doesn't sound like a good deal to me."

"As we see it, you may not have many choices because, as you said, the bank wants this property for itself. If it forecloses on you, it becomes a matter of time before you walk away with nothing at all. Listen, think about it. We are putting up all the money, paying off your loans, hiring you for life as the manager, rebuilding the place from scratch, and furnishing it with high end appointments. We're also offering you 40% of the profits, a salary with benefits, a new car and whatever else that will make you happy, but we must own the lion's share of the business or it's not good business for us. Now, we have the resources to undercut you by having the bank call in your loan and then, my friend, you are shit out of luck. This way you win, we win, and the bank loses. Think about it and let us know so that we can go down to the bank and clear all the debt and begin talks about rebuilding. Think about it."

"Sir and Ma'am, you guys run a hard bargain, but it seems that, if you're on the up and up, there might be room for another discussion."

"As a matter of good faith, we will go with you to the bank and clear up the debt right now. If you think we are crooks, then that's another issue. We will just shake your hand and wish you good luck. We like it here, the private notion of the place, and our only demand would be that a few times a year, the place will be vacant for two weeks so that our families can meet and enjoy the weather and the beach. Unless you think we're playing, do you have any other options?"

"Frankly, I don't, but I'm not going to jump into bed with a bunch of strangers that I don't know a damn thing about."

"Thanks, Mr. Carter. We enjoyed ourselves here, and hopefully, when we try to come back, you will still own this magnificent place. Thank you." Mallory and Monica started to walk away when Mr. Carter inquired, "Any play in the ownership percentage?"

Mallory answered, "Tell me what you want. I will propose it to the others, but you have to consider what we have offered to you at no cost."

"Were you serious about going to the bank and closing out my debt?"

"As serious as a heart attack!"

"Then, Mr. Smarty Pants, let's go. You're going to do this without any legal papers to be signed and all of that?"

"Mr. Christopher Carter, we ran a check on you when we first checked in. If a handshake and an agreement note on a piece of paper isn't enough for you until my wife can draw up papers, then I guess we're back at the beginning of this conversation. We trust you, Mr. Carter. Besides, you see all those big strapping guys that are a part of our group, they are not the kind of people you want to piss off. This is good for you and for us. Mr. Carter, we are not a bunch of crooks, or mob guys or thieves. We help people, and sometimes, they help us. In this case, that is what I think is going on with you and me. Okay, let me get our money man and we'll meet you in the lobby in fifteen minutes."

Mallory called the Sarge and told him the results of his talk with the inn keeper and the Sarge told him to proceed. Mallory called Jong and told him that he needed him to bring some account numbers to transfer some money for the purchase of the hotel.

# # #

At the bank, Mallory could sense a problem. Mr. Carter asked the banker, "Can you tell me exactly how much money I owe you people?"

"Funny you should show up here today, Mr. Carter. We were about to alert you that you have ten business days to settle your entire loan or we will foreclose on your property. Let me see, you owe us $122,569.89, and that is the only amount that we will accept."

Jong looked at Mallory and he nodded to him. Jong said, "We are Mr. Carter's partners and we're here to pay off his loan. Here is the account number you can withdraw the funds from."

The banker looked at Jong and proclaimed, "This is unacceptable."

Mallory said, "Let me introduce you to my wife, Mrs. Monica Mallory. Mrs. Mallory is a representative of the United States Treasury Department and is here to make sure that there are no issues with the transfer of the funds, or with your issuing a stamp stating 'satisfied' on the loan papers. Now, I don't know what you mean when you say this is unacceptable, unless you have issues that are not bank related."

"Let me speak to the manager, and I'll be right back."

In the manager's office, a conversation was happening, and a telephone call was being made. Mallory said to Mr. Carter, "These guys are as crooked as shit. I'll bet you a hundred bucks that they probably have a buyer lined up for your property and that's what the phone call is about."

The manager came out and said, "We are surprised by this new development. Let me have them prepare the papers for the transfer and loan satisfaction document. Give us a few minutes and we can wrap up this matter."

Mallory followed him into his office and said, "Stop the stalling techniques. You do this right, or we will have this bank shut down and your people investigated by the Treasury Department. I smell fraud and collusion. I hope to hell I'm wrong."

"Sir, please, let me get this done. In a few minutes, this transaction will be completed."

Mr. Carter exclaimed, "We didn't settle on a percentage."

"Mr. Carter, I know you are a reasonable man and you will come to realize what we're doing is saving you, your hotel, and your life's work. We like helping, but in the long run, we also don't make bad deals with bad people. Are you a bad person, Mr. Carter?"

"I'm a good person who is just down on his luck."

"We believe in luck, but more importantly, we believe in helping people help themselves. This is a natural deal for us and for you, even though you think giving up 60% of your place is high. You come to the table bleeding from every orifice, with a group of bad guys about to steal your place from under you, and you have no way to stop the hemorrhaging. Assuming, you're going to deal with us, you keep your place and will earn a negotiated salary. Maybe in a few years, after everything is the way it can be, you might want to buy us out, at a fair market value price, of course. We don't hustle people, we help them. According to my wife, when the place is rebuilt or refurbished, every celebrity from here to there, will want to have their pictures on your walls. In essence, Mr. Carter, you had few alternatives. Those guys were going to rape you without using any lubricants. Let's just get them out of the picture and you can talk directly with my wife and draw up an agreement that is satisfactory to you. Our main concern is that you don't get plundered, and in the process, you don't try to take advantage of us."

"Are you people crazy or something? Why would you want to pay off a loan without any paperwork to protect your investment, especially, since you don't know me?"

"Mr. Carter, we appreciate the way you treated us, and we recognized early on that you didn't have the funds to operate this place. Insofar as the legality of our relationship, you work that out with my wife once we have gotten rid of the carpetbaggers."

Jong filled out the papers for the wire transfer and in a matter of ten minutes the debt was settled. The manager presented the original loan papers and signed them indicating that the loan had been satisfied. Jong said to Mr. Carter, "We need to open an account. Do you want to do it here or is there another bank in town that we can use?"

"I certainly don't want these bandits involved in our partnership. Let's walk down the street to a bank where the people are friendlier and honest."

"Mallory, how much do you want to put into the account?" Jong asked.

"I think we should park at least $1 million so there are no holdups when work is needed and bills have to be paid." He looked at Mr. Carter and said, "There will be two signers on that account--you and Mr. Jong. He will be with us most of the time and, therefore, once the plans are jointly approved, you can take control of the account."

"Are you people crazy?"

"Once again, Mr. Carter, we trust you to do the right thing. We have a few women who are going to want to work with you from afar to decorate and appoint the place, just try to roll with some of their ideas. We operate as a family and we are inviting you in subject to a few rules and conditions. In time, you will learn and come to realize that this was a great decision on your part knowing that those guys had you spread eagle over a barrel."

# # #

Inside the bank down the street, Jong said, "I would like to open an account and transfer $1 million dollars to it."

The teller sarcastically replied, "Yes, right this way. We have lots of people coming into our bank wanting to deposit $1 million. Just have a seat and one of our million-dollar tellers will be right with you."

Mr. Carter replied to the teller, "I know that sounds rather crazy, don't it? However, these guys are serious and are my new partners." The mood somewhat changed, and Jong said, "I'm sorry, I may have sounded a little pretentious, but I do want to open an account with this bank and deposit the amount of $1 million initially. Is that a problem?"

"Not at all, Sir. What kind of account do you have in mind?"

"We need an account that will allow Mr. Carter to have access to funds to begin and complete renovations on our hotel. A simple two signature account for checks that are over $100k. We're just setting up good business practices that have checks and balances."

"You know, our bank can play a role in this matter and act on necessary issues, if you're not around. To endow a single person in a business relationship with access to that kind of cash can create all kinds of concerns. The bank could play sort of an auditor's role. The bank, respectfully, without getting in Mr. Carter's way, could keep him apprised of balances, needs, and other accounting functions."

"That sounds like a good idea. You and Mr. Carter need to have that conversation. We're just facilitating this relationship, and Mr. Carter has to be completely comfortable with what you propose."

Monica nudged Mallory for his input, and he agreed with that idea. Mallory asked, "Do you have a problem with the bank doing the bookkeeping?"

Mr. Carter nodded in agreement and said, "I think that's a good idea, but I'm in charge, right?"

"Mr. Carter, you are our man, almost in our family, and if you don't like what's going on, give us a call and we will make the change."

#

Jong made the transfer of funds into the newly opened account and the deal was done. They had not finalized the details, but the group either owned 60%, or some to be negotiated percentage, of the hotel.

Once the transaction was completed, Mr. Carter noticed the new account balance, and exclaimed, "Are you people crazy? I haven't signed a thing, and you place a million bucks at my disposal."

Mallory assured him, "Mr. Christopher Carter, we're sure you will do the right thing because in the long run, it's all yours. Why steal from yourself or us? In the future, all you must do is ask us and if it's practical, it will be done. You're in charge. Now, you can use local people to lay out the plans or we can send you people to assist in drafting the blueprints. However, and whoever you use, no charlatans are allowed."

## CHAPTER SEVEN

In Birmingham, Alabama, the group began to meet the people who worked and lived on John Lee's property. Since the death of his woman, the group had installed monitoring devices in his new place which was almost completed. They also installed sensors in the fields and contracted with a security firm to monitor the farm from the various video installations.

In the meantime, Beckmire had reached out to his old nemesis Allen for assistance in locating his former boss. The Sarge asked, "Allen, how on earth have you been and what on earth have you been doing?"

"Hello, Mr. Beckmire. I'm still on the run and, from what I hear, you're supposed to be dead, and yet, here you are speaking to me. How can this be?"

"I guess you'll have to put this in the book of miracles. Let me cut through the chase. Some people tried to do some very nasty things to me and my family. I want them and I need your help. However, the knowledge of my not being dead must not be for sale by you. Tell me where to begin."

Allen understood the Sarge's request immediately, and replied, "You know he wants me dead as well."

"I actually thought he served you your papers. Glad to know that you're still on his hit list. How on earth did he get to become so powerful and protected?"

"That little ass-eating, penis-sucking, scum bag has photos of a lot of powerful people doing the nasty with little people and each other. He has a knack for knowing what proclivities a person enjoys, and he feeds off that knowledge and adds to it by making up devious things about them. The congressman that was charged with having an affair with a seventeen-year-old summer intern, that's your boy's work. The Deputy Director of the Agency that was photographed up in Maine last year with a twenty-three-year-old man in a compromising position. that again was your boy. If you don't play his game when he says it's time to play, keep a sharp eye out for your name or picture in the news. That little shit is the person behind those events. I can't believe that he has amassed that much power and controls people at all levels. Listen, he can make your dreams come true, but when he asks for a favor; don't hesitate, don't pause, just say how soon and for whom."

"Allen, how do I get to save your ass, yet once again? Tell me where to start looking for my cousin."

"Yeah, that cousin shit really freaked me out when I was told what he did to you and your family. I said to myself, 'so much for being related to that damn guy'. Mr. Beckmire, I am so far removed from the grid, but I will make a few long shot requests from some other people who are on the move as a result of your dear cousin. Give me a couple of hours and let me see what I can find out."

"I'll catch you later." The Sarge turned to Jong and matter-of-factly stated, "I know you had plenty of time to figure out where he is!"

"Sarge, the guy is in Atlanta, Georgia and is staying at the Marriott Marquis on Peachtree. Why did you trace Allen's call?"

"I believe Allen made a shit load of money working for Walter and lost a twice as much, messing with us. Now, don't you think that little snake is going to call Walter, let him know that we're alive and that we're hunting his ass. He'll try to sell that information and, perhaps, get back in good graces with Walter."

"That all sounds good, but your cousin is not a forgiving person and would more than likely kill that guy to send a message. I have never seen, nor heard of, a more devious person than Walter. He strapped suicide vests on babies and detonated them. He thought he had killed all of us including the children. Now, do you think he's going to buy information and then say, 'all's forgiven', to Allen? I seriously doubt that, and Allen probably realizes this as well. Let's see what he comes back with, but if I were you, I would ask John Lee to ratchet up his security for the next few days."

"I see your point and it's a point well taken. I'm going to see what he comes back with if anything at all," the Sarge stated.

# # #

John Lee was proudly showing Somara, Yeshida, and Jilkes around his property and pointed out the boundary markers that separated their properties. Jilkes asked, "Why do we have to have property markers, isn't it enough for people to know that our properties butt up to each other?"

Yeshida responded, "Since no one lives forever, it is best to mark those things that can be marked, so those who come after us will know how we lived and how close we were."

"That was well stated, and I agree with it. So, can we make this happen tomorrow if we aren't called to duty?" Jilkes asked.

"Well, that would make me feel really good knowing that we would be really close to each other," John Lee stated.

"Well, we talked about it and I spoke about it with Yeshida and she flatly said, 'I love the idea' and so, tomorrow we get this done. Remind me to clear Jong's calendar, we'll need him to handle the money part of this thing."

"I be done took the liberty of having that there architect fellow come out and talk to you tomorrow along with that guy who be doing the surveying and all that. Now, there be another 6,000 acres of prime property across the road. Would you like to go in with me and buy it before one of them there developing kind of people put a damn mall over there?"

"Done! Just so that you know, I'm letting Yeshida design the house with Eastern and Western aspects to it. I hope that architect is good."

"He should be really good, being that he's a Chinese fellow who happens to like pigs."

# # #

The crew was adjusting to the slow pace of life in Alabama. Courtney said to the Sarge, "Now, this would be a good place to relocate once you've finished saving the world. It's perfect, slow, methodical, and laid back. All you need to do is learn something about farming or raising pigs, and it would be a wonderful place to live and watch those grandbabies develop. Speaking about development, I seriously think we need to quietly move the hell out of Philadelphia and sneak away somewhere. Lord only knows what has happened to our house and the different people who have been through it. I don't know if I would want to call it home anymore. I mean people literally died in that place. Do you have any thoughts about it?"

"Honey, I really haven't had time to think about it because at every turn someone is trying to kill us, however, you are correct. We don't need those kinds of memories in what is supposed to be our home. Let's set aside some time later and discuss options. You know, we must think about Rashida and her child as well. I'm sure she wants to be near you and me, maybe we need an immediate family meeting."

"Great idea and I'll set it up. Thank you, Ben Beckmire, for caring about the entire world." Courtney lovingly hugged her husband, and said, "You are one promising catch."

"The act of promising means that I have promise. At this point I would have thought I graduated from the school of promise to the world of delivery."

"Ben Beckmire, whatever! Let it go and enjoy the compliment."

# # #

Later that evening, Allen called the Sarge and said, "Rumor has it that you people are still alive, and that people are on their way to that ranch to collect DNA samples to verify who really died. It probably created suspicion when there were no funerals. My sources tell me that Walter is hanging out in South Beach with a large security contingency. I suggest you not attempt to engage the man there but wait until he comes back to the DC area. He's in South Beach with his family, but that shouldn't matter to you because he tried to kill your family. I also have to warn you that there are high stake visitors there as well, and everyone has a security detail. I know your people could take on the third battalion, but this one might turn out to be too messy, even for your outfit."

"Do you know the strength of the security detail?"

"I was told that there are thirty-two people guarding his ass."

"Are the taxpayers footing that bill?"

"Who else? Walter is an amazing man and has his hands in all kinds of pockets. I hear he has taken on a new young male confidant as well."

"You mean lover, don't you?"

"They start off with official status, somehow are seduced, bite from his fig tree, and end up enslaved to the emperor. Mr. Beckmire, other than that I have no additional information to provide you. I would like to think that things are good between us and that I don't have to look over my shoulder for you."

"All is good, but if I need you or if you hear anything that could be of use to me, I expect you to send me a message. After all, this guy is out for the both of us."

"Oh, there is one other thing that you might find interesting. You remember his associate Mike? Well, Mike told him to kiss off and that he was going to expose some of his dirty dealings. That was a mistake because Mike's car blew up in his garage, he was able to escape and is now being hunted by Walter and his thugs."

"Do you have any way to reach him?"

"Absolutely not. Remember that guy was sent to put a hit on me but gave me the opportunity to escape. If I knew how to reach him, I would hide out with him. My trail is getting narrow, and people are discovering me at every turn. I wish you would hurry up and make your cousin an artefact. That news would make a lot of people really happy."

"I'm working on that in a way that you wouldn't believe, but I don't want him dead--I want him in misery."

"Oh shit, that sounds too evil for my tender ears, Mr. Beckmire. I'm going to say goodbye. If I hear anything or get a fix on Mike, I will be in contact. You know we didn't start out as people who could trust one another, but I'm happy that we're at a point now when I don't have to look over my shoulder for you or your boys. Catch you later."

# # #

The Sarge took a walk around the property and realized exactly what Courtney was referring to. The place was peaceful and full of people who were out to help you and not take advantage of you. Everywhere the Sarge ventured on the property, people were offering him water, food, or conversation. When he came upon John Lee and Jilkes he said, "I was thinking about giving you two some wet work on South Beach. The issue is that everyone knows about you two."

"I be betting they don't know about us and our new associates," John Lee said.

Beckmire paused, smiled, privately agreed, and announced, "Damn, and if you add Brown to the equation, it might just work out. Listen, the guy who blew up the ranch, with us in it, is in South Beach and I so very much want to get my hands on him. Bring him out here and let John Lee perform surgery on him."

"Sarge, unless you're going to cut that dude into quarters, then there is no sense in placing bad karma on this land. Let us do him there and be done with it," Jilkes said.

"I hear what you're saying, but a guy who places suicide vests on children should suffer a long tedious life without arms, legs and eyes."

"I see where you're heading with that and I concur." Jilkes added, "If we have the two or three ladies with us, I'm sure no one would recognize us because first of all, they're going to wonder how on earth John Lee, and his country ass, woke up with such a beauty on his arm."

"Screw you, minority man. I'm going to change my style and become suave and debonair. It's all a matter of presentation. You know, you and I never really cared about the way we looked until them there ladies showed up. That there South Beach is loaded with fancy places to buy clothes and stuff. Maybe we let them folk down there transmog—what's that there word."

Jilkes and the Sarge laughed before Jilkes replied, "Are you trying to say transmogrify? Just remember the story about the Great Saltie and his transmogrification."

"Jilkes is one smart minority man. I keep learning a lot from him but he don't know shit about land, and farming so, he be learning a lot from me, and that makes our friendship transactional. Like doing good business conducted by true family members."

"Way to go brother, but we have to focus on that SOB that tried to kill us. Is it just us or is it the entire team?"

The Sarge interrupted, "We don't separate and will never begin that practice. I need you two once you have transmogrified, to be our point guys and get this dude so we can chop, wrap, and ship his ass out to sea."

"You be talking about no arms, legs, and eyes. Is that really the way you be wanting to leave that there person?"

"John Lee, anyone who puts a suicide vest on a child is not fit for life on this earth with all their limbs."

"I don't be disagreeing with you, but I be wanting to be sure that we're going to do that to him. I wanted to gut him like I did that Scottie woman, and I want to ask if I can be first."

Jilkes looked at him and said, "We have enough crazy people involved with us. I don't need you wandering off the reservation. Stay focused and let me guide you through some of your mental issues. Don't start liking shit that you can't talk about in public," Jilkes encouraged.

"Anyway, you guys seemingly have a new cover, if in fact, those beautiful ladies want to tag along and get involved in a fight that is not theirs. I think it's the perfect cover for our group. I just need to capture Walter and ship his ass somewhere after I have performed surgery on him, and then place him on a corner to beg his way through life. Jong, make ready the planes because we're going to find out if we can capture and ship this asshole without a lot of loss of life to his people and ours."

"Sarge, the desire to capture him may exceed the need to capture him--just saying. I think we should do this when it is convenient and doable for us. If we are led by sheer desire instead of need, we might get caught up in that revenge syndrome. I recommend that we take a moment and let others decide how we approach this thing because your vision is purely driven by passion seeing the children strapped in suicide vests. The need in this equation might have a different outcome based upon a more rational approach in considering the options," Jong prophetically stated.

"In other words, you're saying that I'm too close to this one to make a rationale decision."

"That's exactly what I'm saying. Let's discuss it before we go traipsing across the country and walk into some formidable circumstances without considering all of the options," Jong suggested.

"Your point is well taken. We'll discuss it further when everyone is present."

CHAPTER EIGHT

Allen received a call from one of his associates who informed him that a friend of his had been hired to do some forensic work on a ranch in the Midwest. The caller also informed Allen that body parts were being assembled and placed in bags for further analysis. Allen called Beckmire and told him about this development. The Sarge thanked him and immediately made a call to Clyde. When Clyde answered the telephone the Sarge asked, "What on earth is going on out there?"

"Well, Sarge, frankly people are out of their minds. People were alluding to the fact that they couldn't find any body parts, or anything related to human remains and it was causing a stir. So, me and a few of the boys unearthed some of those people who tried to kill you and placed them in the field and blew them up. We collected their remains and placed them around the perimeter of Ms. Asiram's ranch. So far, this seems to be satisfying those people in suits who are looking around the property. It may not have been the greatest idea, but it was what we came up with to sort of give you time to reckon with those bad guys who think you're dead."

"Damn, Clyde, that is some amazing thinking because we had heard it was rumored that we were alive and had escaped the explosion. This will indeed give us a few days to handle the matter. I can't, or we can't, thank you enough for being a true friend and patriot. We all appreciate you and your family. Thanks Clyde. Keep me informed."

"Tell Ms. Asiram that those architect types have two sets of drawings they want her to take a look at. One of the suits asked me what was going on with them and I told him that Ms. Asiram's mother wants to restore the place and sell it."

"Good thinking once again, Clyde. I will let her know, and I will get you an email address so that you can send those documents to me."

The Sarge looked at Jong and reported, "Well, Clyde bought us some time. That guy dug up some of those unfortunate souls who died out there on the ranch, placed them in a contained area and blew up their bodies. He and his people collected body parts and proceeded to spread them around Asiram's place. Clyde also indicated to me that this would buy us a couple of days because there were suits on-site trying to figure out why there was a lack of remains. I don't know all of the details, but I will say, we should revisit that conversation relative to need and desire."

"I didn't realize there were people out there trying to find human remains from the rubble, which really could have been a problem for us. Sarge, even after DNA testing, it is going to be hard to name the owner of a part. In my opinion, what Clyde has done is given us a couple of days to try to figure out how to intercept Diablo. Sarge, I need to apologize to you because I feel I was out of order when I suggested that you figure out whether the mission is a need or a desire. We have been through hell and back and I can't believe I challenged you on this issue. I guess I'm weary and tired, but also excited and happy to be needed. It has not been easy for me, but you guys have never wavered in your support. The damn doctors told us that I would never walk again and here I am, running a little. I need you and the guys in my life. I have nothing else and sometimes I guess I rebel against things because I'm the handicapped one," Jong said.

"Wait just a minute! All this time that I have been dealing with you, calling you Mr. Amazing and you're handicap? Well, kiss my own ass, I didn't know that about you. Shit, I thought you were a guy with swagger. I'll be damned, wait until I tell the rest of the group that you're a damn h-capper."

"Sarge, I'm serious about what I'm talking about."

"I'm sorry, Mister, because I am serious about my response. I have no h-cappers in my unit. Perhaps you should apply for a nurse's position since I have no space for h-cappers."

"Sarge, stop the bullshit."

"Sir, I'm not bullshitting you. You're trying to run a hustle on me and get out of doing your fair share of work. If that is what this is about, I mean you being a slacker, that is, then say so. Otherwise, I expect the same dedication and effort from you as I do from the rest of the guys."

John Lee and Jilkes walked into the room and Jong exclaimed, "Jesus!"

Jilkes looked at him and asked, "What the fuck was that for?"

Jong started to say something when the Sarge blurted out, "Guys, do we happen to have any handicap people in our unit?"

John Lee looked at the Sarge and inquired, "Well, I don't mean to sound trifle, but this here black guy is mentally handclapped. Does that count?"

"Do we have any people who have slacked off on their job and placed others in jeopardy?"

"Again, I can only think of one person and that be this here brother who is mentally a h-capper. What be the reason for this kind of inquiry?"

"Someone, and I ain't going to call no names, thinks that he's a h-capper and, therefore, deserves special treatment from the group. He doesn't think that shooting people sitting in their cars is enough excitement for him. I believe he wants to lead the charge, but he can't because he feels that he's a h-capper. What should we do about this situation?"

"I, personally, think that he should oversee capturing that SOB who tried to kill us. Give him that charge and let him run first," Jilkes stated.

"I would do that, but he feels that the decision to capture my cousin is based upon my desire rather than need. Now, mind you, this guy has left the reservation but believes he's here because we are trying to satisfy some kind of quota. He thinks that we should meet first and decide whether my goal is based upon need or desire."

"Well, given the fact that he's going to lead the charge, what's his mission based upon? Is it a self-concocted design or one that has the entire squad's interest at heart?" Jilkes asked.

"Well, I don't know that answer, but he's a great person and has done some amazing shit to keep us coming, going, and happy. I must ask you guys this question, where did that h-capper shit come from? When we go for our runs, do you see any motorized wheelchairs pulling up the rear or leading us in the front?" the Sarge asked.

"This is a perplexing set of questions, Sarge, Jilkes stated. "Perhaps, you should allow this person some personal time to sort out any issues that might be creating this perverse attitude. You know a simple visit home has the ability to heal a lot of things and emotions that humans go through. Give him some time off, and then we'll all talk to him."

"Gentlemen, that ain't going to happen because I need him to provide the alter-ego effect and rationalize situations that are now being described as need versus desire. No, I need this person around because apparently, I may have missed the boat on a couple of issues," the Sarge divulged.

"If you let his demons penetrate your mindset, then you both will have issues, you know. And our missions are too complicated to have issues. The issues are always waiting on us and any mistake, based upon those topics, has the potential of being fatal. Naw, we don't want you to let one of our own share your burden of leadership. One Sarge, one Corporal, and then there is the rest of us; worked so far, so no need in fixing it," Jilkes articulated.

"Can I say something since you people are talking about me as if I am not in the room? Can I say something? Anyways, I challenged the Sarge and after doing so, I realized I was all wet. I circled back to apologize, and somehow, I exposed my own self-pity. Guys quit the bullshit. I'm the h-capper, the Sarge is talking about."

The Sarge screamed at the top of his lungs and said, "Mister, I will kick your ass if you say that one more time." Everyone watched as the Sarge slammed his hand down on the countertop and watched it crack down the middle. He said, "You're not a damn handicapper, and if you are, then we all are because we are one and that is why we have survived the Nam, Brown's father, Gianni and this latest shit. If you must say that, then I suggest you go home and seek redemption and pity. There is none here to be given. I'm done with the subject," the Sarge announced.

"Sarge, the only thing I'm trying to say is that I love you and the guys. This adventure has been so mentally and physically stimulating to me. I am what I am, regardless of how you see me. I just don't want to be a burden or a liability to you."

"Jilkes, you and John Lee get this guy out of my sight before I bust him up. He's the core of our operation and I think he wants to quit. Tell the asshole that I love him, hope that he reconsiders his decision and decides to stay with the group. Tell that asshole that we need him. Tell him that I need him!" the Sarge adamantly stated.

CHAPTER NINE

A newly "transmogrified" Jilkes, John Lee, and Brown stepped off their private jet with three amazing looking Asian beauties. The Sarge looked at Jong and announced, "Now, that's some incredible work you just did. How on earth did you get John Lee to sit still and have his entire look changed?"

"I didn't do a damn thing. Somara told him to stay still or sleep alone, those were her only words. John Lee replied, "Okay honey, if this here thing will make you happy."

"Is he that whipped?"

"Sarge, I don't know what those women did to those three guys, but I would say they're all whipped. Brown is the worst, believe it or not. John Lee is second, and then Jilkes, but they're all whipped."

"That's amazing and wonderful, especially, since those women make those three guys whole. I don't know how but I knew it when they met. I knew that they would be hard to get rid of."

"I would like to visit our discussion of earlier today."

"Unless you want to do mortal combat with me, let it go. They love you; I love you and you're intricate to this team and our missions. You must admit--this is some exciting shit, and it proves that we aren't too old to handle our business. I need you to let that other thing go and stay focused. By the way, have you asked yourself any questions lately, like who do I call first, who do I have do all our business transactions, and who do I send to shoot a driver in the head? Please stop it, and let it go, until we are back in a place where we can all relax."

"Okay, but I'm going to hold you to a real discussion and one where you don't break someone's countertop because you're angry."

"That was showmanship! I was really pissed that you thought this is some kind of charity mission and that you are not important. As a matter of fact, I rely on you more than I do anyone else in the squad. Think about it and get back to me."

# # #

The 'M' property is one of the most spectacular places on South Beach. Walter's condominium occupied half of the space on the twentieth floor, giving him a full view of the north and south perspectives of the beach. It was truly magnificent. John Lee, Jilkes, and Brown were situated in suites, two floors below Walter's spread. They were not yet sure how they were going to capture him. The Sarge wanted his habits to be studied to discern the best time and place to conduct an interdiction. It became obvious to the Sarge that Walter thought he was living in a place and time that did not present an immediate danger to himself.

When Walter proceeded into the bar, five of his security team had already checked the place out and three of his team were strategically placed around the bar prior to his arrival. Walter ordered a slightly dirty Martini, with three olives.

As he scanned the area, focusing on Jilkes, John Lee, Brown and their three trophies, he said to his front man, "I want one of those Asian women. Let me see, they're all sterling, but the one on the far right, I want her in my bed in one hour, no matter the cost. I have never seen Asian women as beautiful as they are. No matter the cost, and I do mean that literally, I want the one on the far right in my bed within the next 60 minutes."

Walter's front man walked over to the group, gave some bogus name as he introduced himself and looked at the fingers of the ladies for any indication that they were married. He saw none and decided to skip the "BS' and go right to the essence of his being at their table. He looked at Brown and said, "I presume that young lady is with you, and that creates a problem for me and my team. My employer eyed your woman and found her to be the most beautiful Asian woman that he has ever seen. He expects me to deliver her to his bed within the next hour." Brown raised up aggressively, but Jilkes grabbed his arm and pulled him back into his seat.

Brown said, "You must be one crazy asshole with a death wish, or a real bad ass. Which one is it?"

"Sir, I'm just the messenger, but my employer is a real bad ass and has a license to kill, now does that qualify him with a death wish? Listen, I can make this thing worth your while and I doubt he touches your lady because he enjoys men. Look around this room. You see those people at the bar? Well, they work for and protect my client. This is a very tense situation; it can end very poorly for you and your friends. I'm sure the lady doesn't want that to happen and would probably prefer to entertain my employer rather than have you guys blown to pieces in this bar."

"So, if I'm not mistaken, you're going to take my woman, let your employer have his way with her and I'm supposed to sit here and hold my dick until she comes back. Is that what you're saying?" Brown inquired.

"I wouldn't put it so graphically; but essentially that is the deal."

"I'm sorry, but that is not the deal, nor will it be. My advice to you is pretty precise, get the fuck away from this table, or have your last drink," Brown announced.

The front man made it a point to show his weapon and motioned for four other members of his team to come over.

Brown was on the verge of going ballistic when Jilkes said, "Sir, we don't want any trouble and we're just going to leave. If you continue to pursue this course of action, then you will have to pull that puppy out of that holster. Before you're successful at that, I will have cut your manhood beyond repair. You make a single move and I will transfigure you into a bitch. Now, you may be fast, but dude I will have your dick before I die. You think you can just walk in here and demand that we turn our friend over to your employer because he's some weird big shot? Sorry, dude, you just messed with the wrong people and we will bleed first before we let you take our friend." Suddenly the table was surrounded by Walter's men with their hands on their weapons.

John Lee exclaimed, "This ain't fair at all. You people got guns and we got pocketknives. Why don't you just let us leave and everything will be fine. No way, in hell, you're going to take any of these women from us unless you kill us in this public place, with cameras everywhere. Unless you're God, then you have no escape plan. This here mess be very dumb and over somebody else's lady!"

Okema said, "No one has considered my opinion in this matter. I often find myself around a lot of this kind of behavior. I just met you, Mr. Brown, and frankly, I'm bored with your conversation that lacks the intellectual aspects of life. I don't know who your employer is, but he cannot order me to his room as if I was a face towel or something to wipe his ass with. I am my own person, and no one can direct my movements, except me, unless they have a lot of rope to lower me into hell. What would be the benefit of such an arrangement with your employer? Your moronic actions are on camera and it's extremely doubtful that you control the 'M's' security system. What is the dollar value to me? That's all I want to know. If the number is not in the high six digits, then I'm going to scream rape, and a bunch of police and other people are going to react to my noises."

"Lady, frankly, you don't have a say in this discussion because we're going to hold guns on your friends until you have serviced our client. So, you can just shut the fuck up and enjoy the inevitable ride?"

Okema winked at Brown and said, "You tarnish my image by your weak words. Perhaps, if you're serious, you will make a stronger attempt to gain all that is left of me since you are unable to protect me from heights."

The Sarge was wired to Jilkes and heard the entire conversation.

He said to Mallory, "Okema wants to lower him from the window. That's twenty stories high, isn't it?"

"Walter is allegedly staying on the twentieth floor, and you know with this guy, nothing is as it's supposed to be. What do we know? There are twenty easy targets in or around the bar or exits. Four are watching over his motorcade, four on street duty, there are at least two stationed at each exit, two at his condo front door and eight inside watching his back. I don't think these guys are going to beg for their lives, so this is going to be messy. I suggest that we get Jong to cut the feed on the security cameras for about four minutes. Guys, what are your thoughts?" Chakes looked at McArthur who shrugged his shoulders. He then looked at Bernstein and Gladstone as if asking them for their contribution.

Bernstein looked at Gladstone and answered, "Why don't we make it six minutes and that way we can be methodical in finishing these guys. I guess we aren't offering any quarters."

"These guys had better die in battle, or Walter will have them killed if they survive. From my vantage point, these guys are true mercs and would probably want to die as such. I suggest we hit them, hit them hard, and make it final. Mr. Amazing, can you and Montomie handle the video and the four watching the motorcade? Whitmore, can you and Gladstone handle the four guys doing street duty, realizing that there are going to be other people walking around? Do you think we can hit them with a drug or something and save their sorry asses?"

"Sarge, why don't we start a small fire on a higher floor or just pull the fire alarm, tap into the cameras, and see what their movements are like before we do anything?" Jong recommended.

"Damn, why didn't I think of that? People, Mr. Amazing is back and I'm happy to welcome him home. I think as skittish as Walter is, he probably has an escape plan in place and all we need to do is watch and learn from it."

"How many different hypotheticals do you want to employ? I mean, he can decide to take any number of turns but, hopefully, we will be at each one to catch his ass. My question is simple--do we let Okema attempt to handle this sadistic son-of-a-bitch by herself, or do we do what we do best?" Chakes inquired.

"My cousin is sick with power, desire, and is a confused about whether he should have been born a woman or a man. I think if he gets Okema in his room, he will probably hurt her because she represents everything that he can't be. People, this is going to be messy, stay with your assigned partners and listen for my 'it's a go' chant—three times before you do anything."

#

Jong and Montomie entered a secure room in the basement of the hotel. The "M's" security system appeared to be under heavy lock and key. Jong said to Montomie, "Tell the Sarge this is going to take longer than projected because the system is controlled by a dual monitoring station that warns the main frame that it is being hacked."

"Sarge, Montomie here. Jong is going to need more time to penetrate this thing. I'll call you back when he has found a solution."

"Tell him that he has to breach it or attend to those guards because we can't let Okema enter that sick man's room."

"Roger that." He turned to Jong and said, "Listen you have a few minutes to break into that shit or kill those guys in the parking lot. The Sarge does not want that lady to enter his cousin's room."

"I understand that, but this is not my design. This is too much pressure."

"Okay, brother, let's pause for a moment. Did you say this is too much pressure?"

"I did! It's like I'm supposed to work miracles or something. He's beginning to work on my nerves."

Montomie stopped Jong from continuing, "Wait a minute, solider. First, who is the 'he', and second, what is the pressure? What's going on with you? If you have now relegated the Sarge to a 'he', and the pressure is becoming too much for you, then I recommend you pack your shit and leave! You should take a break and change your scenery because you're going to get someone hurt with that attitude. By the way, you know it was that 'he', who carried your ass out of that firefight and never missed a step in the three-mile run with you bleeding in his arms. You take care of this, and I will take care of those four in the garage."

"Those are not the orders the Sarge gave us. Listen, give me a couple of minutes with this security mess, then I will pop two and you can pop the other two. I trust the fact that our conversation does not go beyond the two of us. I guess I'm having a melt down with my leg issues. I so very much want to be able to make a solid contribution to all of the things that we do and not just be the errand boy."

"Are you serious? Errand boy? You got the best job in this outfit because the rest of us aren't as savvy or as smart as you are, and besides, I don't remember a skirmish when you weren't shooting somebody. What is the deal with you? Man, you're alive and that's better than being dead, I would think."

"If I was dead, I wouldn't have these thoughts."

"If you were dead, there would be a lot of people who would want to take your place because they love you more than life. Get over the bullshit and rejoin your brotherhood. After all, this is some exciting shit we have fallen into, and it sure beats the heck out of sitting around and watching TV and playing games all damn day."

Jong's eyes filled up with water and Montomie walked over to him and gave him a beast of a hug and said softly, "You know we got your back."

After approximately eight minutes, the fire alarm went off and Okema was on the elevator with two of Walter's security team. As the elevator was ascending, it abruptly stopped on the eighteenth floor, and the general security system issued a warning to take the nearest exit to safety and that it was not a drill. Okema lowered her head and with supreme accuracy leaped into the air and left kicked a set of testicles, and before hitting the floor of the elevator, she right kicked another set of testicles and then confidently landed a secure punch to the first man's throat, retrieved his weapon and fired a single round into each man's head and exited the elevator. As she headed for the exit sign, she passed a person in a hurry who gave her the chills. It was Walter, operating under one of his smoke screens. Okema had never encountered Walter before, but felt that she had just looked into the eyes of the devil.

On the 20th floor, armed men with weapons drawn, huddled around an individual and escorted him to the nearest exit. Everyone tried to discern who the person was, but no one could unequivocally identify the person as Walter. Mallory asked the Sarge, "Do you want to make a move on them?"

"I don't believe that's my cousin. I don't believe he's even here."

Jong and Montomie had a view of each floor and all the action. Montomie said to Jong, "Look at those four guys coming out of that room on the 19th floor, but more importantly, try to zoom in on the guy with the dark glasses." Jong zoomed in on the subject and bingo, it was Walter. Since he owned the condo below, he had steps installed that led from the 20th floor to the 19th. True to form, no assumptions about Walter could be held constant.

Jong called the Sarge and said, "Walter is on the north stairway and making his way down to his caravan. Do you want us to make a move?"

"I want you to commandeer the vans and pick his ass up. We must rescue Jilkes, John Lee, and Brown along with the other ladies, but blast those guys who are decoys. For the moment, you're going to be outgunned, but we should conclude the bar scene in a matter of three minutes and then join you."

Jong and Montomie counted their rounds and Montomie said, "Let's hit them, capture their weapons, but make sure they're loaded. I got the two on the right and you take the two on the left. I'm going to run out of ammo, because I'm just going to wildly fire at them to distract everyone and allow you time to take out the other two. Don't miss!"

Montomie walked into the garage and began to wildly fire at the two men on his right, hitting one in the arm and causing the other one to duck for his life. Jong swiftly finished the two men on his left and began to fire at the lone security person on the right. Jong picked up a fresh weapon and began to spray the area where the guy was seeking cover. A bullet hit the man in the leg, and he threw out his weapon. Montomie walked over to him, retrieved the man's weapon, looked closely at him, and said, "I know you. You were at the ranch. I remember you, your cigar, how you laughed, and how you told the children that the vests would protect them. Yes, you and that red-headed guy. I'm not going to kill you because you were just following orders. But what I'm going to do, will hurt like hell." Montomie shot the man in each elbow and both kneecaps. He then took out his knife and carved his initial on the man's chest.

Jong yelled, "At least carve a 'J' somewhere."

In the bar, a full firefight was in progress and it was being decidedly won by the Sarge and his group. It was methodical and each target had been pre-assigned. Zanthius said to Asiram, "This is your last mission. You're beginning to look like a pregnant woman."

She laughed at him, but her laughter quickly changed to concern. She said, "Honey, I know that guy over there in the corner, the one with the red hair. He was at my ranch and placed the vests on the children." Zanthius secured the area and walked over to the man who was obviously bleeding from his wounds and said, "So, you thought it was funny to tell the children that the vests would protect them?" Zanthius looked around the room and saw John Lee and Jilkes and announced, "I think I have someone you guys might want to do some work on."

Jilkes walked over to where Zanthius was and exclaimed, "Well, I'll be damned! This is the man with the jokes. John Lee, look what I found. You remember that guy who placed the vests on the children? Him and that cigar smoking dude, well, he be here and not dead." After securing the area, John Lee and the ladies walked over to Zanthius, Jilkes, and Asiram. John Lee said, "Somara, I have some special work to do on this here guy and I don't want you to see me do it."

"I will watch you and help you, if necessary. You must stop trying to shut me out of that part of your life that is not pleasant. It is all of you, John Lee, that I admire, desire and am falling madly in love with."

"Well, honey, since you put it like that, I would like to discuss with you what I, I'm sorry, what we, Jilkes and I, want to do to this guy. This here rodent placed suicide vests on the children and told them that the vests would protect them and laughed as he and his partner locked those babies in them there vests."

Zanthius said, "John Lee, you guys secure this area. My father and the others are making their way to the garage and need our firepower."

John Lee looked at the redhead and exclaimed, "You won't have the opportunity to place anything around anyone's body in this life again." He whispered something to Somara and Yeshida and they quickly moved behind the bar and retrieved two bottles of 100 proof rum. John Lee pulled his big blade out and without telegraphing his move, hacked the guy's left arm until it dangled from his body. He then, once again, without telegraphing his moves, hacked his right arm. Jilkes stuffed his mouth with a napkin and when the two ladies returned, they poured the rum on the redhead's wounds and lit a match. They cauterized each severed arm. Somara asked, "Would not death be more fitting for this person's future?"

"Honey, this here person placed those suicide vests on the children. I be thinking that death be too easy in his case, but if you want me to kill this here rat, then I will follow your wishes."

"No, my love, I follow your wishes. There is so much that we don't know or understand and to give input would be to sour the decision. You have made an honorable call to let him suffer and for him to contemplate his role in wanting to hurt innocent children."

Jilkes stated, "I think we might be needed in the garage. Can you ladies manage the clean-up and secure this area?"

Yeshida exclaimed with confidence, "If anyone moves, they will face a second death."

"That's my girl. I think we secured the place, but we might have missed someone, so stay alert."

In the garage, the team waited patiently for the door to open. Brown began to scale the steps to secure Okema while she was in the process of running down the steps to secure him. The two met on the fifth floor and exchanged a powerful and seductive kiss. Brown said, "We have to head down to the garage and secure the rest of the team. Did you really want to lower that guy twenty stories to the ground? I have never seen a rope that long."

"I figured by giving you a challenging scenario, you would come up with a better alternative to make sure that he had no chance of seeing, touching, or abusing what is now considered, for your eyes only, Mr. Brown."

"I am honored, but afraid at the same time. You are creating a terrible void in my mind. The only person that seems to matter to me, is you. I still consider you a Gordian knot. I can't get you out of my mind, but I don't want you to respond right now because we have to get busy and make sure that the others are safe."

# # #

In the garage, and without a shot being fired, the Sarge said out loud, "Cousin, that was extremely dastardly what you and your people did out there at the ranch. How on earth could you place suicide vests on your kin and tell them that it was for their protection?" There was no response and Brown yelled, "Friendlies picking up the rear."

"How many friendlies are you and what names?" Mallory demanded.

"Jilkes, John Lee, Yeshida, Somara, Okema, and Brown, ahead of us we have Asiram and Zanthius."

Okema said to Brown, "I believe the person you're seeking has already made his way out of this place. Just before meeting up with you, I had a strange sensation come over me, that included chills and what I believe was a view of the devil. I think it was your Walter person." Brown looked at her and thought about the vests that were placed on the children; and at the top of his lungs he yelled, "abort, abort, abort."

The team heard this information coming in but were slow to process it. In less than thirty seconds, as they retreated from the general area, there was a detonation that shook the foundation of the 'M' Hotel.

When the smoke cleared, the Sarge gave a weak command to conduct roll call. Most of the guys were disoriented by the blast, especially in the enclosed area. Jong and Montomie were first to arrive on the scene from the section of the garage they were in and the scene was total chaos. Montomie shouted, "What the hell just happened? Where is the Sarge and our brothers? Who, the hell did this?"

A bewildered and stressed out Jong yelled, "Stop asking dumb ass questions and focus, this scene may still be hot. Look out for our guys and don't be too trigger happy."

As Jilkes, John Lee and the rest of their group entered the blast area, John Lee yelled, "You got friendlies asking about our people. Don't move until we be done cleared this place of rat droppings. Can yawl 'roger that'?"

Jilkes looked around and said, "The devil himself did this. He knew that we weren't dead, and that damn guy sacrificed his people to get to us. He'd better improve on his antics because we're going to focus all of our energy on his ass and he has to sleep at some point."

#

At the airport, a bewildered but otherwise healthy group of people stared into space and each wondered, 'what the hell just happened'? The Sarge was unable to communicate effectively but continued to make inaudible sounds, incomplete sentences, and a series of repeated remarks that caught the attention of those who were not in the immediate blast zone. Jong took it upon himself to attempt to calm the Sarge down. He convinced the Sarge that all the team members were accounted for and they were without injury other than concussions, headaches, earaches, and disorientation. The Sarge could only remember his last encounter with Jong and the exchange between the two required monitoring by Mallory.

## CHAPTER TEN

In Birmingham, Alabama, many members of the group remained slightly disoriented. Although some were more coherent than others, the Sarge demonstrated signs of a concussion, and Courtney was watching his every move. Courtney placed six members of the team on inactive status because of their inability to answer basic questions. Bernstein, Chakes, McArthur, Gladstone, as well as the Sarge and Mallory, were all relegated to the inactive status. In the interim, Jilkes and Jong called the shots.

Allen called the Sarge's phone and Jilkes answered it. Allen said, "I'm sorry I have the wrong number."

Jilkes screamed, "You have the right number and we still have an active contract on your ass!"

"I gave you guys all that I had on the 'M' situation, and you people blew it. Why am I being threatened?"

"Last I heard, you were supposed to provide us with complete details. You neglected to include information about the dude's place."

"It's not like he invited me to his place and showed me around. It was confirmed by my people that he lived on the 20th floor and that is exactly what I told the Sarge, and by the way, who the hell is this?"

"You don't need to know who this is, but what you really need to be aware of is, that I control your contract. You, my friend, almost got all my people killed and I will not forget that. I hear Walter wants your ass as well, so I suggest you present your ass to him in a couple of days and give us another shot at him."

"I am only dealing with the Sarge! Screw you, and good night."

Jilkes looked at John Lee and said, "He told me to screw myself and that he was only dealing with the Sarge, I can't let him talk to the Sarge, not in his current state."

John Lee began to say something when the Sarge's phone rang. It was Allen who said, "Perhaps, I was a bit rude in our last discussion, but what would make me feel at ease is if I could hear Mr. Beckmire's voice. He is alright, isn't he?"

"Absolutely, but he is unable to come to the phone because he is handling a serious money matter. As soon as he is available to talk, I will have him call you and I will remind him of the fact that you are one rude puppy."

"There is no reason to be insulting. I have only dealt with Mr. Beckmire in the past and, therefore, I am extremely cautious about changing our protocol. I'm sure you understand that, especially, in the business that we find ourselves. Please, have him give me a call and I will give him my updates. In the meantime, it's important that Mr. Beckmire know that I left this phone and number in a place where his nemesis can retrieve it. Thank you and good night."

Jilkes looked at John Lee and said, "I think I would like to gut that guy, but I guess we need his intel."

#

Zanthius said to Asiram, "I think that was your last mission, Ms. Lady. You're a mother to be, and explosions and bullets flying are not conducive to a healthy birthing process."

"Really, Zanthius? You're going to tell me what I can do now, and what battles I can fight? Really?"

"Honey, I'm not telling you anything other than the fact that I want our baby to be healthy and safe. Being in the middle of firefights is not what I consider safe and I'm sure you will agree with me."

"My husband and lover, never try to tell me what I can or cannot do."

"Okay, you know what, do whatever you want to do, but I assure you, your path will be injurious to our child. Catch you later."

Zanthius left the room in a thunderous manner, slamming the door and screaming obscenities under his breath. Asiram recalled her comments and they led her to tears. She thought the enormity of her body's transformation, as well as her overall look, was beginning to take its toll on her and Zanthius.

Zanthius was smart enough to recognize what was going on. An hour later, he entered the room and found her crying. On his knees, he crawled from the door to where she was sitting, and loudly and tearfully said, "We are the greatest team on earth and what hurts you, hurts me. Let's birth this baby correctly and safely. I love you with all my heart and soul and you are the only person on earth that matters to me. Please stop crying. Realize that this thing called being pregnant is going to make you look different, but to me, you will be the sexiest person that I have ever seen."

"Honey, please don't abandon me in my hour of need. This is all new to me, my body is going straight to hell and I don't like it."

"We're a team, Asiram. As such, I am yours until the end of time, and you're mine through eternity. I love you so very much, but I must demand that you play a safe role and not lead the charge anytime soon. I'm worried because our enemies will use any tool possible to inflict pain on us, just remember the children with those suicide vests on."

# # #

Once the Sarge had recovered a bit, he received a briefing from Jilkes relative to his conversation with Allen. The Sarge called Allen and was surprised when his cousin answered the phone.

Walter said, "You must really be connected with some powerful people to escape that last surprise I had for you. You know, none of this is personal and I take orders from a higher source, just like you do. I really didn't want to do what I did, but it came down to you or me; I chose me. Now, before you start screaming about what you're going to do to me, I just want you to know all of my resources are being focused on you. And, when you talk to your little snitching-ass friend Allen, let him know that he will face a horrible death. That's all for now, Couz, and damn you must really be connected to get out of that shit at the ranch and the garage."

Walter hung up the phone and thought how wonderful it would have been if Beckmire was working for him and not against him.

Meanwhile, the Sarge turned to Jilkes and announced, "I think this thing just got worse."

## CHAPTER ELEVEN

The senator received a call from the colonel who was working with her on evaluating the data disks that were secured from Helga via the 'idiot spy'. He said to the senator, "I'm afraid I have bad news for you about the Carbon Factor. I had two independent teams working on the feasibility of the documents and both have concluded that important segments of the documents have been cut. Someone is sitting on the five stages that will allow us to move forward with strategic testing."

"In simple terms, Colonel, I need you to explain to me what you're talking about."

"Ma'am, someone has taken out an insurance policy. They copied and deleted five strategic sections of the documents that are key to our moving this project forward and testing the results. Someone either knew what the hell they were doing or randomly cut aspects out of the document that are important and simply can't be recreated because we don't know how the process works. I am certain whoever did this knew what they were dealing with. This couldn't have been randomly completed, the sections are too important and plus, five out of five strategic deletions; I, don't think so. Someone on their team has a scientific background."

"Colonel let me get back to you within the hour. I have to make a call."

The senator dialed Walter's number and shrieked, "You screwed up again. The disks are missing five strategic sections that are needed to understand how to construct the process! I need you to cease all hostilities and find a way for me to talk with the people you were supposed to conclude. I need you to stand-down on this problem and get me accurate contact points. They seemingly keep sticking you deeper and deeper in your bowels. You won't need a colonoscopy when they're done with you. Please save yourself, this mission, and stand down. I need you to disappear until I have confirmation of the needed information, and the process. Then, my friend, you can go and do your dastardly deeds to those people."

"I will get you some numbers, but Senator, don't try to sell me out for a short-term solution when you and I have long term obligations and involvement. I hope I'm extremely clear on that point."

"Walter, you remind me every day about how we are connected and, if I didn't know any better, I think that you might be trying to threaten me in some kind of indirect way."

"Senator, I would never threaten you. You're like family to me and our union is a successful one, sort of dependent upon each other."

"Walter, let me just say one thing, I don't know if I want you to consider me as family, considering what you tried to do to your current family. Get me clear numbers and disappear. I hope I made myself perfectly clear that there are no extenuating circumstances that will endanger those who have the key to the Carbon Factor. Are we on the same page on this one?"

"Senator, you do know that they're gunning for me."

"I realize that! That's why I'm suggesting you disappear for a while. Oh, and do take your family because I believe you have put them out there as well. Once I have verified the information, I will support any action you take that does not draw attention to what we're doing here. Until then, my friend, you need to keep a bag packed, a tank full of gas, as well as a wallet full of money. Get me some info within the hour please, and good luck, Walter."

She knew that he was not expendable, as long as he controlled access to key documents that covered up fraud, assassinations, and money laundering. She called the colonel and asked, "What's our exposure to Walter?"

"Ma'am, I would prefer to return to your office and speak to you directly about that matter."

"I'm going to rest for a while, but if you can get here in the next two hours then we can discuss this issue. If not, we will work on the schedule for the week."

"Ma'am, I will be there within the hour."

# # #

Allen, who left his hiding place in a hurry, received a ding on his phone indicating that he had a new email. He knew it was from Walter and decided to give him a call back using the two-minute rule upon calling the number he left. Allen placed the call and announced, "Don't waste your time with bullshit because you're on the clock."

Walter responded, "I need new contact information for your friend. You do this for me, secure a free conversation with the senator, and I will take you off the endangered species list."

"You're not a generous person. Something must be awry. You had the phone that I used to call him on and left for you. Why didn't you use that number? I know you're trying to kill me, but it appears that you need me."

"Yes, Allen, I need you, but you must play one side or the other, your choice. You can come in from the cold and assume the kind of roles that you're used to, or you can stay on that list."

"You know what, Walter, I'm sick of your threats and I don't have a relationship with Beckmire. He has a contract out on me as well, so one way or the other, it appears to me that I am the walking dead. Go blow yourself!"

Allen disconnected the call and knew that he had Walter by the balls. He realized that Walter would never ask for help without bartering something in return. The fact that he was offering him life and the warmth to come in out of the cold, only signaled a temporary relationship. He thought to himself that Beckmire had a better bargaining chip and decided to hear the options prior to committing to Walter.

It was five minutes later when Allen's phone rang again and Walter said, "I guess I have to control my temper, and make sure that any deal I make is for the long term. I know you're on the clock, but I wanted to make sure that you understood that when you come in from the cold, you realize that you are a member of the team, please remember that. Also, I need you to help me keep this guy off my ass, so once again I am doubly committed to helping you, if you can help me. Give it some thought, and I will do whatever to make sure that it is a guaranteed statement without any retraction capability. By the way, I tried that number, and it was disconnected."

# # #

The senator called the colonel and told him to meet her at her second residence. It took the colonel forty minutes to get to her place. When he arrived, he found her waltzing around in a 1970's multi-layered negligee. She didn't offer him a drink but simply fixed him a drink of her choice and spiked it with a chemical that was made to make a man do a hard job. Prior to taking a sip of the drink, he watched her walk away from him and stared at her body as it was reflected through the outdated attire. He thought to himself that if given the opportunity, she was doable. He had no idea that he was going to have to give it a try. The senator sat directly across from him and revealed the right amount of her inner thigh and other attributes, to create an awkward situation. The colonel said, "Ma'am, may I speak freely?"

"Of course, Colonel."

"Ma'am, you have never offered me a drink and I have never been alone in a room with you. I must admit I'm feeling a little intimidated by your presence."

"Colonel, what does that have to do with anything. We are working together on a matter of national security, but that does not mean that our meetings must happen in my official office. I hope the fact that I'm relaxed, and you're in uniform, doesn't create a problem for you. Listen, I think we are adults. I just came home and had a shower, I'm not trying to suggest anything or trying to outrank you, so let me change the atmosphere; I'll be right back."

The colonel was literally sweating his ass off when he heard the Senator's voice, "Colonel, I need your opinion. Can you come here for a moment?" The colonel turned the corner and found the senator totally naked. She said, "I want, and I need, you. As I see it, I'm going to be the next President of the United States of America. So, General, where do you see yourself in my administration?"

"I see me doing and being all that I can be to satisfy the President of the United States of America."

"Great answer." The senator walked over and began to assist the colonel in disrobing. She sucked his breast and guided his hand down to her love zone that was dripping wet. She backed her rear up against the colonel's member and he, without warning, rammed it into her zone. The Colonel was well-heeled and the initial thrust from him sent the senator into convulsions. He was so deep in her love canal, that on his second thrust he misaligned her uterus causing an extreme amount of pain. She fell to her knees and said, "Something's wrong, my entire body is in pain. Call my assistant and tell her to get here. I need to get to the hospital."

# # #

Allen called Beckmire and told him that something was not right. He shared that Walter had offered to bring him in from out of the cold and restore him to some semblance of yesteryear. Beckmire asked him, "At what price, is your soul no longer for sale?"

"That's exactly what I'm talking about. This guy takes out a contract on me one month, and the next month, he wants me to help him set up a conversation with you about the Carbon Factor. I barely trust you, and I, for damn sure, ain't going to get back in bed with that snake. Why does he want to talk to you about the product? Did you give him the full package, or did you purchase yourself a long-term insurance policy?" Allen hesitated for a moment and realized that the Sarge had not responded and said, "I think I might be getting warm on this matter. You kept some aspect of the package and now they need it, but how did you know what part, if any, to keep? Is someone in your group a scientist?"

"Allen, you ask a lot of questions, and I realize that, if you were tracking me you would know by now where I am. I'm trusting you to keep that a secret between us. To your other point, yes. We do have an insurance policy, and I'm happy that your ex-employer was probably told to stand down, especially since the product requires a series of steps that we just happen to have in our possession."

"Absolutely, fucking brilliant! That's why he wants to welcome me home so that I can gain your trust and betray it. I once told you that you would never have to look over your shoulders for me! I meant that. Neither one of us is safe as long as Walter is alive and is taking orders from someone on high. I used to think he took orders from the senator, the soon-to-be president. However, I heard him belittle her to her face and decided that it was someone else, more powerful, but probably extremely low-key. So, how do you want to play this one and what do you want me to do? I have nothing to lose because Walter is a double-dealing piece of shit that I don't trust. You, sir, on the other hand, are at least clear about the alternatives and have kept your word. So, I'm counting on us to eliminate your cousin so that we both can inhale fresh air once again without worrying about who is watching."

The two men continued their conversation and strategized about ways and places to begin a full search for the elusive Walter. Allen realized that if Walter couldn't have his way, he would retreat to dark places in his mind with the help of opiates and a certain kind of woman who could also play the role of a man. Allen told Beckmire that he had a soft contact that he could put feelers out to. They would simply have to wait until Walter reared his ugly head or his footprint appeared on some dastardly crime.

## CHAPTER TWELVE

John Lee's people prepared a feast for the group, as well as the addresses to the houses, where breakfast, lunch and supper would be served daily. Although not feeling 100%, the Sarge asked John Lee if he could set aside some time so that the entire group could meet and discuss some new developments.

After lunch, the group met and the Sarge provided them with his latest intel on the state of their existence. He indicated that the very person who ordered the vests placed upon the children had indicated to him that all his resources would be coming to bear on the group. He also stated that he had received a call from Allen who had exclaimed that Walter was interested in conversing with him about some missing data. He added that the group should thank Mr. Amazing for having the foresight and knowledge to strategically remove important aspects of the Carbon Factor specifications. The Sarge concluded that he wasn't sure, but after the call from Allen, it looks as though the missing information was tantamount to a secure insurance policy.

Brown asked, "What are the terms on the policy and is it renewable?"

"I'm not sure if it's active. I believe that Walter and his group have been told to stand down until all aspects of the specifications have been reviewed and are working. This is just a guess on my part because no one has called with a sense of urgency asking about sections two or three of the process."

Zanthius stood up and said, "If those sections are critical to the process, then perhaps, we should be looking for an insurance policy that pays an unambiguous premium—Walter."

The Sarge said, "I see where you're going with this and I think it's an absolute no-brainer to make that a part of the policy."

"Pops, I would also place a number on each section to assist us in rebuilding and refitting our fleet, homes, projects in the sewers and anything else we can do for mankind."

"I thought it was you who said that we should not be doing this for money."

"That was back when I was naïve and didn't have a wife and child to think of. I have matured since then. After they blew up my ranch, my farm, and shot up my house in DC, we need policies and pre-paid premiums. My only fear is that Walter will not be actively made a part of the policy, but strategic information is just as important to finding him. He's a ruthless person, and I personally want to draw straws for his ass."

"Sorry, Son, but the design for Walter's demise has been discussed and ratified. It was agreed that death would be too good and swift for him and that another form of existence would suit him better and hopefully, make him a more moral person."

"Would you care to elaborate on that statement?"

"Not really; there are women amongst us."

Courtney stood up and announced, "Zanthius, your father wants to cut the man's arms off at his elbows, cut his legs off at his kneecaps, and blind him during the process."

"Now, that's pretty drastic. I've heard this before, and I'm sure he's not planning that."

The room got quiet and Zanthius asked, "Really? That's what you want to do to him? Sounds like a message from the bush. I like it and I'm for it. How about you, Honey?"

"I used to think I did some crazy things to people, but you people have me beat. I'm no extractioner; I'm merely a person who scares the shit out of people, whereas you people plan how someone is going to live after you catch them. What a sick family, but I'm fine with it as well."

"Anyway!" Beckmire continued after considering something else. "It is apparent that they realized that key aspects of the formula were missing, and they're interested in having a discussion to find out if we know anything about it. I would like Asiram, Zanthius, Bernstein, Mallory, and Jong to discuss the notion that Zanthius raised relative to pricing and indexing. In addition, I want to reflect on the monetary and psychological costs associated with being homeless and at the same time not inviting guests over for dinner. I would also like for Jilkes, John Lee, Brown, and of course, their lovely associates, to look at our overall security and discern where the holes are and how to correct them. We need some weapons. Can you make that happen, John Lee?"

"I have a few toys around here, but I'll need to make a run to town and pick up some stuff from my buddy. I be thinking that everybody down here needs to know how to use a weapon and, therefore, I'm going to get those new little shooters for the ladies."

# # #

Later in town, Jilkes and Yeshida strayed away from John Lee and Somara and encountered four young bucks feeling their oats. As they walked by the group one of them said,

"Damn, she be fine. We should take her away from your black ass."

Jilkes turned around, but was pulled away by Yeshida who said, "No need to worry about them. I will attend to them once I have secured you in the store."

"Wait a minute, I'm supposed to protect you, not you protect me."

"Yes, this is true, but your rage would probably lead to one of them getting hurt badly and then there would be police involvement. Not what I consider strategic thinking. Now, if I go, and one of them slightly brushes me, then I can give them a less than severe beating, but no one will have their neck broken. I think it's a win-win situation, however, I may need you as back up."

Yeshida walked back to where the guys were sitting and said, "I'm afraid you have hurt my companion's feelings and I think it's only fair that you guys go to him and beg his forgiveness for being rude."

"Are you out of your damn mind? That punk sent you over here to ask us to apologize?"

"No, I volunteered to intervene because I did not want to see him, how do you say it, 'whup your asses'. Now, if you apologize, all will be forgiven and forgotten. If you don't, then I am afraid that I will have to honor my companion by beating the living shit out of your asses."

One of the guys tried to sucker punch Yeshida. The move she put on him was incredible and consisted of a round kick and a disabling slap to the crotch. Subject number two swung at her, and as his blow was caught, she violently turned backwards and swung hard enough to knock his friend down. The fourth subject said, "I be on my way to apologize for those guys who just got their butts kicked by a woman. I would like to be free to do that without any pain. Is that alright with you?"

The young man walked over to Jilkes and asked, "Does yo woman have any sisters? I be needing me a girlfriend like that. Them there guys whose asses she beat, well they be dope smokers, but they still be my friends. I knew it was a bad idea, but when you find out how to stop stupid, you will realize that you just solved all the world's problems. I apologize because I'm not stupid and I just don't, randomly, like being kicked in the ass by a wonderful looking woman."

"So, you think my woman is all that?"

"Well, from the look of my friends, I be saying she is that plus a lot more."

John Lee meandered over to Jilkes and said, "I see you be done met the local smart boy."

"I guess you're right about that because Yeshida just kicked his friends' asses."

John Lee started towards the kids and Jilkes said, "Everything is good, let it go." The kid said to John Lee, "I told them it was a bad idea, but have they ever listened to me?"

"Why you be hanging with them there fools?"

"Them fools be my friends since I was three years old and I like them, not what they do and say."

"That be fair enough, but you tell them that I have a special ass whupping to give them for insulting my guests. Now, gone; git. What was that all about?" John Lee demanded.

"Just guys being guys, nothing more."

After loading up his truck with a shitload of guns and ammo, Somara said, "I like this slow life and I want to stay here. Only you must get over the sadness that the old house brought you. Are we a couple, or are we an object?"

John Lee looked over yonder and announced, "We be more than a couple if you like. You make me happy as my favorite pig did so there ain't much more I be needing."

# # #

As the group arrived at John Lee's place, Okema was walking around in front of the house having, what appeared to be a heated conversation on her cell phone. Brown was on the porch looking at her but was unable to hear precisely what was being said. Jilkes walked over to him and asked, "What's up, bro, everything all right?"

"Not sure, but whoever is on the other end of the phone appears to have pissed her off." Okema, in her native tongue, summoned Yeshida and Somara and began to give them a summary of the call. Okema said, "You guys may have to go back, but I'm not leaving here unless Mr. Brown is unhappy with me." She looked at Brown and he threw his hands up in the air as if he were asking what is going on. She smiled and said to her friends, "I have no obligation and I want to stay here and be done with that work."

"Perhaps the tasks that we are needed for can be accomplished with Mr. Beckmire and his group. We can act as mercs and offer our services for a price. We are surely underpaid for the work we do, in comparison to the male morons we work with, we are surely underpaid," Somara stated.

"Now, that idea stirs merit, Somara, but it must be sanctioned by Mr. Beckmire. Let me speak to Mr. Brown and in the meantime tell our handler that we will get back to him within the hour," Okema indicated.

Okema walked over to Brown who was standing next to Jilkes and reported, "There is a situation in London that our agency, or rather former agency, feels that can only best be handled by the three of us. I am not willing to go back to a place where low life morons make more money than we do because they have a penis. Although the issue relates to a potential terrorist strike, I, or rather we, are investigating a new life here with you people. I would like to propose that if they need our services then they certainly could use your group's services as well. In essence, we will all become mercs for a substantial price. What are your feelings, and is this something that you could broach to Mr. Beckmire?"

Jilkes looked at John Lee, and then at Brown, and said, "There is only one problem with that proposal, we can't leave the women and children alone while we're across the ocean."

"Hell, son, we take them all on this journey like we be doing all along," John Lee announced.

"You know that would give us time to get from under the guns of Walter and try to figure out a new strategy for dealing with and capturing his ass. I say we take this to the Sarge and Mallory and see what they have to say."

#

A few hours later, the group met with the Sarge and Mallory. Okema presented their proposal, the risks, costs, timetable, and benefits. The Sarge and Mallory were mentally high on the notion that they could do this international work, get paid for it, and in the process keep the group active, together, and alive. The Sarge exclaimed, "Hell, I like this idea, and given our current situation with my cousin, we might be able to pull this thing off and disappear for a while. Okema, the major problem I see is that we don't work well with bureaucrats; that may be a sour point of this idea."

"Mr. Sarge, if I can control the information flow and how we get things done, would that make for a better relationship?"

"Okema, you, my lady friend, are one of us and as one of us, we can follow your directions subject to our commonsense approach to hostile situations."

"Mr. Sarge, then I would like to make the call to our former employer and give him the parameters of our working with him, as well as the requirements of our new partners and organization."

"Before you do that, young lady, I need to meet with everyone and broach the subject and get their approval." There was a knock at the door and Jilkes walked over and answered it. Zanthius asked, "John Lee, where can I take my pregnant wife to have some fun?"

John Lee looked at the Sarge and replied, "How about we be taking a trip to London?"

"Now, if you were serious, I know she would love to go there. Wait a minute, you are serious. What business do we have in London?"

"That is the subject of our dinner meeting in approximately one and a half hours. Can someone find Mr. Amazing and tell him I need his input on helping our friends across the pond?"

## CHAPTER THIRTEEN

The locals provided the team and their family members with an awesome meal. The desserts were off the chart--key lime pie, pecan pie, apple pecan pie, apple pecan cake, and moonshine. The moonshine was the best. The Sarge said, "Before we get too giddy on this moonshine, and damn, I have to agree, this is some good 'S H I T', I need to make a proposal to the group, including the women and children.

"First of all, let me set the record straight. We have all given up our lives and lifestyles in order to protect each other and those that we love and hold dear. My poor daughter-in-law will never invite me to her home again because I am the cause of two of her most favorite places being destroyed. I don't say that lightly because there are some things that money can't buy. It can't buy you loyal friends who will die for you. It can't buy you a family that will kill for you. And it won't buy you the love of a woman who believes in you. Now, that I have covered everyone's weaknesses, I must inform you that my cousin Walter knows that we are alive and has decided to commit all of his resources to see that we don't miss his show the next time around. That is the bad news.

The Sarge looked around the room before continuing, and said, "The good news is that Mr. Amazing, aka Jong, through input from the 'idiot spy', McArthur, and mysterious others, randomly cut out sections of the product that we picked up in Japan. Those 'cuts', are essential to the government's testing this product. My cousin suddenly wants to have a phone meeting with me to discuss the missing aspects of the Carbon Factor, which means that someone has ordered him to abdicate his objective of destroying us until they have control of the sections that we have. Now, this story gets even crazier as it goes on. Our lovely friends and converts, Okema, Somara, and Yeshida are caught in a very precarious place since there is a threat to their homeland. Their former employer is demanding that they forget the love quest that they are on and go back to help protect the Empire. Okay, I told you this was going to get crazy. Somara suggested something to Okema, that she in turn suggested to Jilkes, Brown, and John Lee, and then we had a meeting to discuss this proposal. Now, the real crazy part of this thing is, that Okema's proposal provides us with protection and a safe harbor while we negotiate the value of the missing sections of the Carbon Factor that we have in storage."

Beckmire paused before adding, "Okay, my son walks into the room and asked John Lee where could he take his wife since she was bored, or something to that effect. John Lee astutely said--come on people take a guess, what did John Lee say to Zanthius?" Before anyone could answer, the Sarge replied, "John Lee said to Zanthius that he should take her to London."

The place broke into pandemonium. As Beckmire continued, "Now, I told you this was going to get really crazy, didn't I? Okay, the crazy part is that Okema, Somara, and Yeshida worked in London and they have received credible information that a terrorist attack is imminent. Which brings me to this point--we can offer to help, but our families must be protected, not here but there where we will be if her agency accepts our rules of engagement. My question to you people is, as I'm really beginning to feel the effects of this moonshine, shall we go and help our friends across the pond, if we can?"

Pandemonium once again broke out in the room. The Sarge turned to Okema and said, "Well, there's your answer from this side of the world, but once again, we need strong security around our families and we must know all of the details, and I do mean all."

Zanthius walked up to his father and said, "I have an idea that might make it harder to track us." He turned to Okema and asked, "What if we flew into Rome, and were seen getting onto a bus that was seen leaving the airport. But then that bus leaves the grounds, turns around, and we pull the tape off its sides, and it takes us to another terminal, where we board one of your military or private planes. Can you make that happen if this scenario is a go?"

"I'm sure they're going to want to make this happen because you guys are without, please forgive me, I was about to make a statement that could possibly injure your feelings," Okema paused.

"Make your statement and if your head is still on your shoulders when you finish then you know you didn't offend us."

"Fair enough." She continued, "I was going to say that you people don't need a tremendous amount of protocols and operational guidelines to do what you do. That is what I must convince my people that its necessary to allow you to, well, essentially, 'do your thing', without people looking over your shoulder. May I continue to speak freely, Mr. Sarge?"

"By all means, spill your guts."

"I am not sure I want to spill my guts, Mr. Sarge."

"Okema, it's a metaphor, which means, let it all hang out—backchannel discussions, you know—be straight forward.

"You people have the look of hippies in that you're all colors, all races, all genders and all crazy. I say that with admiration."

"Okema, make the call and get back to us because we might just go to London for a brief vacation. Oh, Jong, have we started to do stuff on the island?"

"Mr. Sarge, I will have some pictures for the group tomorrow to approve and, I must say, that place is going to be fabulous and under budget without cutting back on quality and convenience," Jong replied.

"Mr. Amazing is back in the gym. By the way, do you have any family members in London if we need to back door those people?"

"We are universal, Mr. Sarge, and as soon as you ratify this mission, I will let them know I'm coming, but quietly. It would help tremendously if we helped an old uncle make his bail and bribed a few bad politicians."

"Why bribe them? We should be exposing, them my brother."

"You're so damn right. Okay, it all depends on whether we get the job."

# # #

It appeared that everyone had enjoyed the moonshine except the women who were of Asian descent. Okema walked over to Brown and said, "I need to talk to Mr. Sarge, but I will not do so unless you sanction it."

Brown looked at her and said, "Okay, let's dump one of your practices, Mr. Brown, Mr. Sarge, and Mr. Everybody Else must end at this moment. Can we agree on that?"

"Yes, Mr. Brown."

"Didn't we just agree to end that 'Mr. Brown' stuff?"

"Mr. Brown, that can only be ended in one's bed after one has made love to confer conclusion on the formality."

"Okema, we made love and I thought we confirmed our relationship?"

"I did not hear the words, 'I love you', Mr. Brown."

"Oh, my God! Okema, I love you! Okay, so let it go."

Okema walked over to Somara, and Yeshida and said, "Mr. Brown has now indicated that he loves me. I think that I am okay with his approach. I'm going to make the call to our people and let them know that we will only come back if our chosen team is allowed to operate without oversight, on our own and for a sizeable amount of money. I will let them know that if they want to hire male morons to operate huge schemes and neglect the rights of women, then we will play on the outside and that will cost them an organization."

Okema saw the Sarge and walked over to him and asked, "Mr. Sarge, my contact might ask me what the price of such an endeavor is. What shall I quote them?"

"Ask that moron, what will be the cost if the terrorists succeed in their mission? Is he prepared to second guess the lives of many civilians against a few measly pounds?" The Sarge inquired.

Okema asked again, "What should we charge them for our services?"

"Mr. Amazing, if we stop a terrorist attack and save many lives, as well as prevent the destruction of precious monuments, what should the bill look like?"

"That's a hard question. Perhaps, we would fare better by trying to figure out where the terrorists are getting their funds from, and make those people pay if it's a legitimate group. I think we should ask for a flat rate. Maybe we should ask for six million euro and the ability to keep all assets recovered from the terrorists and their supporters."

"Why does your brain think like that? I know of no one else that thinks like that. You want to get paid for the job and, just in case there is a tip involved, you want to be able to escape the taxes on that as well. I like it, but everything is subject to a final approval. We must develop an exit plan for us, as well as our families."

"Mr. Sarge, if we do this well, everybody in the free world will be looking for us to provide them with a cleanup function. I suggest that we handle all of our future business on the down-low; we don't need to be famous; we just need to be smart," Okema stated.

The Sarge looked at her and then Jong. Jong said, "She is absolutely right. Maybe, if we accept this job, we need to find a different mode of transportation and leave our fleet just where it is. People can track us by where our planes are, but they can't track a private jet that we engage."

"Okay, I see where you two are going with this and I'm getting sober just listening to you. Jong, we're going to have to work on that one. Okema, if they want us to do the work, they have to find a way for us to bypass all that passport and ID mess. Is there any way they can smuggle us into the country, and I do mean all of us--women and children? We need one of those freaking planes that people like Paul Allen had for his sports teams."

"We should discuss the notion of trading in the new planes and getting one that can carry us all, like that Embraer

145, that could certainly seat all of us including the women and children. We should have a serious conversation about this soon," Jong said.

"There is a bounty on the person who is allegedly planning an attack on us. When your generals placed pictures of those wanted in Iraq on playing cards, one of them was roughly worth $20 million—the cost of one of those jets," Okema stated.

"Jong, I see those eyes of yours getting bigger and bigger. You must budget each job we do and make sure that each section of the Carbon Factor that we have is at least worth $10 million. Then, work the deal with the airline manufacturer to sell our current fleet, or maybe not. The people who tried to kill us are the same people who want those sections of the package that we erased. They tried to kill us as well as our babies. Let's keep the two G-650s and order the higher end model of that jet and make those assholes pay for it before we send them to hell."

"Now, Sarge, I like that plan because I have never felt so out of control and as sad as I did watching them place those vests on the children. I will make them pay through the nose. By the way, when are you going to call Allen again?"

"I'm glad you thought of him, why don't we call him now. But first I need you to come up with a figure for each of the five sections, and I really mean a number. Those assholes tried to kill us to obtain what they want and need; it is going to cost them plenty."

The Sarge, in an extremely inebriated state, called Allen. When Allen answered, the Sarge said, "I hope you're not giving out any more of my sworn numbers."

"No, Mr. Beckmire, I'm trying to keep all of us alive until we can decimate our common enemy. I hear he got official orders to stand down on his quest to see you dead because it is obvious that you have something they need. I wonder what on earth that could be? It was a brilliant move on your part and a lifesaver at that."

"I need a way to find Walter. Do you have any ideas?"

"The man's an enigma and is, basically, self-controlled in the sense that he calls most of his shots."

"Who calls the other shots?"

"You want me to sign another death warrant? Mr. Beckmire, that is classified information and I really don't have a clue as to who pulls, or who can pull, his strings." Zanthius was standing nearby and whispered something to his father.

Beckmire said, "Allen, I need to call you back."

"Pops, I overheard your conversation, and it is clear to me how to get access to your cousin."

"What's your suggestion, son?"

"We have four sections of the Carbon Factor that they need. As a function of the agreement, you could say three sections are for sale and the fourth one is contingent upon the delivery of Walter to you unharmed and unguarded. Listen, you know a lot of people have died trying to get their hands on what we have and what we have is a huge bargaining chip. Let it be known, each section is a separate negotiation and the fourth is non-negotiable."

"The 'idiot spy', eh? Son, that's some quick thinking and a great plan. I need to run it by the group and see if they agree with it."

Jong heard the exchange and said, "I got to tell you, the apple doesn't fall too far from the tree. That was quick, and as a matter of fact, the kind of thinking that you used to be able to do. Just kidding, but that was phenomenal."

"You know, Jong, he's really a smart kid. I need to get him, and Larry involved in more of the details because the two of them really don't think like you and me. They always have a 'what if' scenario up their sleeves."

"You know Sarge, that's important for all of us because their thinking and actions have gotten us out of a lot of messes, as well as in this whole mess. I mean we usually go in and 'bang, bang, bang' and it's over. Today, these guys figure out the modern world rules and apply them before we go 'bang, bang and bang'. It's a different time and we're different people and a helluva lot older."

Okema knocked on the door, bowed and asked, "Mr. Sarge may I speak with you and Mr. Mallory?"

"Yes, you may, Okema and how much longer are you going to use that 'Mr.' mess?"

"I'm coming to the end of it because Mr. Brown has indicated his love for me—tee-tee."

"We're happy to hear that, now how is the other thing going?"

"Mr. Sarge, my former agency does not know your work history and, therefore, they are reluctant to enter into a long-term relationship with you. However, they are willing to make this one-time offer of an equivalent of three million dollars for a clean and final conclusion of their need. I told them that they pay idiots more than that to create problems and, therefore, I could assure them that their offer would be quickly and permanently declined. One of the main idiots raised the price to $5 million with a safe habitat for the children and women. I told him that I would call him back within the hour." The Sarge looked at Jong and inquired, "Can you find Mallory? I want him in on this decision because before we agree, I need to know the who, what and why. Okema, we operate in an old fashion manner and perhaps that might be our downfall. We don't care about the politics of the issue, just who needs to be stopped and what are our security concerns. I'll leave all of that political stuff to you once we figure out how the terrorists are going to hit their targets."

"Mr. Sarge, the agency is aligned with highly trained groups who can help. Is this something we should request?"

"Okema, we do not work well with strangers. Give us the relevant intel and let us figure it out. With you and the other ladies providing us with input, we don't want any new groups or situations other than a bomb disposal unit on standby. Why can't they handle the situation themselves?"

"Mr. Sarge, in the UK there are a lot of different groups finding themselves in the country daily. The strategy of the UK was essentially to divide, conquer and enslave, and therefore, every aspect of our government has watch dogs and whistle blowers that are rewarded handsomely."

"I guess it's a real problem when you have too many ships trying to conquer too many places for precious metals. No need to talk about the addictions, diseases and slave trade that were created," the Sarge indicated.

Mallory walked into the room and the Sarge said, "Can you talk to Okema for a few and get the details of what we would be up against if we attempt to help them with that problem?"

The Sarge's phone rang and it was Allen who reported, "Apparently your family member has decided to go off the reservation, and, in essence, to tell all who think they handle him, to kiss his ass. He is clearly aware of your hate for him and has decided to pursue you first before you attempt to get to him. His reaction to the Carbon Factor was quite simple and straight forward; 'screw the Carbon Factor and Ben

Beckmire; may they all rest peacefully in hell until I get there, and then we can shake things up again'."

"Are you telling me that he is telling his handlers to kiss off?"

"Mr. Beckmire, you can't handle a handler; it becomes confusing and an unachievable action. If Walter has told the world to kiss off, then he is committed to seeing you in hell, and everyone else for that matter, including yours truly. I think a huge statement has been made and I suggest you people make yourselves invisible. You guys are well endowed, try Spain, go back to Australia, or play more in Europe; just don't tell me where you're heading. Also, I am about to sink this phone in the toilet and activate a new one. I suggest you do the same thing after I call you back with a new number."

Mallory and Okema seemingly agreed about certain aspects of the mission. He said to the Sarge, "I don't like the concept of this effort, but I think if Okema and the other two ladies are our single source contacts then I feel better about this project. I don't like our odds if some stranger is trying to tell us where to turn. By the way, did Allen have any new intel about Walter?"

"As a matter fact, he did, and we have to get out of dodge. Walter has left the arena and is operating on his own and has expressed that he wants us dead. Allen indicated that his handlers had told him to stand down, but he has told everyone to kiss a certain part of his anatomy. He knows that I want him dead, so he's not going to let himself be a part of any bargain where he surrenders to us peacefully." Okema was about to say something when the Sarge asked, "Can you get us a plane to secretly fly us to London after we land in Spain or Italy with jets that can't be tracked?"

"Mr. Sarge, if you get us to an airport in Italy, we can immediately put the group on a military style plane to Heathrow where you will be whisked away in a military convoy. I have already attended to that matter. The obvious concern is, are you willing to take on the task of eliminating a terrorist cell operating in a not so nice part of London?"

"It behooves us to leave this area immediately because our nemesis is on a mission to see us dead. Jong, call the pilots and have them start the engines. As for our destination, we will say Rome, but will develop an alternative plan once we get confirmation back from Okema's people on the ground."

"I'm on it, Sarge. Are we taking everyone?"

"Ab-so-damn-lutely; can't leave any one behind to be captured by my sick cousin. By the way, do we still have the copy of him doing the nasty with several different people?"

"I didn't delete it, Sarge. Are you thinking about putting his actions on YouTube?"

"Indeed, I am, but only to draw him out and disorient him so that we can pick the venue rather than fall into his trap. Hopefully, this job won't take us forever to figure out and conclude. We can also plan his capture and decapitations. By the way, are our planes ever left unattended?"

"Hell, no! Three-on and three-off. The planes are also watched by remote cameras that were set up as a back-up review mechanism. This was that little lady's idea, as well as the three on, three off surveillance. Now, as a part of their checklist, the cameras are scanned before all take offs. They figured that wherever we travel there are usually dead bodies left behind and people looking to get revenge."

"Mr. Amazing suppose you were called Mr. Unreliable and something unfortunate happened that should have been attended to. I hope I'm making myself clear about relevance and need. We all love you, and we never give you an assignment based upon what you can't do because we all know that you can do whatever the hell the rest of us can do," the Sarge stated.

Jong looked at the Sarge and asked, "If that's the case why am I saddled with the rebuilding project? That seems more like a job for one of the ladies."

"Oh, my goodness! So, this is what all this shit is about? I'm sorry, brother, but you are the only one who handles our finances and makes sure that none of us get into any shitty deals and that due diligence is conducted on each transaction personally, as well as organizationally. You have the most trusted position in our group. Think about it, Mister. You could write yourself a hefty check and disappear, and we would have to spend an eternity trying to find your ass. I think you're confusing trust and brotherhood with pity and safety. First, your shit ain't safe because you must shoot assholes just like the rest of us. You haven't gotten any pity on our runs and walks. As a matter of fact, people say to your face, quit slacking, although in a tender fashion. That place is going to cost us a significant amount of money and I need you to do this because no one watches the beans better than you. Look at our new fleet of planes. Who did and suggested that? Every time we get into trouble, we must call on your extended family to help us out. Listen, if you tell me the essentials of the deal, I will take it over myself, but you will have to act as my assistant."

"You always rope my ass in. I was going through male menopause," Jong announced.

"I think men have a much more elegant name to their mood swing; it's called evolutionary melancholy. Seriously, I will take over the hotel project and you can focus on trying to corral my cousin."

"Sarge, the hotel is done. It's being raised as we speak, and all of the necessary construction materials are either there or are on their way. It doesn't hurt to add a completion and delivery incentive to the negotiations. I am meeting with your wife, Ava, Monica, Asiram, Rashida, and Yvett to go over the color schemes and appointments and will conference in Mr. Christopher Carter. I got this and I'm going to have cameras hidden all over the place. I told you to let it go, I'm done with that previous conversation. Mr. Amazing is back and keeping watch over everyone with a new focus of trying to find the devil.

"Thank you, brother, we all need you, but secretly, I need you the most."

## CHAPTER FOURTEEN

Later that night, the entire group boarded their planes for the long ride across the pond. This trip would be less than a vacation for the group.

Three beautiful private jets landed at the Charles de Gaulle Airport in Paris. The group was seen disembarking from the jets and entering customs. On their way to customs, the group was redirected to a bus and was seen leaving the airport. Twenty minutes later the group boarded a private plane for London. Their jets would remain in Paris under the watchful eyes of their pilots.

In London, most of the women and children boarded a bus and would be cared for on a private estate. The entire team, including Carlos's people, the three Asian ladies, Larry, Zanthius and an insisting Asiram boarded dark vans and were driven to the Best Western, formally known as the Grosvenor House, on Buckingham Palace Road. Their rooms were pre-registered, and the group entered the dated hotel through the service entrance. In a parlor suite, Okema's contact awaited the group and wasted no time telling them about the seriousness of their concerns. The group was shown photos of the possible terrorists and their last known locations.

John Lee asked the question that no one else seemingly wanted to ask. He inquired, "If you have these here pictures, and you know where these folks be hiding, why don't you just swoop down on them and arrest them?"

"That's a good question, old chap. My name is Ivan Moncheloff, and I'm not sure you Yanks have been paying attention to the news over here. We have been the butt of a lot of criticism about the way our minorities and immigrants are treated. If an armed police unit entered the area in mass, there would be riots that would consume our time, efforts and distract us from our other duties. Our presence would provide a cover for those who would place the civil rights of others in jeopardy. We considered using mercs, but they are too noticeable. Okema told me that her new friends specialized in this kind of thing and could fit into any place without suspicion. As I look at your people, I agree totally.

"Our problem is that we can't have another event take place in that area or it is going to go ballistic. We need a small sophisticated group to extract the perpetrators alive or leave them very dead, with a preference for the latter. There have been five shootings by special law enforcement groups, and the area is almost without police presence. They burned down our substation, and all cars that enter the area are frequently shot at. What is more than critical to us is the nature of the product that is being developed for an alleged detonation. Our only intel is that it has a strong respiratory impact on those who are near it, but we don't know the components. We had a person enter the hospital with symptoms that we couldn't initially characterize. We performed test after test but couldn't figure out what was wrong with the guy. We still have his body, but it's decomposing at an accelerated rate. It's like something out of a sci-fi movie."

The Sarge asked, "Is there any way we can get copies of these photos?"

"I can have them here within the hour. This group is as diverse as any I have seen. I know your history and the things that you accomplished in Vietnam, as well as your drug dealer elimination program. As I said, I know your history. It is with admiration that I say, frankly, you chaps are what the Queen ordered—an amorphous group without identity."

"What about weapons. We know that all of your bobbies don't carry weapons. What's the ratio, one to five?" Mallory asked.

"Okema made us aware of your needs and when you take your tour of the area later in the day, you will all be armed," Ivan stated.

Jong asked, "Are there any elevated places where we can provide long distance coverage?"

"There are a few such places, but all are on top of the flats where the very people you're after will have eyes as well. I can get you an aerial of the area with close ups of people sitting on the roofs all day long, looking for police types."

"Do you have any friendlies in the area who can provide intel? Are there any transplants from America who live in the area?" Mallory asked.

"We have several friendlies, but we wish to keep them from harm and unknown to their neighbors. I'm not sure about Americans. Why would any American want to live in this neighborhood?"

"Most of America is not paved with gold, just a few neighborhoods. It would be great if we could get a couple of our people in there to scout out the place, especially, where the source of this headache is living and where the place of product development is. Do you have any idea where they might be trying to build the alleged bomb? Do you think they would do it in the place they live?" Mallory inquired.

"Let me get you the photos of the individual who wandered into the hospital and is decomposing at an exponential rate of speed. We are recording his status every five minutes because the differences are that significant," Ivan indicated.

"The body does not decompose quickly unless it is in a heated environment," the Sarge stated.

"This body is frozen, Mr. Beckmire, and it is still decomposing at an accelerated rate," Ivan indicated.

"Please, get us the pictures so that we can try to figure out what the hell we're dealing with and whether or not we should make ready hazmat suits. Are you certain that this individual is key to the people plotting the attack?"

"We aren't sure about anything, but it does draw attention to where the man went for medical assistance. He showed up at the general location where our radicals are, and to make it really interesting, the gentleman had no fingerprints."

"Oh shit, now you're talking. Get us the aerials and any other needed information. Also, make sure Okema gets all possible escape routes. If we can obtain the target, terminate it, and figure out where the product is being developed, I would need your people to be ready to shoot anyone who shows up on the street with a weapon. I want it all documented on camera, so get your tech people ready to give us some long-distance coverage. Jilkes and John Lee, you people feel like taking a walk through the park?"

"Sarge, we would love to be your guinea pigs. The problem is that we have to take our women, or they won't allow us to go."

"Are you shitting me? You people are that smitten?"

"Sarge, we now fold their laundry; go figure and stop humiliating us. We can go, but they go with us. We need a plan as to why we are there or a connection with someone."

"Oh, my goodness, I can't believe you two are P-whipped." The Sarge's phone rang and it was Courtney who said, "We are staying in a castle and it is magnificent. I wish you were here, my king, to enjoy it with me. I love you baby, be safe and stay focused."

The Sarge mumbled, "I love you too, baby."

Jilkes inquired, "What did you just say? Did you just tell your wife you loved her?"

Courtney asked, "That's Jilkes, why is he up in your business about telling me you love me?"

"It's nothing, honey, I'll call you later. We're in the midst of a meeting."

# # #

Approximately an hour later, Ivan presented pictures of the decomposing body to the group and most walked away from them. The Sarge, Mallory, and Jong studied the differences in the five-minute intervals and were astounded. Zanthius walked over and looked at the photos and said, "Wow, his metamorphosis is being generated by exposure to a powerful accelerant. Did he purposefully drink HCL, or a like substance?"

His father inquired, "Son, what is HCL?"

"Pops, it's hydrochloric acid--a strong corrosive acid. Trust me, it's the kind of thing that you don't want to touch or inhale."

"I presume you're the one called the 'idiot spy'?" Ivan asked.

"I am Zanthius Beckmire De Lombardo, and I am no idiot."

"Sorry, if I offended you. I would like to hear more about what you think is going on with our dead body. Our forensic scientists are baffled by what is occurring."

"Listen, I know that when you freeze a body you think that you have controlled its state. I find it hard to believe that my friend the cockroach survived the ice-age and everything else. Based on those pictures, I think this guy inhaled an acid-based gas or swallowed an acidic base substance. I'm no scientist, but I know the results of acid, especially HCL. There are so many different chemicals that you can mix with HCL and create a devastating conclusion of human life, it's toxic as hell. Perhaps that's what your people should be researching. Who has obtained large quantities of HCL and for what reason?"

CHAPTER FIFTEEN

Jilkes, John Lee, and their companions were touring Leicester in the United Kingdom under the pretense of developing a business and using local talent. Leicester had a significant population of people who migrated there. It took in a lot of people from Uganda, as well as migrants from Somali, and the Indian subcontinent. Within these various groups, came a lot of problems that the government was not prepared to deal with. The hodgepodge of religions and ideology didn't do well in terms of making the settlement in a new country smooth. The jobs that were available, in the minds of the locals, belonged to them and often created friction about the employment of immigrants.

An old saying that seemingly held true through all the immigrant's trials and tribulations, was 'an idle mind is the devil's workshop'. This was never so true as when it came to the unemployment rate among young able bodied men and the schemes that were put in place were designed to keep them busy--making ping pong paddles and doing other menial tasks.

#

Jilkes, John Lee, and their companions attracted a lot of attention, especially, when they turned onto a street and were in the middle of a neighborhood that was divided by a simple crossing sign. The sign was confusing, and the group stood there and debated what the sign meant; where they were, where they needed to go, and why the hell so many people were looking at them.   John Lee said, "So, Somara and Yeshida, you know we ain't got no guns on us, and if this gets too crazy, you gals need to go into them there purses and pull out the heat."

As John Lee was about to say something, Jilkes exclaimed, "Well, I'll be a dumb ass Yankee. Somebody is playing with chemicals in the area!"

"What the hell you be talking about, Jilkes?"

"Brother, haven't you ever driven by a landfill or other such places where you get that rotten egg smell?"

"Not sure where you be going with this, but I be thinking I know what you mean. I just got a whiff of something that smelled like rotten eggs."

"Ladies, do you guys smell that stench? Because if you do, I think we are near the place where someone is trying to develop a dirty bomb. I don't want everyone to look at the same time, but there are a shitload of wires running to one building. The one with the sign that says it's a shoe factory. Oh shit, everyone come closer to the map. I just saw a reflection from the adjacent roof. We are in their scopes."

Jilkes said, "Yeshida, point to the street behind you, and John Lee, you look at the map and point to the street in front of us." As John Lee looked at the map and pointed in a direction, he too saw the reflection from a scope on another building and said, "We be of interest to those people because they be having scopes on us from all directions."

"I think we should not walk in the direction of those wires but walk down the street that bypasses the place of interest. Oh shit, is that Asiram and Zanthius walking down the street?" As the couple got closer, it became obvious that it was not

Zanthius and his bride, but a look alike couple who could pass for them in public.

The group stopped at a local pub and asked for directions to the museum. Okema recorded their location on her phone by using GPS settings. In the pub, John Lee asked, "Why don't we at least have a beer since we're here?"

Jilkes asked the barkeep for four pints. There was no fanfare or problems until John Lee asked the barkeep, "What on earth is that strong smell?" The barkeep appeared to become agitated and said, "Mate, I have no idea what you're talking about, enjoy your beer."

# # #

Once they finished their beers, and as the group was prepared to leave, there appeared to be a gathering of people on both sides of the street. John Lee whispered, "Looks like we might have to fight our way out of this mess."

"Yeah, but no gun play because that will really make us look suspicious." Three young men walked over to the group and one of them asked, "So, what are you people doing this far away from home?"

"Oh, we not be that far from home, hell, it just be a plane ride across that there Atlantic," John Lee stated.

"So, you people are Yanks?"

"I prefer to be called an American, not sure where you be getting that there Yank stuff from."

"Do you always talk like that?"

John Lee looked at the guy and answered, "What be wrong with the way I be talking? You be trying to pick us up or something. We be with our dates."

"Mister, if you want trouble, then I can make it happen," the guy said.

"Listen here, Sonny, before you can raise a finger, I could snatch the life from you in a bloody manner. Why don't you just run along and leave us be. We be tourists and don't want to have a problem with muggers."

"We're not muggers, but we're suspicious of visitors who come here looking around."

"We ain't no visitors, we been here before you were born. I be done had family that were from here and my friend here had ancestors as well from here. So, as we be seeing it, you be suspicious, and you be the visitor that won't leave us be. Now, we be wanting to make our way to the museum. Is that a problem or do you want to be hanging around with us?"

"Where are you from?"

"Now, didn't I just tell you deft ass, where we be from?"

"No, man, relax. I mean in the states?"

"We be from Birmingham, Alabama."

"Him too?"

"Now, there be two things you might not want to do. Don't refer to him as him, and never say anything about our ladies. We fought in Viet Nam together and you are about to get yo ass handed to you."

"Governor, why are you so aggressive? We just like to know what strangers want in our community."

"I ain't no governor and I be done told you that we were here before you came here in a spaceship. This be our community and you ain't seen aggression yet. We be tired of this here inquisition, and we ain't got no mo to say."

"Listen, the museum is two kilometers down this road. Try to be out of the area by night fall."

"You mean we can't visit where our folks be done lived?"

"Not if day is about to turn into night!" the guy emphatically stated.

"Well, that message be loud and clear and perhaps we be better off just leaving the area now. We have our ladies, and they are rather soft if you know what I mean." The men started to walk away and Jilkes said, "I have a question for you, why do you walk around the streets carrying weapons, are you the police or something?"

"That was your first and last question. Enjoy the museum and don't let the night find you on this side of the street."

"What about on the other side of the street? Is that okay?"

"No more games, be out by nightfall."

Jilkes looked at John Lee and said, "We have marked the area. Let's get out of here before that guy understands that you called him a punk with a gun."

As the group headed for the main street, the person with the weapon that did the interviewing asked, "Leaving so soon?"

John Lee stared at him and replied, "This here place is not how we be remembering it. It be like the old Alabama; backwards, obtuse and in need of a change. We don't feel safe here. So, we be going back to our hotel. Y'all have a nice day, now." The person asking, and apparently directing people in the vicinity, nodded to two individuals to follow the group.

Jilkes asked John Lee, "Those rookies are following us-- do you want to split up and capture them?"

"That wouldn't be the mission we were given, but if we be annoyed with those assholes then I say we grab them and see if Asiram wants to work on them. They seem like small time drug dealers. They don't be looking like someone who wants their asses blown off."

"That's what I was thinking, they're just punk kids with big handguns. Something is not right about this Op. Now, I distinctively smell sulfur, but you can ride around Wilmington, Delaware and, get the same funky smell. I'm no damn scientist, but I do know that there is an 'H' in the hydrogen bomb, there is an 'H' in hydrochloric acid, and therefore, there is an 'H' in hell. We need to cleanse this place of the 'H's' and move on, but there is something else going on here. You asked the barkeep about the smell and he became agitated. I think there might be terrorism and drugs in the same place. Besides, where the hell are the police? This is the bad lands and the bobbies dare not enter without backup, they have lost Leicester and they don't want to acknowledge it to the world. John Lee, when you have a problem that you can't fix, what do you do?"

"I be calling a specialist."

"Exactly, we need to raise the price of this mission now that we know what the real deal is, and that the government is afraid to move on this diverse population with the press ready and willing to cry racism. How did you get over the notion of racism?"

John Lee looked at Jilkes and his eyes filled with water. Jilkes embraced him and said, "I love you more than life and it is you who makes my life worth living, not the money, Yeshida, or anything else, my brother; just you."

Somara said, "Is everything alright?"

John Lee replied, "It is now, we reaffirmed our love for one another in a man's way. You will not know how much that means to me considering the other things that have happened to me. Now, I know if I die today, my best friend will be there to make sure that I'm attended to properly. Love you Man!"

Jilkes, Yeshida, John Lee, and Somara decided to separate at the end of the area that was "V" shaped. John Lee told Somara, "Hang loose and look in the windows. We don't want to take these guys until we see signs of our people and then we want to get their phones from them before they can speed dial that there is a problem."

Jilkes and Yeshida hastily made their way towards the meeting place and ducked into an alcove. As the person following them briskly walked by, Yeshida stepped behind him and power slapped him unconscious. Larry and Carlos were standing close by to give assistance.

John Lee and Somara didn't have the luxury or a place to secretly confront their person and decided to walk towards him and disable him. John Lee threw a thunderous punch into his solar plexus, and the man went down for the count. Gladstone and McArthur were there to assist them.

In the van, John Lee said to their captives, "I guess you don't see anything funny anymore, do you? When all of you little rats were together, you acted like you could take us. I'm going to give you the chance to take me and if you succeed in kicking my ass, I promise you, them other fellas will let you be, but you got to beat my old ass."

The Sarge stepped in and announced, "That's not how we treat our friends and the person who is going to tell us why they hassled you guys on your way to the museum. Who did you think they were? Why did you mess with my family? I guess you're not going to talk, so let me say this--the next person you see will make you talk or stick your little dick in your big-ass ear. I'll give you a minute to think about it."

"You Americans don't scare me."

"We don't want to scare you, but I bet you'll change your tune once you meet the 'Extractor'. Take a minute and say your prayers."

Five minutes later, Asiram climbed into the hot van. She never said a word but began to cut at the guy's pants until she exposed skin. Still not asking a question or making eye contact with the guy, she made a cut close to his penis and another slit on his left testicle. She said, "I need my damn glasses, I can't see a damn thing, and by the way, are we castrating him or just cutting his nuts off?"

"Ask me anything and I will tell you the truth!" the man exclaimed while shaking.

"Oh, I don't do answers, my job is to cut and bleed you out until you die slowly and in a lot of pain. Besides, I have a dinner date with my baby's daddy so I'm going to cut major arteries so you will just bleed out faster."

"Wait, get the boss-man in here or whoever I must talk to."

"They told me that you would never talk. Don't go nowhere, I'll be right back."

The Sarge entered the van and said, "She must have felt sorry for you, she only nicked you. You will answer my questions truthfully or you will never enjoy the pleasure of a woman or a man again."

In the other van, the second young man was attempting to be a tough guy.

The Sarge asked his captive, "Why do you guys just hang around and hassle people on holiday?"

"Unless you saw some magnificent factory churning out a product that the entire world could use, then this is as good as it gets. There are no jobs, and the schools are useless. The government prefers to have us contained and be violent to each other rather than running the streets and being a menace in their productive cities. They pay us to make ping pong paddles and other stupid products in their antiquated manpower schemes."

"How did you get mixed up with the guy who displayed his weapon to my people?"

"Again, if you see a plant or a college that's enrolling and/or hiring, then gangs are what rule and govern this area, mate."

"What do you know about a major attack on London by extremists?"

"Governor, I don't have that kind of clearance, I'm just a foot patroller."

"What do you know about the constant smell of sulfur of late?" Beckmire continued his questioning.

"Again, Governor, you got me there, but where there is smoke, there is usually fire. I used to think that these guys were all hot air and used their terroristic notions to fleece the local shop owners of a protection fee, but I'm not sure that is the central theme anymore."

"What does that mean?"

"Governor, is there any way in hell, you can get me out of here and to some place where I at least have a chance to make it legally? If you turn me free, then I am already dead and just don't know it."

"That depends on you and the information you give us."

"Listen, Governor, these blokes done left religion and have sworn allegiance to the devil. They have been secretly radicalized and apparently have direct contact to a leader in the most wanted group in the world. Governor, you said it depends on the information I give you. Well, I'm about to run out of credible information unless you want to know a few names and flat numbers."

"What is your name?"

"Ali Maamoud."

"Ali, what is the source of the smell and what are they brewing there?" Ali dropped his head and said, "I fear they have found a formula that mixes carbon and sulfur with other elements to create an extremely devastating dirty bomb. It must be successful because they sent a prototype description to Somalia a week ago for construction and testing. These guys are radicals, they use the notion of religion to justify their killing of infidels. Whatever they have configured, it's huge, but I'm sure it's not nuclear or nothing like that, I don't think."

"How many people are in that place where they are brewing their potion?"

"How many more questions will I have to answer before you decide if you're going to help me or kill me?"

"Touché! We will help you get out of here, but there are so many conditions that you might want to strap on a vest before you agree to what we expect of you."

"I would never agree to strap on a vest, Governor. I cherish my life and the lives of others, and that is why I'm so desperate to tell you anything to get the hell out of this place."

"How old are you and where are you parents?" Again, Ali's head dropped, and he murmured that he had no idea where his parents were. He said, "When we left Africa by boat, the children were placed in one hole and the adults in another. I never saw them again after the boat ran aground in Italy and everyone tried to escape. I believe I am twenty-two years old, and I am good in mathematics."

"How many people work in that stinky place and is that the only one?"

"Wrong question Governor!" As he contemplated a response, he said, "I would have asked, how many people in the community support that stinky place and will die protecting it?"

"Okay then, you asked the question now give me the answer."

"There are fourteen to twenty people there at all times. There are probably four on the roof tops pointing in all directions and ten to fourteen in windows that are routinely rotated around. The dumb thing about the window positions is that they all wear neon colored headbands, so they don't shoot each other, but they become easy targets for their enemies."

"I will be right back, make yourself at home but don't go nowhere."

"With these straps on my legs and hands, I will definitely be here until you get back, take your time, Governor."

The Sarge called the squad together and told them about what they had discerned from their captive and asked Mallory if they were able to glean any information from the one, they had. Mallory told the group that their captive was a tough little bastard but realized that being a martyr with a decapitated dick may cut back on the quality of what you get when you get to wherever they go after hurting innocent people and dying.

Zanthius said, "Give me three minutes with him alone and he will either talk, or I will blow his head off. We are wasting too much time and we have a madman hunting us. That is who I think we should be focusing on."

Asiram gently touch her husband's arm, and said, "Calm down, dear, you have demonstrated to us that you don't have the temperament to engage in debriefings or interrogations, so I believe the team has taken a silent vote against you working

alone with any hostages. Let John Lee and Jilkes deal with
him for a minute, once he sees that damn knife of John Lee's,
I think he will want to join the union."

The Sarge said, "We're getting a lot of information from
the guy we have, but I need to corroborate the information
before we make a move. Okema, your people need to figure
out what kind of detectors they have developed to detect
sulfur. There's no way they can seal that element in a
container without it blowing the roofs off nearby buildings.
Now, what's scary is the fact that the kid said that a prototype
description has been sent to Somalia for testing and production
using our dear old friend, carbon. I think a cheap dirty bomb
can be produced using carbon and sulfur, but I'm no chemist."

Okema called her handler and told him what they
suspected would be used if an attack on London was to
happen. She casually mentioned the words carbon and sulfur,
and her handler yelled for her to stand down because the stakes
had just been increased and that he had to conference with
other members of MI-6.

He hung up the phone and Okema said, "I hate that little
bastard. He told me to stand down because he had to
conference with the head of MI-6, yeah right. I mentioned
carbon and sulfur and he left in a hurry. I do not think that the
Carbon Factor formula is a simple description of a process to
create a dirty bomb. On the contrary, our intel indicates that it
is a powerful concoction that uses a simple but complex
alignment of elements, minerals, hydrogen, and heavy water
to create a massive explosion that sucks up everything that is
hydrogen based."

"What in the heck, did you just talk about, and what is
heavy water?" John Lee asked.

"We know that you guys had the Carbon Factor formula in your hands and gave it up to some really suspicious characters, but there is no way in hades that these locals could replicate the process of making a carbon based bomb. Getting the scientific equipment needed to compartmentalize the components alone would have drawn international suspicion. Mr. John Lee, heavy water has an extra hydronium iron added to it, and it becomes D_2O ."

"Honey, how do you know so much about the Carbon Factor?" Brown asked.

"Mr. Brown, we were assigned to capture it while it was thought to be in St. Moritz. Obviously, by the time we got there, it was long gone and our friend Helga Spengatsenburg quite dead."

"Why didn't you tell me this beforehand?"

"You didn't ask me about this. When we, I mean Somara, Yeshida, and I, decided that we were defecting—well, sort of leaving that business—I thought we had severed all ties with the Carbon Factor until this matter came up, and Mr. Sarge Beckmire indicated that it would give the group an opportunity to escape the person hunting you guys. Did I say or do something wrong to offend thee, Mr. Brown?"

"Yes, you continue to call me 'Mr. Brown', and I thought that after we had consummated a certain event that you would not address me in that manner."

Beckmire asked, "How well did you know Helga?"

"We knew, and everyone knew, that Helga was a double agent, but that did not stop us from socializing with her or her with us. In our business, it is sometimes necessary to ah, how do you say it, ah, yes, sleep with the enemy in order to gain information."

"Is that what you're doing with Mr. Brown?"

"Mr. Sarge Beckmire, I find comfort with the man whom I plan on marrying and I regret your insinuation."

The Sarge walked in front of Okema, looked her in the eyes, and reverently bowed asking for forgiveness. She noticed that his bow indicated he was sincere because it was a low bow that indicated his respect, much lower than if she had been conducting it.

The Sarge said, "If I have offended you, please ignore my small mind and realize that I, and we, have accepted you, and yours, as one of us. As part of our group, sometimes information will require, or at least suggest, a follow-up discussion."

Okema bowed and said for all to hear, "You are a great leader, and we are yours to command, but faith must be a part of the sunrise as trust is a part of the sunset."

"That is completely understood by all of us, and we too have a saying, which is faith should be a part of all humanity, but trust is earned and not taken for granted."

"Touché, as you say."

# # #

Okema, Yeshida, and Somara were discussing the Carbon Factor when Brown walked over and asked, "What are you guys talking about?"

"We're trying to figure out how someone in Somalia got aspects of the Carbon Factor, there may be several paths that are being explored for the use of carbon. Somehow, someone has a connection in Somalia and they're not part of a tribe. If I had to guess, it is the same person who is seeking your heads. He, I thought, was just a common GS 15 or 16 for your government but it appears that this person has more power than those who are elected to run your country. This person appeared on the radar after a plane, with his signature, dropped some mercs off in the middle of nowhere in your country and aspects of their bodies were found amongst the rubble at a ranch," Okema stated.

Yeshida added, "Our people began to wonder how he could escape all the checks and balances. After using facial recognition technology, we know this person has shown up with many people on lists that are not favorable to Western nations. He has been everywhere and nowhere, I mean he is recognized in Germany, but is pictured in New York at the same time. He is recognized in Madrid but is pictured in San Francisco sporting a beard. There is another situation when he is seen in Gibraltar and at the same time in pictures with the Democratic Presidential nominee in the United States. He is connected or has a twin. We are talking about the Carbon Factor being connected to a person in Somalia who will test the efficacy of what might be used here in London."

## CHAPTER SIXTEEN

What a small world! In Somalia, weapons with a US registry were unloaded from a freighter that pirates had captured. Although in the scheme of things the arsenal wasn't considered major, it did, however, provide a local warlord with modern equipment and ammunition to engage in terrorist activities. Stacked on top of the roof of the bus transporting the illicit booty were two large cases of C-4, a tracking device, and four crates of grenades. During its ride to the village, the GPS system as well as the cameras that were encased on each of the products, were activated. The recipient of the products was an old friend of Walter's who refused to pay him for some old items and services. Hysan was a terrorist, as well as a freak. He and Walter shared the same secret proclivities. Stupidly, he had threatened their relationship with exposure unless Walter provided him with certain products—grenades and other weapons that would help him 'fight diseases' in his territory. Unfortunately, he was the same person to whom the shipment of arms was on its way to. In addition to, and coincidentally, the prescription for making a dirty bomb using carbon and sulfur was also included in the same delivery. The so-called hijacking by pirates was a three-party relationship developed by Walter with the captain of the ship, the pirates, and Hysan. Hysan was Walter's nemesis and, was the final threat to Walter's sanctity, privacy, and manhood.

Leaders do not open their gifts or look under the hoods of their cars. They have someone else take care of those tedious and potentially dangerous chores. Hysan had the contents of his shipment examined individually. Once he was satisfied that all was in order, he began to inspect the well-oiled weapons himself and yelled into the night, "I love you, Walter."

Three minutes later, the night was awakened by an incredible blast. A brightness filled the sky which dissipated slowly. Walter once again had demonstrated that he was in charge and in control. There would never be an accumulation of body parts to assemble Hysan, but his DNA was all over the perimeter. Hysan's essence was disseminated across a large aspect of his home territory. Enough of him would never be gathered, if such a thing as a proper funeral, were to be held. Walter made the dice sing again in his favor, but the roll would become difficult as time went on.

## CHAPTER SEVENTEEN

Leicester was calm and extremely hot. The night air was stagnant. Okema's people watched as two vans left the area and made their way towards London proper. The Sarge presented her with a hypothetical, asking, "What if those two vehicles are decoys? Is there any way of isolating sulfur, like we can isolate nuclear materials?"

Okema made a call to her handler and presented two different scenarios. One, she told him if the two vans were decoys and were apprehended, that would indicate that their scheme is being monitored. Two, on the other hand, they could be the real thing. She also asked whether there was any way to monitor a strong presence of sulfur.

The person on the other end of the phone answered, "It is unlikely that Her Majesty's security forces are going to bet on decoys, considering the potential deaths of hundreds of British citizens. We not only need to be sure of the threat, but we need to be precise in dealing with those people who are planning this devious act. If this happens in a bad way, you know, your American friends will be blamed exponentially for any screw-ups and loss of life. I think you should be querying them about decoys. Remember, this is their operation, and we will indict each one of them if things go poorly for the people of London."

"You are, and will always be, a magnificent asshole. Goodbye, jerk," Okema stated.

"Thank you for the vote of confidence; we aim to serve and please."

Okema spoke with the Sarge and Mallory and told them how this thing was going to go down, and that if there was a loss of life and failure to execute, they would be blamed and indicted. Mallory inquired, "What else is new? We're used to being blamed for the collapse of the Wall, the losses in the stock market, and the Kennedy, King, Kennedy assassinations; we are completely comfortable with this sort of bullshit. Listen, we sent Larry and Zanthius on a mission to intercept the trucks, with Yeshida and Somara as backup. They have explicit instructions to cut throats and run the vehicles into the damn dirty ass water, if need be."

"It's important that I ask this question. We appear to be splintered in our approach. Is it more efficient if we work with a common understanding and purpose? I also directed two of our intelligence personnel to follow the trucks and to apprehend them when they entered the city limits. Does this appear to be amateurish?" Okema inquired.

The Sarge looked at her and announced, "That's exactly the image I want to create if it keeps oversight from getting in our way. We know what the hell we're doing, and, so far, we are on point. Those trucks are decoys, I'll bet Mallory's life on it. Can you find a real old spy, with a phone to hit one of the damn things when it gets close to London and blame it on the texting?"

"No one told me that you are clairvoyant. We have an older woman and a person of short stature following them. The smaller person is in an oversized car seat and he looks like a child; however, they are both armed to the teeth. If we communicated a little better, we would not be working at cross-purposes."

"We know that you have handlers, and that's why we are feeding you information that we need you to know. When we make our move on these guys and ladies, it is going to be final and destructive. Your people are racists and hate immigrants, that's the image we want you to keep until we extract vital information from these people about who they are aligned with and whether there are other attacks being planned."

"Mr. Sarge Beckmire, you are my people, if in fact, Rich Brown is a member of your team. We follow protocol and your people write the script for it—no rules, no procedures, just results."

"Okema, tell your people that we are going to blast that place in ninety minutes and for them to keep all friendlies away from the target area. When you talk about decoys, I find this entire discussion full of issues that we can't resolve. If I had to guess, I would say that this place is a front and that there is another location we should be focusing on. Can you check with your people and find out where the suspects go when they leave the area?"

## CHAPTER EIGHTEEN

Zanthius asked, "Hey, Larry, would you smoke a cigarette around a bomb that emits vapors?"

"Not at all. Both of those guys are smoking." Larry's phone rang and it was Mallory who told him to be on the lookout for older woman in a car with a small human posing as a child in an oversized car seat because they are friendlies.

Larry said, "That was Mallory who told me to be on the lookout for an older woman and a small man in a car seat, he indicated that they are on our side."

Zanthius asked, "Can I ask you a personal question?"

"Depends on how personal the question?"

"When your wife was pregnant, did you ever get the feeling that she hated you sometimes?"

Larry acknowledged, "Zanthius, look at the transformation their bodies go through, wouldn't you hate yourself and the person responsible for the daily changes in the way you look? Even though people say shit like, 'oh, you look fantastic being pregnant'; the real translation is you look fabulous being fat."

"I guess I get the point, but her damn mood swings are enough to make me want to jump ship."

"Zanthius, some women don't do well during this time and what they are begging for is real support and no bullshit. You must change your habits my brother. Begin to focus on her and the baby and show her that she is the only priority in your life.

"This roller coaster ride is probably worse for her because she is not grounded in one of her homes. As you know, because of dad, she is homeless, except for one place that she swears he will never see or set foot in," Zanthius replied before conceding, "I guess I have been rather nonchalant and cavalier at times. Look, Larry, a car is coming up on us and in a hurry. By the way, thanks for the chat."

Both men made ready their weapons and saw that it was an older looking woman with a guy in a car seat. The guy in the child seat frantically made gestures pointing at the trucks and made signs suggesting that Larry and Zanthius handle the second truck. As the two brothers attempted to figure out what was going on, the lady passed them and slammed her car into the first truck causing the second truck to slam on its breaks, creating a perfect scenario for Zanthius and Larry to disable the second truck.

As the truck came to a halt, Zanthius snatched his guy from the seat and began to put an old fashion ass-whupping on him. Larry shot his guy in the left leg, placed the hot barrel on his right leg and fired a round into it. Zanthius then pulled his guy around to the other side of the truck and pulled out his knife. Larry placed wire-ties on them as Somara and Yeshida pulled up behind their vehicle. Zanthius asked, "What are you guys doing here?"

"A third vehicle was following these two trucks. What are the contents?"

"We were kind of busy and didn't have time to explore the contents. Why don't you guys check that out?" The two women went into the back of each truck and realized that they had been set up because there was nothing in the back of the trucks. Somara left the first truck and called Okema and reported, "Decoys; nothing in these vehicles unless the vehicles are the bombs."

Okema said to the Sarge, "I reluctantly report to you that there was nothing in those trucks unless the trucks are the weapon. If I had to guess, the product is being assembled in parts and pieces in different places."

"I don't understand what you mean when you say in parts and pieces."

"I think that aspects of the product are being transported to another location and are being assembled there."

Mallory looked at Okema and asked, "How would you transport parts of a bomb that are basically made of products that are liquid? People would have to carry containers filled with different chemicals, right?"

"I'm not sure how it can be done, but if the product is not on the trucks then it is either already in place or is still in the confines of those buildings."

Meanwhile, the two surviving members from the other truck were hustled into cars as fake accelerants and small explosive devices were placed in them. It had been rumored that Zanthius has a short temper when it comes to interrogating someone and demanded of one of the captives, "Where the hell is the bomb?"

"What bomb? Mister, you have us all wrong, we don't do bombs, we are students, and we drive trucks at night to pay our expenses."

Zanthius smiled at him and said, "You're wasting my damn time, now I'm going to make you bleed. I know you think that there are going to be plenty of virgins waiting on you when you die, but unless they give you a new dick, that won't matter." Zanthius slashed the guy's inner thigh and asked, "Are you married?"

"No, sir, please sir, don't do this to me, I'm a student trying to earn honest money. Please, sir."

Zanthius took his knife and ran it right above the guy's shaft and said, "I'm going to make the letter 'T' in ten seconds and once I start, I will not stop until I place what is left of your dick in your mouth. Tell me, where is the bomb? Where is the bomb?" As the man began to cry from pain and/or the likelihood that he was going to be neutered, he mumbled, "Purgatory."

"What the hell are you talking about? Purgatory; that's hell. What the fuck are you talking about?"

"All praise be to the one and only—the bombs are already placed in the theatre district and will go off tonight after the final scene in Dante's Inferno."

"Where were you heading?"

"We are decoys." Zanthius looked at his associate who was bleeding profusely and acknowledged, *Dante's Inferno*, eh?" Well, my friend, here's your purgatory--bang, bang, and bang. He placed his weapon down and said, "That was too fast, don't you agree? I mean he's dead and didn't feel a thing. Now, you my friend, you're going to feel every little sensation that I have to offer, so let's get ready to have some fun. I want your leader's name and all those who are a part of his cell. I want foreign names and addresses, sister's, and cousin's numbers. I want to know about the people who are willing to kill people for unknown reasons!"

"Sir, I beg you, please don't hurt me any further. I have given you all the knowledge that I have. In two hours, there will be four huge explosions. Two detonations by those wearing suicide vests and one by a street vendors cart and the fourth, I am not privy to its positioning."

Zanthius stepped away from the captive and called the Sarge and announced, "There will be four explosions at the end of *Dante's Inferno* in the theatre district tonight." He then continued to report the intel the man had shared.

"Good work, Son, we're on it. The only thing I'm concerned about is whether he, or she, is using the Tube as an escape route. I think we have missed the primary person. I need you guys to get to the nearest Tube station near London's Palace Theatre. I'm sure he or she wants to watch the results of their masterpiece in person."

Somara said, "We're thirty minutes away. Who are we looking for?"

"You're asking me? I have no idea what the leader looks like. It's your ball game and you don't know who is pitching. It's okay, it would take an act of God to discern who the responsible person is before this event. What we must do is get up close and personal, which exposes us to danger while looking for people outside of the blast zone who have a ringside seat. Listen, there are six of you along with Carlos and three of his people waiting to assist, that's ten people who are sharp and love what they do. I need you guys to head there and with luck, stumble across the ringside seat while we try to put others wearing unusual clothing for this time of year, out of their misery. We might spook them, and cause panic. They may get to detonate their vests, but they won't get to hurt the brunt of the crowd leaving the theatre. Okema can you contact your handler and request that he place shooters on all four quadrants, and give them the okay to head shoot people wearing too many clothes? I know that's a tall order, but we need to minimize their ability to detonate their devices. I mean, a clear indicator would be to attempt to track people with wired hands, but you really can't see that from afar, now can you?"

"Dad, what I hear you saying is that those of us close by will have to make a less than scientific decision to execute people randomly, based upon the nature of their attire, am I correct?"

"Son, you are right on the money."

"Head shots are perfect for that, but if the detonators are pressure released, then you, or whoever does the shooting, is going to be obliterated."

"Son think of how many lives we can save. Our business model is extremely profitable, but it comes with a tremendous amount of risk, each of us knows this and so should you, by now."

"Dad, perhaps we need to rethink our approach to this shit. Let me start by saying, we don't have a clue as to who the real villains are and we're going to execute anyone who is overdressed. Now, that does not sound like a smart plan to me, especially since we must get up close and personal to decide who is overdressed, and by the way, that idea is totally subjective in nature. What I think we must do is distance ourselves from the immediate area and take aim from afar. What you're proposing sounds more like a suicide mission or one where people will be remembered as martyrs. Please, just think about it. Why should we be up close and personal with people who are willing to kill themselves for some archaic political reason that is guided by some philosophy that means truly little to you and me? Pops, listen, give Larry and me the ability to call out targets and let those souls that we identify fall upon our shoulders. You can't walk among hundreds of people and hope to find a person housing a suicide vest. We have a purpose and it's not to play a stupid hero. More likely, it is to provide governance over those who depend upon you as their leader."

"Son, sometimes you have to play in the dark to know what scares you."

"Pops, we aren't scared. We enjoy what we do, it keeps us together and it also allows our family to grow--Somara, Yeshida, Yvette, and Okema. If you must hear me say it, then I will, we all need you and don't want you in the middle of shit that could prove conclusive."

"Where is all of this emanating from? What on earth gives you the idea that I'm trying to jump off a cliff?"

"I, or rather we, thought we were hearing some stuff that sounded terminal."

"Are you people out of your mind? My wife would preemptively kill me and you if she thought that we were on a fatal mission. My problem is that I must be able to answer the same call that I ask of my guys, and now you two. A leader who sits on the hill and merely watches the results is not much of a leader. I think respect is gained and maintained when you're actively engaged alongside your men during the heat of a battle. That is why those eleven guys are here and will follow me to the end of the world. They know I would take the heat for them on any given day. So, you people need to know how we roll, we play to win and that is all we do."

"Pops, you can't lead the charge, that is the end of the conversation. If you want to orchestrate our approach, then all is well, but you cannot lead the charge. Those remaining will need your calm and know that vengeance will be theirs in this life or the next."

"Zanthius, I love you and appreciate how you have corrupted Larry. He would never have come at me like this."

"Sorry, Dad, those were Larry's sentiments, I just reiterated them." The Sarge inquired and Larry indicated that what Zanthius said was accurate.

## CHAPTER NINETEEN

In the midst of the crowds walking around London, Larry and Zanthius appeared to stand out more than any unknown terrorist. On the other side of the street, Brown and Bernstein appeared to be lost tourists, with Somara and Okema following close behind. Zanthius called base command and said, "Pops, I know you're monitoring this transmission and I need to know places in close proximity where people could stage their operation."

"This is all commercial. They would have to come already loaded or already have a safe haven within the general vicinity. Check with Somara and her people and see if they have eyes on any suspicious areas."

"Roger that. We only have forty-five minutes before the show ends."

"Son, I'm good at telling time, and as long as you and the rest of my people are out there, I'm going to do my best to end this thing without a bang."

Zanthius turned to Larry and asked, "Do you have any idea who we are looking for?"

"I'm looking for a person who looks like you with a constant smile of contentment on their face. It is that person I will focus on because they have concluded their life and are willing to conclude a multitude of others in the process."

"Why must he look like me? Do I look that crazy?"

"No, my brother, but you do wear a perpetual smile. You appear happy and content and ready to meet your maker. That guy over there to your right reminds me of you with that look of contentment." Zanthius looked at the fellow and noticed his smile but was more attracted to the cumbersome bag that he was pulling.

Larry said, "He looks happy and dangerous at the same time. Oh shit, oh shit, look at the wires coming from the bag and leading to his hand."

Larry called the Sarge and said, " Dad, this is Larry. We think we have located one of the suspects and we're seeking guidance as to how we handle this one."

"If you're sure, or reasonably convinced, that this is one of the individuals, then you need to walk up to him from different vantage points and place two shots to the head. You also might want to hit the deck because if it's a pressure release switch, then I'm going to have to say a prayer at your funerals. Can you engage the target from afar without the loss of innocent life?" the Sarge inquired.

Larry looked at Zanthius and asked, "Can you make a strategic hit from afar? Have you ever made such a shot?"

"I am good at what I do, but I don't want to attest to my shooting capabilities, there are too many innocents hanging out here," Zanthius replied.

"Okay, if we can get close enough to the target, I will need you to focus on his hand and make sure he does not have an opportunity to open his fist after I place as many rounds as possible in his head," Larry stated.

"I think I can handle that," Zanthius announced.

"Brother, I need you to focus on his hand, or we are both going to be blown to hell in a hurry. You keep your hands where he can see them and distract him. I will do the shooting, but I will need you to catch him before he releases that trigger, if in fact, there is one."

"Damn, that sounds so conclusive, but I understand exactly what you expect from me. I can grab, control him and allow you to terminate him, but please don't shoot me in the interim."

"When you grab him, exert all of your strength to keep him from raising his arms. Be sure to keep his fist closed. Once you have him in your clutches, close your eyes and turn your head so that the splattering of flesh and bone does not create a problem for you."

"That's going to be a close corner shot, are you sure I'm going to be safe in this process?"

"I can only say that I love you, and that I don't want the notion of your demise on my conscience. I will be as fast and as swift as you are in terminating target number one."

Okema watched the movements of the person in question and signaled to Zanthius to abort. The suicide bomber fumbled with a small clock that had wires leading to his vest. She called her handler and told him that the subject just activated a clock, and the bomb squad truck needed to be ready to move. She was told that the truck was around the corner from them. Okema instructed her people to have the truck come to their location because the subject might have two detonation devices on his vest.

Okema signaled to Zanthius to make his move. As the two men headed towards the subject, he appeared to be in a daze or silently saying his prayers. Zanthius and Larry were clowning around when Larry said, "On my mark—three—two—one."

Zanthius grabbed the subject's hands, fell to his knees, and held them close to the man's side. Larry fired two shots into his head just as the bomb disposal truck pulled up next to them. The wires were cut, and the guy's body and bag were flung into the bomb vehicle and it drove off. It happened so fast, no one realized what had happened. Zanthius had blood spatter on his shirt and face, but other than that, it was a clean hit. Zanthius called the Sarge and reported, "I believe we got one of them. Any intel on the other perpetrators?"

The Sarge replied, "Chakes and Montomie are following a woman who is wearing the full garb, but they aren't sure about her at this point, McArthur and Gladstone are following a young man who doesn't have a package but keeps looking for someone or something to arrive. That's all the intel we have right now, rather thin I'm afraid to admit."

Chakes called the Sarge and reported, "I believe the woman we're following is wearing more than underwear under her outfit. She keeps looking at her watch and the last time she looked she had to pull her sleeve up and Montomie said he thought he saw a device taped around the middle of her arm."

"Is there a clean shot available, and what would be the damage if she detonates her device?"

"There are a lot of friendlies around, and depending on what she has strapped to her, I estimate a quick twenty to thirty dead and another fifty to seventy-five injured."

"Shit, that is way too many lives to gamble with. Let me find out where the other bomb disposal truck is. Stand down for now unless you see a problem. We have thirty minutes left before the theatre lets out so, hopefully, she won't exercise her options until that time."

Okema made the call to ascertain the location of the disposal unit and was told that it was parked directly in the alley next to the theatre. The Sarge called Chakes and told him to eliminate the subject but with minimal loss of civilian life.

"Sarge, no disrespect intended, but how the hell do we do that?"

"That's exactly why you are who you are. You are where you are because you guys are the best, can figure shit out on the move and can stay safe. In other words, first stay safe."

Zanthius interrupted the transmission and said, "If she is strapped like our guy was, then there are two mechanisms: a handheld pressure release switch and a clock timer. I suggest, or rather highly recommend, that one of you grab her arms, keep them down by her side, while the other one puts two solid slugs in her head. Make sure the disposal unit is close so before she hits the ground, you can cut the wires and then you can throw her ass in the barrel to self-destruct. Don't mess around. Distance yourself from her as soon as possible after you dump her in the truck."

"Just have that box close to dispose of her ass as soon as you place the rounds in her head. As a matter of fact, they're watching you and waiting for the action to go down," Okema indicated.

Chakes discussed the method of operation with Montomie and they both seemed to be on board with the plan. Montomie would hold her arms by her side, fall to his knees, and Chakes would put two shots in her head. As the two men converged on their target, and as Montomie grabbed her and held her arms tightly by her side, he realized that the woman was pregnant, and the device strapped to her arm was her cell phone. He violently swung her away from the line of fire and his head became the target for Chakes. Montomie yelled, "Abort, abort, abort—she's pregnant." It all happened so fast; the woman didn't have time to scream but fainted in Montomie's arms.   Chakes was a nano-second away from placing two rounds in her head.

The subject, that McArthur and Gladstone were following, turned the corner and saw his lady friend in the arms of a stranger. McArthur ran up to him and said, "If you want to see her again and live to see another day, you will do exactly what I tell you to do or I will blow your head off."

As the makeshift ambulance pulled up to their position, the two young people embraced in the ambulance and spoke in their native tongue. Chakes said, "Only English. We thought you were suicide bombers."

The woman looked up at him and mumbled, "I thought you were a terrorist. There was a woman I encountered in the loo, who after washing her hands, made an adjustment to something that was saddled on her body. She didn't see me, but I saw her and began to wonder what was going on."

"Your English is perfect, where did you study?" Chakes inquired.

"Temple University."

"Oh yeah, that's in Baltimore, Maryland," Chakes stated.

"It is not. It's in Philadelphia, Pennsylvania, and is located on Broad Street," the lady stated.

"Just checking, I know that. Listen, I'm sorry we had to gather you guys up like that, but some unbelievably bad people are planning a horrific act here tonight. You led my associates to her, and we followed her, so it all worked out. Can you give me any details about the woman you suspect?"

"You walked right past her as you began to accost me. She had the full garb on but had a purple sash."

Chakes called the Sarge and said, "We blew it. The people we followed are clean but there is a female with a purple sash that may be one of the bombers. We need all eyes searching for a woman in garb with a purple sash who left our location two minutes ago and is probably heading towards the target zone."

"Okay, keep those people safe and out of the way and keep your eyes open for suspicious movements and locations. I'm assuming that they are not trying to communicate with each other, because if those vests are radio controlled, it could prematurely detonate the devices. These are my orders and are not to be questioned. If you see any individuals who are suspicious in nature, shoot first and ask questions later. Okema's people didn't want to do this job because they knew it would be a problem. This way we take the blame and perhaps the legal outcomes. Now that we are clear about their strategy, again shoot first. Once we are safe, then we will collectively try to figure out why we did what we did."

"That's a tall order, Sarge, and could be a costly one," Chakes indicated.

"Gentlemen, and I'm including the following, Chakes, Montomie, Gladstone, McArthur, Larry, and Zanthius, follow my orders or resign your posts."

"Sarge, have you gone off your meds? We heard you and we usually obey you. What's up with that resign your position?" Gladstone nudged Chakes and told him to conclude the conversation. Chakes said, "Roger that Sarge, and I'll call you back in a few." Gladstone said, "I think someone else was on our line which is why the Sarge went left. Call him on his cell and see what happens."

Two minutes had expired and the Sarge called Chakes and said, "That channel was compromised and was being recorded. Someone is monitoring our actions. In the meantime, do not use the radios--use cell phones. I have to speak with Okema and see if her people are wiretapping us."

The Sarge called Okema and asked if their radio transmissions were being monitored and recorded. She told him that it would make good business sense for them to monitor and record the transmissions. After all, their people could not randomly assassinate people. However, we are out to make a statement and to avoid a catastrophe."

As the clock continued to tick down, Okema reminded the Sarge that there was less than twelve minutes left before the end of the performance. The Sarge said, "I want everyone on the streets looking for the woman dressed in full garb with a purple sash, she should be moving east at a distinct pace. Wait a minute, the person that Larry and Zanthius neutralized was coming from the north. I bet you $1 that the other subjects will be moving from west to east. John Lee, you and Jilkes got to figure that one out on the fly. Oh shit, I bet there is someone on the inside who is going to detonate a bomb and force people onto the streets, then subjects from east, west, and north will continue the carnage."

Larry, I need you and your brother in that theatre. We have less than ten minutes people to wrap this thing up or some rich people are going to wish they had stayed home, drank Scotch, and slept with the maid. I need everyone to call in when they have targets in sight, so that I can have that bomb-mobile ready to help these crazies end their lives. I hope, to heaven, I'm not missing something obvious. Does anyone have another strategy?" Hearing none, he continued, "Okay, eight minutes, people, let's try to save as many lives as possible, including our own. I love you all, be safe and swift."

## CHAPTER TWENTY

Okema received a call from her people who adamantly stated that there was no bomber inside of the theatre, and that their intel was specific about how this thing was going to go down. Okema turned to the Sarge and relayed the information to him. The Sarge said, "Tell your handler that if they want to conclude this event based upon his intel, then we will stand down and disappear. Tell him he has four minutes to figure this shit out or shut the fuck up and let us work."

Okema politely hung up the phone and said, "We will all rise or perish together, Mr. Sergeant Beckmire."

"Call your people and tell them that I need immediate access to the place through the rear entrance with two ranking officers, who might have to calm down the crowd."

The Sarge sent out the three-minute warning and everyone felt like they were looking for needles in a haystack. Suddenly, John Lee snapped his neck around and said, "That there be too many clothes for this time of year and that guy looks to skinny to have an upper body like that."

Jilkes exclaimed, "Grab his arms and I'll place the rounds!"

Carlos called the Sarge and said, "We need the bomb-mobile two blocks west of the theatre. Now!"

Jilkes said, "Carlos, if anything goes wrong with our approach, don't waste time blowing his head off."

John Lee staggered across the street and positioned himself six or seven feet in front of the guy and Jilkes ran full throttle from the rear with his pistol aimed and ready. John Lee abruptly yelled, "Jilkes, now!"

Jilkes fired two shots on the run that entered the man's head and before he could stagger and/or hit the ground, John Lee had hoisted him off the ground by his arms with his fists closed. People that witnessed what happened, began to scream. The bomb-mobile appeared, and after severing all the wires, the disposal unit experts asked John Lee and Jilkes to throw the subject into the belly of the vehicle.

Before they responded, Jilkes and John Lee gathered the subject by his feet and arms, and they threw him into the bomb-mobile. Jilkes turned around and saw a cart, unattended, near the entrance to the theatre. He called the Sarge and said, "I see a cart and no vendor. I pray to God that there is not someone, somewhere controlling the trigger. Tell my woman I love her!"

Jilkes started towards the cart, and John Lee began to advance. Jilkes, looked at him and waved him off, and said, "If I blow this, take care of my family. Love you man but stay the fuck back!"

Jilkes approached the cart as the bomb mobile followed him. He looked at the cart and realized that he could not lift it by himself and beckoned one of the drivers to assist. John Lee, vociferously yelled at the driver, "Stay the fuck in the truck! We got this." He looked at Jilkes and said, "When I die, I want to be with my woman or you. You know this is how we roll."

The two men decided to gently place the unit in the bomb-mobile and get the hell away from it in a hurry.

Jilkes called the Sarge and advised him that the train from the west was terminated and no further service would be provided from that area. The Sarge asked if they could lend assistance in the rear where Larry and Zanthius were sniffing

out what they hoped, was a dead animal? Sarge radioed in,
"We have two minutes before the show ends, and I wouldn't
want anyone to see that issue. The men agreed and began to
hustle to the rear of the building. The bobby stationed there
was apprised of their visit and quickly ushered them into the
place. Larry saw John Lee and signaled him to sniff out the
other side of the venue and then held up three fingers. John
Lee held up one finger, and Larry smiled.

John Lee whispered to Jilkes, "I think this here problem
is just a ruse to force people out on the streets, so that those
crazies could have done their thing. What would you do to
make someone run out of a place?"

"Duh, set off small explosives. But if I wanted to hurt
people, I would string a couple of grenades from the lights
and--Oh my God, Oh my God! Let's get the hell out of here.
Look what's attached to, what appears to be, the main curtain
lines." John Lee saw it and looked for Larry and Zanthius but
didn't see them. He ran across the back of the stage and saw
a stagehand and forcefully asked, "What or who controls the
opening and closing of the curtain?"

The guy looked at him and replied, "What are you doing
back here?" John Lee placed his weapon to the man's head
and said, "Look up in that corner that I'm pointing to. Do you
know what those are?"

"Bloke, I'm just a stagehand."

"Last time, who or what controls the curtains?"

"The same person that controls the lights and sounds, and
he's sitting in the middle section of the auditorium."

"Listen, if he closes those curtains, you're a dead man.
How the hell do I cancel his command in the next two
minutes?"

"We have to get to the other side of the theatre and shut off the main breaker. That is the only way to negate his command."

"Can we get there in less than two minutes?"

"I can get there in one minute. Let's go."

Larry and Zanthius saw Jilkes and John Lee moving fast. John Lee stopped and made eye contact with Zanthius and made the signal for them to abort and abandon. Zanthius said to Larry, "Look, I think John Lee wants us to get the hell out of here." Larry turned around and saw the robust signals of John Lee and said, "Brother, move like there is no tomorrow." The two men plus a bobby made their way towards the exit.

Meanwhile, John Lee, Jilkes, and their new best friend, made their way to the main breaker and Jilkes pulled the lever. Larry stopped in his tracks and said, "They must have found the bomb, but the performance is still going on." It was less than a minute when Larry said, "Brother, we should prepare these people for what may come next. To save our lives and forfeit theirs without any attempt to help is not the way I want to live or die. You and the bobby get the hell out of here; I got this."

Zanthius lowered his head, looked up and said, "Larry, if I left you here and you died, how many times do you think I would hate my decision? Anyway, don't answer that, let's go and commandeer a microphone."

On stage and in the presence of royalty, Larry yelled, "My name is Larry Holland, and this is my brother Zanthius Beckmire De Lombardo. If you panic and run out of here, you will probably be blown to smithereens. This bobby will confirm that there are grenades ready to explode at the closing of the curtains. Wait, I need you people to listen to me or we are all going to die. We are experts in dealing with terrorists

and were invited to assist in keeping you safe. Now, I know
that some of you want to run right out of that door, but I need
you to trust me, my brother, as well as the bobby. Get down
on your knees, place your hands on your head and put your
head as close to your midsection as possible. We have
neutralized two subjects and have discovered the grenades, but
a fourth has eluded us and is carrying a horrible device that
can cause significant damage. If there is a mass exodus from
this place, many of you will die needlessly. I need you to look
up in the right and the left corners of the stage. You will see a
string of grenades that would have been activated if the
curtains had closed. Those are not props. They are the real
thing!"

Jilkes and John Lee retrieved the ancient fuse from the
switch that controlled the lights and curtains and walked out
on the stage where they were surprised to witness absolute
calm and understanding. Larry announced, "These are my
associates and apparently, they control the switch to the
curtains. I need you people to stay on your knees until this
bobby comes back in and tells you it is safe to leave the area.
This is not a media event, and until we find out who, where,
when, and why this happened, you might just want to keep this
experience to yourself."

The four men descended the stage and methodically
exited the building with their weapons drawn only to face a
lone bomber who was expecting chaos and carnage from
within. Zanthius saw her purple sash first, and announced,
"Your fellow bombers have been neutralized in the worst
possible manner, is that what you desire to happen here? We
will not let you become a martyr! We are far enough away
that the damage will be superficial, and we are probably the
best shooters in the world. It's your choice, but the slightest

twitch will cause us to fire upon you. As you can see, there is no one here, but you, us, and four weapons pointed at you from afar. I don't know your cause, nor do I care about it. I will say that you have picked a coward's way out of life but we're willing to assist you in this being the last thing that your miserable life remembers." The woman began to cry when she realized that she and the others had failed, and that those who planned this event had failed but would live to try it again. She released her hand-held switch and detonated her ordinances. Although covered with blood and body parts, the team members were without injury and no civilians suffered from the misguided strategy.

As the event concluded, Okema called her handlers and announced, "I believe we have honored our commitment, as well as saved the lives of many of your rich, powerful, and famous citizens, despite your flawed intel. I will send you details as to where to forward payment. I must alert you that a perpetrator is still out there and that he or she probably has more puppets to exploit and explode."

"You and those Yanks did a pretty fair job of locating and concluding the threat. Our people could have accomplished the same thing," her handler announced.

"Yes, Commander, your people are experts, but are handicapped by rules of engagement and two million rules concerning the use of force. The 'Yanks', as you refer to them, don't consider these rules. They are free to execute on location and will shoot a pregnant woman and her child if it means saving a lot of lives. They don't take kindly to people stepping on their territory once they have marked it with their urine. Goodbye." As Okema was about to hang up, her handler cautioned, "One final piece of information before you disappear. A certain person by the name of Walter has been paying handsomely for information about your group's whereabouts. Your planes are under security and are not officially in Italy. The Italians are interested in certain trade sanctions against the French and are using this episode as a bargaining chip. Walter, on the other hand, seemingly has a hard on for your people. You have forty-eight hours before the location of your planes will be made public. I wouldn't waste anytime wining and dining. I would extract my group immediately, if I were you."

"If you need to get the Italians attention, tell them that a major terrorist organization is operating in their country and that we had plans on rooting them out and ending their careers. However, with this new information, we will let them step on each other's heads until they figure it out or lose a significant number of their people to a horrific bomb."

"Okema, is this true?"

"We ascertained the information from one of our captives. If they want to mess with us indirectly, through others, then we will close our eyes and disappear within the next ten hours. Sergeant Beckmire was going to conclude this problem for them because we had intel, but since they want us to get out of dodge in a hurry, tell the bastards that their problem can be made whole for $15 million US in cash. Call me within the next thirty minutes because we will have to expose that we had intel of an impending attack and passed it on to you, the Brits, who failed to communicate it to the Italians because you felt there was no credible intel or logical connections, even though we just successfully concluded a group here in the United Kingdom. Once again, your choice. You can manifest this thing anyway you want, but the terrorists are in Italy, and we were going to visit them for free, but now that politics have gotten involved, it's going to cost them. You have thirty minutes.   Then we will collect our planes and be gone from Italy."

"I am so sorry to learn that you have acquired many bad manners from the Yanks."

"These Yanks tend to go straight for the action without a lot of 'bs', mate. Get back to me."

## CHAPTER TWENTY-ONE

At the airport, the ladies and children were happy to see their men folk. Much of the conversation was about the spectacular castles and boring foods. Courtney asked the Sarge if he had missed her and he said, "Like my ring misses my finger or my finger misses my ring." The two engaged in a kiss that made the grandbabies say, "Ugh." Asiram walked over to Zanthius and said, "I think that I have created a master spy in you, Mr. Zanthius Beckmire de Lombardo. Give your wife a kiss."

"Oh, my goodness, you are really developing into a pregnant woman, I so love you and I missed the crap out of you. Is everything okay with you? Any strange pains or sickness? Do you think we can make passionate but deliberately cautious love?"

"Zanthius, my dear husband, please go and give your mother a hug and kiss before she assassinates me."

"Oh, yeah, but get used to the fact that you're my new momma in ways that my mother could never imagine. Love you, be right back."

Also, at the airport, a special vehicle was there to collect and immediately destroy all the weapons that had been used or touched by the group. Mallory said, "I hope this is really happening and that they aren't using our prints to involve us in any future ruses that they can manifest."

Okema was on the phone with her handlers and was told that Walter had been sighted in La Romana, Dominican Republic.

She pulled Beckmire aside and asked, "Can you ask Mr. Mallory to join us as well?" The Sarge motioned for Mallory, and he joined the group. Okema reported, "I have committed you and us to an enterprise that impacts our hidden identities in this part of the world. The Italians are using the fact that we have landed planes at their airport, and since there is no record of them, are blackmailing the British into cajoling the French into some minor trade deal. I told them that we had obtained credible intel regarding a terrorist cell operating in Italy and that we were going to eliminate it for free. I also told them that since they wanted us out of their airport immediately, the cost of the service would now be $15 million. I did not have time to contact you because my handler was on the phone acting smug. I apologize for my actions and promise never again to act for the group but there was also information about the Walter person that I wanted to gather."

She lowered her head and Beckmire asked, "What was the discussion about Walter?"

"He is currently in La Romana, Dominican Republic." Beckmire looked at Mallory and the two men silently thought in unison, "Where is Jong?"

Okema quietly stated, with her head bowed, "I must admit, there is a small terrorist cell in Italy that I personally would like to see eliminated. It operates near the airport which is the cause of my concern. I thought they were just voices, in the night, until I found out that they attempted to develop a chemical bomb. They are a bunch of college students mostly from the United States, who are trying to sympathize with radical religious groups."

"Perhaps we beat the shit out of them without killing them, you like that idea?" Mallory asked.

"I love that idea, because one of them is my sister."

"Your sister is a sympathizer?"

"She is more than that. She is the leader and has innocent blood on her hands. It is only fitting that I be the one who provides her with everlasting peace."

Mallory looked at her and asked, "Are you sure you're up to that kind of mission?"

"I have Mr. Brown to help me recognize the bad that she has done, the good that I do, and how the world will be better off if her mindset is unable to actively create the horror that is inherent in her. She was a demon as a child and has only grown to envision more horrific ways of destroying innocent people. I have considered facing her for years and have reconciled with the fact that I will have to kill my own sister, who I love so much. My parents have commanded me to be the one who provides her peace."

"Listen, Okema, if you have precise information and we can provide backup for you and your friends, then we will do this thing. We have no intel on this matter and, therefore, can only operate in a backup role."

"Mr. Sergeant Beckmire, you had no intel on this matter, but you led the charge. Is it a matter of money?" The Sarge stood up and walked in front of her and bowed extremely low indicating that he had offended a friend once again and wanted to know how to make amends.

He said, "Okema, you have helped us and provided intel, as well as firepower for us, and we have, on the peripheral, thanked you. This thing that you need done in Italy, we will provide cover, or advance movement for you once the details of the location and subjects have been described to us. As a matter of fact, I will be willing to honor your family as well as Mallory. The notion of concluding a family member's life, regardless of circumstances, is a thing that will never leave you. I suggest you allow that action to be carried out by a randomly selected member of our team. No one will ever know who did the work, if you were to assist in this matter it would make for bad karma."

"Please allow me a few hours to consider your support, especially in light of the fact that my parents have appointed me to purge our family of the evil."

"Your request is our command. You tell us who and we will provide the terminal event, as family. And, as family, it is the same as you following the edict given to you by your parents, even though your new partners carried out the event. It is much easier for one of us, randomly selected, to carry out your obligation to make your family whole. Even if you are remotely involved, you will be burdened for the balance of your life. Let us help you and let us carry your burden."

"Mr. Sergeant Beckmire, a thousand thanks."

As the group boarded the private military jet for Italy, Beckmire's phone rang. It was Allen who said, "I can't talk long, but don't go chasing fish in an orchestrated pool. Your cousin is in the Dominican Republic. I just heard and confirmed this matter but, I also know it taste bad to me. Too many people know about his whereabouts on this one. I highly recommend that you let the Dominican Republic notion, pass. It's a set-up with support from the military; goodbye."

# # #

Once the group landed in Italy, two obvious looking agents approached Okema and asked her if they could have a word with her. She walked away from the rest of the group and was informed that there was the strong likelihood that her sister was killed while trying to assemble a suicide vest. The agent's attempt to ease Okema's burden about the details of her sister's demise, didn't reconcile with her. Okema knew that her sister was a chemist, a brilliant one at that, who knew what elements could spark a chain reaction. She also knew that her sister was too smart to die because of a simple mistake in outfitting a bomber. Okema asked where the bomb site was and whether she and a few of her companions could take a look and see what happened.

At the site of the explosion, it became obvious to Zanthius that the whole thing was staged. He said, "Pops, why would someone take the time to place all of their personal information in a bag in a corner?"

"Keep that information on the down-low son. I noticed that and wondered why myself? This whole thing seems staged to me, and I bet you $1 that the body parts here are from innocent homeless people."

"Pops, don't look now, but there is a camera located at three o'clock."

"There is one at nine, twelve, and six as well. I think we're being observed. Hey, Mallory, I can't take this scene. Can I talk to you outside for a minute?"

When the two men stepped outside of the bomb site, the Sarge said, "I saw four cameras in that place but not sure they were recording."

"You must have missed one old man, there were actually five and the fifth one had blinking lights on it."

"No shit? Where is it located?"

"It is directly across the street, panning this place. Get Okema out of there. Let's plan a strategy because I don't believe her sister's remains are a part of this charade."

When Okema came out she pretended to be crying and upset and said, "Let's get out of this place. My sister is somewhere watching us."

The Sarge placed his arms around her as if consoling her and she whispered, "Is this a good acting job? Do you think we sold it?" Okema asked.

"Well, I must admit, you did a great job of pretending to be in mourning. I think for the untrained eye we might have a fifty-fifty chance of cajoling someone."

"How does one cajole someone?"

"By acting the way you did and by me consoling you over the loss of your sister. We are trying to trick people into believing that you are upset that your sister is dead. At the same time, we looked strategically around the area and tried to figure out where they are watching us from."

"Oh, I see! So, you saw the six cameras as well?"

"I only saw four, Mallory saw five and now you say there are six?"

"There are five cameras inside of the blast area and one focused directly on the site from across the street. My sister is a very unusual individual who believes in dotting every 'i', and crossing every 't'. If this was the precursor to her devious act, then her real act is going to be horrific."

"Why is she so troubled and willing to hurt innocent people?"

"If you can believe in fantasy for a moment, then her trouble began when she designed a product that became a household item for fighting germs without the use of a bunch of chemicals. She gave it to her boyfriend, at the time, and he sold it to a large pharmaceutical company for untold millions of dollars. He dumped her and changed his identity, and she hasn't been right ever since. She met some nutty people in school, started smoking pot, listened to a lot of political tapes, and watched dysfunctional documentaries about religion. When she was dumped by that guy, her mission in life was to find him and dissect him. This is exactly what she did. In small and logical sections, she disconnected him from life. He has never been seen or heard from by anyone since then."

"I assume when you say she disconnected him from life, she cut him into small pieces."

"No, she did not cut him at all. She connected him to another one of her inventions and sucked the life out of him and I do mean literally, sucked the life out of him. She placed his bones in another concoction that she developed that changed his matter into a liquid. I know all of this because she wants me to share both processes and other devious developments with the world once she has passed on."

"I'm wondering if I should talk to Brown about this?" The Sarge inquired.

"That will not be necessary. I told him about how smart she is and what she did to her boyfriend who jilted her."

"That sort of thing doesn't run in the family does it?"

"No, Mr. Sergeant Beckmire, we are total opposites," Okema confessed.

# # #

As the Sarge, Mallory, and Okema compared notes, the night sky was brightened by multiple explosions that left everyone wondering, what had just happened. At the airport, hundreds of people had been senselessly murdered or injured by an unknown party without a stated manifest.

The Sarge announced, "We have to get back to the airport and check on our people. Mallory, give Jilkes a call, and see if all our people are accounted for."

Mallory placed a call to Jilkes but received a busy signal each time. He tried to call Jong, McArthur, Gladstone, and Chakes and received busy signals. He deduced that people were trying to call for help and/or call to check on their loved ones. He told the Sarge that the telephone lines were tied up and that they needed to get to the airport as soon as possible.

# # #

At the airport, Okema was met by a local confidant. Okema stridently said, "I think this is the work of my sister. I need to put these two gentlemen in touch with her group so that they can attempt to catch her before she flees the country. Also, if I know my sister, she has a finale in store, and you need to tell people to stay low and be observant."

The baffled agent said, "I need to clear this request with my superiors." As he attempted to reach his boss, another explosion occurred that superseded the previous one at another part of the airport. The Sarge said, "We have got to help these people, this is insane."

Mallory said, "We're chasing a ghost who knows how to blow shit up with simple matter. Okema, we need to hear everything there is to know about your sister and attempt to figure out her next moves. Apparently, she is using low grade materials that are not detected by the security systems."

"My sister is a brilliant individual who understands simple matter and how to connect or disconnect matter to make it good or bad. As a child, she was able to play with things and make them constructive or destructive. She is a fanatic. That makes our challenge even more difficult because if she suspects that I'm on to her, then we will have to bury a lot of people before we find her. She knows that my parents want me and only me, to kill her. Therefore, it has become a game, but she has no intel on my new best friends, which jettisons me to another level. I mean, she considers me methodical, and I consider you guys everything but that, which will help us find and conclude her unknown purpose."

Zanthius looked at Okema and said, "If she knows that your parents, who are her parents, want her dead, then perhaps one of her targets are your parents. If she is driven by so much rage that is unfocused, then perhaps, she desires to hurt that thing or those persons who she feels abandoned her. After all, your culture has some strange and challenging customs that are hard to relate to in this day and age."

Okema looked at Zanthius, and started to walk away, turned to say something, but didn't, began to walk away again, and finally said, "Your title, that of the 'idiot spy', has much merit Mr. Zanthius, because who can decide between genius and idiocy? That is, nothing you articulated has merit, yet may be the very thing in play as we speak. She has always resented my parents for showing me favor. My father did not want girls but had two and despised both of us, but one more than the other. We were considered useless in his world and proved to be just the opposite. I am sure my sister would love to wire them to one of her inventions and end their misery."

"Even though that sounds a little far-fetched, it may be a real link to finding your sister. She has hurt and killed a shit load of people tonight, if in fact it is her conducting this destruction. I think her final portrait has not been painted and perhaps it will be of your family. If I were a betting man, I would think she wants to do a family farewell shot, or at least make it look like one," Zanthius reported.

"Mr. Zanthius, why do you think in this manner?"

"Okema, I have been in some bad mindsets that almost made me complete the final act. I believe that your sister is desperate and needs healing, perhaps an escape route. Either way, termination is in that equation somewhere; the question is, are your parents the target? I didn't do the things that your sister has done, but I thought about ending my life as well as my former wife's. Loneliness, time, and booze can create monsters out of all of us. Where are your parents now?"

"They are approximately two hours from here on the outskirts of Rome."

Zanthius looked at the Sarge and said, "Pops, I have an idea, but I'm not sure what tactical plans you and Mallory may be considering."

"Son, you're doing a lot of deducing and, seemingly, you might be on to something. Continue with your thoughts."

"I would like Okema to call her parents and tell them that she is going to drop by for a few minutes to say hello before catching a flight back to the States. I would like to attempt to assess their moods when they invite or disinvite her. If her sister is there, she is going to want to make sure that Okema is there for the final portrait. I'm sure they heard about what happened at the airport and they should implore her not to leave but to come and stay with them until it is safe."

"Mr. Zanthius, my culture or should I say, my father's, does not value female children. I think he would wish that my sister and I reach an honorable death. There will be no welcoming tea ceremony, only slight eye contact, a minimal bow, and off into another room to avoid looking at useless human beings."

"Wow, that is totally not how I, or we, see you. I'm sure Brown doesn't see it that way either, but with parents, you never know what you're going to get."

"And just what the hell are you referring to, Mister? The son who got me off the couch, made me call my dear friends and protectors so that we could safeguard, his philandering ass. Just what are you talking about, Sir?" Ben Beckmire asked.

"Pops, you're the best father I have ever known."

"Considering the fact that I'm the only one that you have ever known."

"May I finish, Generalissimo? This has been a heavenly event for me--reunited with my mother and discovering a father that I never knew I had. You, Courtney, Larry, and Rashida, have been that high that I have been searching for. Now, that I found you, ain't no way I'm going to end these charades if I can help it, because this has been the most gratifying aspect of my worthless life along with marrying a crazy-ass assassin who I love unequivocally. So, parents are not always who you want them to be, but in my case, they are my lifesavers and I love them both."

"Ah, Mr. Zanthius, no matter how my father feels about me, he is my father, and I will honor him as such for the balance of my life."

## CHAPTER TWENTY-TWO

Outside of the flat where Okema's parents lived; Jilkes, John Lee, Brown, and Bernstein took up strategic positions and watched the quiet neighborhood. People from the area watched the mayhem that occurred at the airport on their TVs. As Okema made her way to her parent's flat on the second floor, she noticed two individuals hanging out, much like the members of her team, who didn't appear to live in the community. As she removed her shoes at the front door and knocked like someone who did not want to be heard, the door flung open and it was her mother speaking feverishly in their native tongue. Okema's mother was telling her that her father was sick and unable to get up off the floor. Okema rushed in and found her father sitting in his favorite chair. As the door shut, a familiar voice from the rear said, "Now, we are truly together as a family."

Okema turned around, slowly bowed to her sister and said, "Nice to see you, Fukema. It has been a long time."

"Yes, Okema, it has been a long time, and as you can see, I have been extremely busy. Some things never change, like our father. He still regards us as useless human subjects unworthy in his eyes, a thing I shall remedy for him. Before I embark on that trip, dear sister, I want you to recognize the ordinances that I have taken the liberty to place throughout the house. If you think that you can overcome me, and or wrestle the controller from me, beware of the fail-safe devices that I have installed. So, now that you recognize that, have a seat, and let me entertain you for a minute. How did you like my signature work at the airport earlier? Truly spectacular, wasn't it?"

"Fukema, you and I will never agree about what is spectacular because what I saw happen earlier today was the work of a sick, deranged, fanatical human who lacked the passion or consideration to find a different kind of work; a work that would actually help people."

"Please, let me introduce my associates. They are here to make sure that you don't show any of your lethal skills. Where are the two androids that follow you around?"

"If you're referring to Somara and Yeshida, they are with people who make them happy. Unlike you, my dear sister, you will never be happy because you like making people pay for your pain caused by the lack of love from our father."

As Okema was strapped to the chair by Fukema's companions, Fukema said, "Father, at one point in time, I thought I loved you, even though you thought I was a lesser human being than Okema, and the two of us were less than a male child. We knew that you made our mother service your friends if you lost money gambling. How many at one time, was it Mother? Three or four? Well, Father, the entire world lost respect for you even though they didn't know about your weaknesses and your major fight against your own sexuality. Yes, Father, I am well aware of your encounters with little boys and men, but I guess my sister will never acknowledge any weakness in you. Though we were considered less than human, you never allowed anyone to violate us, although the night you lost the deed to the flat was a scary time for us as the men kept looking at us."

Okema blurted out, "What does any of this have to do with the hundreds of innocent people who were killed and the countless more injured, at the airport tonight?"

"Sentimental, as usual, eh Sis?" I will get back to that scenario, but first, the things I recall Father, are things that turned me into the mentally imbalanced human that I am today, who only likes to kill people in mass and blame it on some archaic religion. What is ever so troubling to me, Father, is the fact that you have never ever looked us in the eye and apologized for the way you treated us. So, here is the reward that you are going to receive tonight, for being a despicable, homophobic, wife beating, child considering pimping father. You will receive the award of blindness, for the balance of your life."

Fukema walked behind her father and placed what looked like a mask on his face and tightened it from the rear. The mask contained chemicals that would create a relaxing sensation but in essence would dilate the eyes to the point that blindness was the ultimate outcome in a matter of minutes.

She looked at her mother and said, "Now, Mother, I can't believe that you were totally innocent in all of this. You knew what was going on. Why didn't you call out for help and report them to the authorities?"

Okema interjected, "The very people you are talking about, were the so-called authorities."

"Stop talking shit, bitch. Don't try to save her."

"Fukema, I knew their names and where they lived. Each man met with a suspicious death. You, on the other hand, just blinded our father and now you want to hurt our mother, the only person who kept him from selling us into servitude. She covered his debt through sweat equity, and she paid dearly for it. She was a beautiful woman and had a remarkable body.

Our father, the poor drunk and an even worse drug user, sold his soul to reach momentary highs of inconsequence. Our mother did all kinds of unspeakable things and withstood all kinds of humiliation to keep us in clothes and fed. So, my brilliant chemist of a sister, you want to hurt her further? That's impossible; she has been hurt in so many ways that you will never know or can even imagine.

"Do you know how many times father attempted to trade us, but it was her cunning abilities and looks that kept the predators away? You don't know shit, Fukema, except hurting people because you were hurt as a child. Oh, my goodness! Grow up and get over what happened to you years ago. What did those people at the airport have to do with your personal issues? Did they plan it or play a part in it? Did they finance it or cheat our father, or was he the fool that he has always been? Listen, you have me here for a reason and I know what it is. Can we get on with this family funeral or must I listen to more of your childhood drama stories, bitch? Make your move but allow the innocent people who live in this place to get the hell out of here."

"Sister, that is not the way this is going to end." Fukema walked over to her father and made incisions on each of his wrists.

"I have never liked you, Okema. I want to make sure that your love interest dies alongside of you. So, I'm waiting on your new best friend and friends to show up so that I can decimate you all."

Okema looked at Fukema and asked, "How do you know about my friends?"

"We all have a mutual friend that I like to call Diablo; in this world he goes by the name of Walter." Beckmire hearing this name, called for a breach of the flat, but was overridden by Zanthius who said, "Pops, sounds to me that is exactly what she wants you to do, charge into the place that is covered with ordinances and allow her to have her wish. The last thing we need to do, Pops, is try to breach that flat. Where is John Lee? We need his dog sniffing abilities, right about now."

#

When John Lee showed up with Jilkes in tow, he said, "Okema's sister is one sick woman. Me and Jilkes have been neutralizing bombs for the last thirty minutes, and the question be, how many more of them things be in there? I mean she, or them, have designed a trap that will kill everyone within a three-block radius. Now, the stuff she be using is the stuff I be using on my farm but at a lower dosage. I mean this here girl done wrote a new book about bombs that can evade them there test people use to find them. I be meaning that in one of the bombs that we found, it was held together by oats glued together with what looked like nitro-by-products, and some shit, that I can't even spell or say. She be a wicked woman with the notion of killing as many people as she can before she is killed herself. She ain't got no regards for life, she just be wanting to kill mo people."

The Sarge who was still in a state of shock after hearing his cousin's name mentioned by a little-known terrorist, said to Mallory, "How the hell can a guy have his fingers on so many dysfunctional triggers? He probably has been engaging nuts for years and financing them as well. This guy is hedging his bets, if one thing doesn't work, then he wagers on another, with aggressive resolve. How could he know about Okema and Fukema unless he has a tainted MI-6 person on his payroll?"

Brown announced, "I'm not prepared to leave the woman that I love in there either, so I suggest you guys pull back to a safe zone because I'm not going to abandon my lady."

The Sarge looked at Mallory and yelled, "Jilkes, John Lee, Gladstone, McArthur, you people are up. Find some sticks and stones to throw because we have one of ours in that place and we damn sure don't leave our people behind."

Jilkes yelled, "Sergeant, sir, we can do better than sticks and stones. We have 9's, plenty of them, and bullets, compliments of our new partners from London."

"Well, hell, Son, pass them things out so we can figure out how to get Brown's lady, our friend, out of this place that is rigged for a massive explosion. Where is Chakes? He knows how to open shit that ain't his, go into places that he's not wanted, and slip into small areas without detection. But, Mr. Brown, you're going to have to kiss his butt and ask him how he would breach this place."

"Naw, Sarge, we cool. Chakes and I will perform the inner workings and try to reduce the potential of detonations, we got this if he'll join me," Brown stated.

"Stop being silly, you know damn well he's going to do his part. Do you think you might need anyone else?" The Sarge inquired.

"I like the way Larry works—independent and methodical and all, but he sometimes reminds me of a lone wolf," Brown said.

"Brown, if you want a super guy other than one of us to back your play, take Larry, he's as good as they get," the Sarge said.

Larry was never more than a few feet away from the center of conversation and listened to all the dialogue. His take on the situation was totally different from everyone else's.

Larry thought the key to ending this problem was not Fukema, but her assistants.

Larry said, "There's a lot of conversation regarding me, but not including me. May I be so bold and make a comment? There are several people hanging around and, I believe, they're part of Fukema's group. Me, personally, I would like to bleed one of those individuals and figure out what is going on in that flat. John Lee and Jilkes are great at bleeding people. Why don't we corral those people who are just hanging out and see what the hell they can tell us about the ordinances that she is using."

The Sarge said almost to himself, "How can one man have his hands in so many pots and stirring them all at the same time?"

The Sarge then spoke to the crew, "We have truly underestimated, my cousin. He is a resilient source of negative energy and I can't wait to get my hands on him. I know he has payments scheduled and rewards posted for all of us, but I feel that if we can bleed Fukema enough to share just a little intelligence, then I think we can cut him off at the pass and figure out how to end his sick schemes."

"Pops, I would like to catch Fukema and see if she is as tough as her actions. I mean blowing up unsuspecting people doesn't seem like a hardened criminal who is hell bent on destroying the human race. First of all, she is a coward because she convinced others to do her bidding. I bet you $10 that she will tell everything that she knows if we can get our hands on her. Her kind, probably, has no propensity for up close and personal violence, just the aftermath from afar. I also bet you that she has an escape plan. That family funeral is bullshit!"

#

Probably fifteen minutes later, Jilkes and John Lee came back with two people who had been hanging around and who happened to be packing. In the van, John Lee pulled out his favorite knife and a wet stone and began to sharpen it. One of the captives asked, "Really, you're going to scare us to death with a rock and your knife?"

Less than five seconds later, John Lee deeply penetrated his leg with the knife.

John Lee asked Jilkes, "Do you think I be done got his attention?"

"My brother, you have his full attention and that of his buddy. I think they are going to be very cooperative. At least, the last one standing will be cooperative after you cut every conceivable part off their bodies that the other one can witness."

"That be sounding like a good plan. I already cut this one, so I guess I have to cut that one really bad."

Before John Lee could put his blade to work, the person in question pleaded, "I beg you, you really don't have to cut me. Just ask me what you want to know, and I will answer to the best of my ability."

Jilkes chimed in and asked, "How many of you are in the flat?"

"There is our associate and two others. Fukema is visiting her parents."

"Are you people responsible for what happened at the airport?"

"We definitely aren't the architects of the plan, nor did we control those who did the work and gave their lives."

"If you people didn't do it, then who was responsible for sending those people to kill innocent men, women, and children?" Jilkes inquired.

"Our associate, Fukema, told us that a great crusader from America was helping us to make a statement."

"Are you saying that none of this was done in the name of a religion or some organization?" Jilkes asked.

"There is no such thing in our organization. Our mission is to bring governments who oppress and murder their citizens, for no apparent reason, to their knees. Ask yourself, why would you shoot an unarmed black man in the leg who is lying on his back with his arms raised in the air?"

"I wouldn't."

"Exactly, you probably wouldn't, but there are police who would and who have sworn allegiance to the fact that only police lives matter and that black and brown lives do not; in the scheme of things."

"And for that reason, and others I'm sure that don't make sense, you sanctioned suicide bombers at a busy airport?" Jilkes intimated.

"No, we didn't sanction or participate in it. Our presence was intended to be a misdirection, making agencies think that we did it, but in essence we had no control over or information about it."

"Well, if you didn't, then who had operational control?"

"I don't know his name or who he is, but he's one of yours."

"What does that mean, one of mine?"

"He's a Yank much like you in color and size, and apparently, powerful. Fukema is the only one who communicates with to him. I saw her facetiming him once and I began to suspect he was the one calling the shots and sending money. He seemed like a pleasant chap, but he is not. He is a person who you did not try to deceive once you entered his chambers. He is like the devil, never forgiving and always in a noxious mode."

"Do you have a name for this person?" Jilkes asked.

"I have heard Fukema call him Diablo, Lucifer, and on one occasion she uttered the name, Walter."

Everyone came to attention once again when that name was mentioned, they were concerned that this event was designed to kill them.

The Sarge instructed John Lee to penetrate the captive's stomach. The captive screamed, "I told you everything I know. I gave you the complete truth. Is this my reward and your code of conduct? Gather your information and then dispose of the source?"

"Tell me how we can get into the flat and minimize the loss of life, and perhaps I will change my code of conduct. Otherwise, it's simple, I just let my favorite butcher's assistant make exploratory cuts on your body."

"He's the assistant?"

"That's correct. Our main source for extracting information will be along soon, and once she starts, there is no turning back."

"Listen, Fukema has the flat and the building wired with a lot of explosives, chemicals and other things that I don't understand. However, I don't believe she's going to commit suicide. We have heard her talk about trying to move her life forward and become more of a humanitarian. That doesn't sound like a person who is going to kill her parents and herself, does it?"

"Are you saying that she is going to try to leave another body and her DNA after killing her family?"

"What better way to begin anew, when all who really know you are dead? We became disenchanted over the past few months when there was a focus on keeping everything Fukema owned in a certain lock box. We began to believe we were expendable and were devastated by the airport event. She has been working on multiple programs, terrorism with Diablo, and creating a need for off the book mercs. She's probably worth at least several million dollars, another thing that we stumbled upon accidently. Now, it appears to me, our Fukema, who has many followers, is planning to make a new life away from our goals, as well as from us."

"How would she get out of the flat in a hurry if she had to?" Jilkes asked.

"Something is going to happen at 10. Not sure what it is, but I believe it is some kind of distraction or an act of misdirection. She has been championing the number 10 for the past two months and felt that it was hers and our lucky number. If I had to make a wild guess, I believe there will be a huge distraction, as well as a misdirected activity, that will gain everyone's attention at exactly 10 tonight. The people in the flat will be decimated beyond recognition by her bombs. A few days ago, I saw a blood transfusion device and I'm convinced that she's going to dispense her blood strategically at the appointed hour and disappear forever, leaving all those who believed in her commitment to the cause to suffer the slings and arrows of abandonment. I truly wish her well, but I'm afraid that in her rush to disappear, she has placed into action, plans to terminate our existence as well. Giving up information about her is easy, and I don't consider my informing you of what I suspect are her intentions, to be treasonous.

"The airport was the last straw, especially since she utilized mentally challenged individuals to carry out the attacks. Insofar as her escaping her parent's home, after she murders them, I assume she is going to let herself out the back window and into the apartment below. After her exit from the building in a full body disguise, she will probably blow the whole building up with all those innocent people in it. Lately, she hasn't been of sound mind except about certain issues; the blood and disguise."

"Is this all hyperbole or do you have substantial proof of this plan that you laid out?"

"Sir, we are radicals. Our plans change from time to time, but the one thing I know is that we have been distanced from our leader and our leader is going to abandon us with the intent of making sure that we are found dead. Someone out there has our number and has been paid to follow through on this. If you want proof, try breaching the flat and see what happens. I think there may be a separate detonator button in possession of someone who I am not familiar with."

# # #

"We have approximately a little over a half an hour to figure out how to defuse the bombs and save those people in the building. Any ideas about how we should approach this mess we have been tossed into?" the Sarge inquired.

John Lee said, "I would like for me and Jilkes to enter the building at one end and Brown, Bernstein, Zanthius, and Larry enter at the other. I would like to see Chakes and Montomie enter the front of the building along with McArthur and Gladstone. I be also wanting Jong and Whitmore to cover them from afar. I be wanting to breach the building in five minutes looking for ordinances and trying to get them there people and myself out in fifteen, giving us a gamble of nine minutes. What be your thoughts about this, Jilkes?"

"Let's do it, but not hang around in case there is another trigger somewhere else."

Yeshida said, "I'm going with the group that's going through the front door because I know how to directly get to her parent's flat."

John Lee admonished, "We be wasting time. If that there person was telling the truth, we have twenty-four minutes to make this here thing happen. Sarge, this here be your call, but this is what I think we should do to get our brother's woman back safely. What say you?"

"Let's stop the chattering and make it happen. Deploy now and look for wires and barrels and all kinds of other things that could contain explosives. Remember, she is a chemist and will probably use some real funky shit that may not need wires or detonators," the Sarge warned.

Somara and Yeshida huddled briefly with their men and told them not to be martyrs. John Lee said, "Girl, I be wanting you the right way and I be wanting you to want me too. I be wanting to be your husband; I ain't taking no chances."

"You come back, and I will be your wife, for I love you so very much. I want to go against my tradition and forget ceremony. I want to be happy and dedicated to you."

"Somara, this here thing is only going to take me a minute or so to figure out. You be holding that thought. I don't want to get confused and miss traps smacking me in the face because I be wanting to be happy. You hold that there thought," John Lee said.

The group entered the building and at each intersection found what appeared to be explosives in various containers.

As John Lee and Jilkes entered the building, Jilkes said, "This seems like a set-up to me--look at the placement of this mess. I think she is going to challenge us with her scientific knowledge. Think about it Big Country. I have no idea what this shit is in this barrel, but there could be other barrels upstairs that will run down and mix with this mess. Who knows what the hell she has concocted?"

"I be smelling gasoline, ether, and kerosene. Y'all be getting any smells of your own?" John Lee asked.

"I'm going to head up to the next three floors and see if the same shit is there," Jilkes indicated.

"Naw, we be heading up together; we don't be doing that solo shit," John Lee reminded him.

As the two men, followed by a few others, entered the third floor of the building, they could see barrels as well as wires hanging in odd positions. John Lee said, "I be thinking that she is going to blow the third floor first and all of this shit is going to flow downwards and create one of them chain reactions on each level. Them there chemicals are going to become more explosive than the one before."

"We need to get as many people out of here as we can. Hit Jong on the radio and see if he has a visual on the subjects," Jilkes urged.

The Sarge came on the line and said, "I'm with Jong and we can't see shit. He's calculating how much line you'll need to break through the windows from the third floor."

"Now, that be a thought. She ain't looking for no SWAT team or nothing like that. If one of us kicks the door in and the other two start blasting, we might have a chance. If we do nothing, I'm afraid Brown is going to go at it alone and we can't have that."

"We have fifteen minutes left—no time for anymore chatter, we go now or wait and watch a new family member destroyed. What's it going to be?"

"Jilkes, you and John Lee have to make that call. I personally have reservations, but I have had them about this whole snowballing program that we have been a part of. Give Mallory and me a few minutes to check out the barrels of chemicals."

"Sarge, we don't have time for an inspection--it is now or never. Send me, Chakes, and McArthur, and get everyone else out of the building. I am going to send them through the window while John Lee, Brown, and I, hit that door with all that we have."

With approximately ten minutes left before the alleged detonation time, Chakes and McArthur ushered the people who lived in the flats above Okema's parents, as well as others, out of the building.

Whitmore showed up with what appeared to be harnesses, constructed by Jong, for Chakes and McArthur. He wished them well and vacated the area.

After clearing the floors, Chakes and McArthur connected themselves to makeshift harnesses and prepared to swing from the third floor to the second and enter through a set of windows that they couldn't see. The Sarge said, "I don't like this plan because we haven't had time to dissect it. You assholes had better be alert and focused. I don't plan on going to any funerals anytime soon. Let's make this an ordinary OP where we do the work and get the hell out without anyone getting hurt. That's what I want you guys to make happen."

Chakes looked at McArthur and exclaimed, "This is a new experience. We have never had to swing through glass windows before. I suggest when you swing over that balcony, you lead with those big ass feet of yours and have that pistol ready to fire."

"Sarge, we be out of here, shortly. Watch our backs!" John Lee exclaimed. Jilkes, Brown, and John Lee positioned themselves three doors from Okema's parents flat. Jilkes called Chakes and said, "On my mark—3—2—1—engage!"

Jong had mathematically calculated the distance and their contact point and was right on target. As the two men hit the windows with great force, Fukema froze for a moment. She was perplexed by the sound and completely disoriented by the feet that took the door off the hinges. As she attempted to understand what had happened in the rear of the flat and what was happening at the front, Brown caught her attention and placed two rounds in her head before her discombobulated mind could process what was happening. As she fell up against a wall, John Lee caught her and Jilkes searched her for devices.

He yelled, "I don't feel any controllers on this woman, we have to vacate this place now; someone else is holding the trigger." He shouted into his mike—"Abort, abort, abort!" John Lee snatched Okema's mother in one hand and her father in the other and proceeded towards the violated windows. He pushed the father out of the window first. Brown cut his woman free from bondage and led her hurriedly towards the window. They landed awkwardly, and once they hit the ground, Brown broke his pinky finger and Okema sprained her ankle.

As anticipated, the ensuing explosion on the third floor released some of the barrels of chemicals that were strategically placed to flow down to the second-floor containers. However, instead of a continuous explosion, only the eastern part of the complex was impacted by the detonation since the chemical containers on the lower level had been dislodged from their position by the team. Okema's mother suffered a sprained knee and her father received justice for all his sins, past and present. In the process of the two-story evacuation, Okema's mother and John Lee landed on Okema's father and broke his neck, a fitting death for a disgraced patriarch.

Outside and away from the complex, the Sarge said, "We will never again be a part of a program that we haven't designed, studied, and agreed upon. This thing was a logistical cluster fuck, but somehow we were able to pull it off without any loss of life other than those who seemingly deserved it."

Jilkes urged, "I think we need to get the hell out of here and meet our people at the airport. We don't want to be around when people who might be controlled by Walter show up and tag our asses."

"Good thinking! Zanthius, call Asiram and tell her to get our people and head to the airport—now!" the Sarge exclaimed.

Zanthius nodded in agreement, "On it, Pops. I think they are an hour from the airport."

"That's okay because we're going to be out of here in the next five minutes. Hey, Mallory, get our people in those vans and let's get the hell out of here before the Calvary gets here. I don't feel like answering a bunch of questions. Oh, shit wait a minute. Okema may I have a word with you?"

"Yes, Mr. Sergeant Beckmire, how can I help?"

"Listen, we have to leave here, but do you need to stay with your mother and console her?"

"My mother expects me to leave in a hurry. She knows that I will complicate the situation if I'm here when they start asking questions. I told her I would see her again within the next fifteen days, but probably in another country. She understands the nature of my work, and according to my people, Walter's guys are fifteen minutes from here. We must go and I must say *sayonara* to my mother and at least recognize my father as he passes from this life to the next. My sister, on the other hand, had already passed from this life to the next, when she murdered those innocent people at the airport. I need two minutes, Mr. Sergeant Beckmire."

# # #

In the van on the way to the airport, Mallory watched as the many emergency vehicles passed them, he turned to the Sarge, and said, "That mission was as screwed up as could be. We sent our people on a suicide mission, but we were lucky because they are as good as it gets at what they do. We can't do that again. I mean I saw the possibilities of errors on so many fronts, most importantly, we can only have one chain of command during a crisis and that person sure as hell doesn't need a lot of arm-chair quarterbacks."

"You know I could use some old-time religion right about now, but when I go to confession, I want to be able to completely confess my sins and that ain't possible as long as Walter's ass is still alive. I am going to gut him worse than what John Lee did that woman. What was her name?" The Sarge asked.

"Her name was Scottie, and I couldn't watch that scene. I mean, I was sick and had nightmares for a week or so. John Lee methodically cut her from her sex organ, to her brain and played in her blood. It might be time for us all to undergo some psychological examinations to make sure that we haven't gone off the deep end without a rope to climb back," Jilkes said.

"Not a bad idea. We could do it as sort of a game for the team to give them something else to dig at each other over. I like that idea," the Sarge stated.

"Sarge, I was joking. If you don't know that we're all crazy as hell, then I suggest you take the test by yourself. Man look at what we just did. Look at what we did at the theatre, and look at what we have been doing since we put the team together again; it's insane to say the least. We're all crazy and you lead the band."

"Whatever! Speak for yourself. I know I'm sane and have always wondered about my team members, but now you have confirmed the fact that you're all crazy as hell and, therefore, I'm going to leave it alone unless someone comes up with weird ideas. Okay, back to work. Collect all the weapons and place them in that box. Okema, what are we going to do with these weapons?" The Sarge asked.

"We're going to give them to a man in a red car who should be passing us in approximately five minutes. He will take them and make sure they are destroyed."

"You know if someone wanted to blame us for all of this mess, they could find our fingerprints on these weapons and target us as the perpetrators."

"You are almost correct, Mr. Sergeant Beckmire, but the filament on each weapon is untraceable, as well as any DNA left on them. We can't be traced because I used a product that my late, crazy-ass-sister, developed. As a matter of fact, I want to market it through our team's foundation once we have officially been inducted into the group. The process is probably worth hundreds of millions of dollars and she has other products that she has sent me and my mother that are probably worth billions."

"Okema, this group is about helping people help themselves. You, Yeshida, and Somara have become an integral part of our team. Our group is not about money. This is about ten enlisted men, a corporal, a sergeant and a few new recruits and friends. The things we have been through can't be measured in terms of money. These guys came out of the woodwork because a member of their group was threatened. I didn't have to ask for help, they automatically showed up along with a woman that I once loved and a son that I didn't know existed in the real world.

"Along the way, there was a woman in Australia that one of my guys fell in love with. Then there was the night in a bar where three of my guys fell for three beautiful and amazing spies who were interested in the Carbon Factor. Not to mention my daughter-in-law, who probably will never invite me to her home again because I am the reason that three of them were blown up.

"I say all of this to say, that we have adopted several non-combatants and combatants on this journey, including Carlos and his men. By the way, Carlos is in love with my son's mother, who in return, is in love with him. Although I mentioned her earlier, there is again the notion of my daughter-in-law--a spy, extractor, and a woman whom I would never have chosen for my son, or myself, because of the nature of her work. Asiram and my son, when on the same page, are the best damn spies that I have ever seen, even though I haven't met many spies before. He catches the bad guys, and you can bet your soul on the fact that she's going to get every piece of information that she desires or cut her subjects beyond recognition into extremely small pieces. She is one helluva woman and I'm happy she is happy with my son—no pun intended. Okay, she is a little out there, or in plain language, nuts. Not the kind of person I would deliberately piss-off."

"I think you missed my points as you made yours, Mr. Sergeant Beckmire. You think I was trying to buy my way into your organization. Fukema was full of ideas and ways to match nature with nature, but discern whatever products, for good or bad, that she was looking for. I have most of her ideas and my mother has others that I'm sure are the real deal. She knew that my mom was not sophisticated and could not understand the concepts. I would deduce that my sister was well ahead of the Carbon Factor and was on to something much more diabolical and destructive. It would not surprise me if her notions are linked to the initial development of the Carbon Factor and many other human annihilating concepts. She left, as you say, the reservation, sometime ago and couldn't find her way back."

Brown walked over to Okema and said, "Enough. I need to tell you how much I love you and that I want you to be in my life forever. I was so afraid that when I breached the flat that your sister was going to hit a switch and we would both die, but not together. That was my most perplexing moment. I breached that place to die with you while holding you in my arms and telling you, unequivocally, that I love you so very much."

"My, my, Mr. Brown. I knew this was not the end, I was aware that there are moments of tenderness and love ahead for us. I am happy that you did what you did, and I am most honored to be the woman who you entered the door of mortality, to save a person you love. My, Mr. Brown, you will find that what we have shared is only a token of the possibilities that lie in front of us. I am yours, Mr. Brown, and I now believe that you are mine."

"The first thing we are going to work on is our communications skills. Some of the things you say don't register quickly enough with me, and I have to ask that damn John Lee to define, 'what on earth, you said, and meant'."

"Aw, he would be the one to consult because although I sometimes don't understand him, I eventually acknowledge all that he has uttered, even in that strange tongue of his. He is an extremely intelligent person with wisdom that supersedes any that I have encountered. He's worth listening to in other words."

# # #

As the family members and children arrived at the airport, the notion of killing and being killed dissipated and people were happy to see their mates. Courtney exclaimed, "Ben Beckmire, if you don't get your butt over here and kiss me, there is going to be another war, one that you can't possibly win!"

## CHAPTER TWENTY-THREE

Jong approached the Sarge and reported, "The pilots filed a flight plan for Baltimore, Maryland, but once we are on our way, we can request a medical or mechanical allowance to change our plans." John Lee overhearing the conversation, asked, "Why don't we go and check on our investment and make sure we don't have to murder that little fella down there?"

"Now, that's a good idea. Courtney and Monica, may I have a word with you two?" As the two women huddled with the Sarge, he asked, "What's the status of our project in St. Thomas?"

Monica methodically pulled out her iPhone and pulled up something that resembled a pert chart. She and Courtney whispered back and forth and finally Monica said, "Other than the fabrics and china, the physical façade should be completed, and it should be available for opening in three weeks."

"This has all happened rather fast, hasn't it?"

"I'm not sure you remember this, but we thought that by operating with crews around the clock we could employ more people, get the job completed faster, develop a training program in building trades, and fund a center to provide certifications upon completion," Courtney said.

"So, you guys are telling me that work on this project is continuous and around the clock? Seems to me the words continuous and around clock have the same meaning. Wow, then perhaps that is where we should head. Do you think we can live in it for a week or so until we find out what is happening with Asiram's places?"

Monica replied, "I don't see why not. Let me give Mr. Carter a call and tell him that we will be there in the morning and will need living quarters for the group."

"Don't you think you should ask him if he can accommodate us?"

"Unless you gave him controlling shares, I don't think so. I mean this is a good opportunity to make sure he's on our side. We really don't know him, and it makes good business sense to drop-in on projects to see the real deal as opposed to some contrived work plan," Monica suggested.

"Okay, we did say that you guys are in charge, so I'm just going to follow your lead, show up at our vacation place and inspect the quality of work that's being done."

# # #

In the back of the plane where Brown and Okema were sitting, Brown attempted to console her over the loss of her father, her sister, and having to leave her mother behind. Brown asked Okema, "What is it you want to do? Do you want to move her somewhere else or move her closer to her family? Tell me what you want to do?"

Between sniffles and tears, Okema said, "I would like to bring her to America, so that she will at least, have me near."

"Sweetheart, where would you like to settle? You see the way we have been living. I assure you I like what I do, and I love being around my guys, but I love you with all my heart. Just tell me what you want me to do, where you want to live, and then we can start making it happen. I love you and will marry you as soon as you're willing to marry me."

Okema began to cry harder and Brown asked, "Did I leave something out? Was I supposed to say something else? Honey, what is wrong?"

"My monthly is fifteen days late."

Brown yelled, "Oh shit, oh shit! Oh, my goodness! Wait, if I already asked you to marry me and maybe you're pregnant, then what's the big deal?"

Okema started crying so loud that Courtney went to the back of the plane and asked, "What's going on with you? Brown get her some water before she becomes ill. What's wrong, honey?"

"I wanted to be married before I became pregnant."

"Well, that sounds like a technicality that doesn't matter if the man has told you he wants to marry you. He has asked for your hand, hasn't he?"

Between sniffles Okema said, "He just asked."

"And you just found out you may be pregnant—duh! What did you think would happen when he got his happy dance on while inside of you? Listen, get some rest, and just be happy that he didn't do a hit and run."

"What is a hit and run, Dr. Courtney?"

"Ask him, but in essence he didn't hit a home run and run all the way out of your life."

# # #

Beckmire asked Jong if he thought Mr. Carter was untrustworthy. Jong answered, "I have developed a telephone relationship with the man and find him to be extremely transparent. Why are you asking?"

"No reason, but I think we should go there and check out what has been going on. Courtney and Monica told me they have crews working around the clock. Did you know that?"

"I did and so did you. Zanthius mumbled that we should build this thing around the clock and give more people an opportunity to earn a living, gain a skill, and invest in their country."

"I have the greatest kids on earth, always thinking about someone else. Jong, do you mind instructing the pilots to set the course for St. Thomas? What is the status of that plane that could hold us all?"

"My King, the plane will be ready by the end of the month. I had them condense the number of seats and make sure that each seat is able to recline into a bed."

"You think so little of me?" The Sarge asked.

"What do you mean?"

"My King, comment!"

"I need some salt water and sun. I know I have been acting strange, but I'm having personal problems and I am not focusing on the details that are essential for our survival."

"Jong, my brother, your problems are our problems, and I hope as a result of your being involved with this craziness, it hasn't cost you dearly," the Sarge stated.

"In a way, I keep thinking that if I were back home, I could have at least chased my wife's suitor off, but I realize that he was only chasing someone who wanted to be chased. My problems with my wife started over four years ago when I did not recognize that she was having an affair right under my nose and without a lot of concern for the ramifications. I guess I have been trying to figure out ways to make it better because I love her but realize that she doesn't love me. Perhaps it's my ego saying that even though I have a disability, I'm not going to roll over, and just let some dude screw my wife and drop her off while I look at them from the window."

"Listen, this is strictly between the two of us. If you want to keep her because you love her, then let me know. If you want him dead, I will personally do this for you while we're in St. Thomas, and no one will know about it but the two of us."

Jong looked at the Sarge and said, "You're one sick person! You would do that for me?"

"I'll cut his dick off and send it to you, if you want, and yes, I will do this, for you because you're my brother. You have killed for me, saved me from being killed and have watched my back since we left Vietnam. If you have a list of people you want to be gone, give it to me now, so that I can make one trip and bring you back to the party. Our brotherhood is the strongest bond that I know. We survived because we depended on each other and knew that we would be there for each other, no matter the problem. Look at me, look at Brown, and look at John Lee. We be family, my brother, and nobody comes between us—nobody."

"Thanks, Sarge. You knew about this didn't you?"

"I did because there are members of your family who consider me family."

"Can I have a hug?"

"You damn sure can, Mister."

As the planes began to reach their cruising altitude, the chatter on the plane began to diminish to a stillness. The team was exhausted and needed the comfort of each other, their families, and their lovers.

## CHAPTER TWENTY-FOUR

As the planes began to descend on St. Thomas, the captains engaged their public address systems and said, "Good morning sleepy heads, we are now on descent to the wonderful island of St. Thomas where the temperature is 84 degrees, with winds out of the Southwest at six miles per hour. I have made the transportation arrangements. One last thing, please make sure you deposit all hardware in the compartments in the front of the plane and have a nice day. As usual, we enjoyed serving you guys and look forward to another rushed trip."

Jong said, "You have to admit, we are not your normal traveling public. Sarge, do you think we should shop before we go to the hotel or come back into town later—I'm seeing a lot of repeat outfits on our guys."

"I kind of noticed that myself, including the pants that I've been wearing for the last three days. Check with Courtney and Monica and see if they want to go into town with us or go later without us."

"By now you should know the answer to that question. No man wants to knowingly shop with a woman unless he's in the doghouse. Therefore, I highly suggest that we have two separate shopping trips. I know, good luck with that one," Jong stated.

"I guess you're right on that one, so why don't we all pile into a couple of the vans and head into town to one of those stores like Target or Walmart. I think that is as good as you're going to get on the island," the Sarge announced.

The group, overwhelmingly, chose Target, in deference to its ownership, and each man knew exactly what he needed-- jeans, shorts, shirts, socks, boots, sneakers and underwear--the things that make survival easy, especially, when you don't have a clue as to where you're going to be from one day to the next.

# # #

As Jong was about to pay the total tab, two locals decided to have some fun at his expense. "Hey, buddy, what happened to your legs?" Jong looked at them and continued to examine the enormous bill that he was presented with. He asked the clerk about one item and she pointed to the back of Brown's head. The local said, "This here man be disrespectful. Man, you no hear me ask you a question?" Jong started to distance himself from the individual, but his path was blocked by the man's friend. John Lee nudged Jilkes and said, "We need to go and give Jong a hand."

Brown said, "Naw, I wouldn't bother unless you need to pull him off those two."

The one guy blocked his path while the other guy snatched the cash card out of his hand and yelled, "Man, when you get asked a question on this island, you had better answer, or it's going to cost you."

"Give me card back and I won't kick the shit out of you," Jong replied.

"Man, you be out of your head"—smack, pop and two sounds of thump, thump and both men were laid out." Jong reached down, picked his cash card up and politely handed it to the clerk. It happened so fast she asked, "Did they hit you?" Jong smiled at her and, signed the bill and left the register.

The Sarge exclaimed, "Such a showoff! Just had to deck those two kids, didn't you?"

"I didn't want to, but you know how I am when someone snatches something from me."

"Jong, you are a showoff. You could have handled it differently. You could have yelled for backup and let your brothers do your bidding."

"Sarge, sometimes it feels good to do your own cooking."

Brown said, "I asked you once before to show me how to do that. If we get a moment to relax here, why don't you instruct us all on that technique?"

Jong looked at the Sarge who said, "I would love to know how the hell you took those two so quickly, with that very strange and unorthodox looking movement."

"When I have time, I will try to show you clumsy people how to utilize your body and your brain, because that's exactly what I did."

"Whatever!" the Sarge exclaimed.

# # #

When the group arrived at the hotel, everyone was in awe. The old façade had been replaced with a new modern building that looked as if it were made for kings and queens. It was surrounded with low-E glass that was bulletproof and fountains and pathways that were handmade. It was a fabulous design, exceptional construction, and was approximately fifteen days away from being completed.

When Courtney, Monica, Asiram, and Mallory saw Mr. Carter, the first words out of his mouth were, "Welcome home, my family." It was then that Mr. Carter was officially accepted into a very strange, but wonderful, fraternity.

The members of the group hugged him and told him what a marvelous job he had done in such a short period of time. He looked at Asiram and said, "It was your husband's idea. He suggested that I engage three separate rotating crews that work around the clock, with Sunday mornings off between nine and twelve, so that families could honor their religion. I promised incentives to the suppliers, as well as retrofitted an old plane, that was just sitting on the runway. They pick up our supplies from the mainland, everything that we needed to finish this project from doorknobs to towel racks, from sheets to the inside curtains because the outside curtains were not approved by you ladies." Everyone looked around at each other and Asiram said, "Perhaps after we get settled, but before dinner, we can go over the remaining issues."

Mr. Carter said, "I have arranged for all dining to be with locals, our kitchen is not finished, and I'm trying to figure out which side to vent the ovens and stoves. I wasn't expecting you guys, but I'm so happy to see you because I have some other ideas, but I didn't get a return call from Mr. Jong. Therefore, I have not concluded specific aspects of the hotel."

Monica said, "I have a question and a suggestion. First, are the rooms habitable? Second, why don't we wait until later so you can give us a full tour and we can make notes and have an official meeting in the morning? Ladies, does that sound okay and reasonable to you? Is that okay with you, Mr. Carter?"

The ladies shook their heads approvingly, but Mr. Carter said, "I need to speak to your guys, Mr. Jong and Mr. Mallory. There is a situation brewing right over that hill that smells like a sweet opportunity for you guys. More importantly, it will save another local like me from that very same bank."

Courtney said, "We will speak with those who need to hear this proposition and set a time for you and the people in question to have a conversation with our leadership. Is that fair to state, ladies?"

Everyone concurred. Mr. Carter said, "If there is a way to consider this new proposal, it will expand your beach front access from .33 miles to 1.15 miles of pristine beach and property, just saying. You could get it at a deal that would be similar to the one we worked out."

# # #

Later, when Mallory ran across Mr. Carter he announced, "I heard about the opportunity. Did you in any way compromise our ability to do good business?"

"Mr. Mallory, I did much better than that. I told him that not only could you people help him, but you could secure him and his family if he were willing to give up the majority interest. I also said that he doesn't have a freaking choice because the bank is going to take it from him and he ain't going to get shit. He is my friend and my enemy at the same time. He's a stubborn old Jew who has run out of options, just like I did."

"We'll get back to you if the leadership thinks it makes sense for our involvement, but cost is a major consideration. We will keep a fair eye open and an honest quote available. Catch you later. Oh, and by the way, based upon what you've done here, I'm going to recommend that your percent of ownership be increased." Mr. Carter looked at Mallory and uttered, "Who are you people?"

#

Asiram kissed her man and said, "Dude, you got a lot of work to get done so let's take a walk on the beach and you can tell me about what happened, wherever the hell you guys were."

"How's the baby coming along?"

"Frankly, my love, I wish I could have shot some shit into you. I would love to ask your dumb ass a question like, 'how's the baby coming along'? A better question is, 'How's the mother of my baby doing'?"

"Honey, you yourself have often called me the 'idiot spy'. I don't know much about this kind of thing, but I do know that I missed the living day lights out of you. All I want to do is make you happy. I recognize that your body is going through a transformation."

"Is that what the hell you call it? Have you lost your damn mind, dude? I'm fricken pregnant and my body will not be mine for another six months; look at this disaster of a figure! Stop smoking that crack."

"Honey, I'm trying to figure out how to talk to you and show you that I know how much your looks are important to you, as well as to me, but I want you to know that I will work with you to regain that magnificent figure that you had and to me, is still there."

Asiram looked at Zanthius and said, "My dear, 'idiot spy', you have no idea how hard it is being pregnant. I thought while you were away and did not call me that, perhaps, this is not what you wanted, and I have put a wrinkle in your perfect little life. Are you ready to be a father, Zanthius, my husband and my freaky lover? I need these three things from you, dude. I need you to plan on and learn how to care for someone other than yourself. I need you to make sure that I'm 'HHH'; Healthy, Happy and Horny every single day. Most of all, I need you to have sex with me every time that dumb ass member of yours can get it up. Oh, and by the way, if it can't get up on its own, then I'm going to feed it that stuff that begins with a 'C' and that other stuff that begins with a 'V'.

"Asiram, you won't have to feed me anything because my love for you is off the charts. When you're not around and I visualize some of our unions, I become so horny. I dream of us making love constantly, so this is not the issue. The truth of the matter is that I must harmonize my feelings of late because I feel that the baby is all that matters to you. Sometimes you make me feel like a simple sperm donor, a thing that I'm not interested in being. Asiram I love you so much and I owe you my life. Other times, I think you feel that I could never pay you enough in blood, sweat, or tears to settle that debt."

"Zanthius, we saved each other. In the interim, we fell in love and you became the focus of my existence. I don't think you owe me anything. I killed for you and you killed for me, a thing that marriages should not be made of. We needed each other, and from the first time I saw you in that airport, my life began to change and at each step of the way you were a part of my metamorphosis. Did you know I even considered assassinating Helga to gain access to you?"

"I'm glad you didn't. She essentially seduced me while you attempted to play with my feelings. She knew immediately what she wanted, but you my love, wanted us to go on a long journey towards courtship."

"Well, what's wrong with that?"

"Can't you see? We did exactly that. We courted and killed, got shot at, and fell in love."

Zanthius stopped her in her tracks, lifted her off the ground and began to kiss her very essence. While in his arms, he kissed her lips, her neck, and sucked her ears. He knew that he had to protect her from sand entering her love zone, so he took off his shirt and ripped it in half and said, "All that we do on this beach must be on this shirt, in one position. We cannot afford a single grain of sand to enter the home of our child."

Zanthius reclined on the deserted beach and Asiram mounted him and began to rotate her body on his member. She sighed with pain, and he asked, "What was the problem?" Asiram told him that he was hitting the house that their child lived in. Zanthius methodically, rotated her body to the side. From the rear, he began to give Asiram control and exciting gratification without any pain, just pure luxuriation.

As the two continued to enjoy the bliss of the moment, Zanthius stroked Asiram and she returned the pleasure, his moment, as well as hers, was upon them. He began to lightly scream that he was coming, and she screamed that she too was coming, and how much she loved him. It was during the moment of their joint orgasms that Zanthius opened his eyes and saw two men approaching them. He attempted to jump up from his position and was hit with a significant amount of power from a taser gun. Zanthius fell to the ground and was rendered momentarily unconscious from the volts from the taser guns.

Asiram was slapped with a slight sedative and hauled off by the two other uninvited guests. Meanwhile, Zanthius was disabled by the volts entering his body. As he fell unconscious to the ground, the owner of the property next door saw Asiram being dragged away and Zanthius being tasered. He called Mr. Carter and shouted, "Some people are kidnapping your guest.

They tasered one of your people and two people are hauling a woman away."

Mr. Carter yelled, "Someone is kidnapping your people on the beach." No one asked any questions. Okema and Brown headed towards the beach from one direction and saw what was happening to Zanthius. Chakes and Montomie headed out of the south entrance of the hotel and headed full steam towards the direction of a waiting van. Montomie stopped and called the Sarge and exclaimed, "North entrance to the property on the right, a getaway vehicle is waiting for Asiram!"

As Asiram was being dragged in the sand by the two people, she saw her opportunity when one of them said, "I need to catch my breath, let's stop for a moment and besides, she's out like a light."

Asiram began to say, "Water, I need water."

"When the boss gets to your ass, you will need more than water. I feel sorry for your dumb ass." The leader of the two-man group urged, "We got to get moving." Asiram realized that her dead weight was difficult for the two men to handle and increased her odds of watching them tire, as well as gave her an opportunity, to gain her resolve to conclude the two fools. The other guy looked at her and announced, "Oh shit, she's pregnant. We have to be careful with her."

Meanwhile back on the beach, the two men who were tasering Zanthius saw that they were being surrounded by a group of fierce looking individuals. They dropped their tasers and threw their hands in the air. The Sarge walked over to his son and saw that he was burned out. He looked at Larry and said, "Take Jilkes, John Lee, Gladstone and Whitmore and bring my daughter-in-law back alive, with her captives in tow."

The group headed out with Larry almost an eighth of a mile in front of everyone else. As he turned the bend on the beach, where the action was allegedly taking place, he accelerated his pace when he saw the footprints of two people dragging a third on the sandy beach. John Lee stated, "We can't let this here kid beat us every time. Can't we show up at the same time at least once?"

The group headed off behind Larry in a full sprint and were determined to arrive at the same time, or close to the same time, as he appeared on the scene to rescue Asiram. As they got closer to the where the people were resting and hauling Asiram, Larry saw their image and turned on the after burners. Jilkes and John Lee went into warp speed after seeing people drag their friend on the beach. Gladstone and Whitmore pulled out their pistols and Whitmore said, "This is going to be a record setting shot because if we miss, we are screwed because, we won't know who sent them. Aim small, hit large; that's what we're going to do."

As the lead individual disrespectfully dropped Asiram on the beach and proceeded to pull out a pistol, Asiram stood up from behind them, cocked her head from side to side, waved off everyone and began to give out a butt-kicking that would be remembered by the people receiving it. There were a series of high kicks, low punches, groin spikes, knee disablers and ball shattering blows. When Larry reached her, he asked, "Why didn't you just call for Uber to come pick up the remains?"

# # #

As Mallory and the Sarge began to harshly interrogate the kidnappers, they consistently said that it was about the money, nothing else and vehemently stated that there was no knowledge of a Walter.

Larry said, "You violated my brother by tasering him. When he awakens, he's going to want to cut something off you, I suggest that before he comes to, you might want to have a peace offering in mind to settle his rage. You people dragged his pregnant wife on the beach, and I can assure you, he's a master at dissecting parts of the body. Think it over but realize that you're going to witness his rage."

As the men sat there, John Lee said to Jilkes, "When I saw them dragging Asiram like a piece of trash, it be reminding me of my woman hanging over my balcony. I think you and me can make them there fellows speak some truth. You want to give it a try? I mean Zanthius is just going to methodically shoot them and that don't do nobody no good, we need to find out who is behind this here mess."

"Let's have a word with the Sarge and see if he'll give us one of them for demonstration purposes?"

The two men huddled with the Sarge and Mallory, and he said, "You're correct, my son is going to execute them without gaining an ounce of information. Pick one of the guys who was dragging Asiram and, well, just do your thing."

Jilkes asked Larry to find them some plastic bags so that they could clean up their mess. As Larry was walking away, John Lee yelled, "I be needing some gloves as well, see if you can find me some. Thanks, Larry."

Ten minutes later, Larry returned with the plastic bags and gloves for John Lee and Jilkes. He handed a pair of gloves to Jilkes who said, "No, Larry, I don't do this kind of work, my boy is the expert and has a certain proclivity towards doing it precisely."

The Sarge said to Mallory, "Tell Mr. Carter to give the workers the rest of the day off with pay and a $400 bonus for the progress they've made. What do you think?"

"Sarge, we need privacy, this is a good way of getting it. In the meantime, I think it would be a great time to meet with the man next door and see if we can make a deal with him that will save his property and gain us a new associate and more eyes on the property. I will meet with Jong and make sure that Mr. Carter, the neighbor, and hopefully, the women, go into town within the next hour or so. I kind of doubt that's going to happen after what happened to Asiram. I think you might want to save one of those poor souls for her," Mallory suggested.

"I'm trying to get my daughter-in-law out of that business, but I will let her make her own decision about these assholes. I would appreciate it if you got Mr. Carter and the neighbor to go into town with you, and please take Monica and Courtney as well. If the rest of the ladies want to go then by all means that will make sure we can deal with this shit quietly. By the way, we need to place armed guards around our people until we have a chance to meet with those who think they run this, that and the other," the Sarge acknowledged.

"Gotcha! Let me see what I can do, and I'll get back to you later. I would like to make a tentative offer on that property if Jong and I agree, subject to your approval and that of the group," Mallory stated.

"Mallory, this is not my group. This is as much your group as the next man's. I was appointed to a leadership position and as I recall, so were you. We all make these decisions; none of us stands a chance alone. We are a family with a few rules, just let us know what you think are the best options for us."

"You know, Sarge, we have been together a long time. Even when I disagree with you, I agree with you because you have seen all of us through some funky times. Your leadership and love for us has saved our asses on more than one occasion. It makes us a unit when we have a single leader. Knowing that each man is a leader, we resigned to that single point person notion, and it has worked. Don't try to get out of this by trying to disavow your responsibilities."

"Stop the bullshit! Have Carlos and his people shadow our families in town, and I think we can also put the pilots in play while we're here. Speak with Jong and see if he feels that is something we want to do with our pilots," the Sarge stated.

"Listen, the entire crew has made noise about the way their days are structured and how they have to babysit planes. I will speak to them and see how they can ensure our safety and join us at meals and everything else. The one thing I will not relent on is our safety, and if they don't want to watch the planes, maybe they can work for someone else," Mallory indicated.

"Mallory, there has to be a win-win situation available to all of us. Please explore it before you go ballistic, fire everyone, and we'll have to catch a damn boat home," the Sarge cautioned.

"Funny you should mention the word boat, we have guys who want us to buy a yacht from the proceeds from the West Coast. Guys come to me to buffer their concerns because they feel that sometimes you act like a king or a deity or something."

The Sarge stood up and said, "Let's have a meeting tonight. I no longer want to be in charge of anything and I'm going to cast my vote for you, my brother."

"Why are you being so dramatic? They need you to make the right choices for them. I need you to make the right choices for me. Get the shit over your ego! Realize that we're here because of you, and some of us haven't seen our homes in an exceedingly long time. Okay, Mr. Clump, don't dance in a place where you can't see who you're rubbing with. You're it, so get over that ego shit and lead us on, Brother."

"I like the idea of a yacht but there are so many of us and we keep growing due to emerging relationships or pregnancies."

"Speaking of pregnancies and I'm not sure if you heard the latest, Okema and Brown are expecting a child and they want to get married ASAP, as well as evacuate her mother, from where we just left."

"We don't have enough money to buy the Queen Mary, do we?" The Sarge asked.

## CHAPTER TWENTY-FIVE

John Lee, Jilkes and Larry methodically placed plastic bags underneath the individuals who were dragging Asiram. John Lee said, "That be a really bad thing you did to that there pregnant lady, dragging her on the beach and dropping her like some piece of trash. So, me and my friends are going to make an example out of you guys by cutting you into little pieces in front of each other. Now, who be wanting to go first?"

One of the guys who tasered Zanthius said, "Man, go screw yourself, Yankee. You no be scaring us with this plastic and shit. Man, you not know where you be and you damn sure don't know nothing about me friends. You hurt one of us and we kill all you people, women and children and pregnant ladies too."

Jilkes looked at him and said, "Man, you sound really scary, but we be the devil's left hand and we know how to make a boy into a girl. Now, you my friend, are being saved by the bell until that dude you tasered gets his wits about him and then we will see how bad you be. Now, in the meantime, I want you to watch my man work on your friends and he be damn good, Man, at what him do. Him going to make your friend a bitch first, then gut him from him dick to him brain, and man, you got a front row seat to witness it. We be scared, Man, but we no be scared of you. The demon that haunts us, kills the women and children first, and then looks for us. That thing you tried on the beach will be the last thing you ever try. If you no be the boss-man, then you will scream his name out to minimize how we violate you, my scary brother. No Man, you no see scary until you watch how my man makes your friend into a pussy."

John Lee put the gloves on his hands and said, "My name is John Lee, but you people will call me Jason, as in that scary guy with the mask. Now, my man be done told you about you two who tasered our friend. You guys get to watch because our friend will relate to you later. But you two are fair game and I'm going to start with you in the black shirt with the scary skull and knives on it. Have you ever been cut or stabbed?"

Jilkes interrupted John Lee and said, "I be having to go to the bathroom, have fun."

Larry looked at him and asked, "Are you serious, you're going to leave now?"

"Larry, I need you to come with me unless you want to enroll in a biology class that dissects living human beings. He's going to butcher those guys and if you don't have a strong enough stomach for blood and guts, then you don't want to be here."

"I'm not going anywhere. I want to see what he does to these guys."

"Larry, you're a good man and I wish you luck. His methods can cause you sleepless nights. I've been there with him and he's not a forgiving soul, but it's your choice. I'm out of here."

"That bad, eh?"

"Larry try your luck. He's going to cut that guy in ways that you can't imagine, the other three guys will tell us how to find their mothers, fathers, and everyone else. John Lee has become an artist; he makes a statement with each dissection."

"I want to watch him at work."

"Then you will learn about things that will limit your ability to sleep. Enjoy the picture show, but don't complain about the ending."

As Jilkes began to walk away, Larry yelled, "He's your friend, aren't you going to support him?"

"Naw, you take the job if you can mentally survive the trip, he's going to take you on."

John Lee positioned one of the people who dragged Asiram across the beach in front of him and asked, "Why did you pick our friends to attack? You be working for Walter?"

The first guy replied, "I don't know no Walter."

John Lee pulled his long knife out of its cradle and sliced the other guy on his leg and said, "This here be some random game. You answer correctly, I cut you, but just a little, and if you answer incorrectly, I cut him until someone says, 'I'll tell you everything you be wanting to know!' Listen up boys, I have wasted a lot of time, and therefore, we be having to increase the timetable." He raised his knife in the air and stabbed one of the guys in the leg, penetrating him all the way through to the chair. Larry saw that and walked out of the area momentarily.

Everyone in the room screamed, but not as loud as John Lee. The people who tasered Zanthius were horrified by what they just witnessed. While it was fresh in their minds, John Lee, forcefully, pulled the blade from his victim's leg and slammed it into his other leg. John Lee exercised control when he pulled the blade out of the guy's leg and cut the guy's pants away. He uttered the words, "Anyone who treats a pregnant woman the way you did deserves no mercy, and no quarter will you be given."

John Lee, after extracting his huge blade from the guy's other leg, said, "I'm not going to ask you to answer any questions because I know you will tell me all that I be wanting to know. I want your three friends to recognize and realize that they be next." With power and force, John Lee slammed his blade into the guy's scrotum and began to vigorously work his way up to the guy's head, all the time while yelling, "You had better look at your future because you be next."

Fishermen know how to fillet freshly caught fish, but few people have perfected the art of filleting a human being. John Lee was their huckleberry; he had pain to spare. In plain sight of the other three kidnappers, he exposed the inner workings of the body before them. As he completed his task, he screamed, "Who's next?"

As his guests began to squirm in their chairs, regurgitate, urinate, and defecate on themselves and make unintelligible sounds, John Lee said, "I know who's next. It's the other person who disrespected a pregnant woman and dragged her on the beach."

As John Lee approached the other individual who was dragging Asiram off the beach he said, "You're going to be my poster child. I'm going to cut you into little pieces and then you and I are going to go fishing. Do you like fishing?"

# # #

Jilkes asked Larry if he was alright and Larry exclaimed, "Hell no! I'm not alright. He gutted that guy like a pig or something."

"Yeah, I knew he was going to do his best work after he found his woman hanging from his balcony. He has kind of left the reservation and I'm going to have to reign him in and have a long discussion about his new hobby. You know he and I weren't always as close as we are now. If we are ever out and you make an aggressive move towards me, it might be your last. I love that guy so much, and now that we have met those women, we both like a lot, I'm waiting to hear him tell me he's in love and wants to spend the rest of his life with her. I know that Brown has impregnated his lady and is going to have a quick wedding, so she doesn't lose face, not that it matters here."

"What about you, Jilkes, are you playing her or being played? Are you really into her, or is she just a maybe?"

"Well, Larry, and this is between us, I adore that woman so much and I love the way she makes sure that all is right with me each day. My mind, body, and my soul. Then she whispers to me, 'I love you, Mr. Jilkes, and I am yours to command, and love, but never to abuse and misuse'. I'm waiting for my partner to get the bug and then I want to do a double wedding and maybe triple if Brown can hold off for a while. Now, Larry, don't make me send you to John Lee. I gave you information that no one else has a clue about. I would hate to make your children fatherless and your wife a concubine."

"Damn, Bro, leave the wife and children out of it."

"That's a metaphor Larry; your family is my family."

"I know that, and, by the way, I can't thank you guys enough for coming to my pop's rescue, he's a proud man. You know better than me, he doesn't like to reach out for help, but what's interesting is that this whole scene gets bigger and bigger with new family members. I think we should get a bigger jet."

"Okay, Larry, here we go again. We are planning on getting one that will accommodate all of us, including the children. It's on order and may be waiting for us when we get back to the states. If you mention this, I swear, I will let John Lee box you for two rounds."

"Why just two rounds?"

"After that, Larry, you're either maimed or dead. He is a fierce competitor and one that you want to keep near and dear to you. I have seen him take on five enemy soldiers with just his knife, and brutally demolish them. He's a beast and the only way I keep him under control is by letting him know that I once beat the shit out of him."

"Bullshit!"

"I'm telling you I did. At camp, he called me the 'N' word and, I mean, we fought until the next blow was going to be his last or my last and someone was going to go up for murder. We worked it out and haven't spent many days apart since we went to Vietnam. Now, the rest of these guys Larry are some freaky people. I'll try to give you the low down on each one later because they all like you, and it is important that you understand them. Let me just say one more thing, each of these guys can be like your pops. Every last man can make the right decision because that is the first thing your father taught us to do--rely on the man next to you, behind you, besides you and in front of you. If you see he's on the wrong footing, call him into a huddle and convey your thoughts. That's our way, Larry, you need to figure out how to fit within their thinking. They were amazed at how well you handled that DC thing, as well as how that reflected so well on the Sarge. We are simple folk, Larry, but if you cross one of us, then you bring out the devil in all of us at the same time."

## CHAPTER TWENTY-SIX

John Lee started his next session by saying to the other guy who was dragging Asiram on the sand, "So, you never heard of Walter, eh?" As he was about to continue his preparations to unmercifully kill this guy, Zanthius burst in and said, "John Lee, did you kill that guy?" John Lee looked at the body and said, "I be the one who did that one. I be saving them there two over there for you, but I want to finish this one because something about him reminds me of what that person must have thought about when they did that dastardly thing to my woman in my house."

Zanthius looked at the two men and exclaimed, "You are going to wish that you had a heart attack prior to my coming in here! My wife is resting peacefully, but you're going to suffer for a long time." As Zanthius was about to leave the room he looked at John Lee and said, "Let's see who can do the best work."

"My masterpiece is yet to be painted, but with this here fellow, I might find the vision to paint it."

#

In Asiram's room, all the women had gathered to support and console her. Courtney said, "I'm so glad the guy next door had the presence of mind to call here to alert us that someone was dragging a woman off the beach and tasering a man. How on earth could four people sneak up on you guys and catch you in a vulnerable position? What on earth were you guys doing?"

Asiram looked carefully around the room and said, "Ladies, I was having some of the best sex I have ever had, and we thought we were safe. I know that when Zanthius interviews those guys, he's going to be really pissed because just prior to them tasering him, he was in the midst of, te-te, an orgasm." Ava looked at Courtney and said, "Perhaps we should leave you alone with Asiram to make sure those tiny grains of sand are purged from her baby's house, what are your thoughts?"

"Ava, I think you and I need to do some internal washing, can you help me with this?"

The two women examined Asiram and sprayed water into her womb to flush out all remnants of sand. Ava turned to change her gloves and saw that Asiram had an open sore on the bottom of her foot. She asked Courtney, "Can you look at this sore on her foot? It looks as if it's infected."

As Courtney turned her attention to Asiram's foot, she said, "Call the Sarge and Zanthius and get me some boiling water and a cigarette lighter. That open area has been compromised by a worm that wreaks havoc on people.

"I think it's a hookworm or Cutaneous Larva Migrans CLM. I'm going to need someone to go into town and get a prescription filled for albendazole and mebendazole. In the meantime, I'm going to need to sterilize this damn thing and I need a lighter and someone to hold her down because this is going to hurt like hell."

When Zanthius walked into the room, he stridently, asked, "What the hell is going on?" Courtney responded by saying that, "I think your wife picked up a hookworm on the beach and we need to move in a hurry to kill this thing."

"What the hell is a hookworm?"

"Zanthius, I don't have time to give you medical definitions at this point, but, believe me, it is the worst infection a pregnant woman, or anyone, could have. Listen, get someone to call the pharmacist in town and let me speak to him. In the meantime, I want to create a hot zone for this thing, so that we can localize it before it lays its larvae. Asiram, honey, this is going to hurt like hell, but this is what I need to do to control this thing."

"Suppose you're wrong with your prognosis?"

"Suppose I'm right, Zanthius. Get with me or get the hell out of here."

"Mom get her arms and pull them back to you. She's going to scream for mercy but don't give in until the doctor has done whatever, the hell she's trying to do to my wife."

"I'm trying to save her life and the life of your baby. If you have some other plan that is better than what I'm trying to do, then by all means, try your luck."

The Sarge walked into the room and asked, "What the hell, is going on in here?"

"I don't have time for questions. I need you to look into your daughter-in-law's eyes and assure her that you and everyone else, including the woman who is burning her, loves her, and respects her dearly."

The Sarge knows his wife and knows her well and said, "You people had better realize that this woman is one of the smartest and most learned doctors that I know. She is brilliant and I trust her actions, even though I don't know what they are. I trust Courtney because she is a Beckmire and she is smart. Any questions or concerns?"

"I love you, Ben Beckmire, talk to your daughter-in-law."

# # #

Meanwhile, John Lee was preparing to operate on his next subject when Mr. Carter walked into the room, got on his knees, and said, "I need you to be merciful with this person. He is my sister's only child."

"He be done dragged a pregnant woman across the sand to kidnap her. Where be his mercy?" Never far away, Jilkes walked in and said, "I must have missed something. Mr. Carter, why are you on your knees?"

"I'm begging for mercy for my sister's only child who fell away from education and ventured towards being a tough guy. I have often told him that he doesn't know what tough is, and now he's facing the ultimate notion of tough."

"John Lee, I need you to take a break until we have a chance to work through this situation. I need you to summon the Sarge, so we can at least listen to Mr. Carter plead for his family member, and let the Sarge, as well as Zanthius, make the decision about this guy's life. Are we good with that, Brother?"

"Jilkes, I saw this dude drag Asiram across the beach like she was a piece of driftwood."

"I know, my brother, but we have a chain of command that helps us sort through the difficult decisions. Will you at least wash and put your favorite knife in its case until we have a chance to work through this parlay?"

"That be a strange word to use, my brother, but because we are brothers and you be moving in on that property next to mine, that be a real conclusion, right? Since all this is a formality, then I be waiting to assist Zanthius in the disposal of those other two, realizing that there might be a way to gut this guy and cut his eyes out before he dies." The other two kidnappers continued pissing their pants because they saw his work and knew it was only a matter of time.

# # #

In the makeshift hospital, Courtney began cauterizing Asiram's foot and pressing downwards on her legs and veins to keep anything that got in, at its lowest level. At the site where the hookworm entered, Courtney made a small incision on Asiram's foot and literally tried to bleed her until the uninvited guest was out of her body.

Meanwhile, McArthur and Gladstone made their way to town and picked up the hard to pronounce medicines. When it came time to pay for the medicines, neither man had any cash or a credit card on them. McArthur said, "I'm sorry, I don't seem to have any money."

Gladstone stated, "I didn't bring any either."

The owner looked at them and said, "Just pay me on your next trip to town." They both looked at him and Gladstone said, "We will definitely pay you, and we thank you for being understanding. Our people will really appreciate this, and we will get back to you shortly. We are part of the ownership team at Mr. Carter's new place."

"I knew that. We know everyone new on this island. Whether they are bad people, like those bandits at the bank, or good people, like you guys. Okay, run along and get this medicine to the patient."

# # #

Asiram had developed a temperature, but, otherwise, was okay and Courtney used the medicines that were provided. In the meantime, the Sarge walked into the butcher's shop and asked, "What seems to be the problem and why is there a civilian in the room?"

Jilkes said, "Mr. Carter, here is your opportunity to plead your case."

"Mr. Beckmire, this guy is my sister's only child and I'm begging you for his life. He thought he was tough. As I look at him sitting in his own piss and shit, I know he's just a wanna be. I am begging you to spare him with conditions, but please spare him."

John Lee said, "This here guy be one of the guys who was dragging your daughter-in-law across the sand like a piece of driftwood."

The Sarge looked at the kid and slapped him so hard that he ruptured his eardrum. He said, "That's for disrespecting my daughter-in-law and endangering the child that she's carrying." The Sarge instructed John Lee to fetch Zanthius and let him be a part of the decision-making process.

As John Lee disappeared, the Sarge turned to Jilkes and said, "He's off the reservation and we need to bring him back. Mr. Carter, if my son says that your nephew must be punished then I will not go against his wishes. I will plead for your family member, but if he, John Lee and Jilkes want his blood then I suggest that you leave the room because what comes next will not be a pretty sight. I can't promise you anything."

The Sarge looked at Jilkes and said, "Get Mallory down here and Jong. We may have to buy Mr. Carter out because of what might happen to his nephew."

#

Later and as the group assembled, the Sarge explained the conundrum that they were presented with. He told Jong that if the group decided against Mr. Carter's plea then he didn't think that he would be a good partner in the future and, therefore, they needed to make him an offer that he couldn't refuse. The Sarge said to Zanthius, "Son, his life is in your hands. I prefer that you at least question his motives and find out who put him up to this mess, while the rest of us decide about our business relationship."

The Sarge knew that Zanthius was going to decimate the kid and that their deal with Mr. Carter would fall apart and end unpleasantly and be final. As the Sarge attempted to explain how the group worked, and their respect for each other, and especially, the women and children he said to Mr. Carter, "Frankly, I don't think there is a chance, in hell, that my son is going to excuse the actions of your nephew."

"Sarge, if it were my wife, I would decapitate that little moron. He's my sister's only as she has already lost one to drugs. I had to beg for his life on my knees; he's basically a good kid, but stupid as hell. If only I could have made him work for me and been able to pay him, then I might have been able to save his life. I have told my sister, time, and time, again that he was going to break her heart because he wanted to fit in with that scum from the hills. She never listened because she was too busy smoking herself into oblivion."

Zanthius walked out of the room and announced, "Dad, we have to clean this mess up, body parts all over the damn place." Mr. Carter's head fell in sorrow, and he began to sob.

Zanthius asked, "Mr. Carter, why are you crying? I didn't hurt your nephew because my wife said that he showed her compassion when he realized that she was pregnant. That doesn't excuse his behavior, but it lessens my resolve for revenge in this matter. My father believes that sometimes it is righteous to spare a life, even though, they are out to hurt you."

"Your father is a wise man; I respect and thank him. I have suggestions for my nephew here on this property that might keep him out of trouble in the future and make him realize how close to being terminated he was," Mr. Carter stated.

"One problem with my son's decision is that we now have two witnesses to a crime. We need to find out where the so-called leader lives and end this reign of terror on the island," the Sarge stated.

"Sarge, neither my nephew nor I will talk about what happened here today. As a part of his penitence, I will make him help me take the remains out to sea and dump them, therefore, making me and him complicit in this matter." The Sarge looked at Mallory, then John Lee and asked, "What say you, John Lee?"

"I say that Jilkes and I agree to spare his miserable life if you will take the remains of these other guys out to the deep water and weigh them down and dump them. You be alright with that suggestion, Jilkes?"

"I be alright with most things that we decide as a group, but I want pictures to show they are involved."

Zanthius said, "Your nephew might need a doctor because he is bleeding from his nose and ear. I think it's from someone slapping him. Now, those other two fools, well, let's just say they won't be tasering anybody any time soon or ever."

## CHAPTER TWENTY-SEVEN

The group enjoyed seven days in St. Thomas and purchased a bunch of water toys for potential future guests to use. They also performed a few extractions of those who would create problems on the island, and left a few messages around town that essentially said, "Do wrong—wrong will be done to YOU!"

# # #

As their planes touched down in a small airport outside of Baltimore, Zanthius said to Asiram, "Honey, right now your new rebuilt home is the only place that we can house all of these people."

"Zanthius, don't you live there and aren't you my husband? If the answer is yes to those questions, then I go where my man takes me and where we have coverage." He kissed his wife and rubbed her stomach and asked, "Do you think we have to give up this life of adventure once we have the baby?"

"At some point in time, I want to settle down and raise our child properly."

"Sorry, love, I want the same thing, but you have to admit, these have been some exciting times. I love and trust all of these people; met my father who I was told was dead; my mother has a new lover who I have known forever; I met a spy who seduced me, bewitched me, made me fall in love with her and, at some point, made me impregnate her. What a bruja, and I love her so much." He kissed Asiram again, and she began to weep.

Zanthius asked, "Are those tears of joy, or are they tears of sorrow that reflect you're not happy with me?"

"I'm so proud of you, my love, for sparing that kid's life in St. Thomas. I knew that my husband had learned empathy and clemency. You made me happy by not brutally killing that kid. He was crying when he was dragging me and saying, 'we have to be careful, she's pregnant'. Now, that was a turning point for me, especially, after what you said to me on the beach in St. Thomas. I love you, husband, and I want you to be more forgiving than I could have ever been."

# # #

As the group loaded into special vehicles that resembled minivans but were bullet proof and compartmentalized with weapons, the Sarge asked, "Jong, when we talked about state-side security, you didn't take any shortcuts, did you? Are we loaded, and to what degree?"

"Sarge, this is a ten-passenger minivan equipped with automatic weapons on each side, front and rear and can be operated by a single person wearing the Facebook virtual reality goggles made by Oculus."

"Jong, stop the bullshit, what is real about these hideous things that you bought?"

"Sarge, everything I said is true. Sit in the passenger's seat and put those goggles on your head. I must turn the system to simulation or otherwise you will be firing live rounds. I also took the liberty of having them place some of that 007 shit in the vans, such as, oil slicks, tire piercing spikes, attaching grenades and fire breathing machines to ignite oil."

"Who in the hell built this shit?"

"My cousins. They loved the way we did business in DC. On their own, they developed the armor made from extremely light alloy metals that when combined create a substance that is bullet resistant."

When Asiram got into the vehicle, she announced, "I guess we must have made a few bad investments, but I still have funds stored and saved."

Courtney said, "Your father-in-law would never be in such a position and I'm sure these things are more than they appear to be. Jilkes, why are you and John Lee in this van with us?"

"There seems to be some new technology that has been installed that we are trying to master," Jilkes responded.

"Girl, what did I tell you? I told you these things were more than they appear to be. I wouldn't be surprised if they have guns hidden in these things."

John Lee said, "You be more than a doctor because you be smart as can be. This here vehicle is supposed to have a couple of machine pistols or guns, and I must figure out how to use them. Ms. Asiram, how you be feeling?"

"So nice of you to ask. I'm feeling good considering the fact that my mother-in-law hates me enough to attempt to set me on fire and perform an exorcism while my father-in-law and husband watched. Other than that, and not knowing who I can trust, I'm good. How about you?"

"Well, ma'am, I just be thinking if anything happened it was in the best interest of the entire group. Our decisions are usually more concerned with the total pie and not just a small piece."

"John Lee, if I wasn't certain, I would say that you just dismissed my issue and minimized it in the scheme of things."

"That there might be a fair assessment of the truth as well as a realization of how we operate and protect our own. We all love you, including the person who tried to burn you alive."

"Okay, John Lee, you're stoking a fire that will blow up in your face. Let it go, man," Jilkes suggested.

"Where are we heading by the way?" Asiram asked. Jilkes told her that they were going to check on the progress of the rebuilding of her farmhouse.

Asiram said, "It won't be ready for another month or two."

"Well, I guess we'll all have to make do in the barn and in the fields. I think Jong took the liberty of having his family members secure the place and stock it with provisions for the short time we will, probably, be here."

"So nice of you people to let me know what's happening with my farm and what food stuffs I want in my house. Thank you very much."

Courtney slid close to her and said, "You do know that I love you, don't you? As well as the fact, that I had to improvise back there and make sure that little worm was localized and cauterized, you do know that those things were necessary, right?"

"Courtney, I was just joking, I'm glad that you were there and helped me out of the problem."

"I will confess one procedure that was not necessary was the one when I burned your butt! Courtney joked."

Zanthius entered the van and said, "Hi, baby, how are you feeling?"

"I'm feeling okay, just the butt of a lot of jokes, that's all."

"Well, I'm here to protect you now. I think we can leave, guys. I think my dad is waiting on you to give him the okay signal on the intercom system." Jilkes looked at John Lee and they both studied the instrument panel.

Jilkes finally asked, "Where the hell is the switch to engage it?"

"Look at the panel in the middle of the dash mounted on the inside of the roof. Hit the green button and you can talk to all of the vans at the same time or just one in particular."

John Lee mumbled, "What happened to cell phones?"

Zanthius told Asiram that he knew the farm wouldn't be ready for at least another thirty to forty-five days, but it was the best place to strategize against an old and never concluding nemesis—Walter. As the caravan began its journey, the Sarge said, "I haven't heard a word from anyone about the Carbon Factor. Is it possible they found a way around the information you deleted?"

Jong said, "Funny thing you should ask me about that, because it's been on my mind ever since we left Europe. No one has contacted you about the product which leads me to believe that they must have figured out the formula without the aspects that we have. What are your thoughts on it?"

"That is exactly why we're brothers. I've been thinking about this mess every day wondering why no one has reached out to us. What I have come up with, is they don't know how to reach us. Can you believe that? I'll bet you 100 bucks that there have been multiple calls to a phone that is probably at the bottom of the ocean. Can you call Mallory and tell him that I need a throw away phone to make an important call?"

Mallory got on the intercom and asked, "Do I look like a telephone man? Sarge, I gave you three phones. Have you used them all?"

"No smart ass, I need another one because the other ones are broken. I like this intercom set up."

Jong looked at him and said, "We need to stop and turn around, so if they attempt to triangulate our position, it will show that we are heading north and not south."

"Way to look out for us. You guys pull over to the right up there and after that next exit I will make a jug handle and drive north and make the call. Then get off at the next exit and head back to you guys. Catch you in a few."

The caravan stopped on the side of the road. Mallory handed Sarge another cell phone, and his van made the U-turn and headed north. The Sarge called the senator's private number and was not surprised when she answered the phone herself. He said, "This is Sergeant Beckmire. How are you?"

"Sergeant Beckmire, we have been trying to reach out to you for about a week and were surprised that we only had old numbers for you. It's important that we talk about our little project because our people are completely stumped. Of course, we tried to figure out the aspects of the design without your input but returned to square one on each occasion." Jong placed his watch in front of the Sarge and whispered, "thirty-five seconds and then disconnect."

"Senator, I'm having a bit of car trouble at the moment. I will try to call you tomorrow at 10 am, if that is okay with you. Right now, I must figure out if my vehicle is on fire and whether I need to abandon it. Hit you tomorrow, Senator."

The Sarge disconnected the phone and Jong said, "We gave them five seconds to attempt to track us heading north. Let's pull off at the next exit and head down to the farm."

As the Sarge and the rest of the people in his van came across the others on the side of the road, he quietly said, "Let's

proceed to Asiram's place for fellowship and to get me back
in her good graces."

## CHAPTER TWENTY-EIGHT

When the vans made the left turn off Route 211 and on to Ida Belle Boulevard, everyone woke up from their deep sleep and realized they were going to a place that had lots of great memories, as well as a few bad ones. Asiram said, "I, at least, hope the pool has been repaired."

Zanthius lowered his head and said, "Honey, from what I hear it's going to take another two months to redo the façade and the structure of the pool. I'm just going by what the people have been telling me. I don't want you to get upset because you have one idea, but reality shows another. Please realize that we're just temporarily stopping here." Suddenly, Zanthius yelled, "Hold up a minute." He asked Jilkes to broadcast his comments. When he was communicating to the other vans, he said, "I think we need to abort this mission because my wife expects to see something that is not there. I recommend we turn around and proceed to the hotel. A few of us can come back tomorrow and survey what has been accomplished. I don't want to provide her with more grief."

"Honey, I'm okay. Let's just go so that I can see where we are in the rebuild."

Zanthius said, "On the other side of the equation, if you see things that you don't like, we can have them changed. I just need you to have an open mind, baby, until me and my dad can make this right for you."

As the vehicles headed towards the farm, Asiram said, "I hope someone has been taking care of my horses. I'm such a disaster, I never thought of my precious horses. Honey, we may have to stay in a hotel because I'm emotionally spent."

"Baby just at least look at the place and let me know what you think. By the way, the Midwest ranch is almost completely rebuilt. They expect that project to be over in the next few months."

"I'm sorry, husband, but two months is a long interval."

"Let's just focus on this property first. See what is needed and then move to one of our other homes, don't forget the place in Philadelphia."

"Oh my, I completely forgot about that one. One day I'm going to gut your father. He blew up my farm, had my house in Philly shot up and burned, and had my ranch house blown to pieces. One day, my love, I'm going to punish your him for crimes against me." In the other vehicles, everyone was listening to the rant.

As quiet settled on the airwaves, the Sarge quietly asked, "Asiram, is there any way I can make this up to you, short of you practicing your trade on me? Honey, I love you so much and I want to make sure, that as your father-in-law and your baby's grandfather, that we can coexist. Please, think of something I can do to make sure you won't hurt me."

She turned to Zanthius and asked, "Did you know I was broadcasting?"

"Honey, your beef is with Jilkes and John Lee who are in the front of this vehicle. I'm back here with you. I didn't know those guys were broadcasting our conversations."

"Daddy-in-Law, I love you so much, that was just idle conversation. We can talk later if you want, but I was just kidding. It was much like your wife when she said she was trying to set me on fire. We are all one big family, filled with all kinds of jokes."

#

As the vehicles rounded the bend that leads to the farm, Asiram said, "At least they have kept the trees out of the road and, wow, the lawns are all manicured, how nice." As the caravan rounded another set of bends, Asiram said, "Oh I see, they made the path to the house more direct, instead of going up this hill another thirty yards and then making a left turn and coming back to the same place." She was about to say something else when she broke into tears, because her farmhouse had been transformed into a property that was twice the size but used the original footprint as a benchmark. It had notions of a Midwest ranch including a guest house and an adjoining tunnel that was underneath the pool but was vented miles away. The experience of what had occurred at the ranch shaped the design and security of the reconstructed farmhouse. It was completed, the pool was larger and yes, eyes and ears were everywhere, but nowhere to be seen. The latest technology in security and spying had been incorporated into the design. The workers were not allowed to leave the property and were trucked to their worksites in container vehicles without windows.

As Asiram stepped out of the mini-van she was riding in, she, announced, "Daddy-in-Law, I love you so much. Monica, Rashida, Yvette, Okema, Yashida, Somara, and most of all my two Mother-in-Laws, Ava and Courtney, thanks ladies for being a support mechanism that these knuckleheads will never understand. Ladies, I would like to invite you to join me in my elongated pool for a swim, drinks, and hor d'oeuvres. Zanthius, get your butt over here."

Zanthius said, "I wanted this to be a surprise. I have been working so hard on this project from afar and didn't want you involved because I wanted you to focus on our baby. Asiram, the spy, I love you so much and I dedicate my life to you. I know you had this place way before me, but I hope all of the changes I have made, meet with your approval, as well as make it a bit more comfortable, for our extended and expanding families."

"Zanthius, my husband, my 'idiot spy', my lover, and my baby's daddy; I love you so much. From the first time I saw you in that airport so far away, I knew that by hook or crook, you were going to be mine, just didn't figure in the Helga card. Just joking sweetheart, she played her game well. I tried to be to cool and paid the ultimate price."

Zanthius held his wife's hand as he said, "No, love, you did not pay the ultimate price, Helga did. Can we move forward to today without conversation of a dead comrade? I must tell you that my father told me that if I didn't get this done, as well as the ranch in a prescribed amount of time, then he was going to demote me to 'maybe he's my son'. Oh yeah, he would call a meeting and say, 'I know the projects are on schedule, and then instruct me to talk to Jong about advanced security features. Spare no expense but have it ready according to and before schedule'. That's how this process was completed on time."

Zanthius added, "Jilkes and John Lee told me that my dad would kill, or try to kill, prior to his own death, anyone who attempted to harm his children, his family and his friends. Jilkes told me about a mission where he and John Lee were cornered with no ammunition left. The Sarge slipped away from the remaining squad and walked into the enemy's camp and single handedly slaughtered with his knife and pistol, eight to ten men before they could react. I'm telling you he would disrupt the rotation of the earth, and back track through time, to place a major ass whupping on anyone who was suspected or capable of hurting you, me, or any of his men. Sergeant Ben Beckmire is a beast when mad and makes Diablo look like a Sunday school teacher. He loves him some Asiram and bleeds about the things that have happened to your properties. If you get a chance, cut him a little slack, so that he can focus on keeping us all alive and making you a happy daughter-in-law in the process. Also, you should pull him, and Courtney aside, not together, but separately, and just blast them with your feelings.

"You will be amazed at their responses—'screw with mine and I will kill all of yours'—just a saying I heard that from the horse's mouth."

Asiram began to tear up and said to her husband, "I joked about Courtney trying to burn me alive, but she did her best. I guess that was a mistake, right?"

"Sweetheart, you crushed her feelings without knowing it. My dad said she cried herself to sleep that night because she feels you don't understand her and that she doesn't understand you. She is, apparently, a brilliant doctor who fell in love with a Philadelphia police officer and hasn't looked backed since. They adopted Rashida and Larry, turned those two around and made them great human beings.

"Larry was a hustler and Rashida took a ride one night with a guy who basically did everything he wanted to do to her and then kicked her to the curb. He also raped her dope addicted mother, kicked her to the curb, then her mother settled in with a dealer who wanted to do the nasty to Rashida. You have got to talk to them because I can't tell you the story about the children. Only my dad can tell you the story of his friends who have left their homes to join this journey. Not a one has left. Think about it, dear, no one has had a family emergency or a plumbing problem or a small fire or anything? That's a little amazing and too weird to brush off as chance. No, these guys are a dedicated group, and I think you know how they protect each other. Sweetheart come down to earth and smell the same roses they do. You might learn a thing or two. Get to know them better, honey, they apparently are going to be around for a long time."

"Zanthius, are you saying that I act stuck up?"

"Just a little, baby, but enough for people to notice. They know about most of your homes and have lived in them. You welcomed them, but did you spend any time with them trying to get to know them? See where I'm going with this, dear?"

"Thanks, honey, just one more question. Do you really love me, or is the new addition what's keeping you around?"

"Asiram, if you don't know how I feel by now, then you will never understand my feelings for you. I want you to rest for, maybe an hour, then I will come and get you and take you on a tour of your remodeled home."

# # #

Courtney saw Zanthius and asked how Asiram was doing. He told her that she was doing okay. Courtney suggested they take her to the nearest hospital and make sure the wound was sealed and the worm or worms were dead. Zanthius thought that she was making a big deal out of the issue when Courtney abruptly asked, "Do you love your wife and want to make sure your baby is okay? Then, Mister, I suggest you get her, and two guys to watch our backs, while we are in the hospital."

Zanthius entered his room and Asiram was half asleep. He said, "Honey, Courtney wants us to go to the hospital and have a doctor take a look at the wound to make sure that all is okay."

"Tell her we can do it tomorrow."

"I can assure you that she is not going to accept that response. I think you need to get out of bed, and we need to attend to this issue and be sure that all is well with you and the baby."

Asiram looked at Zanthius and said, "Give me five minutes, she's absolutely correct and I need to start listening to people who are smarter than I am in certain areas."

# # #

The Sarge asked Jilkes and John Lee to escort them and have three of Carlos's men follow behind them. As they pulled up to the hospital, they saw two guys in suits and sunglasses hanging around the entrance. Jilkes said to John Lee, "Those guys are packing."

"Yes, I be seeing that, but they don't seem to be looking for anyone they just be standing there like they be protecting someone. You understand what I be saying? They be looking like protectors."

Jilkes checked out the environment and concluded they were indeed there to provide security to someone who was already in the hospital. Jilkes called the other van and instructed Carlos's, men to keep those two suits in their eyesight. Jilkes pulled into the emergency room circle and got out of the car first and waited for Carlos's men to pull up behind him. Jilkes opened the door as John Lee got out of the van and opened the sliding door for Courtney and Asiram. Carlos's guy got in the vehicle Jilkes was driving and drove the vehicle to the parking area followed by the trailer. At the threshold of the automatic doors, one of the suits said, "Only the ladies can go into the emergency room."

John Lee looked at him and said, "You best be moving away from that there door, Mister, or there is going to be some trouble right about now."

His partner saw that they were out gunned and said, "We have a VIP in there and we can't let you go in there with weapons." Jilkes had the presence of mind to ask him the status level of the VIP?

"VP daughter," was the response.

Jilkes said, "Not making light of the situation, but do you know what state you're in? This is one of the most gun friendly places in the country. May I see your ID?" The agent showed him his ID and Jilkes said, "To us, our pregnant lady is a VIP. John Lee, call Carlos's guy back to collect this hardware."

"You sho' bout that?"

"I'm not sho about a damn thing other than Courtney feels that Asiram needs to be looked at and, according to that suit, the Vice President's daughter is in there as well. How much attention do we need?"

"I be seeing your point." As the van pulled up, Jilkes unloaded his pistol onto the passenger's seat as did John Lee who said, "I be feeling really naked about now."

#

In the emergency room there were more suits standing by the doors and watching people as they entered the area. A nurse asked Courtney to fill out a ton of papers on Asiram. She decided to fill them out with Rashida's information in mind thus keeping Asiram's identity momentarily disguised.

A sympathetic doctor was passing by and asked what was ailing the mother to be? Courtney responded that Asiram picked up a hookworm in St. Thomas and that the procedure used in extracting it wasn't done in the most sterile environment. They were checking to make sure that she was alright as well as the baby. The doctor told Asiram that he and his wife just had a baby girl five days ago and that he was in a baby watch and help mode, and for her to come on back. Courtney said, "You have a VIP in your emergency room, and you didn't provide service to her."

"My colleagues are attending to her. I hear she apparently has some real issues and is under observation. Anyway, what makes you sure it was a hookworm?"

"It's proper name is cutaneous larva migrans CLM and I was a practicing doctor in Pennsylvania until I retired."

"Impressive, Doctor. Did you apply fire to the entrance?"

"I did, but I wanted to make sure that we got all of that little creature and that is why we're here."

"Did you, by chance, administer any medications to the patient?"

"I did as a matter of fact, albendazole and mebendazole, not really friendly to pregnant women, but a must if in doubt."

"If you think about coming out of retirement, we need a learned doctor down here who is smart, calm, attractive, and has a beautiful friend who is pregnant."

"Wait a minute, I thought you said you were married?"

"I am, but the day I can't look at two beautiful women is the day that I want to be buried."

The doctor extracted blood from Asiram and performed a few other tests including taking cultures of the internal and external parts of the wound. He asked Courtney if the phone number she stated was a good number, or a don't bother to try to trace me number? Courtney told him that it would work for a couple of days or so. The doctor told her that he would try to analyze the data as soon as it came back from the laboratory and give her a call from a number that was not hospital related. He also told her that he was confident that comrades of hers had made a huge donation to the hospital and, therefore, if she was with a guy named Sarge, everything was good and covered.

# # #

As the group left the hospital, the guys in the suits were still there and the smarter of the two said, "I'm so damn happy that we didn't have an incident."

Jilkes said, "Those are my sentiments as well. Some minds go for the gusto and others try to figure out the cause, I'm glad we connected. Have a great day."

As the men loaded the vans and as Carlos's men secured their exit, John Lee said, "We need to give them there fellows more credit than we do."

"What and who, the hell, are you talking about, John Lee?"

"I be talking about Carlos's men; they be diligent and on task and are good at protecting our backs."

"I agree with you. I don't think we have given them their fair due, nor have we acknowledged all that they do for us. We might want to bring this to the Sarge's attention. I think he believes that when they get that check at the end of the month that is all they are looking for. They have joined the family, but we haven't certified them yet."

# # #

When the group arrived back at the farm, the Sarge was in the middle of one of the fields accompanied by Mallory. He was on the phone with Allen who was telling him that his nemesis was planning a trip to St. Thomas but was persuaded against that action because of the recent drug busts and their connections to US citizens. Someone convinced him that if he shows up in that part of the world, he would be detained and that no matter the person in power, he would be locked up and subjected to island rule, a thing that foreigners don't speak about once they are released.

Allen also advised him if he sent his planes on a trip cross-country, but stopped at the airport miles away from the ranch, it would throw Walter off and have him running to every location that was presented to him. Allen said, "So far, I have been straight up with you, but I feel he's closing in on me. When he accomplishes that task, you must realize that he is going to bleed me until I tell him every little detail of our conversations—just saying."

The Sarge thought for a moment and said to Allen, "Give me ten minutes and I'll call you back." He conducted a quick but decisive conversation with Mallory, and they concluded that they would send a plane for Allen.

The Sarge called Allen back and said, "I am a butcher, and my people are really good at slicing people and keeping them alive at the same time."

"Why are you telling me this, Sergeant Beckmire?"

"I'm about to make a proposition that will enhance the longevity of your life. I propose to send a plane for you. I'm going to give you the opportunity to help me catch our problem and then send him some place to never be heard from again."

"That sounds like a coffin."

"For him, but not for you. It sounds like your freedom and our freedom from a person who has amassed too much power over others and is trying to control the world with a simple device that could destroy it. No, I'm not trying to kill you, Allen, although there are a thousand reasons why I should. Let me know when you want to be extracted and I will make it happen. But if you try to play me, Allen, my resolve will be nuclear."

"Sarge, I'm on the run from a crazy man who wants to kill me, you, and your entire family. He's not the kind of guy who invites you in from out of the rain and offers you coffee. No sir, it will be him or us."

"Allen, why don't you plan on making that trip across country in one of our planes, stopping near the ranch, then heading on to San Francisco, and then on up to Seattle somewhere for a week or so? I mean, it will give you an opportunity to clean up and take care of some of your short-term obligations. Also, if you need actual cash, there is always $50 to $100k on the planes."

"Now, that's a great idea and one that I will gladly act on. Let me hit you back in a few."

# # #

Zanthius, decided to let Asiram sleep and wandered around the farm. He was eventually joined by Larry, Jilkes, and John Lee, all with an interest of inquiring about the security functions of the farm.

Zanthius said, "There are some really significant changes to this place, such as the new bungalow on the other side of the new pool. The pool was actually moved by twenty feet, and what once was the pool is now the guest house with its own water well and backup generators."

John Lee asked about security, escape measures, and said, "We sure don't want to get trapped like we did out west!"

"I think we have the same basic floor plan as out west, but we have survival compartments. The old pool was ten feet at the deepest end. Ten feet below, that is, the entrance to our bomb shelter, which is equipped with tools, enough oxygen for thirty people in that compartment, and thirty people in the bunker under the main house. There are three sources of oxygen; one is pumped from natural air into the compartments and can operate literally forever. A second source of air is the individual tanks, the third is from tanks that are buried below the pool that can provide forty-five days of air to both bunkers. Of course, the bunkers have telecommunications capability that are hidden, and handprint activated.

"No one knows this but you guys, so far. I even took the liberty of installing a Morse code for you old-timers." Jilkes looked at him, but it was John Lee who put him in his place by telling him that if it weren't for these old people his ass would have washed up to shore without a life vest.

Jilkes asked, "What's the quality of the windows?"

"Funny, you should ask. The windows can withstand large caliber rounds and the walls are thick enough to retard large rounds as well. We spared no expense in rebuilding the farm and the ranch house. Jong and I thought that this might be the kind of place that we can enjoy and want to do so, for as long as we can. Therefore, we still needed this place, where our families could congregate but be safe.

"You guys are aware, that we purchased that property where the Senator lived which expanded the footprint of the farm. Security wise, I have pop up cameras, like those sprinklers people use to water their lawns. There are also listening devices, pressure sensitive paths, spots where you couldn't find sensors, if I showed you where they were hidden, and cameras that are built into the fabric of the environment."

"What the hell does that mean, Zanthius?" John Lee asked.

Zanthius pulled out his phone, pulled up an app that resembled Siri, and asked it to key in on the cameras in the vicinity of his phone. The app asked a series of security questions and within thirty seconds showed the team where four individually powered and monitored cameras were placed. Zanthius followed the arrow that appeared to be like the format of a navigational system, and it led the group to a tree.

John Lee said, "So much for that there high-tech camera mess."

He and Jilkes began to laugh when Zanthius said, "Guys, look up in the tree or, better still, look at a picture of us on my iPhone."

The astonishment of the tree and the iPhone pictures took the steam out of Jilkes and John Lee and they became more attentive students. John Lee asked about equipment and Zanthius said, "When we get back to the farmhouse or the guest house, I think I will be able to get an 'Amen' from you brothers from another mother!"

# # #

Allen called the Sarge back and asked, "Is this move full of trust, or is it clouded by past misdeeds?"

"Allen, I am, or rather, we are offering you a little more of that thing called living than you are presently experiencing. Text me the coordinates and I will have my pilots fix a location and indicate to you what airport they will be arriving at and at what time. You will ask, 'are you picking up someone else'? Nothing more, just are you picking up someone else? They will give you a secure number to text your longitude and latitude headings and they will know where the hell you are and the estimated extraction time. Hang up and call me on the other number I gave you. This one has had a lot of use lately and I don't want to compromise your departure."

"Understood, Sarge, and I must tell you something, I tried to kill you people and now you're offering me immunity. That's incredible and saintly. Nevertheless, I am deeply in your debt, and I know of a place where Walter has hard cash stored. Now, if you want to draw a rat out of a hole, I know the way to do it and make a ton of money doing it."

"First, let's get you extracted, and then we'll figure out how we get this guy. Allen, you won't be afraid to pull the trigger when the time is right, will you?"

"Sarge, I have been living like a homeless person, and I'm not quite use to this way of life. I'm looking for salvation and the appropriate time to kill my archenemy."

"Okay, I'm going to give the phone to Mr. Amazing and he's going to connect you with our pilots. Stay safe and, hopefully, we'll see you soon. By the way, where is your family?" A long and silent stillness occurred and was only ended when Allen uttered, "I don't know. I truly don't know, and this is by design."

"I understand. See you soon," the Sarge replied, grateful that his own loved ones were so close.

# # #

Asiram said to Zanthius when he returned from walking with the boys, "Mi amor, I need to visit that state of mind that was so rudely and dastardly interrupted by those people who attempted to kidnap me and electrocute you. I was in the midst of having a phenomenal orgasm when they surprised us. I think it would be great if we try to make it up to each other, but this time we take a blanket and pistols."

Zanthius shook his head, laughed and said, "I see you're feeling much better, my love. Would you like to take a walk in the woods and explore nature with me?"

"Oh my, I love exploring nature in the woods. It is always so raw, penetrating and rewarding. Yes, I would love to explore the countryside."

# # #

Later that evening, dinner was catered by a seafood restaurant that provided the group with crabs, mussels, clams, oysters, lobster tails, corn on the cobb, fried potatoes, and shrimp. It would be a high cholesterol kind of event, but everyone would have a marvelous time. As the manager of the restaurant asked McArthur who would be paying the bill, he said, "You stay here, I'll go and fetch him for you. I must say the people who you selected to work this party were friendly and respectful. I am sure our business manager is going to make this night worth their while."

As the manager of the restaurant looked around the front of the property, Jong walked out of the door, saw the manager, and asked, "Are you the person that we pay?" She turned around and damn, Jong's heart fell to his feet and struggled to rise to its appropriate holding place. He stammered and said, "Sorry, you took me by surprise."

Being ever mindful of come-ons, she asked, "How can I take you by surprise at your party? Really!?"

A blushing Jong replied, "Your beauty is beyond my comprehension. When you turned around, I felt confused for some reason. Please forgive me, may I see the invoice?"

As Jong made his way towards her, she could see that he had sustained or inherited major issues with his legs. Although not feeling sorry for him, the manager asked, "What happened to your legs? Were you in a car accident or something?"

"What do my legs have to do with my ability to pay the invoice?"

"Nothing, Sir. Sorry, I intruded." As Jong reviewed the bill, he could feel her eyes piercing his very soul. He abruptly inquired, "Do you always stare at people with such intensity?"

"Only when I'm fascinated by them. Please sign the bill and I'll be on my way." Jong looked at her and said, "Leave me a copy please."

"Sir, as you know, this bill is an estimate, and the final bill will be calculated tomorrow when this event is over and done with."

"Fine, thank you. I look forward to reviewing it again tomorrow.

Goodnight."

#

In the field Zanthius and Asiram were making whoopee again, but this time they were interrupted by Jetty, one of her horses. As Zanthius tried to bring the deal to closure, Jetty began nudging him on his butt with her mouth. Asiram yelled, "Not now, Jetty, not now." The horse not understanding English kept nudging Zanthius and finally became aggressive. Zanthius slowly rose up from the position he was in and realized there was a moccasin moving in his direction. He reached down and aggressively pulled Asiram up and started firing at the snake, finally hitting it.

The response from the people at the farm was immediate. Larry was first to arrive with a pistol in hand and asked, "What the hell are you shooting at and why are you out here with your ass exposed to the world?" Everyone broke into laughter. Jetty had quickly retreated at the sound of gunfire.

Zanthius exclaimed, "That damn horse alerted me that a snake was near. Can you believe that? A horse told the story."

"We're going to get one of the mules and feed Jetty treats until she runs away. That could have been catastrophic. That could have been fatal! Oh my God! Whatever that horse wants, I'm going to make sure she gets it."

## CHAPTER TWENTY-NINE

The next day, at 11 in the morning, the doorbell rang. It looked like a courier with a package. Courtney naively opened the door, and the person said, "I need to speak to Mr. Jong, I made a mathematical mistake on the invoice, and I need to make it right. We honor our customers; we don't rip them off. I will stand here until he acknowledges the fact that we made an honest mistake, and that he will at least consider us if you have another event."

Courtney said, "Wait here a second, while I try to find him."

Three minutes later, Jong appeared at the door and was surprised by his visitor. She said, "I presented you with the bill last night and there was a $200 mistake on it. I took the liberty to correct the bill and ask you to consider us in the future, if in fact, you have another event like last evening. Somewhere in the kitchen, two orders were confused, and you were charged for more beer and shrimp than were delivered. The mistake was totally mine. I just want to make sure that you realize that it was not a blatant attempt to rip you off."

"You drove all the way out here to tell me that? Why didn't you just call me? By the way, what's your name?"

"My name is Mary Alice. When I realized the mistake I made, I felt it important enough to drive here and apologize in person." Jong noticed how her hue began to change and recognized that she was nervous. He asked, "Would you like to have a cup of tea, I was just in the process of fixing myself a cup?"

"That would be great since I haven't had a cup yet."

"Please, come in." As he walked into the house, people were staring at him. Jilkes bellowed out, "Wow, Jong, what a cutie."

Just what he didn't need to hear since he was nervous, and it certainly brought attention to Mary Alice's presence. As they entered the kitchen he said, "Mary Alice, this is Courtney, that is Monica, this is Rashida, and the one with child is the owner of this farm and family member, Asiram. Oh, and that guy hanging behind her is the 'horse-follower'. A snake was on target to bite him in a peculiarly exposed place when Jetty, one of the horses, nudged him to vacate the area." Mary Alice spoke to everyone. Courtney broke the ice and asked, "So, you made a mistake on the bill and thought that you needed to drive out here to make it right, eh?"

"That's exactly how I felt. I also wanted to put our bid in for any future events that you might hold. We enjoyed making it happen. We were treated well, and no one was offended. Sometimes when we cater these affairs, people get a little too friendly, but your guests were respectful at all times."

Jong interjected, "I just want to fix us a cup of tea and discuss the bill out back, ladies. Please forgive me for taking her away from you."

On the back deck, they briefly went over the bill, acknowledged the error, and began a general discussion. Mary Alice asked Jong, "So, which one is your wife?"

"Who said I was married?"

"No one said it, you just look like a married man, am I right?"

"I would have to answer that question like a weather person; you are fifty percent correct and fifty percent wrong. According to the law, I am still legally married; that is your fifty percent correct. Emotionally, I am single, and this is your fifty percent wrong. My wife is involved with other men. Therefore, she has concluded our relationship and it is not about saving face or respect. It's about I don't like her anymore on any level, and when we settle this ship down, I will pay her off and be done with her. How about you, where's your husband?"

"I guess he met your wife, and they are living happily ever after. He hit the bars, found a younger woman, and started smoking pot to be cool, I guess. Anyway, he spent every dime that we saved for a house on drugs and booze. Then he tried to become a drug dealer and now he's doing time in state prison."

"Do you go and see him?"

"Mr. Jong, why on earth would I go and see someone who betrayed our vows, stole my money, and cheated at will? No, actually, he can rot in his appointed hell, and frankly, I have erased him from my mind completely."

"Okay, tell the truth, why did you come back out here? Please don't tell me some fabulous fable about a mistake on the bill?"

"You have managed to put me on the spot. In all honesty, my sole purpose was to find out whether or not you were married."

"I don't see how or why that would bring you back out here. I also see that no matter how I approach it, that's going to be your story and you're going to stick with it."

Mary Alice looked away and said, "The farm is so beautiful during the day. This is a magnificent farm and truly modern in every aspect. Mr. Jong, I saw you earlier during the evening when we were setting up. My mind first and then my body became excited without you knowing it. I have no idea how the moment came to be, but I can assure you, I have never had a man take over my body and mind like that. Let me ask you a question, when you turned around and saw me, what did you think? I recall you said that my beauty was beyond your comprehension. I have never heard words like that spoken to me. I confess, I saw you first, so if you want to have a follow-up meeting it's on you to find me and convince me that we should continue our conversation. Please, Mr. Jong, don't think this is about some freakish notion of sex. I'm only about eternal love and not just sex. Good day, Mr. Jong, nice to meet you."

Mary Alice walked through the house and saw that people were trying to readjust from their positions of eavesdropping on her conversation. She said, "Nice to meet you ladies and gent."

Courtney walked out and exclaimed, "My brother, you do have trouble to contend with! That is one fine woman who likes one fine brother. Are you going to pursue her?"

"Courtney, I can sometimes barely walk. Why would a woman like that want to be bothered with a man who can barely walk?"

"Really, Jong, are you kidding me? Okay, brother, this is what I have to say about what I overheard and what I saw. If you let that one get away, then I'm not sure you can manage the organization's business interest when you can't manage your own personal affairs. That feeling sorry shit, well, give it to someone who is a cripple. I only see a man who I admire and who is admired by everyone he works with. I have got to tell my husband about your sorry response."

"Come on, Courtney, don't tell him anything because he's going to put me on leave and make me go and settle issues at home. I'm not ready to do that."

"Jong, if I were you, I would get a van, take two friends with you, and seek her out. Start the conversation today, not tomorrow. That woman came looking for a man that provided her with a vision of someone she could trust and love. I mean that was some serious stuff she told you out there, buster. Not that I was intentionally listening."

Jong walked into the kitchen and saw Jilkes with his head in a plate of food and said, "Since you like embarrassing me in front of people, then you, your boyfriend, and your lady friends, can accompany me into town to find that woman. If the Sarge approves the mission, be ready in forty-five minutes."

# # #

On their way to town, Somara asked John Lee if this was a mission or an outing? John Lee told her that he wanted to take her to town and let her shop for a few basic things. In her native tongue, she told Yeshida that they were going shopping. Jilkes nudged Yeshida and said, "Sweetheart, we agreed that we would speak in a language that we both understood."

"I'm sorry, my love, but sometimes it just naturally happens. It is natural to converse in my language with my friends like you do with yours."

He looked at her and said, "You are absolutely correct. We're a couple and they're a couple and, therefore, we don't have to know what each other is saying or doing every minute, except that this trip is really about trying to figure out where a person of interest to Jong, is." Yeshida said to Somara in their native tongue that Jong was trying to get laid.

Somara jabbed John Lee in the ribs and said, "You said we're going shopping. We no go shopping, we go sex hunting for Jong."

John Lee looked at Jilkes and then at Jong and said for everyone to hear, "Sometimes you see people and you be concerned that they don't be like you. I mean me and that there black fellow had a helluva fight before we came to realize that we needed each other where we be heading. Our friend Jong is not on a sexual mission, but on a mission of legitimacy, much like the one that Jilkes and I went on with you two. I want to be with you forever and I will never answer for him. Jong had a strong reaction to that lady and needs to follow-up, according to our smart doctor. In the meantime, you can go and get some farm type clothes because you two, look like a carton of eggs on a football field."

The two women looked at each other and attempted to decipher the metaphor when Jilkes said, "You guys look like foreigners."

Somara said, "Mr. John Lee, we are foreigners."

"Never mind, don't worry about it. We got your backs."

"Is there something wrong with our backs?"

Jilkes said, "Okay, guys, let's focus on Jong for a minute and forget this road we are on."

In town, Jong rode past the catering company, drove around the corner and to the rear of the place. It was immaculate in the rear and no aroma of food stuff in the air. He drove to the front and pulled into one of the parking spaces in front of the business. Jilkes said, "We're out first, people. Somara and Yeshida, you guys got the front and John Lee, and I got the back. What we're looking for is sudden movement in the place while our man is in there. All radios on channel 4. Let's make this seamless and easy. Eyes open and no channel chatter about love and marriage."

Somara walked Jong inside of the business and looked around. Yeshida took a seat on a flower bed ledge outside of the catering business. Jong walked in and said, "I would like to speak to Mary Alice, please."

"May I tell her who is calling?" The clerk replied.

"My name is Mr. Jong. She catered an affair for me last night and I need to speak to her."

The guy said, "Well, this is her day off. Is this a social call or business related situation?"

"This is a combination!" Jong exclaimed.

The guy said, "In that case, you might find her at the Pancake House, which is a couple of miles up the road on this side of the street." Jong started to walk out of the door, turned around and said, "Thank you for your help, I'm simply trying to figure out a way to take her to dinner." The guy screamed extremely loud, then placed his hand over his mouth and yelled for the rest of the workers to hear, "Mary Alice has a suitor, and he speaks our language."

He turned to Jong and said, "Sir, drive 2.2 miles up this road and you will see where she is having a meal." Everyone heard the information and met in front.

John Lee asked, "Well, you be having them there directions, why are you sitting here waiting for Jilkes?"

"Last I heard, he was still a part of the team."

"Yeah, but he be holding you up from your destiny. He's a big boy, he will know how to find us." Jong looked at him and said, "You know you cannot sleep without him near you, so shut up and call him."

#

At the Pancake House, Jong saw Mary Alice, through the window, having a conversation with two guys and decided that she was busy and began to walk away. She saw his image in a mirror and for a moment was elated that he was in town, perhaps, looking for her. She then watched him turn around and head towards his vehicle. She excused herself from her present company and bolted towards the door. She yelled across the street, "Mr. Jong, you're in town and you couldn't take a minute, to say hello?"

Jong paused for a moment and said, "Are you serious? I received a call from our mechanic about one of our planes and have to get back to work. You know like, making a mistake on a bill, you must attend to the issues at hand. Wouldn't you agree?"

"Nicely put Mr. Jong. Since you're here, do you think we could have dinner sometime soon?"

This caught Jong completely off guard. Jilkes nudged him and said, "Oh yes, I think I can make that happen."

"Your voice sounded different. Are you okay?"

"It sounded different because it was not me. It was Mr. Jilkes trying to help me out in this very embarrassing situation."

"If you're feeling a little nervous, think about how I felt when you asked me why did I really come to the farm? You talk about peeing your pants? Okay, my question to you and not Mr. Jilkes is, would you like to have dinner with me and if so, when?"

"Would it be asking too much if I asked you to have dinner with me at the farm? I know there are a lot of people there, but I'm sure that they will give us privacy and allow us to communicate without them hanging out of windows to hear what we're talking about," Jong stated.

"Mr. Jong, I feel that you are a gentleman, that I can trust you, and I want to invite you over for dinner, but I wasn't planning on it happening tonight. If you're prepared to fix me a simple meal, share a couple glasses of wine, and you can get someone to bring me home without you driving then I'm all in."

Jong looked at Jilkes and John Lee and said, "Those two, plus Somara, and Yeshida are our chaperones. I assure you, and any family that you have here, they will not go against protocol. As a matter of fact, and since they're in town, why don't we commission them to prepare our meal and select the appropriate wine. I can assure you that the two guys have no choice in the matter, but they will have to convince their lady friends to participate in the adventure." He turned to Jilkes and John Lee and said, "Won't you boys?"

"Mr. Jong, I hope I'm not putting you on the spot, but you have placed me on the spot and, therefore, I'm going to be available. Will you be able to have someone pick me up at 5 pm?"

"I have a better idea. Why don't you throw a few things in a bag and you can come with us now? We can go swimming, sit in the sauna and/or steam bath, you can ride a horse, or we can take the mule and explore every aspect of the farm."

"You want to ride a mule rather than a horse?"

"I think I prefer riding in the mule since it's motorized." Jong smiled an unusual smile and laughed. Mary Alice said, "Mr. Jong, I can trust you and your mates to make sure that I get home safely, right?"

Jong looked at her and exclaimed, "We help people; we don't abuse women on any level and that question is almost an insult!"

Mary Alice paused and started to make a comment and paused again. As her eyes watered, she said, "I was promised a safe ride home after a party at a former senator's home, but what I received was less than safe and totally compromising for me."

Jong realized that Mary Alice experienced a situation that was not to her liking, and said, "I will personally make sure that you get home safely."

"Gee, thanks, Mr. Jong, whom I just met. I am just recovering, and I am unusually cautious when it comes to going out with people. I hope you understand my ambivalent nature."

"I have an alternative idea, why don't you invite a friend and I'll invite a friend and we can meet in town at a place of your choice?"

"That seems extremely boring. Just make sure that I get home, and that will be that. I like the idea of coming out to the farm since it is so magnificent and tranquil."

"I will pick you up with two of my friends followed by another two of my friends and we will make sure that you get home safely," Jong iterated.

"Why so many friends coming and following?"

"It is the nature of our work. I will spare no detail in telling you exactly what we do and who we do it for."

#

Later that evening, the group decided to go up the road to eat crabs and leave the farm to Jong with four people hanging around to provide surveillance and protection, if necessary. Mary Alice asked, "Where did everyone go?"

"Oh, they went up the road for crabs and beer."

"I hope they didn't go to that crab shack on 211, that place is the worst, plus it's dirty. They have had several citations from the Health Department."

"My people will sort it out quickly and be out of there. They don't take chances with food."

"What is it that you and you friends do for a living, Mr. Jong?"

"We are a group of humanitarians that help people help themselves and we dispense of people who are less than righteous. I'm going to try to make a long story short, but do I have your word that this conversation will not be repeated? This is a situation similar to my making sure you get home okay. Can I trust you, Mary Alice?"

"Wow, Mr. Jong, in just a few days we are confronted with trust issues and we haven't even hugged yet. Nothing will be repeated that you tell me!"

Jong gave her a sanctioned version of what the group did, how they met and a glorified version of their Vietnam experience, as well as how bad people tried to kill the Sarge, his wife, and the woman who birthed his son, Zanthius. He discussed briefly, their foundations and how they just happen to make the right investments to financially secure each member of the group for four lifetimes, if such a thing were possible. He told her that Zanthius was an unintended spy and that he had stumbled across a new revolutionary formula for making a bomb that would make those dropped on Japan look like firecrackers. He indicated that they were in charge of certain aspects of the formula and didn't quite know who the hell to trust. Mary Alice asked, "So, are all of you people considered spies?"

Jong laughed and replied, "No, just me and one other."

"Mr. Jong, I'm being serious."

"Mary Alice, we are not spies but what we do sometimes involve those in that community. We are what you call, 'friendly intermediaries'."

"Come now, Mr. Jong, what on earth does that mean?"

"Mary Alice, I kind of feel that I'm missing the areas of interest that I would like to focus on, but, more importantly, I would like to light the grill, shuck the corn, wash the clams, marinate the steaks, and steam the spinach. I'm going to have a glass of an Argentine Malbec, is it possible to interest you in one as well?"

"I'm usually a beer drinker, but wine sounds fine."

"I insist on providing you with the beer of your choice, what might that be?"

"Mr. Jong, I'm a simple girl from Virginia, all I need is a Coors Light."

"Oh my, I like that beer as well, and that is the only beer that I like."

"Mr. Jong, I would like to have a glass of wine with you, take a walk, and sit around the pool. Is that something we can do?"

"Mary Alice, we can do whatever you want to do. This is your night and I'm hoping that this is the first of many. I must admit that I was surprised by your beauty when we first met but was a little confused about your inquiry concerning my legs."

"I know, that was truly unsettling to me as well, the words just came out of my mouth. I saw you, and my body and mind just raced. I didn't know where they were heading. When I interacted with you, I guess I didn't think, and that comment just came out. If I caused you pain, then I'm sorry, but I was confused by the feelings I had for you and I guess I went low instead of high. I'm sorry for a lot of things that I have done, but that question is one of my biggest regrets."

"Let me tell you about these legs and those guys out there. We're a family and have been for a lot of years. We all met at boot camp and formed a bond that is incredible and obviously lasting. These guys will jump out of a plane, without a parachute, to save any one of us. They are here because someone tried to kill our leader, and none of us have been home since.

"On our last mission in the Nam, we were outnumbered and there was an explosion. At the center of that blast was little ole me and that is when my legs were shattered. I was told that I would never walk again. These guys insisted that the doctors didn't know shit and that I had to prove everyone wrong by an aggressive rehab and workout schedule. It was amazing and monitored by my friends. I'm not at 100%, but I'm motivated. I don't want your sympathy, so I blew you off when you asked me about my legs the other night. As you probably can imagine, it is a sensitive issue with me."

Mary Alice spoke softly, "I can imagine, as sensitive as what happened to me after a party that was white-washed and blamed on me. Mr. Jong, I understand fully. We just shared different versions of trauma. I will never ask you again about what you suffered, but one day I will share with you what I suffered and still suffer, because it was alleged, that I was the cause of my attack." As Mary Alice began to cry, Jong uncharacteristically hugged her and said, "If you tell me the whole story, perhaps I can make it right for you. I mean, if you tried to seek justice in the courts and received nothing in return, perhaps me and my friends can secure one of the perpetrators and impress upon his sense of morality to speak freely against the others. Mary Alice, there are members of our group who are experts at obtaining truthful acknowledgements from people who have committed hideous crimes. If you're sure you want justice and not revenge, then I can guarantee you justice. That thing called revenge is something that you must reckon with. We do justice, we don't typically do revenge unless it is a function of one of us."

Mary Alice started crying vehemently and screamed; they raped me repeatedly, but yet it was my fault. That good ole boys' network has tarnished me for the balance of my life, and no one cares about it, but me."

"Mary Alice, we can give you comfort and justice, but if we go down that road, it may conclude our possible union. In other words, it becomes you and I, or you and them."

"Mr. Jong, they violated me, and that ex-senator testified that I wasn't invited. He asked his people how did I get in? He then asked me how I got in? After that charade, I was escorted to a part of the house that led to a basement. That is where I was injected with a drug and repeatedly raped by the senator and his people. Mr. Jong, I know that this may end our little infatuation, but it is important that I tell you about this because no one else believes my story. They all think that I'm just a little street urchin that exists to make trouble and screw people for a fee. I'm no prostitute, Mr. Jong, and prior to that night I was still what, most considered, a virgin. They stole my life, ruined it by fabricating the facts, and relegated me to the status of a common street whore. So, if you can help me then I would appreciate it. If you can't help me without risking our exploration of a potential union, then I will not need your help, I will seek my vengeance in another way."

Jong looked at her and felt compelled to state his understanding of what he had heard. He said, "Mary Alice, vengeance is a one-way street. Once you start down it, you can't reverse your direction. Mary Alice buried her head in her lap and began to cry. I don't know for sure who was involved other than the senator, because he was the first one to touch me and violently rape me. As I recall, what he did to me was painful and unnatural. Before I passed out, I remember him saying, 'her ass is going to be sore tomorrow'. After that all I remember is his laughter and then the smell and rough touch of many other people."

Jong looked at her and said, "Well, this is becoming a very humbling first date. We as a group may not help you if your motivation is directed by vengeance. If you know of a particular person who participated in the event other than the senator, perhaps I could find a way for you to obtain what you want, but trust me on this one, you don't want to head down that road, it's a one-way street." Mary Alice listened intently to what Jong said and without any rhyme or reason, she yelled out the name, Blake.

Jong looked at her and asked, "Who the heck is Blake?"

"Oh, my goodness, Blake was there, and he had his way with me. I know it and I remember him saying, 'this is easier than dating your ass'."

"Where is this Blake now?"

"He's probably home with his wife and two fat children. They live about twenty minutes from here. I see his face as clear as daylight, he was one of the men who abused me."

Jong looked at Mary Alice and said, "I have to take a walk and decide if this is a wrong that I want to right." As Jong was about to walk away, Mary Alice said, "Please don't leave me alone, I feel so vulnerable, because I think about whether something I said or did led those people to believe they could violate me and completely get away with it. I need you near me, Mr. Jong. My emotions have begun to create a hell pit for me that I don't seem to be able to climb out of. After that event happened to me, I have refused to be involved with anyone, Mr. Jong. I saw you and my heart began to race and I couldn't understand what was happening but realized that this had to be a positive sign for me since all other signs were negative and filled with hurt. I was far away from you and I really couldn't see your face but felt your spirit and realized that I needed to have faith and to believe that everyone wasn't out to recreate the epitome of that reprehensible moment of my life. Please don't leave me alone for I fear that I will retreat into that place that is not good for me."

Jong looked at Mary Alice and said, "I am totally confused because of all of your associates that you are privy to, you selected me to help you face this issue."

"Wait, I didn't select you, Mr. Jong. My heart said that you were a good man, one that I could trust and believe in. I am also very confused about this whole issue. Listen, I saw that you were struggling a little trying to walk, but it had nothing to do with your physical being, Mr. Jong. I am so afraid of you because I don't know why I like you. I saw you and you conquered me without knowing it. I felt defiled once again because I didn't have anything to say about what was going on in my mind and to my body. This is not an easy night for me, perhaps you should escort me home and perhaps rethink why you and I are here together. I'm totally confused, but I know that there is a solid reason that I'm here with you. I'm hoping that you feel something to help us meet in the middle or we can say adios!"

Jong said, "I need five minutes. Can you wait five minutes and then we will decide what we should do?" He walked away from Mary Alice, installed his earpiece and uttered, "John Lee and Jilkes, I need you at the house now." Before he could say another word, John Lee showed up from the south and Jilkes waltzed in from the north. They said, almost in unison, "Get with the program and stop playing around."

Jilkes reported, "I sent Carlos and two of his people to Blake's house and he should be arriving within the next twenty minutes. This thing that you're going through is very real and you must embrace it. This woman is apparently special, and you know I don't believe in magic, but Cupid shot his arrow, my brother, and it hit you square in the ass—sorry, in the heart. It's now or never and you need to figure out how we clean up this mess in a hurry. Blake's ass will be here shortly if we can find him. I know we can make him give up everyone who was involved in this mess. You and Mary Alice can decide your next steps. John Lee and I will ratify your commitment to the rest of the group, and we'll go from there. This is some serious shit that has landed on your legs, get with it, and make it work. This lady spiritually, physically, and emotionally loves you. I think she wants you to kiss her and confirm the fact that you at least like her. Do me a major favor and forget your traditional practices and walk up to her and say, 'don't say a word and close your eyes'. The rest is up to you, Romeo. Kiss her gently, back off, then kiss her again, and each time she attempts to say something, say to her, 'please don't talk'. I'm looking for a sign from heaven that this will work, and your talking will only interfere with it. Man, kiss her, kiss her, and your body will say what it is you're involved in. You will know, my brother, and it will scare the shit out of you."

Jong looked at Jilkes and said, "You and that country guy are so special to me, but I'm not much of a romantic. We don't do a lot of kissing in my culture."

"That's probably great, but once you find a woman who you like to kiss and she you, then you will learn to enjoy each kiss. This is a test run to see if she is the one, my brother. Go with the flow and forget about tradition, family, and friends."

"You guys are the best and I lower my head in tradition to thank my ancestors for aligning me with you, and the rest of the team."

"Forget tradition and ancestors, go do your work, and figure out if this is a new beginning, my brother."

# # #

In less than forty minutes, Blake was tied to a chair in the barn and the hood was removed from his head. The first words out of his mouth were, "Do you know who you people are messing with?"

Carlos said, "In five minutes, you will be begging for forgiveness and asking for mercy. If it's true what is alleged that you did, then I personally will gut you from your balls to your brain."

"What are you talking about? I haven't done a damn thing. I'm one of the leaders of this town and you can be assured that people are looking for me at this very moment."

Carlos exclaimed, "Shut up and prepare to meet a woman who alleges you violated and relegated her to the bottom of hell!"

Blake exclaimed, "I had nothing to do with her or that situation!"

Carlos looked at Blake and paused. He then said, "Do with what situation and who is her. I haven't disclosed anything, and, yet, you seem to have a guilty conscience. This is going to be informative. If you attempt to deceive us, you will witness a part of your anatomy being cut off, am I clear?"

# # #

John Lee, Jilkes, and Jong walked into the barn. Jilkes said to Jong, "I don't think you should be here because it's your woman that's in question. Why don't you leave this to me, John Lee, Carlos, and his men?"

"Why on earth would I do that?"

"Maybe because the things we hear may turn you off to a potential mate. I just think you should let us handle this and report to you what we discover. Come on, if you hear the wrong thing from this guy, you're going to go ballistic and may even drop the lady before you get a chance to know her."

"Guys, I am more than that. I am substance, understanding and, as such, there is nothing this guy can say to us that will sway me from at least attempting to get to know her. I feel a kinetic connection to her as well as a carnal desire to mate with her."

John Lee looked at him and said, "Dude, animals' mate; people make out."

Jilkes looked at John Lee and said, "Is that what you and Somara do, make out; wow that sounds so high school-ish."

John Lee gave him the finger and Jong said, "Listen, let's go and listen to what this guy has to say about my associate."

#

Jilkes began the conversation by telling his captive that he represented a group of good guys and gals who helped people help themselves. He then said, "I'm going to ask you a few questions that I may know the answer to, and on any occasion, should you desire to fabricate the truth, you will be sliced or a part on your anatomy will be severed. Do you understand the rules?"

Blake looked at him and said, "I don't care what you people call yourselves, but you have no warrant to abduct me and hold me hostage."

"That was your one and only remark that you can share, without a penalty. Now, everything you say is on the record and will result in a reward or a penalty. I'm going to get right to the point. You were at a party given by the ex-senator that used to own a house somewhere in this area, is that right and do you remember the party?"

"I don't remember no party." Jilkes nodded to John Lee who sliced Blake's left leg, who screamed for the world to hear.

Jilkes said, "That was a penalty and a small slice. From this point forward, you are going to be penalized with deep penetrating slices until we start to amputate parts of your body, do you understand?"

Blake watching the blood run down his leg yelled, "Are you people crazy? I have done nothing wrong, why are you tormenting and trying to kill me?"

Jilkes yelled, "Do you remember the night that you had your way with Mary Alice? Do you remember how you and your friends violated her right to exist by drugging her, and sexually annihilating every place that should have been saved for someone who would love and protect her? Who were the other people that participated in that event? Don't fricken lie to me because my friend is going to bleed you bad."

Blake made the unfortunate mistake of saying that he didn't know what they were talking about. John Lee took his favorite knife and plunged it into Blake's foot. Blake screamed into the night, but his sounds were drowned out by the music being played by the late Prince. Jilkes looked at the man's punctured foot and said, "You are going to need attention immediately or you're going to bleed completely out."

Blake recanted and requested, "Promise me that you'll get me to the hospital, and I will tell you how it all went down, and why we didn't suspect that she would have connected friends. Look at my foot. I need a doctor or I ain't going to tell you shit."

Jilkes nodded to John Lee who once again unsheathed his massive blade and Blake yelled, "Wait, wait, please, wait. We did a lot of girls, but never had to be concerned about an inquiry."

Jilkes asked Jong to leave the barn because the shit was about to hit the fan. Jong answered, "I need to hear about this."

Jilkes said, "You have heard enough to substantiate the fact that she is an honorable woman. You need to attend to her emotional wounds if you want to see how far your new relationship can go. Let me and my boy extract the vitals of who, when, where and why."

Jong stubbornly said, "I need to hear him say what they did to her and why."

John Lee looked at Blake and said, "This here next cut be deep and you might be missing a finger or the balance of your foot, it be your choice, but it's going to hurt and what be the matter is how much hurt you can deal with?"

Blake told the group that there were five of them and each did to her what they wanted to do to her. She was spread eagle at first and after that they unchained her and did what they wanted.

John Lee asked, "And what did you want to do to her? Who are the rest of the people and who was first?"

Screaming in pain Blake replied, "Please, I need a doctor I'm losing a lot of blood."

Jilkes yelled, "Did it matter to you how much blood she lost or that she is scarred for the rest of her life? Who was first?"

Blake asked, "What does that matter?"

Jilkes answered, "It indicates who was in control. Don't ask me any more questions. You answer the questions, or I will let my sadistic friend cut you until you bleed to death."

Blake looked at his foot and said, "The first person to have his way with her was a friend of the senators, some dignitary from DC, named Walter. Then the senator had his turn with her. That Walter guy didn't appear to be that much into a comatose woman. He was more interested in the senator, but according to our ritual he had to smoke the peace pipe."

Jilkes immediately asked, "What does 'smoking a peace pipe' have to do with what happened to Mary Alice?"

"It means that if you see it, you have to penetrate it, whether you want it or not." Jilkes pulled Jong to the side and told him to go get the Sarge, and to bring Courtney. Blake had mentioned the magical name that got everyone's attention.

# # #

When Courtney walked into the room she said, "Oh, my goodness, what happened to you?"

John Lee replied, "He stepped on a spike. It's really not that bad." Blake was about to say something when Jilkes stepped behind Courtney and made a cutthroat gesture to Blake indicating the outcome if he were to contradict the fact that he stepped on a spike.

Courtney announced, "We have to get you to the hospital. I'm going to give you a temporary bandage that will get you to the hospital, but you have to leave here in a hurry. You can't hang around here talking with these guys."

Courtney wrapped the foot and secured it with the materials she had at her disposal. The Sarge told her that he would see her in a minute.

As soon as Courtney was out of sight, the Sarge walked in and asked Blake, "How do you know Walter, and do you know where I can find him?"

Blake asked, "And who are you?"

Jilkes exclaimed, "I told your dumb ass not to ask any questions, that's a penalty. John Lee, stab the other foot!"

As John Lee unsheathed his knife, the Sarge said, "Delay that order for the moment. Sir, I'm going to ask you again, how do you know Walter and how can I reach him? He's my cousin."

Blake studied the Sarge's face and said, "I really don't know him, but he's a mean person with a lot of stuff on a lot of people." Blake went on to express how Walter, at a private dinner, made the senator suck his toes in front of six people and proclaimed, 'if I hear of this event in any of my circles, I will slay all of your families'! He then told the senator to enter a room and have sex with the wife of one of the other guests who was a congressman. After the senator entered the room, he said to the group, "Loyalty has its rewards. He cut on a monitor to show the congressman's wife having sex with the senator. He also gave the congressman a duffle bag full of money—$3.5 million, I was told."

Beckmire asked, "Do you know where I can find Walter or who is the best person to lead me to him?"

Blake said, "It would have been the senator, but we all know that can't happen now. If I had to guess who he is in touch with the most, I would guess it would be the congressman. Listen, I have cooperated to the fullest. I need to get to the hospital; I'm feeling a little light-headed."

Jong exclaimed, "Yeah, just like Mary Alice felt after you people drugged and raped her! You be best telling me the truth on this here next question because, otherwise, you won't have to worry about sex in your future. How did you violate her? What was your pleasure with her?"

Jilkes looked at Jong and noticed that he was losing focus and becoming agitated at the same time. Jilkes yelled, "Hold up, one damn minute. Sarge, please take Jong out of here. I'm afraid that if he goes off, there is nothing that John Lee and I can do to stop him. Make him leave the area and assure him that John Lee and I will provide justice and vengeance for the person who intrigues him."

The Sarge looked at Jong and said, "Mr. Amazing, those two guys would die for you and have proven it repeatedly. Your mindset only wants revenge. Let them decide upon justice and properly administer it. I need you to come with me and I need you to do it now, soldier."

# # #

Jilkes and John Lee extracted the names of the other people involved in the atrocities that plagued local girls of moral stature who lacked parental over-sight.

John Lee, out of left field, said, "I think we need to make this family whole by making sure we don't be having no weak links."

"What the hell are you talking about?" Jilkes asked.

"We be having some pilots that know that wherever we go someone usually shows up dead. I believe that if they be wanting to turn their coats inside out, we be been had without any grease."

"Damn, Old Country, that's some powerful shit. Let's call a meeting and deal with it because, apparently, it is on your mind. That is some serious looking out!"

# # #

After discerning the pleasures that Blake had enjoyed with a comatose Mary Alice, John Lee said, "It would be nice to round up them there other fellas and have them do the same things to each other."

Jilkes immediately dismissed the thought, but it kept resonating in his brain until he said to John Lee, "I like that idea, and we should move it forward and see if Jong agrees. But first, let's get our guest to the hospital and leave him in charge of getting his friends who like to have sex with comatose women together in the next forty-eight hours."

Jilkes had two of Carlos's men drive Blake to the hospital. He called the Sarge and told him that they had to meet on a critical issue raised by John Lee.

Jilkes, said to the Sarge, Mallory, Brown, and Okema, "John Lee brought up an interesting point that I believe needs to be addressed. He feels that if anyone would turn us in, it might be our pilots, because they know wherever we go there is usually a lot of mayhem left behind. John Lee feels that we have to bring them into the family and let them take part in some of the things we do so that every hand is not without sin."

The Sarge asked, "Don't you guys just want to go home and sleep without having to look over your shoulders?"

Mallory looked at the Sarge and asked, "Are you out of your fricken mind? We gave up sleep to make sure that you weren't placed in a permanent state of rest. Don't make light of our commitment to you, man."

"I'm just saying this is getting old and we still haven't breached the surface as to where my cousin is hiding. You guys know that I love you and without you I'm a dead man walking. I just want to take a few months off without killing anyone and having anyone try to kill us. We are like a group of homeless individuals and I don't know if this is good for any of us."

Jilkes said, "This has been one of the most important chapters in my life. It has connected me daily to John Lee, and the rest of you, and I'm extremely happy. I have met a woman who I absolutely adore and admire and want to be with for the balance of my life. To me Sarge, this is my life, and I don't want to change it. I'm in the best post-Vietnam shape that I have ever been in. I love the adrenaline rushes, most of all being with the people who love me and will die for me if necessary. It don't get any better than this."

A quiet fell over the room until John Lee asked, "Permission to speak freely without recourse, Sergeant?"

The Sarge said, "Have a go at it."

John Lee looked at Jilkes, walked over to him, shook his hand, and said, "I love you man." He turned to the Sarge and said, "I think you be needing to spend some quiet time with the doctor. How on earth can you say things like that to us? I want to sleep with that there pretty woman of mine, but even she knows that we are on a mission to capture a truck load of fat hogs. Some of us be done gain some things and others of us be done lost some things. I be one of the ones that lost something. I mean them there people hung my woman in my house, how can you be talking about sleep? I be so upset because I think you just want to quit while I be loving the reunion of our group and new friends and don't forget how much money we be done come into accidently. I mean we already be rich, but we have found money that ain't even been counted yet. The money ain't the thing that ghosts me, it's who we be and who we always have been--brothers to the end." Somara grabbed and led a crying John Lee out of the room.

Jilkes said, "So much for sleeping because we ain't about rest. We be about making sure that people don't shoot you in a restaurant and hang us in our own homes." The Sarge hung his head low and burst into an enormous scream because he realized that he had momentarily quit on his team. He yelled at the top of his lungs stating that he didn't want to kill anyone else and wanted to receive absolution.

Mallory exclaimed, "There are only two places we can receive absolution and one is completely out of reach, but the other is in our reach and that place is called Hades. All the bad that we have done outranks all the good that we have tried to do. Sarge, I think you're having a breakdown and we need to get you to a place where you can smell the salt water. I think we should take one of the smaller planes and head back to St. Thomas for some R&R and forget about the obsession with Walter for at least a week or so."

Courtney, as well as the entire area, heard this man's heart burst and when she walked in, she asked, "What's going on with him?"

Mallory said, "He's having some kind of breakdown, like we all are having. We need to get to the beach and just play until we are rested and ready to make our next move or I'm fearful of us making a tactical mistake and causing everyone to suffer dearly. We must spend twice as much time relaxing as we do on our business. I'm going to leave you to calm your husband and I'm going to find Jong. We have got to get out of here and relax."

As Mallory exited the room, Jong who was in a crouching position, stood up and asked, "Has the Sarge gone off the deep end?"

Mallory looked at him and said, "A couple of us are going back to St. Thomas. Which plane is available?"

Jong looked at him and asked, "Do you people ever listen to what I say? We are supposed to take delivery of that new jet this weekend. We kept two of the planes, turned in the two tainted planes and kept the third one, and purchased the plane that would accommodate all of us and our families. What's wrong with the Sarge? I have never seen the man so discombobulated. Is he going to be alright?"

"The Sarge is tired of keeping us in this game without us having the ability to visit our families and homes. Everyone is trying to protect him from being killed, as well as protect ourselves.   He is overwrought with guilt.   If something happens to any one of us, he is going to be a basket case."

Jong stood up and said, "I will slap him into reality."

"You will do no such thing. Let him be," Mallory stated.

"You don't understand how this shit works Mallory. The longer he is allowed to suffer like this the more it becomes a permanent state of mind. He needs to have his wits about him, and it is a fifty/fifty chance that he can recover on his own or he will go into a depression where there is no return. Do you want to gamble on that?"

Mallory said, "I don't like this voodoo shit, but if you think it will work let me get Courtney out of the room and you do your thing."

Jong and Mallory walked into the room and the Sarge seemed to be 'out there'. Mallory said, "Courtney, I need to have a word with you. Can I speak with you in the hallway for a moment? Jong will watch the Sarge."

As soon as they exited the room, Jong stood directly in front of the Sarge and proclaimed, "When this happens, you are probably going to want to break my back, but I hope you realize what I'm about to do is for your good and the good of the group. If in fact you slaughter me, don't take it personally, just finish the job we started. I love you, Sarge." Jong looked at John Lee and Jilkes and announced, "His reaction is going to be fast and it will be furious. If you can protect me, I would appreciate it, but he's going to come at me with a vengeance."

John Lee asked, "What are you about to do to him, play with his ass or something weird?" As Jong was positioning himself in front of the Sarge he said, "I'm going to slap him back to reality. The response can be deadly for me."

Jilkes asked, "Are you serious?"

"As serious as a heart attack, and you guys know how strong this man is. Perhaps we should get McArthur and Mallory in here as well."

Jilkes made the call to McArthur. John Lee walked outside of the room and said, "Mallory we be needing you in here for a minute. Ah, Ms. Courtney, he be alright after Jong performs his magic on him."

Courtney said, "Hell no, we ain't doing no rituals on my husband."

"Courtney, just give us a chance before he gets to a place where we can't get him back from. You know we all be loving him. Ain't nobody going to do nothing to him that we all don't agree on. Trust us, this here ain't no power play," John Lee stated.

"John Lee, I will shoot everyone in that room if you hurt my husband."

"We be knowing that. We never want to tangle with you and your medicine. I got to ask you one question, does the Sarge sleep at night?"

"Maybe about four hours a night. Then he goes all day long without a nap or any rest."

"Well, I'll be damn, that there be the answer to what be happening. You being a doctor and all, can you prescribe a sleeping pill for him or for me so that I can go and get it for the Sarge?"

"John Lee, I don't like prescribing pills for people, but in this case, I'm going to make an exception. I need my man back. We all need to go back to St. Thomas and just play in the water and have fun instead of always looking behind us for the next attempt to kill us."

# # #

As Courtney watched, Jong slap the Sarge into next week. A few seconds later, the Sarge sprang from his chair and charged towards Jong, but was momentarily restrained by Mallory, Jilkes, and John Lee who he quickly dispatched of. Courtney ran in front of him and shouted, "Sit your big ass down. He got you out of a dangerous state."

"That little sonofabitch, slapped me!" the Sarge bellowed.

"Yeah, better him than me because I was about to knock you into next week. Relax and calm down. I need you to sit down and breathe slowly."

After a few minutes of discussing what had happened, Courtney said, "Sarge, getting four hours of sleep is not good for you. John Lee came up with the perfect solution, low dosage sleeping pills. Despite my resistance to prescribing such things, I'm convinced that you need something to help you sleep at night. It might make me feel better as well because I don't sleep when you don't sleep."

"That, little sonofabitch, slapped me. I need to talk to him."

"Sarge, you had better sit your big ass down or you will really get slapped, by me." Mallory, Jilkes, and John Lee stood in front of Jong, in a defensive position.

John Lee acknowledged, "You see how easily he displaced each of us? That was crazy, that man just brushed us aside like we were paper weights. Can you imagine if he were pissed at us?"

Mallory said, "I tried to take him one night when he was drunk. He beat the shit out of me and eight others before passing out. When he's mad, I try to stay away from him because he's unlike any man that I have ever come across.

He's a beast. If he is angry and if you're the target, you had better have, at least seven, to ten others to support you, or you're toast."

John Lee said, "I have never had to physically relate to the Sarge and now I'm glad that I didn't. That dude just pushed me aside like I wasn't even there."

Jilkes said, "I can't believe what happened to me either. I'm a pretty strong dude, but that guy handled me like I was a little fly. That was some scary shit. I really don't want to tangle with him."

Mallory said, "I knew this wasn't going to end well for us. We gave it our best and he just came back to earth and showed us who the alfa is." Everyone laughed and agreed that when it came time to dealing with the Sarge, the common consensus was--shoot him!

## CHAPTER THIRTY

In St. Thomas and at a special birthday dinner for Yeshida, the Sarge talked about family, community, friends, lovers, and the team. He said that all those things matter, but the team is what matters to him the most, including being slapped by one of his friends, a moment that he can't understand and more importantly, he won't ever forget.

Jong told John Lee, "That is a typical response. It's now important that I slap him on the other side to neutralize the impact of that slap."

John Lee exclaimed, "When you decide to do that, make sure I'm twenty miles away! Did you see the way he manhandled us when we tried to protect you? What we be needing is Courtney in the room to distract him until he levels out, or otherwise this dude is going to hurt one of us."

"I totally agree. I guess I'm going to have to explain to her what this process is all about and hope she believes in hocus pocus. I really don't want that dude attacking me. When his adrenaline is flowing, he's unstoppable and that is what I'm afraid of; the Sarge, the beast!"

"How about we sedate him before you slap him? Does that matter and will it work?" Jilkes asked.

"I just need to slap him from the west side, then he will be in balance. I want the entire team in the room, plus Courtney, when I do this thing because he will definitely hurt me if he gets to me. Drugs are no good because it alters his mind as well as his state of being. However, the Sarge is an enormously strong human being and we all might need a little leverage in helping me stay alive. This is going to be the second time I have slapped this man. If he gets to me, I'm dead!"

# # #

Jilkes began to explain the information he received from Jong to Courtney and said, "Jong has to slap your husband again, but on the other side of his face. He wants the entire team in the room plus you to defuse the situation. Are you ready to play that game again?"

"Oh, my goodness! Are you people certifiably crazy? You want to slap him again? Listen, the Sarge is a strong person and I don't recommend this action. We got away with it last time, but to shock his body and mind again might be problematic for the person doing the shocking."

"That is why Jong wants the entire team in the room when he does it. He keeps stating that there is only a four-hour window before the Sarge retreats to his comatose state. I don't know what is going on, but I believe in Jong and I love the Sarge. Jong is saying this stuff and it was him who got the Sarge in the current position. Therefore, we should let him finish his task, as well as protect him."

Courtney looked at Jilkes and announced, "Let's do this thing now before I have a change of heart. Get him in here and I will sedate him and then we go with the hocus pocus. Give me a few minutes to go to my room and check my bag out to see what I have that will take this big guy out for a few minutes."

"By the way, Jong is fearful of the impact of drugs. He says this thing must be done with presence of mind and spirit, instead of an altered state of existence. He also realizes that the Sarge is a huge and strong man," Jilkes interjected.

# # #

The Sarge was lured into his room and Courtney said, "I need you to sit down."

"Honey, why is the entire team in here, including that little sonofabitch that slapped me?"

"Sarge, your nerves are bad, just relax for a moment."

"There is nothing wrong with my nerves." After that statement, Courtney slammed a needle into the Sarge's arm and mumbled, "I hope this works or I feel my man will never trust me again."

Jong walked over to him and began to warm up for his routine. The Sarge unexpectedly stood up and grabbed Jong by the neck, lifting him off the ground with one hand, then collapsed back into the chair.

John Lee asked, "Did you be seeing that shit? That dude lifted Jong into the air with one hand. That be really impossible for normal people."

Courtney walked over and inquired, "Honey, are you alright?"

The Sarge answered, "I'm not sure, I'm feeling a little out of sorts. What did you give me?" Jong walked over to the Sarge, he jumped up again and charged towards Jong. Chakes unexpectedly cut him low at the knees and the Sarge tumbled to the floor. The drug Courtney injected into him began to take effect and he was unable to get up.

Jong commanded stridently, "Sit him up before he goes completely out so I can shock his west side and be done with him trying to kill me."

Jilkes and John Lee sat the Sarge up, Jong shortened his mental preparations and within twenty seconds, he slapped the Sarge on the west side of his face. As the Sarge fell back he asked, "Why do you keep slapping me, man?" Those would be the last words uttered by the Sarge for the next twenty-six hours.

# # #

A day later, Ben Beckmire woke up with a terrible headache. Courtney inquired, "Man, are you alright?"

"Why wouldn't I be? All I remember is Jong slapping me. That's who I'm going to deal with the first chance I get. Why did he slap me?"

"He said that you were about to go into a deep depression and that he needed to shock you before the medicine I gave you took hold of you completely."

"Honey, what did you give me?"

"Sarge, I gave you a little something that would help you sleep and that is exactly what it did, put you out for the past twenty-six hours."

"Courtney, stop playing. You know damn well I can't sleep for no twenty-six hours. I have responsibilities to attend to. Where is Mallory?"

"If you want him, call him, honey, but you have been asleep for twenty-six straight hours and that is what the doctor ordered. You can't keep a regimen of four hours of sleep a day with the kinds of things you people are involved in. If you don't get at least six to eight hours of sleep per day, you will become an ineffective leader and you're going to get someone seriously hurt. So, I suggest, no I command, that you plan on getting the recommended amount of sleep at night. In addition, when possible, I think you should take a siesta. You are no longer forty-five years old, Mr. Beckmire. What you and the guys do is extremely dangerous and if you neglect your health, you're going to put us all at risk."

The Sarge looked at her and asked, "I guess I have been neglecting you as well as my sleep, right?"

"Let your conscience be your guide, Ben Beckmire. I'm not going to go there yet, but you're close to being divorced because of the lack of affection towards your wife."

"Honey, I'm going to take a long shower, and afterwards, can we just dance around the room like kids?"

"I'll be waiting on you, Mr. Man. Don't take all day in the shower."

## CHAPTER THIRTY-ONE

In St. Thomas, the group was under orders to do nothing but relax. What was perplexing to the Sarge was the fact that no one, seemingly, had issues at home that they had to attend to. He saw Jong on the beach and slowly walked over to him and said, "Mr. Amazing, I don't know what you did to me, but I want to thank you from the bottom of my heart."

A careful Jong said, "I thought that you loved me and would always be there for me."

"I do love you, and I will take a bullet for you."

"Then why did you try to kill me a few days ago?"

"Oh, stop exaggerating! I would never try to kill you."

Jong looked around and yelled to John Lee, "Hey, Big Country, can you come over here for a minute."

John Lee, hesitantly walked to where the two men were and asked, "What be going on?"

Jong inquired, "You remember the other night when the Sarge attempted to kill me, don't you?"

"I sure do, and I thought he loved you more than any of us."

The Sarge interrupted the conversation and exclaimed, "Would you people stop with the wild tales of persecution!"

John Lee said, "You threw me and Jilkes around like we were paper dolls."

"Okay, I don't remember none of this horseshit you guys are talking about. What is it you're trying to accomplish?"

Jong said, "I'm trying to tell you that you tried to kill me, ask Courtney."

The Sarge held fast for a minute and said, "Okay, I'm going to go and ask her right now. I hope you guys aren't trying to pull no shit on me. I would be disappointed in the two of you if you are messing with my mind."

As the Sarge started to walk away, Jong said, "I took the liberty of having our new plane pick us up for the return trip and invited Mary Alice. Do you see a problem with anything that I have done without consulting you?" The Sarge looked at him and they could see that the big man was about to shed a tear. The Sarge turned around and began to look for his wife, but in the interim ran into his grand babies and decided to play in the water with them and Rashida.

Courtney and Ava were having a fruity drink when Courtney said, "I thought I was going to lose my man the other night. He snapped, and thanks to Jong who slapped him into next week, twice, he came back. I gave him something to help him sleep but it was really close."

"Zanthius told me about that. I was worried as well, but I didn't want to show up at your doorstep asking about my son's father until you felt like having the conversation. I knew what happened, but he's your husband and I knew you could handle the situation. More importantly, I'm glad you are comfortable enough with me to discuss him, our son, our daughter-in-law, Larry, Rashida, and the kids and everyone else that makes up this weird group of people who are trying to do the right thing."

Courtney reached over and hugged Ava and said, "I'll still kill your ass if I catch you messing around with him." The two women broke into laughter and clicked their cups together and continued to laugh.

The Sarge walked over to where Courtney and Ava were sitting and asked, "Is it safe to come over here?"

Courtney asked, "Why wouldn't it be safe?"

"Jong told me that I tried to kill him the other night. John Lee seconded that notion.'

"Honey, you did suspend him from the ground with one hand."

"Not funny, Courtney. What really happened? He's extremely cautious around me."

"Sarge, you were out of it and Jong slapped you back into reality. The shot did the rest."

The Sarge looked at Ava and asked, "What's your input, if any?"

"Oh no, you didn't just cop an attitude with me, Ben Beckmire. I suggest you take ten steps back and come at us again. This is not one of your battles. She is your wife, and I am the mother of your son."

The Sarge saw the two extra cups indicating that they had been drinking for a while and realized that he was about to get his feelings hurt. So, he did the smart thing, he took exactly ten steps to the rear and came back with a smile on his face and said, "Hi ladies, I don't know who that other guy was, but this guy is friendly."

# # #

Later in the afternoon, the Sarge meandered up to Jong and said, "I would like to have a conversation with you about our finances. Are you free anytime soon?"

"You tell me when and I will get my notes and we can discuss them."

"No, I don't need you to have any notes. I just need to discuss what we have in reserve, especially since we purchased that big ass plane. I can't wait to see it; did you name it?"

"Sarge, you can't be serious. I would never be so bold to think that I could choose a name to be affixed to that airplane."

"Listen, I'm sorry about the other night. I don't have a clue as to what was going on and I really don't remember suspending you from the ground with one hand. I need to spend more time with my wife and spread more of my magical powers. I love you man, with full mind and soul, and I would never hurt you. I'm here to protect you as you are me."

"It's okay, Sarge, but I have to admit, I enjoyed slapping the shit out of you." The two men laughed and hugged. The Sarge asked, "What time is our new plane due to arrive?"

Jong looked at his watch and reported, "In approximately two hours."

"I think we should gather the entire tribe, get some champagne, christen the plane, take a ride in it to St. Croix, have dinner, and come back. That's a good idea, don't you think?" The Sarge asked.

"It's a short trip and we could have dinner on a little private island that has a nice establishment called Hotel on the Cay, in Christiansted. That would be a great first trip for our new plane," Jong indicated.

# # #

The Sarge ran into Brown who was sporting a long face. He asked, "What's up, my Brother?"

"Not much, Sarge, just trying to figure out women!"

"Good luck with that one, my Brother. When you do, please hold a professional development class for the rest of us so that we can learn how to deal with them."

"Okema is pregnant and now she does not want to marry me unless her mother is present. I told her that I would buy her a ticket and she screamed at me. She said, 'my mother deserves the honor of your presence to ask her if you can marry her only daughter and you just want to send her a plane ticket to travel to cause me further embarrassment? That is bad karma! I will never marry you. I will slip away in the night so you will never find me because you have created a mountain of shame in my house'. I yelled, 'I thought your daddy already did that one'. Anyway, she wants to divorce me before we even marry because she says I don't respect her heritage or her family."

"Brown, you know what bad seeds can do. Look at your stepfather, he sold you to the streets. I suggest that you take this time to tell her that you love her and that you will personally fly to Europe to pick up her mother on one of our planes. I will ask for volunteers to accompany you, but you take one of those fricken planes and go and get that woman— that's a damn order, soldier. I will inform Jong of the trip and he will make sure that all the paperwork is in order and that her mother can travel legally. We're family and if that's what you want, then we're all in."

Brown looked at the Sarge and said, "I don't know what in the world I would be doing right now if it weren't for you guys. When I'm not around the team, my life seems to be about women, booze, and misery. This is my real life and I hope this thing never ends because I'm afraid that I would end up in a bad place with only one decision to make and you know what that is."

"Brown, we're all in the same box. Have you noticed that no one has mentioned going home for any reason? This is who we are, and it only gets bigger and better, and that's why I'm in no hurry, between you and me, to confront my cousin. I love the fact that we're together, forging new relationships and adding to the number of milk drinkers in the world. Hey, get over her issues. Realize that she is one in a million, and she is carrying your child, Mr. Brown, now how damn crazy is that?"

"Sarge, you are a leader because only the right things come out of your mouth. You resolved my issues, made me smile, and now I'm going to go back to that woman and tell her I love her, I want to go get her mother and bring her here on one of our planes. How perfect is that?"

"You the man, Mr. Brown. I will get in touch with Jong and he will assign a plane to you. I also don't want you going at it alone, so I will have a couple of our friends to attend to the retrieval of the mother-in-law for the wedding ceremony."

"Thanks for thinking out of the box, Sarge. You will always be my leader."

# # #

Yeshida and Somara were both walking around with long faces and refused to share intimacy with their men. John Lee said to Jilkes, "I don't be knowing what I said, but that woman of mine is not talking to me and definitely not providing any nighttime romance."

"Hell, man, I thought it was just me. Mine is saying shit like, 'I have a headache or it's my woman time or I'm tired'. I think what's happening with Okema and Brown is causing this craziness. She's pregnant and wants to be married and I think that's what our two women want. If you just like the sex and not the woman, then pull out before you make her pregnant. This is a conspiracy, and I don't like being played."

"I want to make her pregnant," John Lee confessed.

"Have you lost your damn mind?" Jilkes inquired.

"No, I don't be believing that I lost my mind somewhere. I be thinking that I have strong feelings for that there woman. I want to be with her for a long time and that I would like to have some babies running around chasing my favorite pigs. I'm happy when she's happy, and sad, as hell, when I think that I be making her unhappy. I miss my woman that them there people hung, and I be wanting to make sure that this one is close by all the time." Jilkes listened intently to John Lee and recognized that despite all his machismo, he felt the same way about Yeshida.

He turned to John Lee and said, "Don't ever let anyone talk against your feelings unless they have credible information that should be considered. I love you so much man and what you just described is exactly what I want to happen with my woman, but I guess I'm gun-shy and I don't want to be stepped on again by another woman. I want to be loved and treated like a king and that is exactly how this woman treats me. I need to get over my big ass ego and realize that she is all I want and need. I need to go and tell her that I love her and that I want to go swimming.'"

# # #

Meanwhile, Bernstein and Yvette were simply inseparable--where there was one, the other was not too far off. He had gained her trust and demonstrated to her what a real relationship was supposed to look like and feel like under God. He explained to her that there were occasions when he and team members conducted unholy acts against people who were extremely vile. He stated with commitment that he would always keep her near and safe. She loved him dearly but would often have flashbacks of her forced labor requirements. Courtney had become an extremely important person in her life because it was Courtney who talked to Yvette about what love should look like, smell like and feel like. She was a true inspiration to Yvette, and between Bernstein and Yvette, it was hard to discern who loved her the most.

# # #

The Sarge called the group together and told them that he wanted to take them for a ride on their new airplane. Jong being sarcastic and playing devil's advocate asked, "Why do we need more airplanes. Isn't there a better utilization of resources?"

Under his breath and pretending to cough, the Sarge muttered, "Smart ass! That is a great question, Mr. Jong, even though the purchase of the new aircraft was your idea. I just thought it was necessary for us to have an additional plane to carry our ever expanding family. Please indulge me. Let's just go to the airport and take a ride to St. Croix, another idea of Mr. Amazing, enjoy dinner and fly back. Dinner, by the way, is on Mr. Amazing for doing such a spectacular job and keeping us in the forefront of all that he does. Also, since Mr. Amazing is trying to spotlight me, I want to introduce all of you to Mary Alice who you will meet again once we get to the airport."

In one of the few hangars at the airport, there was a brand new aircraft which had extended leg space and seats that turned into beds. When each member of the team entered the hangar, some of the words uttered were a little raunchy.

As they boarded the plane it was apparent that they had just taken a huge step upwards. The temporary pilots of the plane congratulated the team on their purchase and told them they had just purchased a state-of-the-art aircraft that could do some amazing things. He suggested they fasten their seat belts and prepare to witness the aircraft take-off from the small runway with room to spare.

As the push back tug pulled the aircraft out of the hangar, the captain said, "I will definitely want to know what you name this beauty. By the way, where is Mr. Jong and Mary Alice, the woman we brought down here with us?"

Jong exited the restroom with Mary Alice, and it was obvious that he had been kissing her. He had lipstick all over his lips, cheeks, and neck.

The co-captain came out and checked everyone's seat belt and said, "Enjoy the ride." He entered the cockpit and locked the door. Ten minutes later the plane taxied to the runway and was given the clearance for takeoff. Suddenly the roar of the engines could be heard and felt throughout the aircraft. Then a jolt backwards and bodies were pressed against the seats. The plane raced down the runway and it felt as though, only seconds had elapsed before the plane was off the ground and into the air. People were yelling, "No f....... way, this thing is that fast off the ground!"

As the plane leveled off, the Captain said, "Hate to spoil the fun people, but we are about to start our descent into St. Croix, so please keep your seat belts fastened and we will be on the ground in fifteen minutes. Now, folks, you must admit, that takeoff was funky."

# # #

In St. Croix and on the way to the Hotel on the Cay, everyone on the launch was talking about that amazing, but short, plane ride and how nice the interior was. At the restaurant after drinks were delivered, the Sarge asked for everyone's attention and said, "I think this place is secure enough for me to talk. I want to first of all, thank Mr. Amazing publicly for negotiating this deal at no new net money to us, with five years of maintenance and service included in the cost of the plane. We're also going to give up one of the older planes which will leave us with a fleet of three including the big Croc we just rode in on and those two G650s. What's amazing about this whole notion is that we don't owe a penny on any of our planes. Isn't that right, Mr. Amazing?"

"That is almost correct, the costs associated with owning the fleet is nominal."

"Most of you know that we have become identified as mercs and are considered a group who can resolve most problems. I personally don't like that title because it means that we are for hire, and we are not. We have done a few things to secure and protect the Carbon Factor and along the way, we have stumbled onto untold wealth. I just want to say that we have had a few scary moments, but we are all present and accounted for and have added significantly to our numbers, because we have one mission and that is 'to help people help themselves'.

"I want to officially, welcome the new members to our family--Okema, Somara, Yesida, Yvette and perhaps, Mary Alice. I just want to say that the people who you have found an interest in, and they you, are some of the best human beings God has ever created. I think you ladies are lucky and you guys are equally as blessed because from what I hear, these are some very smart ladies. Unless there are other questions, let's just have a wonderful time bonding with each other and getting to know our 'newbies'."

Beckmire went over to Mary Alice and said, "I really didn't get a chance to meet you, but I hear, and see, my friend is interested in you. If you ask me how I know this, it's because he is covered in lipstick. That is what people were laughing about at my meeting." The Sarge looked at Jong and said, "Please go to the rest room and clean yourself up, dude."

The Sarge made his way over to Courtney and asked, "Did I redeem myself this afternoon?"

She leaned over and whispered in his ear, "I was just getting started when you finished, but I'll let you try to redeem yourself later tonight."

The Sarge looked at her and whispered, "It will be my pleasure to pleasure you, my love." As he kissed her gently on her cheek, his phone began to vibrate. It was Allen who didn't waste any time getting his point across.

He said, "Sarge, the man has come back from vacation and has been cleaning up his house. There have been two suspicious deaths of congressmen and two high powered lawyers who were seemingly connected to everyone. He's cleaning up loose ends and I think you're next. He's of the opinion that eventually, sooner than later, the bits of the Carbon Factor that you haven't given up, won't really matter. Why don't you get that shit off our backs and be clear of this mess?"

"It's quite simple, as long as he doesn't have the entire package then he can't kill me, even handlers have handlers. Allen you're invited in from the cold, but you must be dead straight with me. I did hear that you made the trip on our plane."

"Sarge, I trust you, but, I think, I would lead him directly to you and that would be against the bond we created. No, I want to play where I am on the West Coast, but eventually, work from the sewers and see what I can find out and isolate him so you and your people can end this mess. By the way, I didn't want to negotiate this item, but I found out where he has a shit load of money stored and if you would consider giving me a small finder's fee, I would accept it. Also, if we begin to find his stashes, we slowly create anxiety within him and have a chance to flush him out. I have been told about two locations that might hold between $15 and $30 million in cash. That is considered his play money to buy people with, but I hear his get-out-of-jail-stash is over a $1 billion dollars of stolen money. Listen, you and I must play this man before he gets a lock on us. Our success is probably achieved separately, me working the sewers, and you having the talent to take his ass out once we find out where on earth he is. In the meantime, do you want me to pursue information about where he keeps his money?"

"I think power and money are his only weak points. So, if we remove some

of his money, he loses some of his power. Does that make sense to you?" The Sarge asked.

"It does because if he has no money, he cannot buy influence. I will check with a few other people who are on the run from him and see what they're hearing. I think I met his personal banker. If it is the same innocuous person, then he will give us the keys before we slap him once. I'll be in touch. I'm changing this phone and I suggest that you do the same," Allen indicated.

## CHAPTER THIRTY-TWO

Later, the group boarded their new plane and headed back to their villa in St. Thomas. Jong, the person responsible for such a wonderful experience, was in deep conversation with Mary Alice about what this conglomeration of individuals did for a living and how they could own several airplanes, a thing that was unheard of in her circles. She asked Jong, "Are you people drug dealers or something?"

Jong looked at her and asked, "Do we look and act like drug dealers?"

"I don't know what a drug dealer looks or acts like."

"So, why is the first thing out of your noise maker is, 'are we drug dealers'? Why couldn't we be philanthropists who are interested in making the world a better place to live?"

"If I offended you once again, then I'm sorry. Just realize that I was bedazzled by a person, then raped by him and his friends. I have a right to know what you do for a living because I am magically and instantly curious about you and I have feelings for you."

"I already gave you an idea of our work, as well as showed you that I'm interested in you, by flying you down here on our new jet. Our life is about constant movement. We're always on the go. This place in St. Thomas is one of many, that we have in our organization. We root out the bad guys and help people help themselves, as I already told you."

"What on earth does that mean?"

"Mary Alice, we sometimes have to take a life as well as torture captives to protect innocent people. Let me say a couple of things; my feelings for you are real, but my protection of my friends is powerful. We have a bond that is beyond fracturing. Each one of those guys would replace me in a firing squad and I them."

"I don't know you, but I had the most incredible rush when I laid eyes on you. Yes, I saw you at the farm and wondered why you watched me with so much passion, but with little acknowledgement. We are a close-knit group, and we love each other more than we love others, so that may be a thing that you may want to think about. We have significant information about a substance that is professed to have world changing ramifications. We have seen things and committed acts that in the real world are unacceptable. We are rogue agents of sorts and some people would like to see us terminated."

Mary Alice asked, reflecting on his comments, "My question is simple, you said you move around a lot, how will that impact me trying to develop a relationship with you? I don't know what hit me, Mr. Jong, but I like your very being. I might sound like a fool, but I want to be with you, and I can't explain it in words. Maybe I'll have to show you to convince you, but I'm afraid of relationships and intimacy. I have not sought or been engaged with another man since they stole my life away from me. You intrigue me; your group scares me!"

"Mary Alice, to me, the people in this group are the next thing to Gods that I can see and praise each day. They are willing to sacrifice themselves for me and me for them. We fought in Vietnam together and that is where our brotherhood began, albeit in the midst of chaos and turmoil, initially. We are your best friends if you are a good person, and your worst enemy if you take advantage of people. They are gentle men and women, but each will provide protection for the good of the order and that order is the people that you see here."

"What did you do with the rest of the group that violated me?"

"What did you want me to do with them, Mary Alice? Did you want me to give them a kiss or blow their heads off? Which is it, Mary Alice? Did you want vengeance, and if so, were you prepared to end another human being's life? You need to really consider the consequences when deciding to end another's life, the long-range memories will be with you forever. If you aren't prepared to fall asleep with your victims dancing in your head, then you had better be careful about what you wish for."

"They hurt me, defiled me, and laughed at how tight certain aspects of my body were."

"That was then and now is now! You think about it and let me know. If later you decide you want to have nightmares for the rest of your life, then we will make it happen, but we will use them to do the work on each other; sort of a conspiracy theory."

# # #

As the plane began its descent, the captain reminded everyone to make sure their seat belts were fastened and tight.

Fifteen minutes later, the wheels of the new aircraft touched the runway, and everyone breathed a silent sigh of relief.

The Sarge said to Mallory, "If I wanted to annihilate a group of cockroaches, where is the best venue for conducting such an act?"

"I know exactly where you are going with this and I'm on it. I will speak to Jong and make sure that we have around the clock surveillance on the planes."

"I love it when people are mentally in touch with each other, rather than a whole lot of dialogue having to take place. Did you have a premonition or something that makes you concerned?"

"We have a lot of newness around us. We have new pilots, new lovers, new wives to be and a whole lot of other new relationships, such as Walter our arch enemy, Allen our converted enemy, Mr. Carter, our hotel manager and on and on and on. We have forged new relationships with world powers and have assumed three of their agents in our family. I'm just saying there is a lot of new stuff going on around us. Listen, we started with ten amazing recruits and two non-commissioned officers and I'd like to think that we made a shit load of difference over there in the Nam. Now, we have a damn battalion of unproven people that we have to monitor and protect."

"Sarge, we don't tell you everything, but Jong and I run the works on everyone that is going to hang around from fingerprints to DNA to their social security numbers, or whatever is equivalent. You can't just waltz up in here and feel at home. You have to be scrutinized, sanitized, evaluated, before we sing Kumbaya."

"You guys are the best. I mean you make life so much easier for me by doing the little things that won't let us get hurt. Whose idea was that?" the Sarge asked.

"It was really your indirect idea when you brought Asiram, Zanthius, Ava and her people into the mix. We didn't tell you because we thought you might be offended. We ran background checks on the son you didn't know you had and the sudden appearance of a lost lover who happened to just show up. We knew you were blinded by emotions and guilt. We decided to do the due diligence for you, all the time hoping to keep this secure information from you unless the pieces of the puzzle didn't fit."

"You and Jong should run this operation. The shit you people think of far supersedes my need for information. You people are the real spies along with Zanthius, Asiram, and Larry, but we added Okema, Somara, and Yeshida, spies, as well. Yes, I want a new division created and I want you and Jong to head it up. By the way, did we do a check on Mary Alice?"

"I think she's as crazy as they get, but he's over the mountain top for her. I've thrown things at him, but I'm afraid to announce that there is more motivation than his penis, this dude is head over heels for this lady. I think his problem is that he's trying to make history right by her and it only grows, if you know what I mean. He listens to me but ignores me. I'm not the broker on this one."

"Listen, isolate him with Jilkes and John Lee. They will either kick his ass or commiserate with him, at which point you and I will have a problem. He respects them for their down-home approach to everything and loves them because they kept him alive over in the Nam, a perfect match up. Did you get her prints and other DNA stuff?

"I did and expect to hear something about her, later today or tomorrow," Mallory indicated. I believe in love at first sight, I just don't practice it or accept it. My belief systems versus our people's safety is what is of the utmost importance to me. As a matter of fact, we need to consider delegating different responsibilities to our people. You assume too much of our daily operations, to the point that you don't sleep. You and I have been together a long time and we trained a highly effective group of guys that were the best at what we needed. Even after the fall of Rome and the attempted assassination plots against you, you made all the decisions because we really didn't know what we were into," Mallory professed.

The Sarge started to say something and Mallory said, "For once in your life, give me the opportunity to complete, my thoughts as well as express my feelings. You, my friend, have assumed too much responsibility and you have completely neglected your health. Listen, you and I are as old as dirt, but we look good and feel good because we take care of our bodies. In order to maintain that ability, we must assign certain functions to our people.

"You gave me and Jong complete authority to negotiate with Mr. Christopher Carter as well as figure out the best configuration for a new plane for us. Okay, these are two areas out of your expertise, and you yielded responsibility to someone you trusted. What I'm saying, is that you need to give up more of your kingdom so that the king is only taxed with major issues. He will never be out of the loop, but he need not be engulfed in minutia. This is not a coup, but it is apparent that you are overburdened with responsibilities. This is my private analysis, no one else knows about this and I yield to your superior reasoning," Mallory stated.

"You are such a smart ass, Mallory. After we get data on all the people who make up our tribe, then we start assigning responsibilities from educating the children to health care. I am in love with this idea of yours because I need to spend more time with my wife, or she is going to look for a lover. I can't have that, now can I?"

"She is one fine woman. I would hate to see her leave you because I know the world would not be safe. I know how much you love that woman and personally, I would want to be on another planet if she left you."

"Oh, stop it. It's not that bad."

At that very moment, a voluptuous looking Courtney walked into the room and asked, "What's not that bad?"

Mallory looked at the Sarge and said, "You have got to get a reality check because you are in way over your pay grade, Sergeant Beckmire."

Courtney inquired, "Mallory, what on earth are you talking about?"

"I'm trying to figure out how this guy was able to secure you? Did he spray devil dust or something in the air or did you just find him that attractive or perhaps, bewitching. Just trying to figure out the attraction after all these years."

"Mallory, I know that's 'BS'. The Sarge attempts to use it on me all the time. I believe he thinks I paid for my degrees and did not earn them from those prestigious institutions that were represented on my walls. It's okay because I know he realizes what I have had to do for him, and the rest of you, to keep you all alive."

"I don't know if anyone ever thanks you, but I want to say that on behalf of all those who think you're just another pretty face. I want to thank you for the things that you do, often in conflict with your oath, but for the good of the order."

"Mallory, what is this 'BS' all about? I know when I'm about to be hustled."

"Courtney, believe me, I'm not a part of a hustle and I hope your husband isn't trying to lead you in that direction, either. Okay, I'm going to go and work with the guys to figure out who does what and when. Catch you later, people."

As soon as Mallory left the Sarge's room, he ran into Monica who asked, "Where in the heck have you been?"

Mallory, feeling an impending fire storm replied, "Honey, I've been with the Sarge and I need you to do me a favor and come with me." He gently grabbed her by the arm and led her to the Sarge's room where Courtney answered the door and asked, "Back so soon?"

"My wife apparently was looking for me. I need to provide assurance about where my last resting place was and, therefore, I needed her to hear it from you guys."

"Oh yeah, Monica, he came by two minutes ago and asked the Sarge to cover for him if you happen to come on the scene. Girl, I'm just kidding. These two nuts have been here for a while and besides, where the hell, is he going to go after all these years?"

Monica looked at him and replied, "Perhaps back to the mother of his love child."

There was a significant drop in the noise level volume and the mood of the moment.   Mallory asked, "What on earth are you talking about?"

"I had my assistant go through our mail. One of the pieces that she opened was from a woman in Vietnam claiming that you are the father of her daughter and that the child was interested in knowing about her father and his health."

A dumbfounded Mallory exclaimed, "Honey, I don't have a clue about what you're talking about. I have to at least have the opportunity to review the information before you hang my ass, don't you think?"

"Honey, you got it all wrong. I'm excited about it and want to pursue it to make sure."

Mallory watched as Monica approached him and kissed him on his lips and said, "I love you, dude. If this is true, then perhaps it can at least give you a child since we were unable to make that magic happen. No baby, this is fantastic. It gives me something to do until we solve this Carbon Factor mess that the Sarge's love child created. Before you say anything, being homeless, meeting new people and watching my husband realize how much I love him, his friends, and their mission, is extremely powerful and gratifying to me."

Mallory looked at Monica and said with tears in his eyes, "I don't know what is being said or who is claiming me as a father, but I do know that I have never heard you profess your love for me in words that have meant so much to me. I love you, woman, and always will. If you want to figure out my past transgressions, verify them and make sure that all is correct, then I can't imagine anyone else who I would trust that notion of due diligence with. A lot of things happened in Viet Nam, many I don't remember and some I wish I could forget; we had an ominous job. It was to kill people and have no mercy on anyone in that zone. Our lives were filled with pain because we annihilated people for fighting for their right to live and govern their own land. I'm not proud of a lot of things and I must admit, I had a few lovers, but I didn't think that I created new life there. I'm confused and overly concerned about the timing of the information. Honey, I would appreciate it if you took care of this. I can remember the people I had contact with."

"I guess I will never have a one-up on you, will I?" The Sarge exclaimed.

"Dude, if it's true and if he or she is anything like Zanthius, then I'm all in, just like you were."

Monica looked at the two of them and said, "Grow up, would you? Zanthius, your lovely love child has reunited your team and has led us into world war something and the devil is still chasing our butts. So really, 'all in'? I think not until you have the opportunity to make sure that all is right and assess her interest in this which I will do immediately. Remember who the lawyer is in this family."

## CHAPTER THIRTY-THREE

After leaving St. Thomas, the groups new plane landed at an airport in Maryland. Beckmire pulled Jong aside and asked, "Why do we land in Maryland and have to drive to Virginia, please explain the logic of that, Mr. Amazing?"

"Sarge, the whole purpose is to make sure that we have the best possible chance of an unobvious rendezvous. If we landed in Virginia, then they would look for us at the farm, right? I don't like taking this approach, but we have an unbelievably bad person hunting us. If you want to fly into Virginia, then we can just climb back on board and make our way there. What I didn't tell you is that at this airport, we only must list the name of the plane. Since we don't have a name, this aircraft is titled 'Experimental'."

"Please, don't be annoyed when I ask dumb questions, just shoot me."

"It would be my pleasure, but I happen to love you and what this mission has meant to all of us. We're all together again and it's freaking exciting. If you're finished with that question, I would like to throw another one in your face. We have two G 650s and a new Embraer Jet. We have three sets of pilots, each capable of flying them, but none qualified to fly our new jet. I would like to have a conversation with the new pilots to see what it would take to train them on the new equipment. In the meantime, I placed pressure on the others and told them that everyone has to be able to pilot each aircraft and gave them a timetable."

#

The Sarge's phone rang. It was Allen who said, "I have the coordinates of one of our arch enemy's stashing place. For $25k I can get the other, what's your pleasure?"

"My people have demoted me. I will have to take this issue before a coordinating committee, can I call you back in five minutes?"

"Not a smart move on your people's part, but I respect the notion of democracy. I'll hit you back." The Sarge pondered the information he received from his once nemesis but decided to head to the group and tell them what was up.

As he gathered the troops and began to give his onerous account of what was in store, Mallory interrupted him and asked, "Sarge, what on earth are you doing? Why are you telling us about the details of something that is clearly under your purview?"

"It was my understanding that we had decided to assign certain tasks to people to lessen my load. I assumed the committee was providing oversight over certain decisions."

"What's going on with you? There was no such decision made. The decisions that were made concerned our security, our finances, as well as the screening of our ever-growing family. You are our leader, and you make the decisions about where we go, how much we charge, whether we go and who does what in the field. Our talk the other night was about making sure that everyone is secure and there is not a repeat of what happened to Asiram. Dude, nothing has changed, but we don't want you concerning yourself with every detail when some things such as security, planes, finances, and other items can be delegated. Listen, we're not crazy! We know who led our asses in and out of Vietnam. Why on earth would we want to tamper with our good luck charm?"

"Okay, I get it, but I was thinking that I needed a second person to bounce things off of."

"Look in the damn mirror and answer whatever questions are asked by the person looking from the other side."

The Sarge looked upon the group, smiled and asked, "Don't you people have something to do? Why are you sitting around here wasting time talking to me about bull-crap? I do need to speak with Larry, Zanthius, and Mallory asap. Delay that order; get our primary group, plus Asiram, Larry, Zanthius, and Carlos."

Ten minutes later seated in the dining room at the farm, were the people he requested. Jong said, "Sarge, from a tactical aspect, I think we should include Okema, Somara, and Yeshida because they're obviously another line of defense, as well as offense." The Sarge looked at him and then at Mallory who nodded his approval.

The Sarge said, "Let's have a drink while we wait on them, all except my pregnant daughter-in-law, she can only have water."

# # #

Later, as the three women entered the room, the Sarge welcomed them and asked them to have a seat. He said, "We're going to have a formal ceremony later, but I wanted to be the first to let you know, Asiram, the ranch house has been completely restored and I will kill any person who attempts to violate it in any way in the future." Asiram looked at her father-in-law and broke into tears, between sobs she said, "You restored two of my places, what about the third?"

The Sarge looked at her and answered, "One place at a time, my love. I will make everything that has happened to you, other than your being pregnant, better than it was before. Besides, Rome wasn't built in a day."

Asiram smiled and wallowed over to the Sarge and whispered in his ear, "We have spent a lot of money on things and there really was no rush to restore the places."

"Sweetheart, I am the cause of two of your homes, sorry, three of your homes being demolished. We have, with the help of God, discovered untold amounts of money that have helped us and other people as well. You are my love and probably the most beautiful pregnant woman that I have ever seen, I love you so much." Asiram cried harder and Zanthius walked up to her and escorted her back to her chair.

The Sarge said, "Wow, I love my daughter-in-law, and we all should thank her for the sacrifices that she has made in order to protect and house us. Let's all give her a hand." The group gave her a thunderous applause.

The Sarge announced, "I have to take this call." It was Allen who said, "What's your wish, do you want to buy the other location as well?"

"Consider it done."

"You don't have to talk to your new bosses?"

"I am the boss. Try to be around in the next forty-five minutes so we can discuss details, catch you later."

The Sarge entered the room and found McArthur and Gladstone aggressively facing each other with no one attempting to intervene. He asked, "What in the world is going on and why aren't you people attempting to defuse this situation?"

Bernstein said, "We were just illustrating how you came at Jong a while ago."

"Anyway, I have a play that will probably draw out our cunning enemy, who doubles as my cousin. Our old enemy, and hopefully, a trustworthy convert has the coordinates for two places where Walter stashes lots of money. I want to hit both locations at the exact same time and leave him, if possible, with only, $500. It is thought that there might be $15 to $30 million between the two places. Now, once we do this job, we must be ready for Freddy because he's going to come for us in broad day light with a damn tank. My reason for having you all here, and especially you Asiram, is we can either take him south to John Lee's and Jilkes's new place, fortify your farm, or take him out west where we can smell them coming." Asiram looked at the Sarge with disdain and then whispered something in Zanthius's ear.

Zanthius stood up, tripped over himself, and said, "I'm the woman of this farm, I mean I'm the man of the farm." There was initial silence, then everyone broke into laughter and started whistling and making cat calls.

Zanthius said, "Let me try that again. I'm the man of the farm, not funny Jilkes, and as such, I commit the full resources of all of our assets to this cause." The laughter stopped. After about thirty seconds of silence, John Lee began to slowly clap his hands and was eventually joined in by Jilkes, the Sarge, Yeshida, Okema, and then the rest of the group.

Zanthius said, "We have all benefited from this alliance and it is the most exciting adventure that I have ever been a part of. This is the stuff that little boys and girls dream of at night. We commit all of our resources to this group."

The Sarge walked over to his son, kissed him on the cheek and said, "That was large Son, that was large." He also hugged Asiram who whispered in his ear, "If there is a single broken window, I will employ my trade on you, my Daddy-in-Law."

After the group settled down, the Sarge said to Jong, "I'm going to need as much as $200,000 to provide to Allen for payment to the people who have located the stash houses and to keep him mobile. Have we concluded the business on all of the planes?"

"Sarge, that business is done," Jong stated.

"I'm not sure, nor is anyone sure, of the amount of money that is in each place. Once I have secured the coordinates and we have scanned and walked the area then we will decide when it's a go, if it's, a go. Okema, Brown, and Somara, you guys are our walk about people. Mr. Amazing, can you get body cameras so that their movements can be monitored?"

"Consider it done, but I'll need at least a day to have the products shipped to us."

After cogitating and reflecting for a moment, the Sarge said, "Change of plans. I want this thing to happen tomorrow, people, how do we make that happen?"

McArthur whispered something to Gladstone who in turn stood up and said, "Sarge, I would like to request that you reconsider using the ladies in our walk about because I'm sure their pictures might be on the list from Europe. You must assume that they have all of our records on hand as well. We need a new bee to do the walk about."

The Sarge looked at him and Mallory stood up and said, "Damn good point and you can bet your last dollar that if your cousin has that kind of money stashed then he's going to have the latest information and facial recognition capability to use."

The Sarge said, "I have the perfect people, if they want to play in the game." Mallory hunched his shoulders as if he were waiting for some heavenly input. The Sarge said, "Larry, do you think Rashida might want to get some exercise and,

Jong, what about your new friend? Do you trust her enough to ask her to do some surveillance work for us?"

Larry looked at Jong and was about to respond when Jong said, "I will put the question forward and get back to you within the hour."

Larry said, "Ditto, Pops."

# # #

After receiving the coordinates from Allen, the Sarge gave them to Jong. Later, Jong pulled up the coordinates on Google and enlarged it on a large television screen. He called the Sarge, and Mallory and asked them to come to his room.

As the two men walked over to the newly constructed guest house, the Sarge and Mallory saw a reflection in the distant sunlight. The two men never altered their course nor reacted to the light, but Mallory called Jilkes and reported the incident.

Jilkes called Carlos and asked him where his people were positioned and realized it was friendly cover they saw. Jilkes called the Sarge and said, "It's a part of our new security detail. Plus, they have listening devices with cameras placed all around the farm, but they will not be turned on until next week. From what I've seen, we can hear a hawk coming from a mile away and smell a rat from two miles away, we just need to get it turned on."

Jilkes felt uncomfortable about what he had said to the Sarge and stated, "I'll talk to Jong and make it happen by tomorrow. Sorry, about the lack of attention to an important detail."

In Jong's room, the two men watched in real time as he displayed the location of the first site on a massive screen and then reduced its zoom and showed both sites side by side. Mallory said, "We don't need anyone to do an on-site walk about because if this is true to form, this is as good as it gets. Jong, tell me exactly what I'm seeing at this precise moment."

"Mallory, you are witnessing an evolution and the advancement of technology. Gentlemen, what you are watching is the target area that is in question and the activity that is currently happening as you watch in real time. I took the liberty of playing the activity from the last fifty-five minutes. You will see an astonishing pattern, there are four people walking around the area at all times, on different sides of the street and it looks like cameras are facing every aspect of the buildings."

The Sarge smiled and said, "I like Walter's layout, because if we're successful, I want to stand in front of one of his cameras and put a single dollar under a can and I want the asshole to see me."

"Well, Sarge, it appears that there is enough photographic equipment in the area to catch everyone and everything that comes and goes. What we should try to do is blind the cameras or cut the power. I believe if we cut the power, they will probably have a company of armed people on site in minutes. Let me call my cousins in DC and see if they need to make a few dollars," Jong stated.

# # #

"Later after others were invited into Jong's room, the Sarge said, "I want everyone who is participating in this event to be disguised. Jilkes, John Lee, Somara, and Yeshida, I want you guys to figure out how to make the farm impenetrable. I know we have listening devices and cameras, but everything is not up and working. Check it out, but if someone gets close, I want them to receive extreme resistance."

Jong exclaimed, "You people heard the man, get busy! By the way, I haven't toured the place completely, but did they install a new safe in the basement?"

"I don't know, but Asiram is by the pool, why don't we ask her."

The Sarge and Jong walked over to the pool where Asiram was trying to catch a few rays, he said, "Sorry to interrupt, but we have a simple question, did they install a new safe in the house or tunnel?"

"Frankly, I don't know. Let's take a walk and see. My husband was supposed to outfit the place, but who knows what he did. By the way have you seen him?"

Jong replied, "He and Larry were going to run to the main road and back. That's been a while so they should be returning soon."

As the group entered through the basement door, they began to look at the improvements to the structure. Instead of wood, steel was used as the support beams. What was once a crawl space was now divided into two double rooms with two double beds. Asiram said, "I don't even know if the tunnel is complete and if so how to access it. For safety's sake, why don't we wait for them to return and let Zanthius give everyone a tour? I think we were so anxious to get to somewhere and sleep and relax, we kind of forgot about the essence of our survival, and that is being prepared."

Once out of the basement and with Larry and Zanthius near, Asiram said, "Oh, there they are."

When the two men approached the porch, Asiram asked, "Honey, we were trying to figure out if there is a safe in the house and how to access the tunnel?"

"Well, it's about time someone showed an interest in this place because it is high tech. Okay, I'll show you guys and then you can show the rest of the team. If there are any questions, we can all meet, and I will attempt to bring clarity to all issues. Honey, I didn't want to bother you with the details because all I want you to do is rest. There are escape tunnels that lead two hundred yards into the woods from the east and the west. There is a secure room that can hold forty people with enough provisions to last for three months and it has plumbing.

The tunnel that connects the main farmhouse and the new guesthouse is the way into the escape tunnels. There is a new fire retardation system in place, as well as bullet proof glass, in both houses. There is also a missile detection system that will raise two steel plated barriers to take the initial shock of three direct hits each, before they become ineffective.

Zanthius paused as he studied the crew's approving faces. He continued, "Each tunnel is complete with weapons and munitions as well as a few grenades. Air to the tunnels is provided from two distinct sources both situated at least four football field lengths away from the house and impossible to locate with the human eye. I took the liberty of adding a high-tech surveillance system that differentiates between animals and humans.

There are forty-five listening devices and ninety cameras that record once the sensors have discerned the difference between man and animal. I think we have an open fortress here that does not require us to sleep in the fields, only a single person to monitor the system directly or remotely on his or her iPhone. The barn was tricky in that it was developed to allow the horses complete freedom and refuge from storms. Oh, and by the way, since we now own the property adjacent to us, you know the one where the senator used to live, I have contractors from far away developing a secure tunnel to our new place that can handle a lot of the overspill, in terms of people. It is clear that we all can't fit in these two places comfortably, but once the ex-senator's footprint has been demolished, it will provide us plenty of space."

Jong asked, "How can the system discern the difference between an animal and a human?"

"Animals don't carry weapons and the system looks for any known metal content such as lead, brass or silver."

The Sarge barged in and said, "Impressive, but is it reliable, and Glocks aren't made of metal?"

Zanthius looked at his father and then his wife and said, "My wife and my child, as well as the rest of the crew, are something that I would not throw dice at to get an answer. This thing is backed up, supported and certified, by signals and sensors that protect, not at this time, our most valuable citizen, the President of the United States of America."

# # #

Much later, the Sarge asked, "Mr. Jong, why are we traveling around in those soccer mom cars?"

"Simply because, we don't want to draw attention to our detail. Simple is better and better is simple."

"You are truly, Mr. Amazing, and everyone knows how important you are to us."

"What I like most about those vehicles is that they are bullet proof and that they can save our lives in a battle. Of course, successive hits to the same spot weakens the protection, but the likelihood of hitting the same spot is 1:2000; great odds, if I must say so, not to mention the fact these cars can go from zero to sixty in less than four seconds. They may look like soccer mom cars, but they have the power and the fire power that a group like ours need."

The Sarge continued, "So, in essence, we have bullet proof living arrangements as well as transportation. Good luck with all of these comforts, I prefer to rely on the people I have grown to trust and not blindly depend on any of these protections and contraptions."

"Sarge, these protections and contraptions have significant value because we always have kids and women folk around. These things just make us a little safer, that's all," Jong stated.

"Don't get me wrong, I believe in these things, but I believe in you and the others more than I believe in these artificial products, but they are well received and appreciated. Let's move on. I need you Jilkes, John Lee, along with Somara and Yeshida, to focus on how we breach and secure whatever Walter is hiding in those two locations, and I need this done within the next three hours. I want to simultaneously hit both places. Zanthius, can you ask Asiram if she would like to assist in figuring out how to breach these places? Now, that I know we can withstand a small arms attack, I need to agitate an aggressive family member and make sure that he comes for us. I would like to place all the non-combatants on our new plane, send them to the west coast, and then to my homeland where I know they will be safe. We must draw him out to this place and end this charade."

Jong saw two alerts on his phone and said, "Sarge, here is an example of the security systems capabilities. Okay, let me enlarge the screen on my phone and you will see that the first breach is an animal because the light is green, and the second breach is a human who happens to be driving a metal-based vehicle and carrying a small weapon. It's the caretaker, and if we tap on the image it will give us a clear picture of who it is. Wow, and bingo, there he is."

"That's impressive! Wow."

"No, Sarge, what's impressive is that if he were hostile, I could have engaged any number of weapons systems and cut him in half by tapping the target, engage, clarify, and conclude."

"What do you mean weapons systems?"

"Zanthius, you didn't tell your pops about the weapons systems?"

"You know, Jong, I wasn't going to mention it until we received the suppression devices, but by all means please show him our 'outfield defense systems', better known as ODS'."

"So, Sarge, let me target the caretaker and tap target, then tap engage, and for safety sake, tap clarify. If I hit conclude he would be cut to shreds. We literally have fifteen machine pistols/guns loaded and ready to fire from various angles on the farm. The computer hands the target off to the nearest weapon and within seconds the target is destroyed. We did not want to test them because we didn't want to create the sounds of World War III. We're waiting on air cooled suppression devices and, hopefully, by tomorrow they will be here, and we can field test the system."

"You're telling me that from anywhere on the farm I can target, fire and kill a person?"

"No, we're not telling you that. What we're saying is, from anywhere in the world we can activate and terminate an intruder, all within less than a minute with 100% accuracy."

"That's some real scary shit. Where did you get it from and who installed it?"

"If we told you that, we might have to kill you, but they are never too far away from us and will always be there for us. The installers are my cousins," Jong announced.

"The same dudes that helped us in DC?" The Sarge inquired.

"The very same dudes, as you call them. Also, they custom built those vehicles, and they're not stolen. I insisted that we buy them with real money and in front of real people."

"Son, you were a part of this action?"

Jong profoundly stated, "It was the 'idiot spy' and my cousin's daughter who handled the design and implementation. I only asked the proper questions that you would have asked and made the payment."

"The 'idiot spy' and Mr. Amazing, what a combination. You two get out of here and get back to me on how to breach my cousin's places. If possible, and if we think we can get it done, I would like to engage tomorrow."

## CHAPTER THIRTY-FOUR

The Sarge made a call to Allen who did not answer. He checked the number and decided that perhaps he dialed the wrong number. He dialed the number again and no answer. He looked at the phone, shrugged his shoulders and said to himself, 'damn I hope you're safe'.

Five minutes later, the Sarge's phone rang from a number that he didn't recognize, but assumed it was Allen. The Sarge said hello and Allen began to chide him about paying attention to protocol. The Sarge apologized and said, "For a guy I was about to gut, you sure have a whole lot of shit to say to me."

"For a guy I tried to kill repeatedly, you don't do well with following directions. We have been on this line for sixty-five seconds. Hang up and I'll call you back."

A few minutes later, Jong walked back into the room where the Sarge was sitting and announced, "This call is for you; it's Allen."

A puzzled Sarge said, "Hello, how did you get Jong's number?"

"Sarge, I'm a damn spy and I thought I was a good one until I met you, your band of misfits, and the 'idiot spy'. There is a place near Sears that has clean phones, send one of your inconspicuous types to get a box of them. Use the name Mr. Smith, from Smithville, and we can be in constant communication. Times up, hang up."

The Sarge inquired, "Jong, can you find Larry? I need him and Zanthius to make a run for me."

"Sarge, I can go, plus it will give me some alone time with Mary Alice."

"If I send you, I'm going to have to send someone to cover you. How about I make it possible for you to take her to dinner tonight at a place of her choice knowing that a couple of us will be nearby?"

"Great idea. I'll get the boys, plus Jilkes, and John Lee," Jong stated.

"Naw, Whitmore and Gladstone, I want them to buy us Halloween masks. If you get where I'm coming from. You let me know about tonight. Find out where she wants to go, and I'll have some of your best friends nearby. By the way, how is that going? Do you think you want to bring her into the family?"

"Sarge, I'm in love, but she has a couple of issues related to what happened to her. I don't know how to get beyond that conversation."

The Sarge paused, smiled, looked at Jong and vehemently stated, "Jong, hit it head on! Don't say dumb shit! Say that you will support her and honor her, but she has to honor the new choice that she is considering while selecting options, the future is the only item of relevance; the past is prologue."

"Damn that's sweet. How the hell do you come up with this shit?"

"I feel for each one of you guys. Find out where she wants to eat so that we can either include her in our group or discount her based upon your assessment."

"Sarge, some things might not fit into our pattern, but should be considered."

"It's your choice and only yours. We want you to do, without judgement from any of us, what you think is necessary. Listen, I know you want to make whoopee like the rest of us, but if she ain't right, then she ain't right and you must let her go, like a conejo that grew too big for its cage. I think if you take her to the limits about the issue of now, is now, and that past is an epilogue, then I think you'll find the solution. It's your choice and yours only."

Zanthius walked in on his father and Jong and said, "I think all we have to do is just walk into both places and determine where Walter has stashed his cash. The first site is an old abandoned apartment building that is scheduled for demolition next year around this time, by a company that has direct links to Walter. The second site was an old Italian bakery. Both sites are abandoned and heavily watched from the ground, and by cameras. There are people allegedly working at each site around the clock, but nothing gets removed and nothing gets delivered. So, I'm wondering, what the hell, is going on at each site. I think your cousin is so arrogant and he thinks no matter what he does, no one in their right mind will screw with anything with his footprint on it. Pops, I think this shit is a walk in the park. The only thing we need to take with us is something to empty his money into. My only problem is that I don't want to kill people who are only hired to patrol and guard a place. I would like to stun them first and have our people, from afar, be prepared to conclude them if the stun guns don't work."

"Son, do you really think that guy is that bold?"

"Pops, I'm telling you from the intelligence I've received from people in the neighborhood, it's a shell game played by a very bad dude who will kill your family if you're caught near his property."

#

Jong reported, "I got dinner plans for tonight, but I must tell you that inadvertently, I was told that your cousin has a place thirty-five miles from here under an assumed name."

"What does that mean, under an assumed name?"

"Sarge, your cousin has a place down the road with two women who are lovers. It's alleged that he ventures there from time to time to watch them take care of his farm, if you know what I mean."

"How can a single person control, and be a part of, so many nefarious venues? Doesn't the government have any oversight over its employees? This is insane! This guy has more shit attributed to him than there are windows in the White House. I can only conclude that my cousin is like a part of the Constitution and, each President inherits him like the FBI did with J. Edgar Hoover. This dude is sanctioned."

Jong stated, "If that's true, we need to back off and disappear. We can't place a hit on a sanctioned individual. That's above our pay grade."

"Jong, he wants to get us and our families in his crosshairs. I think the Constitution needs another amendment. We aren't your normal mercs so when we call this dude out, we had better be ready to take on the antichrist. I'm not sure we can match his resources and wit."

"Pops, we may not be able to match his resources, but his wit, well, I'm up for the challenge because throughout this issue, he has made so many tactical mistakes that we have learned from. Now, his resources are another thing, and I agree, we are not a match for them. However, this property is secured by a system that mirrors the Aegis Weapons System that was played around with at General Electric Company and finally developed by its subsidiary, Lockheed Martin. If I had to present a combat scenario to you about an invading force, I would have to state that if four hundred men divided equally from the north, south, east and west attempted to breach this property, there would be four hundred dead bodies, concluded by technology. Sarge, our weapons have the capability of targeting and concluding a vast number of hostiles. It's an amazing system, but its downside is that if you press the conclude button, then that is exactly what will happen. No matter the number attempting to breach the property; all will be slaughtered," Zanthius said.

The Sarge asked, "Now, is this the technology that we have at our fingertips?"

Zanthius answered, "It's beyond technology, it becomes a moral issue that we have to be willing to deal with. Your cousin doesn't give a shit. We do, and that is why it's important that we make sure that all of us are on board with this technology and security. We can kill a shit load of people. The question is whether or not our minds and souls can handle and reconcile those we have concluded?

"Pops, this place as well as the ranch out west are fortresses. If you come here to place us all in a tube and then burn us, there are consequences to the invaders. There is a shitload of C-4 in secure compartments in case the decision is made that we are concluded. If there is consensus that our lives are over and that is the only alternative, then we push the little red button three times and hear an explosion that supersedes the hearing capacity of most humans," Zanthius stated.

"You guys sound like dooms day peddlers. If we're under attack, do you think my soul will sit back and pray over each person that I kill? I think not! If you come for me, you had damn better be ready for anything that I can throw at your ass. This is not a try out gentlemen. We made this commitment and if we are to survive it, we must be the aggressors who give no quarters. This shit is real, and one mistake and we're all gone, including the babies. Why haven't we tested the systems?"

"Pops, we're in the country, not in another country. We have neighbors and until we get suppression devices, we dare not fire those things. The noise level would sound like an invading force firing their weapons simultaneously," Zanthius indicated.

# # #

Asiram, Jilkes, John Lee, Somara, and Yeshida all concurred that both sites of Walter's appeared to be easy targets and that there would be minimal loss of life for those guarding the place. The one thing that concerned them was that everyone knew that Walter never played by the rules and, therefore, wondered if he had the places rigged to explode. The group reported this information to the Sarge. The Sarge decided to call Allen on one of the new phones and said, "Allen, I don't like to threaten anyone, especially you, so I'm going to ask you straight up; is this a set up?"

There was a pause on the other end of the phone and Allen replied, "Mr. Beckmire, you and your people bested me, my people and spared my life. My family is in hiding, and the only way I exist is through the crumbs you throw my way. Walter is a snake and a protected one at that. He has people looking for my family with a kill order. Do you think I would deceive you and play ball with a guy who is known to end relationships without a reason? Mr. Beckmire, I need the commission for providing you the information about the two premises that are alleged to hold cash. I haven't been there, and my sources are underground as well, because they too are on his hit list. You are the only people I trust because you are not in this mess for the money or for power. You were dragged into this unbeknownst to anyone by the 'idiot spy'. I'm desperate, but you saved my life from a torturous death. I pledged my loyalty to you, and on my children's lives, I swear to you that I am legit and trustworthy."

"Damn man, you went from 'A to Z' on a simple question. I will be sending my people on those missions. I hate to have to come and find you and yours if this thing is contrived. You understand how important my tribe is to me. Okay, on another matter, if you need cash then let me know. I know your accounts are probably being monitored, so banking for you is off limits. If you need a million now and let's say 20% of what we can gather from those places with a cap of $5 million, then I think we have a deal. After all, I want to draw him out for a finale. When you mess with a man's money, he's subject to do anything. Plus, we are the extractors, and you should earn a finder's fee to cover your costs."

"Sarge, back to the other question. I have little left and until he is dead, I am living in sewers and eating things out of cans that I don't know about. I am a bum and homeless, but where I live there are some good people who are down on their luck. If there is any way you can manage to provide some type of job or character building training for these guys and gals, that is more important to me than trying to find a place to stash a million dollars."

The Sarge said, "Well, I'll be damned, the senator is calling me. Hit you back."

# # #

"Senator, so nice to hear from you."

"Listen, we can pay you any amount of money you want for the balance of the product, but we cannot be a part of providing you with a civil servant that does his job extremely well. The Russians are preparing to do their third test of the Carbon Factor, and we haven't attempted our first, because you patriots are trying to figure out who the good guys are and where the bad guys hang. Listen, you don't want to incur my wrath, so I suggest you give me the remaining parts of the formula for the Carbon Factor without conditions."

"Senator, I respect your position, but I do not respect the fact that a certain civil servant has you in his pocket. Now, before you begin to scream, let me attempt to calm you. You have received many benefits from this so-called civil servant who is actually a sanctioned individual who is allowed to corrupt and kill individuals at his discretion. I hope your phones are tapped because I'm going to call his name out; Walter, is a bedeviled individual who you, nor anyone else, can control because he has video, audio and records of you taking bribes and offering favors, and in essence, selling your office. Now, the thing you might want to consider is how we find a global network to disseminate your shenanigans to the world. So, let's start this conversation again, but this time, I will set the agenda. Are you still on the line?"

"I am here."

"Let me start by saying there is an apparent function for the Walters' of the world, but there is also a timeline and lifeline that should be placed on their existence. Our purpose in this whole equation is not to support stupid, but to encourage fairness. On many venues you have not been fair because you have been handled by Walter and his handlers. We think we can help you by eliminating some of your stress. We also believe that most of your stress emanates from a sole source—Walter. That son-of-a-bitch tried to kill my family including my grandbabies. I'm going to catch him, but not release him. I'm going to cut him into small pieces and fish with his flesh. Your problem is that you gave him the authority to conclude my family, which makes you a target for me as well. Senator, if necessary, we'll execute a $10 million bounty on your head and his, as well as your families. Yes, I'm saying it over this medium because you have succumbed to people of ill repute. It is clearly your choice, but you have to be prepared to have a new handler, a person that you might personally know who will, at least, not influence you to do wrong, but provide you with consensus information and not dictatorial demands. Senator, this is not a negotiations session. This is a picture of you about to be unveiled to the entire world. If you think I'm blowing smoke up your ass, then take your best shot. We have records, purchase documents, salaries, and they don't add up to what you earn or steal as a United States Senator, oh and not to mention a video of you with the now deceased senator and a congressmen. Your choice."

"Can we meet in public?"

"I don't advise such a thing, but if you want to meet in public that's on you. Just remind yourself that I'm not the wizard. I'm his apprentice. If you think that my demise concludes what is available, then you're really a stupid person and we will make your death simple and horrid."

"Are you threatening a sitting US senator?"

"Not at all. You have admitted that you are mentally unbalanced and that you want to end your life in a dramatic fashion. Listen, you are fooling with a group of people who

have killed so many people that we can't count. If you think
that you might be safe if we're terminated, then you're wrong.
We have a $10 million insurance policy on your head from a
group of Russians that we resurrected from the dead and a $5
million policy from our Far East friends. Don't screw with us
if you want to see tomorrow. Senator, you have one hour to
consider your choices, or attempt to circle your wagons.
Remember one thing, this can be private or over the internet
and, in each case, you will look like Walter's bitch. By the
way, we have several pictures of you in compromising
positions. I can send you a copy over this unsecured medium,
it's up to you."

"I will contact you within the time frame you proposed.
Please do not do anything to incriminate me, give me a chance
to have further dialogue," the Senator pleaded.

# # #

The Sarge decided to call Allen back and when he
answered, Allen asked, "Shit, what was that about?"

"She threatened to throw down her wrath on me."

"Get the hell out of here. She can't be serious. Did you
tell her about all of the substantiated information that you have
about her, her finances, her ethics and her lovers?" Allen
asked.

"I casually mentioned those things to her. She asked me
not to do anything to incriminate her until she had a chance to
get back to me. I think she needs to cool down from that hot
flash I just gave her ass. I told her it would be necessary for
her to have a new handler that was a little more pro-democratic
and a little less prone to kill people who didn't agree with
him."

"Do you have anyone in mind?"

"I do. I thought I would ask one of my loyal associates to take over the role, when we terminate my cousin. I thought about someone who was on the fringes of our organization but decided against it. I really want her to exercise her judgement without political influence from the left or the right. Allen, can I trust you to phase yourself out of that job once we clean up all of her shit?"

There was a long pause and Allen replied, "Don't mess with me, are you serious?"

"I believe you can fill a totally different role until her shit is cleaned up and disposed of. Can you handle it? Your question to answer is, how many other people have you pissed off and can you make amends?"

"I have done a lot of bad shit and I don't want to be back in that arena. I like working with you and in the sewers to help people. My wife has a new lover. I am okay with that. My daughters are relatively safe, but I really want to try to get some of these people who are down on their luck out of these sewers," Allen acknowledged.

"I think you made a wise choice because you can operate without protection and help other people. That is all we wanted to do until someone tried to kill my son, my entire family, and friends. Allen, I know exactly where you are and can reach out and touch you at any time. We placed a sensor in your body that we track by the hour. Sorry, guy, but you were not always our friend."

"I know, but can we meet so that you can get this shit out of me?"

"Do you want to be a part of the siege on Walter's places?"

"Sarge, I don't think that's a good idea because he may offer me a deal once he is attacked. If so, I can be your ears and eyes on issues such as where the hell he is. I want to leave it as is and learn more about what is happening to everyday Americans who fought for this country, but seemingly received the raw end of the stick. Now, I will admit there are a few basket cases down here and in other parts of the city, but by and large, these people are down on their luck. You should come down and hear the extent of their reasoning and conversations, a lot of powerful ideas down in those holes."

"You have a date and hopefully soon. Guess who's calling me at this very moment?"

"Let me know the content. Take care, Sarge."

The Sarge took a deep breath before answering the phone, "Senator, nice to hear from you again. I hope we will be civil and work on those issues that compromise the both of us."

"I'm here to attempt to offer a solution that everyone can exist by."

"Do you mean live by?"

"You may use whatever word you like. It appears to me that we are playing on three different ball fields at the same time--the international one, the local one and the one that keeps me from doing my job without a threat, the underworld one. I'm going to embarrass myself and tell you what you have pictures of as well as video. If I'm not mistaken, you have pictures of me in bed with both women and men, including the dead senator. I am going to give you a couple of options because once this goes viral, my husband is going to kill me and himself. I don't need another master, but I do so desperately want to get rid of the one I have. You are correct, he has me in his pocket and threatens me every damn day. I want to go home and tell my husband, who is ill, that I have been compromised and that I'm ready to check out and it's all over."

"Senator, I don't want you ending your life, or your career and leaving your children scarred for the rest of their lives. You work with me to capture that vessel of ill will and I will handle his complete demise. When I say demise, I mean there will be no DNA left of the person. As a matter of fact, I am going to extract his soul from his body and take it to a magical place that you wouldn't understand."

"Mr. Beckmire, I want peace! I want to complete this term if possible, without any more threats. More importantly, without a handler and I will also drop out of the race for the highest office in the world, the Presidency. That guy invited me to a party, then he and his friends molested me and took incriminating pictures when I was under a drug induced state. Why I'm telling you this, is without reason to me because you and I are not on the same page."

"Senator, we can be on the same page and attempt to receive the same benefits if you decide to play ball with me and assist me in eliminating the cancer that has you under its control. I have, and my people have, nothing against you, even though its alleged that you authorized the suicide vests for my grandbabies. I recognize you as the vessel by which my evil cousin operates with impunity. We want him, not you. We do not want you to drop out of the Presidential race. We can clean the slate for you, and no one will know or have any data that incriminates you."

"Let me consider the consequences and recalibrate my mental stability. I will give you a heads up and tell you that he's employing people from far away to come here and conclude all that exists in your life and before your very eyes. He is a sick person and one who is without any remorse. He made, and I'm not proud of this, another senator screw me in front of cameras while I was in a comatose state. He is the epitome of evil. I also think I know where he keeps his records, and a lot of cash so I hear, but it may be conjecture."

"Where might that be? We heard of two of his places yesterday that have $30 to $40 million. That kind of money sure could help our Vets living in sewers to retool their skill sets."

"I was thinking more in the neighborhood of $250 million or better."

"Senator, if we extracted that kind of money from him, he would first come for you and that would be ugly because he knows about our negotiations in relationship to the Carbon Factor. How do you know where he keeps his cash?" There was a silence on the phone that the Sarge broke, by saying, "I think I understand."

"You couldn't possibly understand, Mr. Beckmire. The things he personally did to me are unspeakable. He violated me on so many different fronts that it is hard to look in the mirror sometimes and I just want to kill him and myself at the same time."

"Senator, I am going to violate Walter like no man has ever been violated. In ways and times that you couldn't possibly understand. My cousin's head will eventually be miniaturized, and a bone placed between his lips to seal his evil forever. You can count on that. By the way, to change the subject, an old Russian comrade of mine has indicated to me that the formula they are trying to recreate is in shambles because the original manifest was transferred from one computer operating system to another. In the process, the files were scrambled. I think they are blowing smoke.

"I would like to table the conversation about those funds until I have had a chance to consult with my crew. That's a lot of ill-gotten money. Let me say one other thing and then I will let you go. Senator, my cousin Walter is the devil, Lucifer, diablo, a whole bunch of other names and I'm going to have his soul. He is from the deepest parts of hell and is out to control and will destroy all that is good. His problem is that I am his nemesis and ordained to end his miserable life as well as extract his soul from his body.

"I know you don't believe in hocus pocus, but Walter and I are descendants of the Aborigine people from Australia. He is defined as a bad spirit. I am the person who puts his soul in a bottle and buries it so deep that no mortal or animal will ever see or witness his evil.

"I will send you another aspect of the Carbon Factor for analysis, but the final piece will not be delivered until Walter's soul has been extracted from his body by me and buried. Your payment will be made in the form of a sole source proposal to develop training programs for veterans, former police officers and people who are down on their luck. It will be sent to you from another former foe by the name of Allen. Nice to hear from you. Your admissions, to me, are as private as if you spoke to yourself in a dream and recaptured what had happened to you from the individual who is the antithesis of evil. You are on break, and therefore, you aren't required to speak about anything. Stay focused and develop all your strategies because your competition is ruthless, a thief, a liar, and he has no idea about foreign policy and hates everyone who doesn't look like him. I hear the Native Americans want all of us out of their country. Good day."

## CHAPTER THIRTY-FIVE

The Sarge said to Mallory, "I want you to divide our forces into two groups. I want to put our non-combatants on planes, and out of here for the next week or two. What are your thoughts?"

"I like the idea because if Walter tried to kill the women and children once, he damn sure won't hesitate to try it again. I say we load them up and ship them out before we attempt to breach the two sites. That way we won't have to worry about them if this thing goes south on us."

The Sarge looked at him, rubbed his chin, and said, "You're right. With them gone we can focus on the mission, lead the trail back to the farm, and get ready for his onslaught. If these sites do hold his cash, then he's going to be mad that I took it and he will want to come and take it back and get revenge, at any cost. So, I'm thinking one of two things here, it may not be that significant to him or it may be his way of finding out where to hit us. I really can't discern what motivates this dude. The senator talked about a more lucrative site that is alleged to hold as much as $250 million. Can you believe this mess?"

"Sarge, I think we both realize that it ain't about the money because he apparently has enough of that stored around the world to pay off and control his many bribes."

"You're absolutely correct, but how dare we take from the king? This will cause him so much anxiety that he will want to erase the name of Beckmire from the books, I guarantee you that. He's a sick person, so we must assume that there is nothing that he won't do. On another note, I think we need to mark this property with proper fences and signs."

"Talk about moving from A to Z in a matter of seconds."

"I mean we have added the former senator's property and we should have topographical images of what we own and its boundaries, don't you think? I mean records are the things that keep you out of trouble, right?"

"I will speak to Mr. Amazing and let him figure it out," Mallory replied.

"I'm going to speak with Courtney, and you can speak with Monica and let's place them in charge of orchestrating this trip abroad until we have settled this matter with the devil. I don't want them near, I want them safe."

"I agree and I think if we breach his places, he's going to have an ego attack that will hopefully cause him to make poor decisions and we can capitalize on his anger. I can only imagine him saying some shit like, 'how dare he'," Mallory stated.

"Cute, but I have mixed emotions about my resolve on this asshole—do I want to cut his arms to the elbow off, legs to the knees off, and gouge out his eyes; or do I just want him dead and in small pieces. I want to spread him from the east to the west and in the deepest part of the water. This man is as evil as they come and nothing is sacred to him, nothing," the Sarge noted.

The new phone that the Sarge received rang and he answered it by saying, "Hello, this is me. Who is this?"

"Cute, Sarge, it's Allen. I told the people who provided me with the information that if this were a bad deal that their entire bloodline would be wiped from the annals of history. I suggested they go up the line and make sure that everyone realizes that poor information is a death sentence."

"Allen, I need you to chill out. I am going to send in my best people; however, all my people are the best of the best. They will discern if they have been compromised or not and will let me know. I trust you Allen because we have a common enemy. As a matter of fact, the people who have the fancy titles seem to need someone to control them and make them rich at the same time.

"If you happen to pass our mental fitness exam, as well as our other tests, I think that I would like to install you as Walter's replacement unit. The only thing you must remember is, what's going to happen to Walter, if we're successful. I am going to cut him into tiny pieces and fish with his ass or decapitate all functional limbs. I will not relent on my passion to kill him or leave him as a shell of a human, in the worse possible way," the Sarge announced.

Allen concurred, "Sarge, I think we all want him dead in the most despicable manner."

# # #

The Sarge entered his room and could sense that Courtney knew something was about to go down. Courtney, without provocation said, "If you think I'm going to get on a plane and hide while you do battle, then you are really a stupid man. Don't bring the subject up to me because I am not going to leave. Where you go, I go, and at the same damn time. So, do yourself a favor, unless you want to be abused, let it go Romeo. Not leaving, not hiding and will be armed."

"Hi, honey, how are you? You appear to be a little tense. Is there anything that I can do to lessen your stress? I wasn't about to suggest you leave my side while I'm in battle. I was going to ask you to conduct shooting practice with the other women."

"I'm a doctor and sworn to save lives, not to end them. However, if anyone comes up on this farm with a weapon, then I will fire on them with the purpose of terminating their life. We have children here, and we will die trying to protect them."

# # #

Mallory entered his room and Monica asked, "Are you here to talk about your love child?"

"No, sweetie, I want to talk about you leaving the compound with the other women, for a while, until we settle this matter with Walter."

Monica smiled and said, "I can't seem to find it! Have you seen it?

Mallory asked, "Sweetheart, what can't you find?"

"My dearest husband, I think you have lost your mind and I'm trying to find it for you. I am not going to yield to my pacifist side while my husband is fighting for his life! It ain't going to happen. If you think I'm going to get on one of those planes with those other women while you're fighting, you have got to be crazy. I'm not going anywhere, and I will be carrying a pistol full time from this point forward."

"Monica, you don't know how to handle a pistol let alone face someone coming at you with a pistol."

"Sweetheart, I'm not going anywhere, and as of tomorrow, I will become proficient in the use of a pistol. I'm not leaving, so don't come to me with stupid. The only thing I want to discuss right now is your love child and how we confirm the identity."

"Well, what can I say when my woman tells me what she's not going to do? Do I say, 'Oh please, my love, go with the rest of the women and wait until I call you to come back?' I don't think so. I want you to remember that scene in the Italian Bistro when Malik was killed. This next aspect of our life is going to be extremely bloody because our foe is either the devil or his favorite son. We are going to be under siege and his goal is to annihilate everyone and everything connected to this group. I want you to go with the other women until this thing is over."

"Honey, I asked you not to come to me with stupid. I'm not going anywhere. As a matter of fact, I don't think anyone is leaving the compound, including the children. Just saying, but you might want to check into that."

# # #

Mallory called the Sarge's room and Courtney answered the phone. He asked, "May I speak to your husband, please?"

Courtney snapped, "No, you may not, he is getting his ass chewed out for thinking that I'm leaving with the kids for somewhere safe while he takes on his cousin. Has he lost his mind? I'm not going anywhere. Tomorrow, Asiram is conducting shooting practice for all the women. You can try him back in an hour if he's still alive at that point. Goodbye, Mallory."

Mallory passed Jilkes and John Lee in the hallway and Jilkes said, "You seem like there is something wrong."

"Yeah, there is, my wife won't listen to reason."

"John Lee, write that down on our list of things to discuss with our ladies. Really, Corporal? You expect to be listened to? First, is it private or can we discuss what's going on?" Jilkes asked.

"Naw, it ain't private. I want her aboard one of our planes with the other women and fly somewhere safe until we finish our business with Walter. She asked me if I had lost my mind. Now, they're talking about target practice in the morning."

Jilkes said, "Yeshida, Okema, and Somara are going to instruct them in the use of handguns, shotguns, assault rifles, and knives. We had better have the emergency medical people on standby tomorrow." The three men broke into laughter.

John Lee said, "I think it be better if they know how to shoot than to be hung like my woman was." The mood turned somber and Mallory focused on what he had just heard and interjected, "We can't protect them when they are far away, can we?"

John Lee said, "I be thinking we need to take this here thing serious and show up for practice and assist in the process. I be thinking that it will be a wise thing for all of us to do. Perhaps we should suggest that we show them how to clean the weapons, take them apart and the whole school on this here is my gun, always love it and secure it . We got them there children around and we best be securing all weapons, or we be having a problem on our hands. I also be thinking that we only provide them with weapons that have safeties on them, like the Smith & Wesson, and not them fancy Glocks," John Lee stated.

"Who's the lead on their training team?" Mallory asked.

"I think it might be Courtney."

"Courtney? Oh shit, no wonder the Sarge can't answer the phone. She is kicking his big ass. He won't be able to put her on a plane and send her anywhere, just like my wife."

# # #

Later that evening, Mary Alice and her people showed up with a spectacular buffet for the group. As her people set up the warmers and tables, Asiram said to Zanthius, "This is so much easier than us trying to fix a meal every night. I mean lunch is easy enough--hamburgers, fries, sandwiches, and fruit is so easy to prepare." Zanthius appeared to be preoccupied when Asiram said, "Earth to Planet Zanthius."

"I'm sorry, dear, I was just remembering some things that happened while my dad and I were in the outback. Listen, I know you heard the latest rumblings about you women getting on a plane and heading for a safe haven until this thing with Walter is over. What's your take on that?"

"Honey, the only thing I love as much as you is this baby that I'm carrying. If you think because someone is out to kill us that I'm going to leave the 'idiot spy' to fend for himself, then you are wrong. I'm not going anywhere and where you go, I go. Did I state that clearly enough for you, love, or do I need to repeat it?"

"Naw, Baby Girl! Your intentions are as clear as the night sky and as precise as the rising moon. However, I want to say something on the subject. I can't protect you from afar and I didn't do such a great job protecting you underneath me, but I think that from all that I now believe in and what I was confronted with in the outback, we're going to be alright. I need you near me and not far away. I support your notion of fighting to the end alongside your man."

"Did I say all of that? Kiss me man before I sit down and can't get back up."

#

The Sarge called Mallory and said, "I heard you called, and I heard you got an earful from my wife. I've moved on from that discussion and I have nothing further to say about it. If you have some other business, then go for it."

"Meet me in the sitting room for a drink. I think we both could use one."

"Now, that is something I can do, be down in a few minutes." In the background Courtney yelled, "I bet you're going to have a drink, aren't you"? Mallory hung up the phone and thought, 'Wow, he really got his ass kicked'.

#

At a table in the corner, in her sitting room, a voice could be heard saying, "Hey Daddy-in-Law, you look as if you got a tongue lashing or something? Do you want to talk about it with your favorite, pregnant daughter-in-law?"

The Sarge looked at Mallory and asked, "Do you remember in the jungle when we didn't have those people with those once a month issues that turned them into demons?"

"Sarge, can you imagine if one of them demons heard you say such a thing?"

"I know, it's not right and it doesn't reflect who I am, but damn, today has been a kick the Sarge's butt day and only by women. I must go and be further humiliated by my pregnant daughter-in-law, who by the way, I love so very much because she is definitely a cross between a guy and girl in terms of doing the kinds of things, we do so very well. Don't go away. I'm going to call you over and see if Ms. Smarty Pants has an answer on how to breach those sites."

As the Sarge meandered over to where Asiram and Zanthius were sitting he said, "Son, I need you to get lost for a few minutes while I have a frank and honest conversation with your wife."

"Pops, that's rather harsh and I can't let you upset her. Why are you putting me in this predicament?"

"Son, I'm just blowing smoke and I would never cross this woman. Anyway, she's good at her trade. So, my sweet, and pregnant, Daughter-in-Law, how can you be of assistance to us?"

"I want you to know Daddy-in-Law that I had nothing to do with the rebellion that you and the rest of the men folk endured. They drafted me, but I wasn't going anywhere anyways because I don't seem to be able to do those long flights well anymore."

"Are you sure you didn't orchestrate this rebellion? It has your fingerprints all over it."

"Really, I didn't. I want to tell you something that I have been thinking about lately. I accused you of destroying three of my homes, but it really wasn't your fault. Those people had me on their hit list, as well as the 'idiot spy' and if it weren't for you and your friends, I, as well as your son, would be dead. I never took the time to thank you guys. I guess I just got caught up in the notion that everything I owned was going up in smoke in front of my eyes. It was when I first realized that the 'idiot spy' had impregnated me that I found out what was important in this world and it sure wasn't a bunch of buildings, scattered all over the place, nor money stashed wherever. It was about family and community.

"As a spy, I have been everywhere and have seen almost everything, but I have never experienced love and community as I have with you people. You're my hero, Sergeant

Beckmire, as well as my Daddy-in-Law. This has been one helluva a ride and I'm on this roller coaster to the very end—no matter what that is." Beckmire was bawling his eyes out as was Zanthius when, between tears, Courtney walked over to the table and asked, "What's going on? Are you in pain, do we need to get you to the hospital?"

A crying Asiram answered, "We just had communion without you, but you were included in our prayers. My daddy-in-law will fill you in later, but it was the best spiritual feeling that I have ever had, and it was about love and community; this community and this kind of love. Look at the grown men crying their eyes out over love and community. That's why I'm not going anywhere because they need my help."

"Well, girlfriend, unless they want to waste fuel on an empty jet, they need to forget about making arrangements." Courtney stared at Asiram for a moment and said, "You know I've been watching you, and your diet is problematic for me. You are pregnant and the baby needs to eat. You need to forget about those little 'boom boom' bathing suits you purchased in Rio. To me you have two choices--try to produce a healthy baby or one with issues. We need to change your diet; you need to eat for two and stop picking around food."

"I know, but it has only been lately that I've enjoyed food. Mary Alice's food has been the bomb and I did eat, but in the beginning of the pregnancy I couldn't keep anything down."

"Eating is a process and not a competition. Eat as little as you like but eat frequently."

"You're scaring me, Courtney."

"No, darling, I'm making sure that my grandbaby is given every opportunity to be healthy, and nutrition is the key to that outcome." The Sarge saw an opportunity and asked, "Did you happen to figure out how we can breach those two facilities, if I can change the subject for a minute or two?"

Courtney gazed at him and then Asiram, and said, "I will back off if you think I'm too aggressive, but I know what is needed."

Asiram stood up and said, "You will have to spend more time with me and maybe you can draw Ava in as well. I didn't think that you two ladies cared for me. At least I know that you are genuine and have legitimate concerns. I have never been pregnant before and it scares the shit out of me."

"Oh baby, so much is going on around us and I must admit that I thought you were a little stand-offish. I think your other mother-in-law feels the same way as I do but she thought it best to let you reach out to us if you needed to. I guess we all need each other. Zanthius, call your mother and ask her, no tell her, to come down here now."

Ten minutes later, as Ava and Carlos walked hurriedly into the lounge area, Ava asked, "What's wrong? Asiram, are you okay?"

Courtney replied, "Ava, Asiram was under the impression that we didn't like her." Ava fell to her knees and began to gently hug and kiss Asiram's stomach. Courtney watching this action said, "Hell, I'm not going to let you get one up on me, Ms. Lady." She too fell to her knees and placed love kisses on Asiram's stomach.

Courtney said to Ava, "She's not eating well, and we have to help her get through this with a healthy baby. Listen, I don't have a problem with anyone here, I love you all and my husband loves you all and this will be our first baby born in our community. Between us and the fencepost, I hear Okema is in a motherly way. All praise to God and his divine wisdom."

#

Mary Alice rang her dinner bell, and everyone showed up like flies on watermelon. Courtney said to Mary Alice, "In the future, please place a card in front of each item listing ingredients and seasonings used to prepare each dish. We have a few pregnant women with us, and we don't want any food allergies to impact their successful birthing."

Mary Alice said, "That's great news and I only use organic substances with few additives, but I will have my people make detailed content cards for all items offered ."

"Do we have a contract with you?"

"No, Mr. Jong just calls and asks me to prepare dinner for X number of people."

Courtney looked around the room for Jong and when she saw him, she motioned him over to her. Courtney asked, "Jong, how do we make her business exclusive to us and what protocols can we set in place to determine if she has been compromised?"

Jong looked at Courtney and Mary Alice said, "Let me get this straight. You want to know if someone attempted to poison the food. How would we know?"

After the fact, the answer is obvious Jong, that's precisely what I'm asking. By the way Mary Alice, Mr. Jong is madly in love with you. Sorry, Jong but get over it. She is madly in love with you, as well, but I need to know how we can protect our tribe from issues relating to food. After all, it's an easy way to do damage to a group as large as this one. Does it make sense for us to randomly select vendors or should we put our faith in the hands of a sole source contractor?

"Mary Alice, I would like you to bring us a proposal detailing how you can keep us safe. You know your people, but we don't, therefore, this should be Jong's first concern. I acknowledge the fact that he's probably thinking with his little brain, which is okay, but it can be dangerous if it's the only brain being used. I would like you to come out here tomorrow and provide me with the ways you can provide quality food, as well as protect us from contamination. I hope I have not been too offensive, but we have a lot at stake here. You know some of it, but it's important that we know who you deal with and how they can impact our very being. Is that possible to accomplish? Perhaps if we ordered from distributors and it was shipped here and your people came out to prepare it, maybe that too could be considered."

"I will be here tomorrow with a plan and a few ideas to protect and secure the group that is drawing me in on so many levels." She looked at a bedazzled Jong who was speechless.

"Thanks, give us a call in the morning to let us know when to expect you."

Jong asked Mary Alice, "Are we going to dinner after you finish here?"

"I thought we would enjoy the food here and take a ride around the farm in the mule, just enjoy nature and talk. Is that okay?"

Jong looked at the night sky and said, "My pleasure is your pleasure, whatever you want to do is great with me. I have just one task that I must attend to before we take a ride."

# # #

In the sitting room, Jong asked Asiram, "Do you concur with our last conversation about those two sites?"

"I told you then, and I will confirm now, that I see no other possible way of breaching those two places without the loss of life. From afar, a drug laden dart could lay them out, but it would be obvious when they hit the ground."

Jong broke in and inquired, "What if they never hit the ground and we provided a hick-up to their camera system? My cousins are looking at their software and are trying to determine the version, origin, and whether it can be hacked. I will have conclusive information in approximately thirty minutes, so I would like to wait until then to offer any other input that I may have."

## CHAPTER THIRTY-SIX

Jong received a call from his cousin who instructed him on how to download the software that controlled the machine pistols that were placed around the farm. He was told that a central station was needed, and that the system could be utilized by as many as fourteen individuals logged into the same portal at the same time. He was further told that each would be given a code and a password and that would be their access information to the system. His cousin cautioned him on the precarious nature of such a weapons configuration placed in so many different patterns of targeting. Jong asked his cousin if the units would signal if they were brushed or disturbed by an animal or a fallen branch as opposed to humans. He was told that they could discern whether the unit had been disturbed, and a self-correct signal would be issued to reboot.

His cousin yelled, "What the hell you try to do, start World War III? The magazine capacity for each of those weapons is 120 rounds. If you multiply that times fifteen machine pistols, you have 1,800 rounds of ammunition to fire at people you no like. If that no sound like World War III, then I go back to China and make noodles instead of weapons for you."

"Ah, but cousin, you no make the money you make on noodles that you make on helping your family member with weapons. What about hacking into that camera system that I sent you the details on?"

"That no system; it is bunch of cameras tied to one computer with no backup. It continues in a loop, and therefore, is senseless to hack."

"How can I shut it down and delay the picture?"

"You no listen! You no never listen when I talk! I say again, camera in loop, show the same thing over and over, again, repeatedly. You understand now?"

"Okay, cousin, hold your damn temper. Is this like my watching a movie, playing it back as many times as I want to watch a scene?"

"You no hear me? In other words, yes. Are you sure we are from the same village?"

"Thanks for the information and as usual, it was good to hear from you."

"Before you hang up, it appears that some Yank is recruiting people from home with certain skills to do some work in this country. You might want to go on-line and look at the help wanted section and see if there is a connection."

"Thanks for the heads up, later."

Jong thought about the information he had just heard and called Mallory and suggested that he get the group together so they could discuss information that was potentially valuable to the group. In the meantime, Mary Alice was cleaning up when Jong said, "I didn't have a thing to eat and now you're packing it all up."

"I saved you a plate. I guess it is getting too late to take that ride and you seem to be preoccupied, so I will hold you to our date, until tomorrow."

"Mary Alice, I'm sorry, but I seemingly have a lot of things to control, activate, and oversee. I will make it up to you tomorrow and perhaps we can go off campus and have a real date without a ton of people watching our every move.

Let me walk you to your truck, and by the way, do you like owning this company, and do you see any way of improving its ability to expand into other markets? Those are just a few of the questions I would like you to consider, in addition to making sure that we all do not eat something and die. I think there might be a business proposition here as well, but I would like to hear directly from you on how you would expand on this business."

# # #

With everyone in attendance, the Sarge announced, "Before I address the reason for this meeting, I would like to say that there was a rebellion today as certain women and partners have decided that they are not leaving the compound for a safe zone while we handle the problem with my cousin. I just want to go on record as saying that I personally accept their determination and fortitude and welcome them as a part of our overall security operation." Mallory looked at him and ran his hand across his throat.

After a few rumblings and other demonstrations of strength by the women of the group, Jong stood up and told the group about the cameras that were situated on the two sites that may hold some of Walter's finances. He explained to the group what his cousin had said, and they just laughed. Jong told the group that the only security was probably people inside the buildings who were low to medium level protection types. He suggested to the group that they cut the power to both places simultaneously and enter the premises with bags and carts to haul what could turn out to be a single dollar.

The Sarge interrupted Jong and said, "Listen, Allen gave me this information and I believe he's on to something, and I trust him. Y'all know that I'm trying to end this thing with my cousin, and if he has funds stashed in those places, I'm sure we are the last people he wants to handle his cash." He apologized to Jong and asked him to continue.

Jong said, "I'm expecting suppression devices tomorrow and I am anxious to test our outfield defense system. It consists of fifteen machine pistols with magazines that hold 120 rounds each and are controlled by computer-assisted-targeting or manually, by the twelve people who have access codes and an iPhone. It's truly revolutionary, but the field of range in relationship to the targeting is all downhill, meaning there are no weapons aimed up, only towards the ground. Rounds can be fired semi-automatically or fully automatically. Oh, and by the way, my cousin indicated to me that someone from America is trying to employ individuals with martial arts and ancient fighting skills from my old country. If I were to guess, they are looking for ninjas and samurai, and if I were to further guess, I would put my money on it being Walter. I suggest that we do this job in broad daylight and let the Sarge unmask himself for the cameras if they work. I also suggest using small weapons and stun guns. Is it still necessary to have a walk about of the places?"

"That was a good report, are there any questions?" Asiram raised her hand and asked, "Jong, what's your take on recruiting people from abroad, and what makes you think it's Walter?"

"My cousins are creative people and have their ears close to the ground back home. If you think about it, we have handled pretty much everything they have thrown at us, including surviving the devastating explosion at the ranch. What he has done in my opinion, and I will confirm this tomorrow, is unearthed, a supposedly, supernatural triad that is powerful and they only sign onto jobs that are, hypothetically, impossible for mere mortals to accomplish."

John Lee exclaimed, "That sounds like the boogeyman!"

Jong turned to him and said, "That's a close description."

Asiram asked, "What are our chances and are we out manned?"

"I heard a rumor and evaluated what we have done to Walter's hired people so far and, I just thought if I were Walter, I would call up old ancients. I have no empirical information, just my guess," Jong stated.

The Sarge said, "It does not matter who is sent to hurt us, we will defend our community from devils, demons, and cousins. If we do this thing tomorrow, we need to get back in fighting shape, and I will assign Mallory to that detail. We have been drinking Pina Coladas in St. Thomas, eating crabs, shrimp, lobster, and other wonderful foods, and now it's time to get ready for work people. I am suggesting we start twice a day work outs. Are there any questions on that notion?"

No one asked any questions. The Sarge said, "Okay then, Jong, I want to make sure that our outfield defense systems are online, tested tomorrow, and every one of us knows how to access and utilize them. I would also like to waltz into those sites tomorrow and extract whatever my cousin has in them. I am also interested in attending the planned sessions on the utilization of weapons by our female counterparts tomorrow morning, as well as participate, in our getting back into shape sessions. The only people that I have seen exercising are my two boys. Have you guys done any kind of exercise?"

No one answered, but everyone knew that their strength and survival skills were dependent on their group being fit and alert.

The Sarge said, "Let's start tomorrow, prior to visiting my cousin's places."

The Sarge addressed a myriad of other issues, including dividing the forces to hit the two sites at the same time. He stated, "We will reconfirm assignments tomorrow and abort or proceed with the issues as need be."

Asiram said, "I think we should investigate Jong's information a little more intently. I have seen a few things in my day and if this is a triad from a certain region, then I think we all should be in our best shape.

"Once, on an assignment in Japan and the actual work took place in China, I saw a group of invisibles run through a well-trained regiment and kill eighty men without firing a shot."

John Lee asked, "Did them fellas surprise them or frag them?"

"No, the fifteen attackers took out all eighty soldiers in less than three minutes." Asiram shuddered slightly, "I don't believe in demons and devils, but I know what I saw and if this is what's coming our way, we all had better be in shape and sharp. The memory of what I saw, still frightens me today. I mean, it was incredible and stimulating to watch so few conquer so many in such a short period of time and with such dynamism."

The Sarge meandered over to Asiram, hugged her and said, so that all could hear, "They sound foreboding, but I can assure all of you that when we were in Vietnam, the ground rumbled when our name was mentioned. My name is Sergeant Ben Beckmire and I am the leader of eleven individuals who won't die without a fight, and when you come for us, you had better bring your A+ game, for we rise to the occasion." Asiram looked at her father-in-law and smiled. She realized he was a proud, strong man and, it would take an angel from heaven, not a demon from hell, to defeat this man.

She yelled, "I give my all to my father-in-law because I know he will protect us or die trying." The rest of the group gave a roaring ovation, and the die was cast. It was shaping up to be a defining moment for the good guys or the bad guys. It was obvious that one of them was going to control this activity.

## CHAPTER THIRTY-SEVEN

The teams designated to penetrate the two sites included seasoned veterans that were good at what they did. Walter, on the other hand felt that his aura was more prescient than it was in reality and, refused to believe that anyone would dare enter his sanctuaries and fleece him of his bounty. At exactly 0930 hours, the two facilities were breached, and teams invaded the confines of the buildings. There were four guards at each site, two with antiquated weapons and two with night sticks. Both guard teams were held as hostages while back rooms with multiple locks were breached and the contents bagged.

At one of the sites, the Sarge gently removed his mask and stood directly in the path of one of the cameras and gave it a four-sided view of who was violating the premises. At the other site, he instructed his people to stay covered. The Sarge paraded his image in front of the camera and positioned all aspects of his body to be viewed with a final turn revealing the third finger extended from each hand. Walter would get the message and know exactly who permeated his sanctuary.

The act of breaching Walter's refuge was simply too easy, and everyone wondered when the places would explode, or if one hundred armed men would surround the place and slaughter them. It was quite the opposite and huge cases were filled with cash. A total of twelve oversized bags and cases were taken from the first site and another fourteen from the second. The Sarge radioed Mallory and said, "This was simply too damn easy. Why would he have all of this money in cases just waiting for someone to take?"

"As I think about this action, I'm feeling the same way you are. What the heck is the catch here? Do you think they're rigged? I have heard if you want to hide something, place it in plain sight without a lot of people protecting it. If Walter had guarded this place like a bank, then it would have drawn suspicion, perhaps he got the same email I did."

"Your guess is as good as mine, but I need Jong's cousin to x-ray each bag and case. Jong, did you hear me?"

"Roger that, Sarge. I'm making the call as we speak," Jong stated.

After all the bags and cases were loaded into the extra vans, the group loaded their personnel and disappeared into the morning sun. The entire operation took nine minutes. The Sarge, Jong, and Mallory were in one van and John Lee, Jilkes, Montomie, and Chakes were in the other. The rest of the group were told to find high ground and provide surveillance work at the meeting place with Jong's cousin.

After the vans pulled into an alley in DC and backed up against a loading platform, Jong's cousin came out screaming and yelling in their native tongue. Jong in essence told him to shut up before he was sent back home—a thing that would mean instant death for his cousin. Jong said, "Do not ever address me in that tone in front of my brothers. I will have your lowly person sent back to people who I have paid off on your behalf. You will do what I ask, and you will do it right and quickly. Never show off in front of my brothers."

His cousin fell to his knees and in their native tongue begged for forgiveness and blamed his unbalanced wife for his tirade. He said to Jong, so that all could hear him, "I am glad you are here with most of the vans because I can electronically change how they look by pushing this new remote control. I beg you, cousin, not to send me back to that place where our forefathers and their fathers were born and labored to make a single man powerful." Mallory started to say something but the Sarge elbowed him so hard he thought he heard a rib crack. Jong said, "I need to know what's in each of these bags. I'm looking for explosives, tracking devices, and anything else that's suspicious."

"I have been insulted by two of my workers and I will make them open each one in my gun range."

"That's not necessary. I want to know what the contents are in each case. What happened to that x-ray system that I hustled for you?"

"I was going to use a handheld x-ray device, but I will get the big brother out here and do it immediately."

"I have important people with me, and they don't like to wait. Move your low life self quickly or you will be sent back in the morning."

Mallory asked, "What on earth was that all about?"

Jong turned to the Sarge and said, "Thanks for that intervention, you saved his ass. Corporal, there are times when one should never enter another's conversation. I publicly spanked his ass because he provided me with a useless system that was not tested, nor did it contain all its parts. In my culture, when one is being whipped, no one dares to question the nature of the incident, no matter how small. My cousin was supposed to provide me with suppression devices a day ago and he did not. If I allow him to miss due dates, then he might miss a crucial one that might mean death or injury to a member of our community. What I did was to tell him about good business versus bad."

"Jong, I'm sorry. The thing about our community is that we never stop learning about each other's quirks and customs. Please forgive me, my friend," Mallory stated.

Jong's cousin was back on the scene in less than five minutes with shields and other contraptions. Jong asked his cousin about one of the items in his hand and he said it was a Fido X3 Explosives Trace Detector. "Now, what I'm going to do is use this device first to attempt to detect any operative explosives, then I will scan each case with the x-ray unit, then physically inspect locks, latches, wheels, handles, and seams."

"I don't want to hear all of this mumbo jumbo—get it done before I make good on my notions. I want five of these cases delivered to me in two days."

"Cousin, it is coming up on the weekend. Can you extend that idea to four days?"

"No! I give you two days!"

Mallory looked at Jong and asked, "You're kidding, right?"

Jong approached Mallory and whispered, "Corporal, you must learn to keep your thoughts to yourself. If he suspects that you can provide protection for him then he will find some way to impress you and beg you to do his bidding. I suggest that you follow the Sarge's temperament and keep your mouth closed. Just kidding."

Forty or so minutes later, Jong's cousin showed him, Mallory, and the Sarge, the bags that had been booby-trapped. He showed them the armed handles that were triggered if the bags were moved significantly away from the adjoining bags and explained to them how it worked. He also marked each case that had tracking devices in them.

Jong said, "You look puzzled, why?" His cousin did not immediately respond and remained completely focused. Jong called his name twice, loudly, and he still did not respond.

He looked at Jong and said, "These cases are rigged with explosives and tracking devices. This case is laced with a powdery substance, but what's puzzling me is that the contents are not the same, look at this computer-generated picture of those cases holding tracking devices and explosives. The images look identical. Now, look at this case containing that powder. See the difference? This case is filled with George Washington bills and the cases that are rigged are Benjamin Franklins; $1s vs $100s. Give these cases back to the owner or take them somewhere and burn with HCL in an enclosed chamber."

"Do you have access to such a chamber?"

"Oh, cousin, your simple and low life cousin has heard of such a thing but can't remember where he heard of this tool." The Sarge motioned to Jong to have a private word with him and told him exactly what to say.

Jong said, "Perhaps if my cousin was guaranteed a good life and freedom in this country he might recall where he saw or heard of such a system."

"Ah, you are a very wise man, my cousin, and if I were to hear such a guarantee, I'm sure it will spark this old brain of mine."

Jong said, "Then if those are the words that will regenerate my cousin's brain cells, let it be known and witnessed before my brothers that if my cousin was to figure out how to destroy that evil white powder, then I will make sure that he is never bothered by anyone from our home."

Jong's cousin exclaimed, "So, it has been stated and so, shall it be done! I now remember where I heard about such a tool and where I saw it. If I am not mistaken, it is in the next loading bay to this one."

Jong looked at his cousin and yelled, "Seems like you played me for a fool!" His cousin fell to his knees once again, placed his head on the ground, and said, "No, cousin, I want to live, I want to serve you and your brothers. If I offended you with my loss of memory, then I apologize and beg that you forgive me for I know that there are people looking for me back home."

"How long will it take you to diffuse the explosives and remove the tracking devices? If you talk shit, I will save a lot of people some expenses by dispatching your low life ass myself."

"Cousin, it will take me four to six minutes for each bag with the explosives and two minutes on the bags with tracking devices. Do you want to watch me work?"

"I do and if you think that you want to dispense of me, those two massive androids over there will hurt you really bad."

Jong walked over to the Sarge and Mallory and said, "I need you guys to step far, far away. My cousin and I are going to do this together, he's trying to 'save face'."

Mallory and the Sarge left the area and the Sarge said to Mallory, "Those two assholes are back there laughing their asses off. Jong was demonstrating to us that he is in control and his cousin is a low life. It is all a game played by people who in their culture must show who is the overlord. It is clear that Jong is, but it is necessary for them to play the game. Jong will slip his cousin a significant amount of money and his cousin will continue to supply us with information, guns, and technology.

"Jong will come to me later and confess to the penny how much he paid his cousin. I will yell at him. He will give me examples of how much his cousin has helped us. I will say, don't do that again and he will swear on all that is dear to him that he won't violate my trust again, until the next time and then we start the game all over again."

"You've heard the saying, 'if it ain't broke, don't fix it'," Mallory stated.

## CHAPTER THIRTY-EIGHT

The cases taken from the first site contained $17 million and there was a whopping $22 million in the cases from the second site. Jong's cousins laundered the money and made sure there were no traces of white powder on the bills. The Sarge called Allen and told him that he had a nice pay day coming his way. Allen asked him what was the take and was told that it was $39 million. Allen yelled, "Are you fucking kidding me?"

"Allen, there was even more, but some of it was laced with what we think was anthrax and we sure as hell didn't want that shit going public. My friend, as I said, it was $39 million." There was a pause on the phone and the Sarge asked, "Allen, what's going on?"

"I was online, and it looks like someone is recruiting anyone who believes they are a ninja or are remotely related to one. I can only think this is your family member doing this kind of deal," Allen confessed.

"I hope he prepaid them because he just lost a shit load of money."

Allen replied, "I think what you have accomplished is to remind him of his vulnerability, and you can be assured that the rest of his assets that are rumored to be in excess of $500 million will be well guarded. Sarge, I need you to send some funds to my family. The information I give you will allow you to access my family, but I am trusting you with their lives. Do

I have your word as the gentleman that I think you are, that you will keep them safe?"

"Allen, we know where your family is. If I were in the business of killing women and children, my team would have abandoned me long ago. No, we don't do families, and as a matter of fact, we hired a couple of our friends to keep an extra eye on them."

Beckmire paused so the weight of his words would be fully understood by Allen. He began again, "Allen, I know where you are at this very moment and have known about every place you have tried to hide. I like the fact that you're playing in the sewer and keeping your eyes and ears close to the ground. My man John Lee vouched for you when we had you and were preparing to cut off your penis. He told me that you could be trusted and that is the only reason you are still alive. Your problem, and my concern is that my cousin remains a powerful individual who controls institutions and the individuals who are supposed to manage them. Listen, I have, and my people have, killed a lot of people, and we literally laughed at your contingency of mercs because they were all over the place and without leadership. In my community, any one of my guys can decide and we go with it. It's not that I sit here alone and make policy, no, I listen to them and then we decide who does what, when and where. My guys, and now girls, are the best machine that I have ever had the privilege of working with. These people are the best and I trust their judgement and anyways, your ass was always under our thumbs. Get over it!" the Sarge amplified.

"You know I had several opportunities to cut a deal with the devil!"

"No, you didn't! All you had was a simple way of surrendering to him and watching your family be eviscerated before your eyes. Between the two demons, I think you picked the gentler one." There was a long pause and the Sarge could discern that Allen was crying and sad about his behavior and his treatment of his loyal associates, his wife, kids, drivers, and everyone else that he had treated like shit. He said to the Sarge, "For a few moments, I thought you were as ruthless as Walter until I figured out why you were merciless in relating to the mercs that he hired. You have given me a new lease on life, and I didn't think that such a thing was possible. I owe you so much, and on so many different levels, and I swear my allegiance to you."

"Did you swear an allegiance to Walter?"

"I did not. I told him that I was interested in making money and playing in the big league. I never said that I would not deliver him to a higher evil and that's exactly what I'm trying to do, deliver him to the anti-Christ, resurrect my family and try a new occupation."

"I'm not the anti-Christ, Allen. I am just a guy who does not like to be threatened and have members of my extended family hung in their own home. I seek a justice that court systems don't adhere to. There's room for people like you who are smart and willing to change their mantra. We like your notion of the homeless issue and need someone who has played in the sewer and understands their plight. We live in luxury while many of our fellow arm bearers are on the streets and are trying to figure out where their next meal is going to come from. We should be able to use a significant amount of this new booty to secure them financially, and as a matter of fact, I'm going to recommend to my people that we employ you to create new venues to help former veterans and others who are down on their luck. This extraction of resources from my cousin could be the catalyst that starts a whole new effort to help former military and police officers, as well as the homeless at large. The question you have to consider, is this something you would be interested in pursuing once we all have been washed in holy water?"

"I want to be purified, brought in from out of the cold so that I can live to love my children, friends, and be a better person than the one I once was," Allen announced.

"It's all about positioning yourself around a better group of people, besides your natural family, and you, will find that this group of people is a great example of a secondary family," the Sarge indicated.

"Sarge, thanks for all that you have done to make me whole. I sent you a text about where to send those funds for my family as well as the amount. I would appreciate it if you made that happen."

"I know where your people are, and I am going to have one of my associates who is responsible for keeping an eye out for them to arrange a place to drop off the amount you requested. Oh, by the way, I will have my man place in our books your finder's fee, minus the amount we drop off to your people. I have to go, but I expect you to keep me abreast about everything that is rumored about my cousin, and especially, if in fact, he's the person recruiting assassins to come to this country and eliminate us."

"I am forever in your debt and whenever I hear rumors, whether I can substantiate them or not, I will inform you. I really think that the person doing the hiring in Asia is Walter, but I don't have confirmation on that yet. Give me a couple of days and I will hopefully have some notion of who is recruiting mercs. Thanks again for being generous, a true friend who could have executed me and my family and never looked back. Thanks for recognizing that some who look bad, aren't always bad."

Jong knocked on the Sarge's door and when he answered it, Jong said, "I made mistake. There was $40 million extracted from the two facilities."

The Sarge looked at him and asked, "Are you sure there wasn't $42 or $45 million? Anyway, you are our man with the money and all of us trust you, Mr. Amazing, to do the right thing."

"Sarge, you and the rest of the guys are my brothers. I remember that thing with Rich Brown's father that we had to deal with, and I swore to myself that I would never corrupt my soul and injure my friends for a few extra dollars. Therefore, you will never have reason to think that I'm skimming my way to the top."

"Mr. Amazing let it go. What you do and why you do it is on you and I don't need an immediate or latent count of our assets. If you want to rip us off, then by all means enjoy the fruits of your decision. I, on the other hand, have consistently said that if a member of our team wants to steal from us then the rest of us will completely turn our backs on this person throughout eternity."

"I can account for every dollar that has been expended. I am my brother's keeper, and he is mine. It was my brothers who carried me out of the fire when my legs wouldn't work. I don't need money or fame; I need my family of brotherhood that has been my only true family through thick and thin."

"Mr. Amazing, I know you got our backs and we yours. I will never question my brother's integrity. I believe if he needs absolution, then he will proclaim his error and, therefore, the situation is capable of being resolved. We are like one, and if all we have been through means so little, then so be it and good luck in your new life, but never try to come back to the herd."

"Sarge, I would like to ask you one question? Do you personally think that I have acted to increase my own wealth?"

"Get the shit out of here. You are my brother and there are eleven others that I would place my life, and that of my families in their hands. Don't bother me with your bullshit. If I thought you were having a financial issue, I would have approached you head on and not through some bullshit notion of trying to trap you in a fable. Let it go and get out of my sight."

"Thanks, Sarge, I was hoping no one questioned my control over the finances, such as my relationship with my cousin for weapons and technology, and other such things as airplanes. I do what I do because you have a lot on your plate, and, on some fronts, I can assist beyond your imagination."

"Mr. Amazing, I know what you're capable of doing and one of the things I know from the bottom of my heart is that you are not capable of messing over your friends. Let it go, Romeo. I'm done with this conversation."

CHAPTER THIRTY-NINE

The Sarge, after having a drink with Whitmore, Gladstone, and McArthur, went back to his room and saw his lovely wife lounging around in a permeable garment. He said, "Now, that garment is going to make me forget my name."

He approached Courtney and whispered in her ear, "I love and need you so much and I'm happy that you guys made the decision to not leave the farm. I know I haven't participated in your drills, but I have a feeling that we're all going to be under a lot of stress in the upcoming weeks. I'm going to mandate that we all practice along with you guys. We are a community honey, and somehow, you and I are the leaders."

Courtney kissed him tenderly and said, "No more talk, Ben Beckmire, no more talk." He kissed her and she kissed him and the only sounds that could be discerned were those of pure and unadulterated love-making.

# # #

Later that evening, the Sarge and Courtney went for a long walk in the woods where they stumbled upon a handgun. Courtney reached down to pick it up and the Sarge yelled, "Honey, before you touch, inspect the environment first. It could be booby trapped. Never think you have just found something when people are trying to find and hurt you, always suspect that there is a problem and, in fact, become paranoid because it is that sense of awareness that may save your life."

He marked the area and said, "We must have this entire farm swept because the kids play in these fields."

When they returned from their walk, he directed Jong to take Brown and Bernstein in the mule to the spot he had marked. He told him that a suspicious weapon was lying there and to check and see if it was booby trapped.

The Sarge's cell phone rang and it was Allen who reported, "I have some bad news to share with you."

"How bad can it be, we're all alive? Anyway, let me call you back, I want to secure a weapon that we found in the fields."

The Sarge redirected his mind to where the weapon was located and told Jong that a white handkerchief was near it and pointed to the marked trees. The three individuals took off in the mule to where the Sarge directed them. In the meantime, he dialed Allen back and said, "What's the bad news you want to share with me?"

"Your cousin had the people guarding his money killed. He also has doubled the bounty on your head and the 'idiot spy's head. He wants you taken alive and will accept the head of Zanthius as a down payment. He will kill any man or woman and their families that brings you harm. I am under the impression that he wants to do some bad things to you. The worst thing he has ordered, is to have his people video Asiram's child being cut out of her. He has declared war on you and your entire clan with a $50,000 bounty for each of the kid's heads. I'm getting this stuff piece meal, but from what I can discern from reliable sources, these are your cousin's edicts. In addition, I believe the senator wants to know what your final position is on the Carbon Factor."

"First of all, is there any way you can engage someone to locate the families of the men he killed that were guarding his money?"

"I can do that, Sarge. What is it you have in mind?"

"I want to endow those families with some of Walter's money. Secondly, I talked to the senator and we have a common understanding. I am not saying that we trust each other and will sing songs together, but we are equals and have dialogue going on where no one is leading the conversation. She recognizes and understands the threat that Walter poses to her sanctity and our longevity. We have a common desire to conclude his miserable life. I am concerned about her, because he has, as I may have intimated, a video of her and she's the star of a few of his sordid films. Now, the last thing she wants to do is have her husband find out about her sex life and conclude her and his life. It's a mess, but I'm of the belief she can come out of this smelling like a rose with our help. Allen, this is truly confidential information.

"Now, insofar as my cousin is concerned, he is one mean-spirited person. What normal person would put a bounty on a child's head? He is a cancer that I am going to rid the world of, and I will make sure that none of his DNA will be found. He threatened all that I hold dear in this world. If he were a man; a fight between just him and I would save a lot of lives, but that won't work because he is too soft and he recognizes that I would break his back immediately. There is no place for him to hide because we are going to put a $10 million price tag on his head just for confirmation of his whereabouts. He is currently masquerading as a human, but he is beyond dead. I will extract his soul from his body."

# # #

Courtney said to the Sarge, "Honey, you have a lot on your plate. What can I do to help? There must be something I can do to help eliminate some of the responsibility and stress that will be the cause of your demise."

The Sarge looked at her and replied, "Just keep loving me the way you do. That's all I need."

As the two embraced, there was a bright flash in the sky and a thunderous explosion that shook the earth that knocked the two of them to the ground.

the end

www.ingramcontent.com/pod-product-compliance
Lightning Source LLC
Chambersburg PA
CBHW021433240626
47153CB00001B/135